DOMAIN

MIKE BARON

WFP
WORDFIRE PRESS

EBook ISBN: 978-1-68057-474-6
Trade Paperback ISBN: 978-1-68057-475-3

Cover design by Janet McDonald
Cover artwork images by Adobe Stock
Kevin J. Anderson, Art Director
Published by
WordFire Press, LLC
PO Box 1840
Monument CO 80132
Kevin J. Anderson & Rebecca Moesta, Publishers
WordFire Press eBook Edition 2022
WordFire Press Trade Paperback Edition 2022
WordFire Press Hardcover Edition 2022
Printed in the USA

Join our WordFire Press Readers Group for
sneak previews, updates, new projects, and giveaways.
Sign up at wordfirepress.com

CONTENTS

DEDICATION

To my mentors:
Peter Brandvole, Franklynn Peterston,
and Judi K-Turkel

ONE
THE BIFURCATED GIRL

Two boys surfed the sidewalk on Longine Avenue in the Los Feliz section of Los Angeles in August 1990. Phil was tall and wiry with blond Beach Boy bangs, wearing a Butthole Surfers T and cutoffs, his board bearing Brian Pulido's Lady Death. Jesse was short and slight with a nose like a conning tower, wearing baggy jeans that sagged over his skinny butt. His board bore a Big Daddy Roth Rat Fink knock-off. Both boys wore ball caps with the bill backward. It was 9:00 AM, sunny and hot, the air redolent with the scent of jasmine and garbage.

Phil soared off the curb at the end of the block, landing on all fours with a clack and a sizzle. Jesse flipped his board expertly into the air with his foot, caught it, and set it down on the street. His left leg paddled wildly to keep up, white sneaker pushing against the pavement and picking up gum. At the opposite curb, he heel-flipped the board over the lip, came down on the sidewalk, and rolled. The boys were looking to get high. Phil had scored a half lid of primo from a friend's uncle who lived in Humboldt County and grew his own. The sticky burned a hole in his pocket. Soon it would burn a hole in his mind. That was the Plan.

They cruised by a strip mall: pizza, karate, nails, pet hospital, liquor. They cruised by a block of two four-story red brick apartment buildings, named respectively The Alhambra and The Cascades. Cars lined the curbs. Smacking the passenger side mirror on an Olds as he passed, Jesse caught up with his taller pal.

"What about the park?" Jesse said.

Phil stuck an American Spirit in his mouth. "No, dude! There's a nark in the park!"

"What nark?"

"Come on, dude! That dude in the hoodie and the Air Jordans, been there every fuckin' day reading *High Times* pretending he ain't looking. He's straight out the academy."

"You don't know that."

Phil nosied to a stop, pulled a lighter from his pocket, and lit the cig. "You want to chance it? Maybe get hauled down to Juvie, have your mom come pick you up? Why's he wearing a hoodie in this heat? To hide his radio, camera, and gun?"

A sheen of sweat glistened on Jesse's pale forehead. He was already on notice at James Dean High School. He was about to enter junior year under a cloud of suspicion. Last semester he'd been placed on academic suspension for cutting classes and general bad attitude. He lived with his mother and two sisters in a third-floor walk-up. He hadn't seen his father in years. "Well let's find a place. Being straight is bullshit."

Phil swooped on. "There's a vacant lot up ahead."

A pickup filled with Mexicans passed hauling a trailer filled with lawn equipment.

"There go your customers," Jesse said. Phil worked at a Taco Bell.

"I never see beaners at the Bell," Phil said. "They all eat offa those curbside vans that smell like chorizo, park at the jobs. Only people I see at Taco Bell are stoners and fat white guys coming off work."

They came to the vacant lot. Once the home of a stucco apartment building surrounding a courtyard and a pool, it had been razed and fallen into desuetude, thigh-high weeds covering everything except the cracked concrete rectangle of the pool which had yet to be broken up and filled in. A run-down Dodge Stratus listed at the curb. Orange tape bearing the message CONDEMNED KEEP OUT stretched from rebar to rebar, falling into the weeds where it had broken or been cut. Empty bottles and cans glittered in the sun: Miller High Life, peppermint schnapps, Red Bull, Jägermeister.

"Dude," Jesse said. "I could use a Jägerbomb myself." He released a high-pitched cackle.

"I hear ya," Phil said. "We'll get your brother to pick some up. That rag head at Curt's Liquor don't give a shit. We could probably buy it ourselves."

Broken glass sprinkled the sidewalk and the first couple of feet surrounding the lot. Newspaper inserts. Condoms tossed from parked cars. Phil and Jesse flipped up their boards and carried them as they swooshed through the tall weeds heading for a place of concealment. A rat scurried away. They came to a mound of earth and nodules of concrete left over from the razing and sat, their boards at their feet.

Phil removed the doobie from his cigarette pack and lit up. Exhaling a gray cloud, he passed the joint to Jesse who inhaled deeply followed by a paroxysm of coughing. Phil pounded him on the back.

"Don't hit so hard, dude! You'll blow your lungs out."

Jesse frowned at the joint. "Man, it's running. It's running 'cause you rolled it too fast."

"Bullshit!"

"You roll the joints too fucking fast." A seed exploded. "See? See? You're always in such a hurry. You didn't break the bud up properly."

Phil snatched the reefer from Jesse's hand. "Gimme that!" He spit on his finger and applied it to the burning tributary. He massaged the joint and relit it until it carbureted to his satisfaction. They passed the joint back and forth until their skulls felt like pressure chambers. "Hey man," Jesse said reaching into his baggy pants. "Check it out." He withdrew a small, silver balisong and began twirling it around, blade catching the sun.

Phil held his hand out. "Gimme!"

Jesse flipped the knife shut with a flourish. "Nahh. You'll cut yourself."

Phil reached for the blade. Jesse danced away giggling.

"Hand it over you little prick! I won't cut myself!"

"Remember that time you gouged a hole in your foot with that screwdriver? You bled like a stuck pig!"

Phil lurched to his feet. Jesse ran through the weeds, laughing and swinging the knife. He stopped, did a comic wave pulse, whole body whipping slo-mo from the ground up. Phil caught up and looked at what lay in the grass, his eyes refusing to make sense of it.

"Fuck," he said.

Jesse whirled and vomited. He staggered, gagging, knife forgotten. Phil felt as if he were in some cheap horror movie with really crude special effects. If he kept that attitude, he'd be all right.

A girl lay in the weeds; naked, split at the waist. An empty green wine bottle was jammed between her legs. Phil saw into the cavity of her abdomen. Her eyes had been gouged out and laid in the sockets. The pinkie finger was missing from her left hand. It would later be found in her vagina. That's all Phil saw before he turned and ran.

TWO
THE HOUSE
PRESENT DAY

From the street, it resembled a Mayan temple hidden in the forest, one that had lain undiscovered through the centuries. The front of the house was dominated by a vertical glass hexagon formed of cast blocks of concrete in a chrysanthemum design that gave the facade a moiré pattern in the early morning and early evening. The trees and bushes were untrimmed. A FOR SALE sign perched at the curb.

"The gardening service will be out on Friday," the realtor assured Kendall Coffin.

Maureen parked her Mercedes SUV at the curb and got out. She was a plump, middle-aged woman with big hair and cat's-eye sunglasses which concealed twinkling eyes. Kendall got out. He was of medium height and build with medium brown hair wearing a Nexus T-shirt, khakis, and huaraches. The only concession to hipsterdom was a diamond stud in his left ear. He had a narrow face, close-set gray eyes, and a spade chin reflecting his Irish/Scots ancestry.

They walked up the concrete steps between two blank walls to the dark entry alcove, sealed off by an art deco metal gate fashioned of arched panels and chevrons. A thick chain ran through the center posts and connected with a massive Case padlock.

Maureen removed a key ring the size of a quoit from her purse. It carried dozens of keys and must have weighed five pounds. Selecting the proper cylindrical key, she unlocked the padlock and pulled the chain through. The gate swung reluctantly inward with a hair-raising shriek. The main entrance was covered with metal panels, a vortex design with blue glass eyes in the center. A frosted ten-inch cube at face height was the only window.

The door swung inward with some resistance. Maureen put her shoulder into it. They stepped into the foyer. Kendall was overcome with a sense of wonder he hadn't felt since he was a child and first visited Wyrick World in Tampa with his parents. He had always loved the architecture of Roark Dexter Smith, had even planned to be an architect, studying drafting, math, and design at the University of Wisconsin. But somewhere along the line big-breasted women and men in tights seized control of his imagination and he ended up drawing comic books.

There was a box of brochures resting on the tile floor. Maureen stooped and handed one to Kendall. "I'm sure you've seen this."

The color brochure featured a shot of the inner courtyard at night lit by offset lamps and a brief history.

WALLANDA HOUSE

Los Angeles, 1971

Frank Wallanda was a writer, producer, and director best known for his string of wholesome teen comedies in the seventies and eighties, Stylin', The Quinceañera, Prom Queen, *and* Li'l Darlin'. *In 1970 he asked his friend Roark Dexter Smith to design a house that would accommodate lavish parties and entertaining. Smith reacted with what many consider one of his boldest designs, a complete environment redolent of an exotic but undetermined culture. Smith conceived the house as a hacienda built around a central courtyard containing a pool, garden, and Smith's unique plinths and pillars that drew inspiration from Mayan, Aztec, Sumerian, and Egyptian culture.*

The house presents an imposing if not intimidating face to the street, almost fortress-like in height and imperiousness. The entry lies at the top of a narrow stair that lies in perpetual shadow due to carefully groomed juniper bushes, through a pair of lavish metal gates that depict stylized leaves and water, through a door that could have been taken from a Japanese siege castle, opening on the airy, inviting interior courtyard.

Here Smith collaborated with Wallanda to incorporate the magic of stagecraft. The courtyard contains theater lighting, an automatic sliding steel cover for the pool topped with hardwood so it can be used as a dance floor, and even a permanent "refreshment lounge." Smith's unique plinths with erotic nymphs dominate one end of the courtyard. Their eroticism is not immediately apparent.

The interior features five bedrooms, five and a half baths, a library, living room, lavish kitchen, and a basement theater with seats taken from the Art Deco Strand Theater on Melrose Drive, dismantled in 1964.

Ironically Smith stated Wallanda House did not represent his ideal of organic architecture but rather was a flamboyant, self-conscious effort to create a total living environment for his friend Wallanda.

Maureen led the way through the foyer and opened the double glass doors to the courtyard. Like the front gate, the glass doors incorporated an art deco design: lilies and dragonflies. They stepped into the courtyard in the cool of the morning. The pool was full and gleamed blue. The lawn was shaggy, and a few weeds peeked through here and there, as well as in the planters. Pyramidal facades rose at both ends of the court. The house seemed both modern and ancient.

"I apologize for the condition. The yard service will have this all straightened out by the weekend," Maureen said. "I told them I was showing the house. I don't know if you have any experience with these lawn services, but they are completely at the mercy of their illegal labor."

"It looks fine," Kendall said, recalling the crabgrass nightmare he'd left in Nebraska. "Why isn't an architectural treasure like this already occupied?"

Maureen walked toward the pool gesturing. "I'll be frank with you. It's a bitch to keep up. Doesn't even have central air-conditioning, although it's designed in such a way as to make maximum use of shade. A lot of the tiles are loose, and the stonework needs repair in places. People interested in show places don't want to spend a lot fixing them up. They either tear them down or build from the ground up or they move on."

"I can't imagine anyone tearing down a Smith house anywhere," Kendall said.

"I know. It's sacrilege. But this is Hollyweird. Nobody can remember anything that happened prior to last week. They're asking 3.3, but if you make them an offer of 2.9, I think they'll bite."

It was a lot of money. Kendall had recently inherited a size-able sum from his mother, Elizabeth. Liz died of natural causes at the Sunny Brook Nursing Home in Omaha, leaving Nick a jaw-dropping 2.5 mil. Where it came from, he had no idea. She must have won it in the casinos. Every week Sunny Brook sent a bus to the Horseshoe in Cincinnati. Liz's death came exactly one month to the day after the death of Kendall's wife, Shirley. Shirley died from an overdose of Oxycontin and vodka. The coroner said it was accidental. Kendall wasn't so sure.

Two point five wasn't two point nine. There would be closing costs, moving costs, repair costs. For a while, Kendall was making over six figures a year drawing comics, particularly Marvel's Dr. Strange, for which he had become famous, but he had fallen out of the system. As in any branch of entertainment, there were one thousand eager beavers standing in line to take his place. His favorite editor was fired along with Kendall's future Marvel prospects. The new editors brought in their pals. Same old same old.

Kendall chose a paradigm shift: moving from Omaha to Los Angeles at the invitation and promise of his old college buddy Nate Polis, now a big shot at Wyrick Pictures. Nate said he could get Kendall work storyboarding and designing. Nate dangled an

Art Directorship in the wake of Shirley's suicide, as many old friends with whom Kendall had lost contact checked in.

With his mother's inheritance, Kendall researched houses online, stumbling across Wallanda House by accident. Internet info was sparse, reprising the brochure. The idea, the dream of living in a Smith house occupied Kendall's mind like raccoons in the attic. An industry friend recommended Maureen. Two weeks after the funeral he landed in LA.

Maureen turned to him. "Would you like to see the interior?"

THREE
AN UNEXPECTED DIVIDEND

The enormous kitchen could have served a small resort. A six-burner gas stove occupied a marble island beneath a copper canopy. An Eskimo family would have found the walk-in refrigerator commodious. Kendall opened the massive steel door, releasing a chill blast which felt good in the morning sun. He stepped inside. His breath formed a white duster in the air.

Rack after steel rack was empty except for a case of Dos Equis, a box of Arm and Hammer, a stack of frozen California Kitchen pizzas, and a liter bottle of Mountain Dew.

"Looks just like my fridge back home," he said, stepping out and shutting the door.

The breakfast nook bulged into the courtyard hexagonally, with a hexagonal hardwood table and chairs—designed by Smith himself—featuring the lily and firefly motif. The study and living room were connected by an elegant stucco arch decorated with Smith's characteristic hexagons. Stone pillars and a jutting mantle framed the massive fireplace in the study beneath a multi-paneled skylight. A framed animation cell from *Velva Visits Venus* hung on the wall.

Most of the rooms featured skylights, including the bathrooms. Built-in bookshelves lined the study. The shelves were filled with books, DVDs, and VHS tapes. Kendall walked to the wall and scanned the titles. Showbiz bios. *Brando For Breakfast*. *Mommy Dearest*. Samuel Goldwyn, Chaplin, Hepburn, Cary Grant. The classics. *Conversations with Dead Movie Stars* by Portia DeManning.

In the center of the wall was an entertainment console featuring an enormous old-school television framed by Harmon Kardon speakers and a Bose CD system.

Maureen removed a framed Picasso print from one wall revealing a circular safe. "I think the number's in here ..." She opened the door. A slip of paper had been taped to the back side. "Yes. Here it is." She closed the safe and put the painting back.

A Steinway baby grand sat in the corner of the den. "That goes with the house," Maureen said.

Numerous vertical windows faced the inner courtyard. The skylights in the bedrooms and bathrooms featured an inter-locking circle design that reminded Kendall of the Olympics or Audi. The massive master bedroom king-sized bed rested on a pyramidal hardwood base with a wrap-around headboard that rose and jutted horizontally over the bed. Kendall threw himself down on the bed raising a puff of dust redolent of the pyramids. The canopy underside was mirrored.

"Wallanda, you old perv!"

Maureen followed Kendall's gaze. "Oh, my. I never noticed that before."

A pair of eyebolts jutted from the footboard and the head-board. The built-in bureau featured a honeycomb motif with a large vertical mirror framed by honeycomb panels. The walk-in closet could fit a Smart car. The other four bedrooms were commodious except for the one off the kitchen obviously intended for live-in help.

"What about the garage?" Kendall said.

Maureen smiled and headed for the rear of the courtyard where a double-gated door opened on a promontory overlooking the Los Angeles basin. "Wallanda bought the house next door, tore it down, and built a heated eight-car unit. Shortly after his death his son, who had power of attorney, sold the lot to a developer who built that Spanish style next door. Let me show you."

She walked around the back of the house, up the overgrown hedgerow, and gestured through the creeping wisteria at the red-tile-topped stucco next door. "Just as well because the property taxes on the house alone are substantial. However, the house is not without a garage. There's a three-car garage at street level where we came in. It's three cars deep, not three cars wide."

"I didn't even notice," Kendall said. "What about the theater?"

"That's in the basement," Maureen said heading toward the rear. They returned to the kitchen.

A door next to the walk-in refrigerator led to the basement. Maureen gripped the handle, turned, and pulled. Her hand slipped off. "It's stuck," she said, gripping the handle in both hands. She tugged, grimacing.

"Let me try," Kendall said stepping up. He used both hands, turned the knob and pulled. The door held fast against all his might. He looked for a lock. There was none. "That's peculiar."

"You know, maybe the house shifted a little, and it got caught in the frame. We have about one earthquake a week out here."

"Seriously?"

Maureen nodded. "Most of them are so minor you don't even notice. It's like a garbage truck passing in the street. You only hear about the big ones."

"So it's only a matter of time before the San Andreas Fault splits like a soggy bag, and the whole state slides into the sea."

"That's about the size of it," the realtor said. "Grab it while you can."

They went back through the house via the other wing. "Why did the last occupant leave all those books and furniture?"

"Well the furniture goes with the house," Maureen said. "Smith designed most of it. As for the books, I have no idea.

They're part of the property now so whoever buys the house gets the books."

"Have you ever been down in the basement?"

"Never have," Maureen held the front door for Kendall, closed it behind her, closed the squeaky gate, threaded the chain back through the holes, and clicked shut the lock. They descended the steep, narrow stair to the street and arrived at the garage, tucked into and under the hill. Maureen searched through her key ring, tried several before finding the right one. She unlocked the garage door. Kendall grabbed the handle and lifted, causing the segmented door to roll back into the ceiling with the sound of a train stopping.

Immediately inside the entrance, a tan tarp covered a vehicle. The tarp itself was covered with a fine patina of dust. Kendall grabbed the end and lifted, revealing the distinctive round tail-lights and duck's ass of a '65 Corvette convertible. They stared at it in silence. The metallic blue fiberglass appeared to be in good shape. The license plate said PRINCS.

"Does this come with the house?" Kendall said hopefully.

"I don't know. We'll have to check the title. Likely its title and registration have lapsed so I would say yes."

Kendall dry swallowed. He'd always loved Corvettes and had long since given up any hope of owning one, until Shirley's death and the insurance settlement. Even then it was just a dream as he planned to sink every cent into the house and his move to LA. His mental calculator spun like a slot machine.

Kendall found a wall switch and flipped it. Harsh fluorescent light illuminated a shotgun garage extending sixty feet under the hill. The garage was much bigger than he'd thought. Beyond the Corvette at the very rear was a door that probably led to the basement, a workbench against the back wall, and an open door to a washroom. Everything the aspiring mechanic could want.

"You could fit three cars in here," Maureen said.

Kendall looked at his cheap Timex watch. He had a meeting with Nate Polis on the Wyrick lot in Glendale in an hour.

"Do you have to get going?" Maureen said.

"Yes. But I love the house. I'll put together an offer."

Maureen clapped her hands. "Wonderful. I know you'll be very happy."

FOUR
NATE

W yrick Studios occupied eight acres in the hills off the Glendale Freeway. Kendall arrived at two thirty in his '99 Avalon with 175,000 miles on the clock. The compound lay on a service road surrounded by eight-foot hurricane fencing topped with concertina wire, like a concentration camp save for the perfect emerald lawn. Kendall pulled up to the stucco guard shack where a uniformed agent checked his ID against his computer and raised the red and white striped barrier.

"Straight ahead. You can't miss it."

Kendall followed Ultra Pigeon Boulevard past moist gardens of bougainvillea, tulips, pansies, and snapdragons, a small pond with a fountain and white swans, to the parking lot in front of the Darryl C. Wyrick Administration Building. Ultra Pigeon and Awesome Possum capered in ten-foot plastic caricature on the facade, the Hope and Crosby of the anthropomorphic world. Awesome Possum was a hideous Gilbert Shelton-like creature. Ultra Pigeon with his bulging chest full of medals seemed more wholesome.

Carrying a thin portfolio, Kendall entered the building through a rotating door. The rotunda-shaped foyer was finished in Italian tile with a marble fountain in the shape of Illeana the

Illusionist holding her top hat from which fresh water tumbled. Fat koi circled the indoor pond. Behind the pond was a curving counter with three clerks like hotel employees dealing with supplicants. Kendall joined a line of four. He checked FB and comicbookresources on his phone while he waited.

"Next!" a clerk chirped.

The guy behind Kendall nudged him. "That's you, bud."

Kendall stepped up to the counter. The clerk was a good-looking young woman with a tight cap of blond curls and dazzling teeth. She wore an Ultra Pigeon pin in her lapel.

"How can I help you, sir?"

"Kendall Coffin to see Nate Polis."

The clerk pecked at a keyboard like a hotel clerk. "Yes, Mr. Coffin. He's in the Brodeen Building." She handed Kendall a laminated visitor ID badge on a lanyard. "Please wear this. If you'll step out front, one of our interns will take you to Mr. Polis."

As Kendall exited the building a blue and yellow golf cart with a blue awning zipped up in front of him driven by a young black man in a blue and yellow uniform wearing a billed cap. "Derrick" was stitched on his chest in gold thread.

"Mr. Coffin?" the driver said.

Kendall got in the golf cart, and they zoomed away, accompanied only by the faint, high-pitch whine of the electric motor. They drove down the spotless blacktop between buildings that merged modern eclecticism and primary colors with Victorian touches such as front porches with swing chairs. Flowers everywhere: n pots, hanging from hooks, suspended from streetlights, and in window boxes. Their scent was pervasive.

"This your first trip to Wyrick?" Derrick said.

"Yup."

"You picked a beautiful day. Stop by the cafeteria if you get a chance. It's all free."

The Brodeen Building was relatively new with a curved roof, an iron bridge over a man-made stream, industrial chains connecting the massive beamed overhang to the iron front porch. Very Bauhaus. Derrick chirped to a stop just before the bridge.

"Enjoy your visit."

"Thank you," Kendall said. He crossed the bridge with a slight booming noise and entered the building through a glass door. It was quiet and chill inside. A middle-aged woman, her hair piled high in a wave and wearing Buddy Holly glasses looked up from her keyboard and smiled.

"Mr. Coffin? Straight back the corridor behind me. It's the third door on your left."

The hall was decorated with film posters: *Stylin'*, *The Quinceañera*, *Grad School*, *Lookin' to Cop*, and *Bite Me*, the latter two produced by Nate Polis. A buxom blond in a short gray skirt exited Nate's office, holding the door for Kendall.

"Thank you."

She flashed a dazzling grin. "Not at all."

Nate sat on an Italian leather sofa smoking a Dunhill Estupendo, one arm up on the sofa's back. Nate wore creased black linen trou, a blindingly white shirt with arrow collars open at the neck, and a black linen sport jacket. He had a good tan. He stood as Kendall entered. Nate was five ten and lean, the shaved skull necessitated by dwindling hair. He had a gold ring in one ear and three gold rings on his right hand. He smiled and opened his arms.

"Bubbelah!"

They thumped each other on the back. Nate gestured around. "Whaddaya think?"

Kendall looked around the office. Floor-to-ceiling windows looked out onto an enclosed courtyard bursting with wisteria and bougainvillea, shaded by palm trees, several picnic benches sitting on putting-green grass. The park was surrounded by office buildings.

Nate's office was square, white walls hung with posters, photos, original art from Nate's movies: *Disco*, *Weisenheimers*, *The Main Man*. The first two featured dogs. The last was a savage black comedy. Not Wyrick's usual fare, but Wyrick had changed after the founder's death.

"I'm blown away," Kendall said.

"What'd you think of Judy?"

"What? The babe? She's spectacular."

Nate oscillated his right index finger in his left fist. "She's my personal secretary. Hey, you want a Dunhill? These puppies are thirty years old."

"No thanks. I don't get the whole cigar thing."

Nate relit his cigar with a gold lighter. "You have come at a propitious time, my friend. We're about to begin production on *Night Shifts*. Dal Lazlo. It's an erotic thriller. The regular storyboard artist died two days ago. Slug fell on him out of the blue. He's in Fullerton, some cholo shoots his nine in Anaheim. I mean, what are the chances?"

"My god," Kendall said. "That's terrible. Did they catch the perpetrator?"

Nate put his feet up on the stainless steel industrial chic coffee table. "Are you shitting? You got a hundred emes shooting their guns in the air to celebrate some gorilla's win in the UFC, just like the rap says. Is it even murder? What an age, eh? *Omnibus locis fit caedes*. There is slaughter everywhere. So whaddaya think? You ready to go?"

"I don't even have a place! I'm putting a bid in on a house tomorrow."

"Oh Kendall, Jesus, man. How could I have been so dense? Really sorry about Shirley. You know that, man."

"Thanks for the case of Scotch."

"'What butter and whiskey won't cure there is no cure for.' Listen. The studio will find you a place while you close. They got a bunch of apartments in the area. The studio will pick up the tab." Nate reached for a cordless phone on the table and pushed a button.

"Judy, we need to fix my friend Kendall Coffin up with some digs for a couple of weeks. Would you see what you've got? Thank you, darling."

Kendall was stunned. He'd passed through a portal into the land of the omnipotent.

"You'll have to sign a non-disclosure agreement. I'm starting you at five thou a week. Is that adequate?"

"I don't know what to say."

"Make hay while the sun shines. This is strictly for the duration of production, you understand, until such times as your services are no longer needed. But don't worry. Do a good job, and you'll never be out of work."

Nate got up and went to his desk, a free-form slab of walnut on steel legs, and returned with a manila folder from which he pulled a short document. He handed it to Kendall along with a pen. "Non-disclosure."

Kendall took the paper and pen. "Nate, don't you want to see my work?"

Nate waved his hand. "Buddy, I've seen your work! Got a guy here who's only job is keep an eye on comics. I know you can do the job. You've been doing it for years."

Kendall could not believe his luck. He'd stayed in touch with Nate since college but sporadically. He hadn't seen Nate in twenty years. When he contacted Nate a month ago—right after Shirley's funeral—he didn't expect much to come of it. Kendall had had a few brushes with Hollywood. When they needed you, they were your best friend. When they didn't, you were a non-person. Kendall guessed Nate needed him, but he couldn't figure out why. It wasn't as if there were a dearth of good story-board artists in the LA area.

It was a standard non-disclosure agreement. Kendall signed it. Nate tossed a script at him. *Night Shifts* by Dal Lazlo.

"Read that. Production meeting Monday the 27th at ten right here. I'm having a little get-together at my place on the 28th. Judy will fix you up with an invite when she puts you on the payroll. You bid on a house? Already?"

Kendall shrugged self-consciously. He wasn't used to spending money. "My mom just died and left me a ton of money."

"Jesus!" Nate said. "You've had to deal with a lot!"

"I wanted to get out of Omaha."

"I know, but most people come out here and test the waters. Don't get me wrong. I'm glad you're here. Timing is everything. So where's the house?"

"Los Feliz. A Roark Dexter Smith design."

"He was a crazy fuck. Like to see it sometime."

"If I get it."

"Right. Well pal, glad to see ya, welcome to LA and all that jazz."

Nate's headset buzzed. His eyebrows went up. "Send him in." He turned back to Kendall. "Hey, my three o'clock's here. See you on Monday. See Judy before you go, right across the hall."

FIVE
MOVING DAY

It was the fastest closing in history. On Wednesday, the seller agreed to Kendall's offer of 2.4 mil. On Thursday, the lender accepted his forty percent down payment. On Friday, they closed and gave him the keys. Knowing the move was permanent, Kendall had packed the old Avalon to the gunwales with plenty of clothes as well as art supplies.

He stayed in the free Wyrick apartment Tuesday through Saturday. It was an airy studio apartment in the Solange Building on Sepulveda Boulevard. On Saturday he flew back to Omaha. Greg Rawlins met him at the airport. Greg wrote comics and novels. Currently, he was writing *Rip-Off* for IDW, *Black Savage* and *Ferroman* for Dark Horse. He and Kendall had broken into the industry together with their own title, *The Ecdysiast*.

Greg met him at the luggage carousel. "How'd it go?" asked the strapping, squared-off writer. He had a Clark Kent presence with square tortoiseshell glasses.

"Thanks for coming," Kendall said, snagging his suitcase.

"That it?"

"Let's go."

They walked to Greg's HHR in the B parking lot. Kendall's house at 5335 SW 126th Circle had been on the market for only a week before it sold. Kendall had ten days to vacate the property. He'd done a lot of packing before heading west, and after that Greg had supervised the rest with his wife Brandy and his younger brother Paul, also an artist. Greg and Kendall hit Omaha just before five. It took over an hour to cross the city. The radio played "Heroes and Villains."

I've been in this town so long that back in the city
I've been taken for lost and gone
And unknown for a long, long time

The song called him west, like all the other Beach Boys songs. "Surfin' Safari," "Surfin' USA," "Dance, Dance, Dance," "Fun, Fun, Fun," "I Get Around."

Go West young man.

Kendall's lawn was neatly mowed and boxes neatly stacked in his two-car garage when they arrived shortly after six. From outside, they heard the noise of a vacuum cleaner. They entered through the front door. Paul was vacuuming the living room. There was no furniture. The fireplace was immaculate. Faint rectangles showed where pictures had hung. Indentations in the cocoa rug showed where furniture had stood. Worm-like cigarette burns covered the living room carpet around the sofa and circled the bed in the master bedroom.

Kendall thanked Paul and ordered pizza delivered. They ate in the screened-in porch looking out on the weed-choked lawn. Kendall had never liked yard work, and it showed. A black wrought-iron table and four chairs remained. The movers were coming tomorrow.

"So I got a gig," Paul said folding a slice of Papa John's.

"What?" Kendall said.

"I'm drawing *Slue Foot Slut* for Hustler."

Kendall swallowed. "What's it pay?"

"Fifteen hundred a page."

"Can't argue with that," Kendall said.

After the Rawlins brothers left, Kendall went into the master bedroom. He'd come home from the gym one day and found Shirley slumped over on the bed, her torso bent forward at the waist and between her legs. Kendall lifted her up. The TV remote had left a checkerboard pattern on her forehead. He tried mouth to mouth. No response. He dialed 911.

The next few days passed in a grief-stricken haze, although the magic had long since gone out of their relationship. Greg shuttled him to the police station where he answered a series of questions. Were there any other drugs in the house? Did Kendall know she was crushing her Oxy up on a mirror and snorting it through a straw? Did she leave a life insurance policy?

Later, clearing out her dresser he heard some clinking, peeled off the top layer of clothes and uncovered eleven empty vodka bottles. What a fool he'd been. There had been incidents of alcoholism throughout their relationship. She'd started drinking as a teenager. She started drinking at nine in the morning. Shirley suffered blackouts while out, miraculously avoiding accidents or DUIs.

A month later his mother Elizabeth died. Greg ferried him through that one too. When Kendall got home from the funeral, he found a message on his answering machine from his editor. He'd been fired. The new editor was replacing Kendall on the series.

God was trying to tell him something. Time for a change.

With his remaining furniture jammed into the garage, Kendall slept on a roll-up futon which Greg loaned him. He had an erotic dream about a girl he met in a cyber-café. She followed him home like a stray puppy. They went from room to room looking for a place to make love, but there were jabbering house guests everywhere. Kendall felt anxious that Shirley would find out. Smoke and shouting filled the room. The house was on fire. Desperately, Kendall pushed the girl ahead of him, but she dug in her heels and wouldn't go. He grabbed her by the hair and attempted to drag her out of the house. The flames were visible now. He felt his skin turn black and curl with excruciating agony.

He jerked awake, the sensation of burning alive still fresh. There was a gray haze in the east.

Kendall rode his bicycle to a nearby coffee shop for breakfast.

The vast Mayflower van arrived at eleven as a crew of six stalwarts, two Hispanic, two Black, two white hoisted and hefted his worldly belongings. He'd written the destination in marker on each box: kitchen, living room, master bedroom. Kendall stood around feeling useless and guilty, comparing the movers' work to his own. All he did was scribble pictures on a page. He'd been doing it since grade school. Half the scripts he illustrated were sophomoric. Some were embarrassing. What legacy would he leave? An Eisner nomination? A handful of funny books? He didn't even have any kids.

One of the movers handed him a clipboard. "Please read and sign, Mr. Coffin."

It was a standard form stating that all his belongings had been loaded and nothing had been damaged. Kendall signed it and handed it back. "When will you be in LA?"

The man consulted a schedule beneath the form. "One week from today."

"Okay, thanks."

Greg drove him to the airport the next day.

SIX
NEIGHBORS

I t was the last day in the studio apartment. Kendall sat at the drawing table Nate had sent staring at the script.

INT. BEDROOM. DAY.
Charlene is tied spread-eagled to the four-poster with a gag ball in her mouth. She looks frightened.

Kendall felt uncomfortable. The scene was mild compared to what followed. The film was certain to earn an 'X' rating, the kiss of death in Hollywood. Kendall had difficulty believing Wyrick had green-lit *Night Shifts*, even with their more adult, "edgy" direction under the stewardship of Maude Cummings, who had become CEO four years ago following the retirement of legendary filmmaker Hans Gropius. Hans had been the last of the "Crazy Eight," the original animators whom Darryl Wyrick had hired for his first groundbreaking feature, *Nudnick of the North.*

Maude vowed to shake things up and had championed a series of adult sex farces with the remake of *Carry on Nurse.* But

Night Shifts went way beyond that. It was an 'A' list porn film with several top stars attached. Dal Lazlo was the "edgy" director of the hour whose *Last Year at Indianola* had steamrolled the critics at Sundance and Cannes.

Kendall stared at the page. One reason he didn't like to draw the scene was because it gave him a hard-on. Sam Fuller would have said that's a good scene. But it wasn't what Kendall liked to draw.

Snap out of it, fool! A job's a job. Draw the damned scene and collect your paycheck!

"I wish they all could be California girls," the Beach Boys crooned from the little Sony Kendall had used for twenty years.

He thought about drinking. It might be easier to draw, but then he'd mess up his sleep and have a hangover.

Draw the fuckin' page. It's just a job. Do the job, and more will follow. This is what you wanted, isn't it? To be part of the Hollywood crowd, go to the parties, date starlets, show up at awards shows.

His phone warbled "I Live for the Sun." He picked it up.

"Coffin."

"Mr. Coffin, this is Phil Bailey with Mayflower. We're about an hour from your place. Just wanted to give you a heads-up."

"Thank you, sir," Kendall said. "I'll meet you there."

He felt like a grade-schooler whose visit to the principal's office had just been canceled. With a sigh of relief, he set down his pencil, stood, and stretched. It was merely a reprieve, not a pardon. The sequence was due on Monday. He had four days. When he started out in comics, he was drawing two pages a day.

Kendall grabbed his backpack containing his laptop, portfolio, and camera and exited the third-floor walk-up. He took the exterior stairs to the courtyard and beeped open the Avalon. He stopped at a Dunkin' Donuts and picked up a half dozen coffees and a dozen doughnuts which he carried to the car in a big cardboard box. The apartment was in Pasadena, a stone's throw but a snail's pace from Los Feliz. Kendall joined the long line of parked cars on the 210, radio tuned to the All Surf Station, WAVE 99.9 on your FM dial.

There was a lot more surf music than most people realized. Kendall had wanted to live in California since he'd first heard "Little Surfer Girl" at the age of nine. He had yet to make it to the ocean.

Forty-five minutes later he parked at the curb in front of the house. The garage sat a mere eight feet from the sidewalk; not deep enough for a car. Plus, there was that Corvette blocking the entrance. Kendall got out, took the doughnuts and coffee, beeped the car shut, walked up the steps, and unlocked the padlock. The gates shrieked like banshees. He unlocked the front door and went inside. The house smelled of dust and curdled futurism, like a museum. He went into the kitchen and set the coffee and doughnuts down on the marble counter.

Shafts of light from the skylights caught the dust gleaming like the asteroid belt. He went through the double doors into the courtyard. The lush vegetation seemed almost tropical, an explosion of green and purple beauty. He didn't like the idea of strangers in the belly of his house. He would do the yard work himself. Maybe some neighborhood kids once he got to know them.

He returned to the Avalon, popped the trunk, and removed a heavy wooden box containing the .45 his father had carried with him throughout the Vietnam War. Kendall was no shooter. He kept the gun for sentimental reasons and because it was an excellent model. He carried the box into the house, into the den, removed the Picasso, and deposited the pistol in the wall safe. He stripped the combination from the back of the safe, memorized it, and stuck it in his pocket.

A vibraphone chimed the intro to the Temptations' "Beauty's Only Skin Deep." With a shock, Kendall realized it was the doorbell. Kendall replaced the painting and went to the front door. A stout, black man wearing a yellow Mayflower cap stood in the vestibule with a clipboard.

"Mr. Coffin? Phil Bailey. Say, this is some house."

Kendall looked over Bailey's shoulder where four workmen stood on the sidewalk staring at the house.

"Hi, Mr. Bailey. Come on in. Would you like some coffee and a doughnut?"

"That's all right. Got plenty of coffee, but I will take a doughnut. Let me just do a walk-through."

While Kendall took Bailey through the house, the movers unrolled carpet runners over the hardwood and tile floors. The furniture arrived carried by burly men like ants returning to their colony with enormous grains of food. Boxes piled up. Kendall's CD collection alone filled six boxes. It took the crew just over two hours to unload the truck. Bailey went through a checklist which Kendall signed. Bailey and one other man got in the moving van, the other four movers jamming into an old Toyota double cab pickup with California plates. As the truck moved down the street, a man walked up the sidewalk from the east and mounted the steps.

Kendall watched with apprehension. The man had the long hair and beard of an old-world prophet, wore Ray-Bans, a screaming red and yellow Hawaiian shirt showing guitars and palm trees, and baggy shorts that stopped mid-calf. Between his sandals and short bottoms, tribal tats climbed up his thick legs. A gold cross glittered on his neck. The man climbed slowly using the rail.

"Hello," Kendall said when the man was several steps down.

The man looked up with a friendly grin. "Well hello, friend. I'm Torrance Skaggs, your next-door neighbor. Thought I'd mosey over and welcome you to the neighborhood."

Kendall shook Torrance's hand. "Kendall Coffin. Torrance Skaggs. Torrance Skaggs. Why does that ring a bell?"

"I used to be in Gearhead. That's a heavy metal band."

Kendall's mouth formed an 'O.' "Gearhead?! Man, I love that band! I've got your first two records. You were lead singer and guitarist! Torrance Skaggs! Come up! Come up!"

Kendall gestured for Torrance to precede him through the gate into the house. Torrance stopped in the vestibule, looked all around, and inhaled deeply. "So you bought the old Wallanda House."

Kendall shut the front door. "That's right. Did you know him?"

"No, sir. Lived next door to the man for six years; he never invited me over. Came to greet him just like now. I even brought him a cake."

"This used to be a real nice town ... you could walk the streets at night ... no bums to get you down ... no drunks to start a fight ..." Kendall rapped.

Torrance grinned and nodded. He'd heard it a million times. "Yup yup, that's off the first album. 'The Badger.'"

"Weirdos started hangin 'round," Kendall continued, adding some shuffle and a little tap. "Hangin' 'round and talkin' trash ... talkin' trash and hangin' 'round ... livin' on that welfare cash ..."

Torrance's grin froze like a charlie horse. He nodded his head like an exasperated teacher. Kendall stopped singing.

"Thank you."

"Was it that bad?"

"Well ..." Torrance said going to the double doors which opened onto the courtyard.

Kendall opened the doors, and they stepped out.

"It's just that I've put that part of my life behind me. I serve the Lord now, and not a day goes by I don't beg for forgiveness, knowing that songs I wrote may have inspired young people to do drugs, engage in promiscuity, or engage in antisocial behavior."

SEVEN
TORRANCE

K endall cringed, recalling a lawsuit that alleged Gearhead's songs had caused a young man to commit suicide. Torrance laughed and slapped him on the arm.

"Relax. I'm not going to ask you to pray with me."

"This is only the third time I've been here," Kendall said walking up to the pool. He stooped and put his hand in the cool, clear water. "Don't even know how to work this pool."

"I've got a pool," Torrance said. "I'll show you. It's pretty simple. Basically, you just add chemicals and skim the leaves."

Kendall stood. "Would you like some coffee? A doughnut?"

"Sure."

Kendall led the way into the kitchen. Torrance chose a cruller.

"Moved next door in '99," Torrance said, chewing. "The year I got out of rehab. You know Ziggy died in '94 from a drug overdose."

Ziggy had been the drummer.

"No," Kendall said. "I'm sorry to hear it. I just lost a wife to drugs."

Torrance's eyes widened. "Seriously? I'm sorry to hear that, brother. I'll pray with you if you like."

"What the hell," Kendall said. "Never hurts."

Torrance took his hand. "It never hurts." He lowered his head and gripped Kendall like a batter. "Dear Lord, please watch over this good man Kendall Coffin and help him in his time of need. Amen."

"Amen," Kendall said.

Torrance let go.

"What do you do, Kendall?"

"I'm a comic book artist. I'm doing some storyboarding for Wyrick."

Torrance raised his eyebrows. "I loved Wyrick when I was a kid."

"Let me give you the grand tour," Kendall said. They went into the dining room. Torrance ran his hands over the back of the Art Deco meets Maya chairs.

"He designed all the furniture too," Torrance said. "Roark Dexter Smith was one crazy motherfucker."

"Yeah," Kendall said. "I got to visit a lot of his houses when I lived in Omaha. We'd go to Wisconsin during the summers, and I'd look at Smith houses."

"You know he was a Satanist."

"I knew he was weird. I never heard that." They walked down the corridor into a commodious bedroom.

"Back in the day, the press was a little more discreet. Everybody loved Smith; America's greatest architect, master of the organic theory, blah blah blah. He treated women like dirt, shafted every creditor, fathered children out of wedlock, he didn't even have an architectural license."

"Really?" Kendall said leading the way into the den with its massive fireplace and Steinway baby grand.

Torrance sat on the polished rosewood stool, flipped up the cover and hit a few keys. He began to play "Rhapsody in Blue." Kendall sat in an overstuffed leather chair, stunned. The piano was in tune and Torrance was masterful. Kendall regretted never having seen the band.

Torrance gave it five minutes before abruptly removing his hands from the keys. "Sorry! I can't resist a set of keys."

They stood. "Don't apologize. I'd love to hear you play the whole thing, or anything you want to play."

"Later. I don't want to take up too much of your time."

"I'm a freelancer," Kendall said. "I make my own schedule."

"What are you working on?"

"Well, I was drawing comics. Now I'm storyboarding for Wyrick."

They stepped back out into the courtyard from the other end. Torrance spread his arms and inhaled deeply. "Ahhh, the smog has lifted."

They approached the rear of the courtyard where a stepped arch in the living room framed the Los Angeles basin. There was a sharp ten-foot drop-off twenty feet from the rear of the house, a ravine filled with gorse and thorns, the roofs and backyards of houses.

"My view's pretty much the same," Torrance said. "We'll have you over soon, and I'll show you what the pool needs. Really isn't much. You've got to clean it and throw in a few chemicals. Every now and then you'll find some dead squirrels or skunks caught in the filter. Hate that shit. I've tried everything to keep 'em out."

Torrance faced Kendall's pool. "Course you won't have that problem because the courtyard is entirely surrounded with house."

"Not entirely," Kendall said indicating the banyan trees. "They can drop from the trees." He looked around. Where was the pump? He spotted a wood block, like a tiny shack, set just off the flagstone on the bluegrass lawn. The grass looked and felt old but was healthy like the lawn you might see outside a stately English country estate. He went over to the box and saw that the top was hinged with a metal handle. He opened it up revealing the pool pump humming away, water moving through plastic tubes, a couple sealed plastic canisters of water purifier.

Torrance found nets and scoops mounted on brackets to the wall. "Here's your nets and stuff. Well, I should be getting back. We'll have you over so you can meet Marge and Tommy. Met

Marge in rehab. Best thing ever happened to me. Tommy's a huge comic book fan."

"I'll walk you out." They returned to the foyer. Kendall offered his hand.

"Say, you know about the security system, don't you?" Torrance said.

"The realtor mentioned it, but I haven't had a chance to check it out."

Torrance looked around, spotted a closet off the foyer. Opened it. Inside was a metal box fastened to the wall. He opened it revealing a series of switches. It was old, something out of the sixties with a Bakelite surface.

"Wallanda designed a system that traps and holds intruders like a possum."

"You're kidding. How do you know?"

"Tommy told me. Said he saw Wallanda letting some scamp out when he was seven. Dude'd been in there all night afraid to cry out because he was breaking and entering. Wallanda and Smith figured burglars would most likely try to enter through the big window wells for the basement, so they rigged them all with a cage-like apparatus that slams down when it's triggered."

Visions of lawsuits danced in Kendall's brain. "Wow. Thanks for telling me. I'll have to have that taken out."

"I wouldn't worry. Probably hasn't worked in years. Just thought you should know about it."

"Are there many robberies in this neighborhood?"

"A few. Kids. Junkies. Plus, there's that nut going around murdering young women."

"What nut?"

"The Kardashian Killer. At least three that they know of."

Kendall thanked Torrance and watched the bearded man mosey down the stairs.

EIGHT
RIDE THE WILD SURF

Kendall stared at the security panel in the closet which was the size of a small bedroom and lined with cedar. Several coats and jackets hung on wooden hangers, and there were dozens of neatly stacked shoe boxes.

The panel was a two-foot square filled with rows of toggle switches, each painstakingly labeled by one of those handheld printers which embossed your message on a plastic tape. FBW #1. Front basement window number one. There were seven large basement window basins, each presumably equipped with a man trap. A faded, hand-drawn map showed a crude schematic of the house and the windows' locations. The legal threat was existential. From the look of the panel, no one had touched it in years. Cobwebs clung to the frame. Spider webs stretched from the toggles, some still holding desiccated insects. A pearly moth glinted in the sun from the skylight. Kendall looked up. The square skylight, matching the shape of the room, had an interlocking rhomboid design and was tinted pale yellow and green.

A box of circuit breakers clung to the wall next to the security system. Each was labeled with plastic tape, all switched to the ON position except for the switch labeled SECURITY. Were the traps spring-powered? Pneumatic? Not that it mattered. Kendall had no intention of activating them. He was surprised the house didn't have something more modern, but that could wait.

Kendall did not look forward to returning to Pasadena. The drawing board waited. The studio waited. He had to get those storyboards in by Monday, or he was royally fucked. He walked through his fantastic house touching the furnishings and the otherworldly stonework. He felt like a character in one of Phillip Jose Farmer's novels. Kickaha in the Overlords' Palace. Just being in the house was a high.

In the bedroom, he looked at the ring bolts inserted in the head and footboards. They bothered him. In the kitchen, he tried the basement door. He would need a crowbar to open it. He glanced at his watch. If he headed back now, he would spend ninety minutes sitting in traffic. He hated that about Los Angeles: the constant press of humanity from every side, the smog a constant reminder of the hectic pace, and crowded conditions. How awful to be poor in Los Angeles—more so than any other city—because everywhere you looked were reminders of luxury, wealth, success. Ferraris and Bentleys on the freeways. The enormous billboards showing impossibly young, beautiful, and wealthy movie stars. The evening news obsessed with the weekend box office.

The check-cashing, pawn shops, and instant money stores were always close. Kendall had seen lines of people outside plasma centers. Tweakers, HIV carriers, junkies, veterans, bums. Who would knowingly use their blood?

There was a constant threat of theft and even death. You had to protect what you had, or some animal would take it away. Hence the gated communities, the elaborate security systems, the private security services. Los Angeles was a steaming cauldron of unchecked desire. Unchecked desire and ruthlessness were the prerequisites of success.

Kendall had never been ruthless. Maybe that was his problem. Maybe he didn't want it bad enough. Now that he was out here, he wanted it more than ever. But was he ready to kill and eat his own mother for it?

Relax, kid. You're an artist. A good one. You'll always have plenty of work.

He went into the library and looked at the books. He pulled biographies of Bette Davis and Humphrey Bogart. Kendall loved biographies. The books smelled deliciously old. He sat in the vintage leather La-Z-Boy and opened the Davis. He was halfway through the book when he realized the light was fading. It was eight thirty. Time to hit the road. Tucking the two books under his arm, he did a final walk-through, making sure the doors and windows were locked.

Locking the front door, he swung the metal gates shut but left the padlock off. He went down the steep steps to the sidewalk. The white garage door caught his eye. No rush. He was used to working through the night, particularly toward the end of his marriage when being with Shirley was like watching someone die.

He removed his newly encumbered key chain and found the garage key, labeled with embossed tape. He unlocked the door and wheeled it into the ceiling with a shriek. Inside he turned on the lights, fluorescents in aluminum shrouds marching back under the hill in ranks of two. He walked by the old Corvette. He hoped he had enough money after paying the mortgage to get it running.

Several olive-painted six-foot steel cabinets lined the wall on the right. He opened one. Row after row of old film in wheel-shaped aluminum containers like a chewing tobacco warehouse. He pulled one out. *Harry and the Hendersons* was written on the lid in black marker. Good wholesome family fun, essential homework for a Wyrick producer.

He put it back and shut the door. Past the cabinets was a large bulletin board on which the previous owner had tacked a Maxim calendar, pictures of cars and babes, a few articles from Variety and Billboard. "*GRAD SCHOOL* CERTAIN TO PLEASE / Although there are a few dissonant moments ..."

From the since defunct Los Angeles Argus Leader: "MAD-

WIRE MEDIA BREAKS GROUND ON NEW HQ/Scene of notorious crime."

Kendall headed back, back under the hill. A wooden workbench occupied the back wall. Above on pegboards was an immaculate display of tools. A band saw stood to the side. There was a metal-working lathe. There were three doors on the right. The one at the very rear led into the basement. The one next to it held a half bath. The third was a closet.

Kendall opened the door and stared. The Silver Surfer by Stanley Mouse. On a surfboard.

NINE
DINNER NEXT DOOR

K endall returned to his studio apartment and worked through the night to finish the sequence, putting his brain on autopilot and slamming coffee. He finished around three, tried to sleep, fell into that shallow hell that is neither sleep nor wakefulness, finally got up, and picked up a stack of comics he'd brought with him from Omaha.

On top was *COPRA*, Michel Fiffe's oddball superhero affair. Fiffe's graphics reminded Kendall of Steranko. He read the whole thing, not really paying attention to the story, studying the innovative graphics. Like most comic geeks, Kendall could rhapsodize for hours about his favorite artists. His own work had been compared to Steranko, Michael L. Peters, and Whilce Portacio.

He dozed off on the sofa and when he woke it was four thirty. He'd slept for eight and a half hours. Kendall showered, grabbed his portfolio and overnight case and booked. Those boxes weren't going to unload themselves.

He arrived at his house—HIS HOUSE—at five thirty, parked on the street, and went up the stairs. He planned to push the Corvette deeper into the garage so he could fit his car in. Kendall let himself in, inhaling that exotic scent. Cinnamon from the

Casbah, frangipani from Costa Rica, Egyptian sands, Martian air, a piece of every movie ever made. Kendall was the master of a house where Robert Mitchum, Ida Lupino, and Sammy Davis Jr. had partied. A piece of Movie History.

He started with the kitchen, slicing the boxes open with a pocket knife, stacking the dishes, glasses, pots, and pans where they belonged. He hooked most of his metal cookware to a redwood rack suspended horizontally over the stove. There were three sinks: a big double looking out on the courtyard and a single on the island opposite.

He unpacked his kitchen radio and plugged it in, setting the dial to WAVE. There was a surf report for the following day, Sunday. "Big breakers at Malibu …"

He set some mugs in a cabinet and turned around. He nearly jumped out of his skin. A boy stood in the kitchen entrance, a tall boy with a platinum fade, tanned face of a surfer, wearing an Explorers Club T-shirt with the sleeves cut off and baggy cargo shorts.

"Hi!" the boy said brightly. "I'm Tommy from next door. The folks axed me to ax you to dinner?"

Kendall came around the island to meet him. "Kendall Coffin. Sure. That would be great. Now?"

"In about an hour. Torrance tells me you're a comic book artist. What have you done?"

"Doc Strange, mostly."

Tommy's eyes went wide, and his mouth stretched revealing copious gum. "Really? I think I might have some of those! I'm sorry, I'm not good on names. What's your name again?"

"Kendall Coffin."

"Oh wow, man! Oh wow! I really dig your work!"

"Tell your folks I'll be over in an hour."

"Awesome."

Tommy left. Kendall thought it a little odd that the kid just walked in the front door without ringing. For the next hour, he put his bedroom in shape, making the bed, hanging towels, putting his clothes away in the bureaus and closets. The master closet was itself the size of a small bedroom and contained the by now expected leftovers. Kendall checked the suits. They were of superior quality and his size. An added bonus. Eight hats sat on the hat shelf. Kendall snagged a Fifth Avenue Bond and put it on. He looked at himself in the floor-to-ceiling closet mirror. Pretty snappy. It was a narrow-brimmed fedora with a red feather. With his loose Hawaiian shirt and white T, he rocked a pose flashing a peace symbol with one hand and Hawaiian shaka with the other.

He wore the hat next door. He went down to the street and walked up the block, the houses separated by eight-foot hedges of tightly woven tensile steel strength evergreen. The Skaggs's house was a traditional two-story Victorian with an immaculate lawn, red and yellow roses lining the stepped stone path to the front porch. The windows spilled a soft glow, and Yes's "Close to the Edge" into the fragrant evening.

Kendall knocked on the screen door.

"Come in," a woman's voice sang.

He entered. A trim middle-aged woman with a tight cap of gray hair came to greet him wearing an apron. "Hello! I'm Marge. Welcome to the neighborhood."

Kendall shook her hands. She smelled faintly of clove. "Kendall Coffin. Sorry, I come empty-handed."

"Don't be silly. Torrance is out back. Would you like a drink?"

"Scotch on the rocks if you've got it."

She stuck a tumbler under the reefer's ice-maker, poured in a couple fingers of Macallan.

Kendall took the tumbler. "Does Torrance drink?"

Marge smiled. "Nope. Not a drop in sixteen years. This is for guests. And me. I like a tipple now and then."

Kendall thanked her, followed the hall to a family room and from there out the sliding glass doors to the pool area where Torrance sat on a bench suspended from the eaves by two tractor chains. He had a glass of iced tea.

"Hello!" Torrance boomed. "Glad you could make it. Have a seat. Hope you like meatloaf."

Kendall pulled up a nylon folding chair. "I love meatloaf. My mother used to make meatloaf."

They sat in a companionable silence for a few minutes listening to the susurrus of traffic on Lincoln, the distant wail of a siren.

"You still keep up with music?" Kendall said.

"Oh, hell yeah. All the good music these days is with independents. The music dinosaurs don't know what's going on. I still get invited to the awards shows. We're even talking about a reunion tour."

"That would be great. I'd come."

"Music ain't what I do, it's who I am. That and the Lord."

"I blame the Beach Boys for me moving out here."

Marge appeared in the door. "Din-din, boys. Din-din."

Torrance and Kendall carried their glasses into the dining room and sat at a walnut table. Marge ferried platters in from the kitchen: baked potatoes, meatloaf, salad.

"Tommy!" she called.

A stooped old man with a Smith Brothers beard hobbled in with a cane.

"Tommy can't make it," Tommy said in a creaking voice. "I, the Great Cornholio, will take his place."

"Tommy!" Marge yelled. "Lose the beard and sit down."

Torrance grinned proudly. "Tommy played Sheridan Whiteside in his school's production of *The Man Who Came to Dinner*."

"Sob!" the Great Cornholio said, peeling off the beard and sitting. He reached for the meatloaf. They loaded up their plates.

Kendall's fork was halfway to his mouth when Torrance put his hands together and bowed his head. Tommy and Marge did likewise. Kendall hurriedly set his fork down.

"Dear Lord, for this food we are about to receive we thank you."

"Amen," all said.

Then they dug in. Kendall waited a few mouthfuls for ballast.

"So, Tommy. What else does the Great Cornholio do?"

"Play drums, of course."

"He's got a band," Torrance said. "The Messerschmidts."

"We write all our own material except for some Gearhead songs."

Marge beamed proudly at Kendall. "Can you believe Gearhead is finally going to be inducted into the Rock and Roll Hall of Fame?"

"That's great news!" Kendall said.

Torrance waved it off. "Twenty years ago, I was mad as hell at being snubbed. These days it doesn't matter so much. It will be a good opportunity to see the boys."

"If you did do a tour," Kendall said, "who would drum?"

Tommy used his fork and knife to play paradiddles on the tabletop.

"Maybe," Torrance said. "I don't want you interrupting your education."

Marge circulated salad. "We wondered who would buy that house. It's been vacant since the previous owner moved out. Four years."

"Did you know him?" Kendall said.

"Yes. He was a writer."

"He murdered his wife," Tommy said.

Kendall's fork stopped midway. "Really? In the house?"

"No," Torrance said, "not in the house. He shot her at some restaurant in Santa Monica. She was with her boyfriend."

"They drank," Marge said. "They fought a lot."

"You could hear 'em even through the hedge," Tommy said.

"Are you seeing anyone, Kendall?" Marge said.

Torrance shot her a look. "Kendall's wife recently died."

"Oh! I'm so sorry. I should keep my big mouth shut."

Kendall smiled. "It's all right. Not sure if I'm ready to date yet."

Tommy heaped more meatloaf. "When you are, Marge will fix you up with one of her lonely, cat-loving friends."

Everyone laughed.

TEN
VOICES IN THE NIGHT

After dinner, Torrance let Kendall use his computer to check his email. The service provider wasn't coming until Tuesday afternoon. Kendall would be cut off from Sunday until then unless he wanted to drive to a cyber-café. It was a blessing. He could get some work done. Facebook was as addictive as coke.

Kendall returned to his strange new house and settled in the library with his books. There was a drawing board in the spare bedroom in the den, but he didn't feel like drawing. He found a legal pad and made notes about his character, Cheap Shot. Cheap Shot wasn't exactly a superhero.

DIRTY DEEDS DONE DIRT CHEAP!

Have you been the victim of a scam, assault, or other crime? Unable to gain satisfaction through the judicial system? I will tackle any reasonable case if your cause is just. Fully bonded and insured. Pick up the phone. I'm always home. Just call me anytime.

• • •

Kendall rummaged through his CDs. He'd stored them alphabetically and labeled each box. He found AC/DC and slipped it in the Sony, filling the room with heavy metal. Kendall wanged air guitar. When the song ended, he turned the machine off and slumped in his chair with a whoosh of escaping air.

Who is Cheap Shot? An inventive former Special Ops/Green Beret/Seal Team Six type down on his luck who hangs his shingle in Pinkerton, inspired by his heroes, the Scarlet Pimpernel and Travis McGee.

Little lady comes to him. The city is using Eminent Domain to foreclose on her house—the house she's lived in all her life—so that it can build a golf course. Kendall envisioned her as a cross between Mammy Yokum and Katy Jurado. Mrs. Peabody. Widow. Her late husband a forgotten war hero.

On the other side, you had Mayor Paloma Bologna whose wife's brother has designed the golf course for an outrageous sum. The more Cheap Shot looks into Mayor Bologna, the more dirt he finds. The dude's into child prostitution, drugs, and bootleg designer goods. But how do you get to the mayor when he's guarded 24/7 by The Sizzler, a monstrous, eight-foot man/robot encased entirely in titanium who can zap you with a hundred thousand volts?

Kendall wanted to do it straight, but funny. There would be tons of inside jokes, but the basic story would be credible, and it must never descend into burlesque. Kendall looked up. It was past ten. He had eight pages of notes.

He went to bed. Kendall slept in his skivvies. He had no use for robes. The strangeness of the house radiated through him, the unfamiliar odors, the sounds, and silences. In his old house, he could hear the kitchen refrigerator while lying in bed. Not here. He felt the immense space around him; the sheer profligacy of it. And in Los Angeles! He worried he'd bought too much house. Mark Twain said that houses had been the ruin of more writers than drink or marriage.

Lucky Kendall wasn't a writer. He dreamt he was with Shirley at a house party. They got separated, and a woman took him by the hand. She had a fantastic body but the head of a werewolf. "I want you inside me, Kendall," she whispered, leading him from room to room. Every room was occupied. Kendall wasn't sure he could get it up with that werewolf head. Suddenly there was a shout.

Kendall shot awake panting. For an instant, he was disoriented. Everything felt strange. Then he saw the soft glow from the art deco lighting in the bathroom and realized he was in his new home.

But the echo of the shout remained in his ears.

ELEVEN
MEETING OF THE MINDS

N ate flipped through the sequence on a rosewood conference table in a meeting room along with the two producers, Desmond Krout and Alice Sommers. Desmond had shaved sidewalls, a hipster trilby, and a diamond ear stud. He wore creased khakis, a whiter-than-white shirt, and handmade Esattos with a two-inch lift and spoke with a Brit accent. When he smiled his teeth jutted like Freddie Mercury's. Alice was the color of café au lait, straight raven hair, pretty except for a grouper mouth. She wore moleskin pants that cupped her buttocks like grapefruit in a net, a man's white shirt rolled up to the biceps revealing her slim, muscular arms, and a pair of cat's-eye sunglasses.

"These are good, Kendall," Alice said. "You have a gift for framing a scene. But they're not specific enough. We want to see stiff penises and penetration."

Kendall's mouth froze in a half guffaw. "Are you serious?" He turned to Nate. "Is she serious?"

"Wake up, Kendall! This ain't the Comics Code! This is the way people behave in real life."

"I don't doubt that, but come on. This is going to get you an 'X' rating. It's practically obscene."

Desmond clapped Kendall on the shoulder with a little squeeze. Kendall wanted to strangle him.

"It's all about context, Kendall!" the producer said as if addressing a vast crowd. "It symbolizes the depravity of the Hellfire Club."

"Why are we even arguing?" Alice said. "You're either going to draw it the way we want, or we'll find another storyboarder."

"He'll draw it," Nate said, looking seriously at Kendall. "Won't you, Kendall?"

Kendall realized Nate's ass was on the line as well as his own. "Of course," he said. "Sorry for wasting your time with this version."

"It's not a waste," Desmond said. "We are very impressed with your layouts and pacing. And the background detail is spot on. Where you from, Kendall?"

"Omaha," Kendall said, his loathing a metallic taste at the back of his tongue. He prayed it didn't show.

"Well, that explains it. Once you've been out here awhile, you'll shake off that small town syndrome. *Night Shifts* is not about titillation. It's a serious critique of where we're at as a society. It's a very moral picture." He sounded like Russell Brand.

Nate clapped his hands. "Okay. Are we all on the same page? Kendall?"

Kendall forced a smile. "No prob. I'll have new pages tomorrow."

Desmond slapped him on the shoulder. "Attaboy."

"Okay," Nate said. "Y'all know about my party Friday night."

"Wouldn't miss it," Desmond said.

"I'll be there," Kendall said.

Alice looked at her watch. "Des?"

"I know. I know. Gotta go. Larry David waits for no man."

Desmond and Alice excused themselves.

Nate looked at Kendall. "Since when did you become such a prude?"

"I'm not a prude. This shit is toxic! Are you kidding?"

Nate shook his head. "The movie will be made, and it will be a huge hit."

Kendall packed up his portfolio. "Okay. What the fuck do I know? I'll see you tomorrow."

"Wait." Nate went to his desk and pulled something from a top drawer. It was a laminated VISITOR pass decorated with Awesome Possum and Illeana the Illusionist. "Here's your free pass to Wyrick World."

Kendall felt a tinge of awe as he took it, a brush of the child-like wonder he'd experienced at his first Wyrick movie, *Awesome Possum*. He couldn't help but light up like a kid. "Thanks, man!"

"You in the new house? What's that like?"

"It's weird, Nate. It's like living in a museum or something. Take me a couple weeks to get used to it."

"I've always wanted to see that house."

"I'll have you by soon. I'm still unpacking."

"Yeah. Come to the party. We'll get you laid."

Kendall thanked Nate and left. He retrieved his car from a company lot and signed out with the guard at the gate.

TWELVE
NIGHT MOVES

K endall stopped at a liquor store and picked up a bottle of Jim Beam. It was the only way to get through the pages. A spasm shot along his spine remembering the old days when he couldn't lay pencil to paper without a snort of blow and a shot of vodka. He didn't blame Shirley for that. They were both coke-heads. God's way of telling you you had too much money. Now the thought of blow made him shudder. Even in his dreams, it made him shudder.

But a little bourbon, hey. 'Murica. He was a freelancer. He could work any damned way he pleased. He could even smoke cigarettes. He'd never smoked. Never seen the appeal. Every time Shirley suffered a setback, real or imagined, she reached for a cigarette. Someone badmouthing her? Outside for a smoke. Bank overdraft? Nothing a cig couldn't fix. Ran up and over the curb in a drunken haze, bashing in the front fender? It called for a smoke.

He parked on the street, opened the garage, turned on the lights, and peeled the tarp off the Corvette. Cherry. Metallic blue with the 427 and lakers. He leaned over the open cockpit and inhaled the scent of old leather and fiberglass. He opened the door and sat in the driver's seat, hands at two and ten, hitting 5000 in third gear.

I was cruisin' in my Sting Ray late one night when an XKE pulled up on the right ...

He put the transmission in neutral, released the hand brake, got out and went outside, popped the Avalon's trunk, and withdrew a hand pump with gauge. He returned to the garage and went methodically from tire to tire inflating each to 40 pounds per square inch. Goodyear blue dots. The rubber was unnaturally dark and supple. He went to the rear of the vehicle, planted his feet against the lip of the concrete opening, and pushed the Corvette deeper into the garage. It rolled without resistance. He pushed it thirty feet in, then went outside and moved his own car into the garage. He went to the back of the long garage and tried the basement door. It would not budge, as if there was something heavy on the other side. He shut the garage door, locked it, and headed up and around to the house.

He could unpack, or he could draw. He unpacked. It was too early in the day to start drinking. He finished with the bedroom and moved on to the library. He unpacked books and records for the next two hours, arranging his CDs alphabetically on the built-in wall shelves. The old-school giant cathode-ray TV was too big for him to move by himself. He thought about asking Tommy. He could pay the boy in comics.

His comic collection nearly filled one of the small bedrooms, the comics arranged by title in long rectangular boxes, the comics themselves sealed in individual plastic bags. He looked at the boxes stacked six deep and five wide. It could wait.

Back to the drawing board. He turned on the radio, poured two fingers in his classic Burger King Star Wars glass, and slugged it down. A nuclear device exploded in his gut. He concentrated on the details, nose six inches from the board. From time to time he pulled his head back.

WAVE played "So Pale and Precious" from the *Dukes of Stratosphear* record. When he pulled back, he saw the entirety of what he'd drawn, and there was no denying his ability with the nude female form. Some of his student sketches still adorned the walls at the Kubert School. His hard-on disturbed him. It wasn't right. They weren't even his own fantasies. They were the lurid quotidian fantasies enjoyed by serial killers and politicians.

Filled with self-loathing, he poured another shot and bent over the board. Sprint to the finish. But a sprint wouldn't cut it. They were paying him the big bucks to imagine the scene in detail.

I vas only following orders.

Distracted and annoyed, he drew. The drums. The drums were all wrong for the song. Was that two stations he was getting? Kendall turned off the radio. The drums rolled with the surf. They were coming from next door. Tommy.

He finished the sequence. The next sequence involved the vacuum cleaner salesman coming to the door. The anvil lifted from his shoulders. He was finished with the filth … for the time being. He was incapable of doing a less than first-rate job. They would love it and ask him to illustrate further sequences which made this one look like *Care Bears.*

Tommy's drumming washed over him like the surf. Hard to believe that he was a teenager, but Mozart had been five when he composed his first songs. Keith Moon joined his first band at sixteen.

Kendall stood, stretched, reeled. He'd been at it for three hours. It was dark out, but Tommy drummed on. The sound was not objectionable. He would not be able to hear it from the other side of the house where his bedroom was. It was ten thirty. Kendall decided to call it a night. He stumbled around the rectangular corridor: running into things, finding his bed, stripping, and tumbling in.

He fell into a shallow sleep with vivid dreams. He had a recurring nightmare where he came home, and Shirley was waiting for him. *Oh no,* he thought. *Oh no. You died. This isn't fair.* In the dream, he swallowed his disappointment and rationalized. She'd turned him into her caretaker. That's just the way it was.

Shirley cried out in her slurred demanding voice. He went to her door and found himself hanging five on a surfboard off the coast of Malibu. Catching a monster coming in fast, seeing a girl with raven hair on an inner tube directly in his path. He wanted to shout, wanted to jump, but instead, he hit her, and she cried out.

Kendall woke up, the echo of her scream still resonating in his head. He sat bolt upright in bed. The echo lingered in the house.

It was real.

THIRTEEN
CALL ME

Nate's place on Mulholland had once belonged to Erroll Flynn. The eight-acre estate was chock-a-block with limos and exotica when Kendall arrived for the party at seven. The casually-dressed valet could scarcely contain his contempt for the old Avalon as he directed Kendall through the house to the patio out back where Nate held court. A babble of voices mixed with music emanated from the open windows.

The house itself was a one-story, quasi-country manor with steep gables and green trim. Suffering the after-effects of his drinking binge, Kendall wended his way through the crowded living room, recognizing some familiar faces. A man was only as important as his party guests. Nate was obviously important. Kendall spotted Nicole Kidman and Keith Urban chatting to a man who looked like a fireplug with a waxed skull.

Kendall didn't know a soul there. He wore the standard Hollywood uniform: white T beneath a black silk sport jacket, blue jeans, huaraches. He went to the rolling bar by the pool and got a gin and tonic from a young man with improbable good looks and perfect teeth. Kendall recognized a famous director talking to a distinguished older man in a blue pinstripe suit. He was torn between fannish fawning and discretion. Discretion won. He looked around for his host.

Desmond Krout leaned into a long-haired beauty by a willow tree in the yard, his hands against the trunk on either side of her head.

Nate held court by the barbecue pit, a massive portable gas grill in a circular stone enclosure presided over by another impeccable youth. Nate had his arm around Judy's waist surrounded by four beautiful people: two men, two women. They had the familiarity of character actors, but Kendall couldn't place them. One of the women, a tall redhead, had had her face tightened a couple screws too far, giving her that cat look so prevalent among older beauties in the plastic surgery capital of the world.

Kendall hovered at the periphery. Nate acknowledged him with a nod and a finger, finished his anecdote to which the assembled responded a little too enthusiastically. Nate excused himself and came over, pulling Judy by the hand.

Nate let go of Judy and embraced Kendall. "Kendall, baby! Glad you could make it."

"I can't believe Nicole Kidman is here!" Kendall said.

"Look around. I think Nicholson's coming over. He doesn't live that far. Well, listen. Have fun. Take a look around. Get to know people. See that guy who looks like a fireplug? That's Dal Lazlo. You have any questions about the script bug him. Listen there're a couple people I need to liaise with. I'll catch up with you later."

Kendall turned and nearly bumped into Ron Perlman. Perlman wore a silk Hawaiian shirt—featuring surfers and hot rods—and had a gray GI Joe beard.

"Whoops," he said.

"Ron Perlman!" Kendall gushed. "Man, I loved you as Hellboy!"

"Thanks. And you are?"

Kendall stuck out his hand. "Kendall Coffin. I used to draw Dr. Strange." It sounded so lame.

I DRAW Dr. Strange. Idiot!

"Oh yeah? I always dug the comics, man."

"I'm storyboarding for Wyrick now," Kendall said, a little desperate, trying not to sound like a fool.

Perlman excused himself. "You hang in there, Kendall."

Kendall retreated to the edge of the yard looking down into the canyons, the twinkling lights of the city in the distance. He was out of his element. He couldn't afford the greens fees at the local golf clubs. He sat in an iron chair and stared into the valley.

He heard the tinkle of ice cubes in a glass.

"Bored, huh?" a woman said.

Kendall turned. There stood a statuesque young woman in a bathing suit that looked like a shark taking a snap of her athletically toned body. Her blond hair framed her face in dramatic bangs. She looked familiar.

Kendall stood. "I'm not bored. I just don't know anybody."

"Me either. Sue Brattles."

They shook hands. "Kendall Coffin."

"What do you do?"

"I'm a storyboarder. I used to … I draw comics."

"Oh. Did you draw Wolverine?"

"No. I draw Doc Strange. What do you do?"

She seemed to lose interest. "Actor / singer / model."

"You're waiting tables," Kendall said.

The corners of her mouth turned down. "You're funny."

Something about her flat delivery triggered a memory. Like a curtain going up, he suddenly realized that Sue Brattles played Dr. Myrna Malloy on the short-lived SyFy cult series, *Day Trippers*, about a group of time-traveling fixers.

"Myrna Malloy!" he said standing.

Sue's mouth turned down in a smile. "Correctomundo."

"Man, I loved that show! I wrote to the network when they canceled it."

"Oh, you were the one," she said, taking a sip of her drink.

"I drew your character!" He reached for his phone. "Would you like to see it?"

"If I must."

Kendall almost panted. He dialed up the picture, too late realizing it was perhaps a bit risqué. It showed Sue wearing nothing but bikini bottoms, her back to the viewer, cupping her breasts and looking over her shoulder.

"I, uh, was inspired by that one episode when you all landed in a lake."

Sue bit her lip. "That's swell."

"I'd be happy to send it to you!"

"No thanks," she said heading back to the patio. "You keep it. If I see you at a con, I'll sign it for you."

With a flutter of panic, Kendall realized he was losing her, the woman of his dreams. He trailed after like a homeless puppy. "Are you going to San Diego?"

"Maybe," she said, looking around for a friendly face. She bee-lined for a cluster of players near the diving board.

"This'll be my fifteenth year," Kendall said keeping up, aware of a body moving to intercept like Champ Bailey. Kendall paused and turned.

Nate came at him with a face like a clenched fist. "What do you think you're doing?" he said tightly, softly.

"What?" Kendall said. Too late for the actress. She was gone with the wind.

"Don't hassle the stars. Don't be a fan boy. Be discreet and listen. You wanna get laid, I'll fix you up."

"Jeez, Nate! I was just talking to her. She came up to me."

"Let me introduce you to a few women."

"What, is she married to a mob boss?"

Nate threw an arm around Kendall's shoulders and steered him toward the house. "No. But she's coming up fast, and there's no way she's gonna go out with a storyboarder. That's not how things are done. I could tell you were getting on her nerves just by the way she was walking."

Shame rose in Kendall's neck like mercury on a hot day. He was lonely and horny. He hadn't been laid in over three years, ever since Shirley's final turn for the worse.

They entered the living room. At least fifteen people stood or sat in febrile conversation. Nate looked around like a practiced scout. Planted a finger in Kendall's chest. "Wait here. Be cool."

Kendall removed his sunglasses from his jacket pocket and put them on. Cool. Nate crossed the room to where two bright young things talked with three guys, at least two of which were old enough to be their fathers. Nate expertly cut one out of the pack and spoke to her confidentially. She looked across the room at Kendall.

Nate went one way. The girl came across the room, smiling, holding a champagne glass. "Hi," she said. "My name's Jennifer. Nate says you're new in town."

She was short and stacked with perfect anime features, auburn hair cut in a pageboy.

"Kendall Coffin. Just moved out here from Omaha."

"The only thing I know about Omaha is steaks."

"Well the only thing I know about LA is what I see in the movies."

Jennifer edged up. She wore a maddening perfume named after an actress. "Need a guide? I'm actually from LA."

"Hey, that would be swell," Kendall said.

"Want to do a line?" For the first time, Kendall noticed the slick under her nose. No wonder she was so perky.

"Ah, no thanks."

She grabbed his hand and pulled him toward the hall. "Well keep me company while I do a bump."

Kendall let her drag him down the wide corridor lined with framed movie posters; Polis' productions plus the classics: *Casablanca, Gone with the Wind, The Maltese Falcon*. She opened a bedroom door. A man sat on the bed with his trousers around his knees as a woman knelt between them.

"Whoops!" Jennifer exclaimed, backing out of the room.

The next room was likewise occupied. They heard snorking sounds from the hall bathroom. Desmond Krout peered out with white-rimmed nostrils, winked at Kendall, and closed the door. They settled on a half bath off the recreation room where Nate displayed his voluminous civic awards and industry trophies. Jennifer pulled him into the bathroom and locked the door. She removed an amber vial from her purse, shook the white powder out on a hand mirror and wrangled it with a credit card.

Kendall felt a visceral shudder. The long, thudding empty hours of sleeplessness by far outweighed the momentary high. Jennifer snorted through a sterling silver straw. She looked at him with manga eyes.

"You sure?"

"I'll pass."

She put her things away, dabbed beneath her nose with a wet tissue, examined herself in the mirror, touched up her lipstick, and led the way back to the living room. They paused at the entrance to survey the room.

"Oh!" Jennifer exclaimed. "There's Jeremy DeKooning. I have to talk to him. Listen. I'd really love to show you the sights. Let me give you my phone number."

She took a sticky pad and a pen from her cunning little purse, wrote her number on Kendall's shoulder, and handed it to him. "Call me."

"I will," he said to her back.

FOURTEEN
THE HOUSE THAT SCREAMED

A h, the classic Japanese luxury marque," the bottle blond attendant sneered as Kendall described his car. The attendant returned in two minutes, pulling up at the front door with a chirp of the tires. Kendall tipped him a buck. Dude stared at it and smiled. Cheap tip for a cheap car.

Kendall got in the car and turned the radio on to WAVE. The Trade Winds's "New York's A Lonely Town" poured like honey from the speakers. Clipped to the sun visor in a CD package were *Pet Sounds*, *The Best of the Beach Boys*, *Brian Wilson*, Explorers Club's *Freedom Wind*, and *Sunrise Highway*. Kendall had taken their advice and followed the sun to the Promised Land, California, the American dream. Land of milk and honey, nuts and fruits, Bikini Beach and Sheryl Crow.

Kendall drove down Mulholland, the boulevard of dreams. Or broken dreams. Attending a party in Erroll Flynn's house. He wished his folks could see him now. They'd probably laugh at him for hobnobbing with the glitterati. He couldn't remember his folks ever going to the movies. They never were keen on the arts. His dad wanted him to become a lawyer. His mother wanted him to become a doctor. As if. Kendall was not analytical. He was imaginative. He always knew he would someday make his living off his imagination. The first time he picked up a comic book it smacked him between the eyes like a dum-dum bullet. *Way of the Rat*. The intricate, accurate drawings of hand-to-hand combat blew his mind, and in that instant, he knew he had found his calling.

Fortunately, he had a talent for drawing; had studied, practised, and polished until he was one of the best comic book illustrators in the country. Him and 2000 other guys.

Kendall had been at Nate's party for ninety minutes, had had no significant conversations, met no one except poor Sue and Jennifer, whose number he had. Good deal. Kendall needed a girlfriend, not necessarily a wife. Although, Shirley had put it succinctly; we marry, or I'm outta here. Kendall figured that's the way a lot of marriages happened. He had bad luck with women. He had a knack for choosing vulnerable-looking dames who turned out to be succubi. Before Shirley, there had been a long string of mostly good-looking women addicted to alcohol, painkillers, meth, blow, smack, nose spray, and chocolate. He had no one but himself to blame. He wished he had all the money back that he'd spent on blow in the nineties.

Oh well.

He pulled up in front of the garage, got out, and opened the door. It wasn't until he got back into his car and turned into the garage that he realized the Corvette was now all the way back at the workbench. Funny. He was sure he'd left it in gear, and the floor was level. He parked his car, got out, and went up to the Vette. He sat in the seat and grabbed the shift. Neutral. He must have been mistaken. Maybe they'd had an earthquake. With a glance at the sealed door to the basement, he went outside, shut the garage door and locked it, and went up the steps to his front door. He would have to get that basement door open which meant he had to go into the basement. It could wait.

Kendall walked through the long dark house feeling like a watchman at a museum. He went all the way to the back and looked out through the pyramidal arch at the city lights in the distance. A million-dollar view if you liked that sort of thing.

Kendall stood in the arch with one hand on each pillar. Samson. It was a million-dollar view, but he was no millionaire; not after purchasing this house. But what a house. He still felt as if he were wandering through a dream. Him! Kendall Coffin; owner of a Roark Dexter Smith house. It was a dream come true.

Like most professional nerds, Kendall was his enthusiasms. He was a creature of pop culture for whom taste was everything. He'd softened from his college years when he used to get into fistfights over who was better, Leftover Salmon or Phish, Wolverine or Batman, Porsche or BMW.

The house itself was the ultimate collection. He could reap a small fortune selling the abandoned items on eBay. It puzzled him that he'd acquired it so easily. Very rarely did a Smith house come on the market.

He circled the house clockwise until he came to the master bedroom, pulled off his clothes, brushed his teeth, and so to bed. He tossed and turned. Maybe he should see a sleep specialist. He'd always been a light sleeper and ten years on blow didn't help, but after Shirley died he started sleeping better. Chalk it up to strange surroundings.

He fell into a shallow sleep. He was on a ship headed for Costa Rica, with a whole bunch of tourists, and in a vast open space surrounded by interior balconies. Kendall hated being at sea. He hated the idea of being confined to a tiny island in a sea of water, the smell of the heads, the nauseating list.

They docked. Not Costa Rica. Portugal. They were issued motorcycles. Kendall could barely keep his on the road, so he adopted an impossible position, torso truncated over the handlebars, trying to thrust his head past the forward most point of the bike. Suddenly back from the ride, staying in a dormitory owned by an anonymous state college. He went into his room and shut the door. He could hear sounds of partying going on all around him: loud music, laughter, women squealing.

A woman screaming, a twisting howl of terror and desperation that brought Kendall out of his sleep like a leaping dolphin. He sat up in bed, sweat beading on his forehead, wild-eyed. The scream echoed faintly down the corridors. Or was it a siren fading off into the distance?

It wasn't his imagination! He could still hear the reverberation. Unless he was going mad. He froze, afraid to make a sound, and listened. The house ticked minutely. He heard the faint echo of a car alarm in the neighborhood. He debated taking one of the Xanax he'd salvaged from Shirley's bathroom.

That was three nights in a row. One way to ascertain whether he was going mad; he could get a sound-activated recorder and set it up in the room.

Eventually, he fell asleep.

FIFTEEN
THE BASEMENT

Saturday morning, after unpacking all his clothes and dishes, Kendall went next door to borrow a crowbar. Torrance led him into the garage where he had a wall of tools and a wood-working shop. Two brand new scratch-built Adirondacks sat on a carpet scrap. Tommy's drum kit occupied the space for the third car. Torrance pulled a crowbar from a home made wooden box.

"What's it for?"

"The basement door's jammed shut."

"Didn't you inspect the furnace before you bought?"

"They assured me everything was in working order. I saw a fresh receipt from a furnace company."

Torrance stroked his beard. "Well, they can't sell a high-end property like that without everything working. Have you used the furnace?"

Kendall hefted the bar in his hand. He could brain someone with it. "Of course not. It's been in the eighties since I arrived."

"What about the AC?"

"House doesn't have AC. Smith never used it. He designed his houses to be naturally cooled. The high, thick walls, the trees. It's been pretty pleasant."

Torrance picked up a sheet of sandpaper and went to work on one of his chairs. "Smith was a weird guy. Read a book about him once. Welsh by birth. Some people believe he was a druid wizard whose houses were surrogate temples."

Kendall chuckled. "You should hear the rumors in Wisconsin. Satanism, orgies, tripping on mushrooms. It's a fact he grew psilocybin mushrooms at Darien. That was his studio in Wisconsin. Been there a buncha times. Well, thanks. I'll bring this back when I'm finished."

"No rush," Torrance said choosing a CD from the stack next to his boom box. Def Leppard followed Kendall down the long driveway. The sound disappeared when he reached the street. He climbed the steep stairs to his own hidden entrance. It was just past eleven. He went into the kitchen and tried the basement door with his hands, bracing one foot against the frame. Even gripping the pistol-style handle with both hands, he couldn't budge it. He wondered if some prankster had epoxied it shut.

Kendall inserted the flat end of the bar between the door and the frame and levered it open. The door sprang out with an electric crack and slammed into the rubber-tipped stopper affixed to the wall. An odor of fried electrics, old film, ancient newspapers, and a hint of rot issued from the dark opening. Kendall felt along the inside and found a switch, illuminating wooden stairs descending into the gloom. Crowbar in hand he descended.

The basement mirrored the house above in that it was in the shape of a rectangle, but only the frame. The center of the rectangle was solid earth except for the pool. Kendall found himself in a long, windowless corridor, all the doors opening toward the perimeter. Light came from bare bulbs mounted in hemispherical indentations in the concrete ceiling, uncomfortably like a prison. He tried the door directly across from the base of the stairs. It fought back, but he forced it open with the bar. Inside was a storeroom lined with steel shelving on which sat thousands and thousands of periodicals, some neatly tied in bundles. *Variety, The Los Angeles Times, Billboard, Playboy, Hustler, National Geographic*. And that was just on the first shelf he looked. One shelf held hundreds of VHS tapes, mostly home-made. One shelf held an ancient 8-millimeter camera and a machine for transferring film to video tape.

Some of those old skin rags might be worth something if he could find the proper venue. Forget eBay. They forbade more things than they allowed. Maybe he could hire Tommy to cata-log, list, and ship the shit. Give him a percentage. He could always use them to get off. Kendall shut the door and moved down the hall to the next door. It was a double door set into a concrete arch similar to those upstairs, with a quasi-Mayan finial. The double door was painted red and had gilt handles like those in a theater. He pulled the doors open and felt a big open space. A cave. He found the switch and turned it on. Inlaid lamps in the floor illuminated the steep little theater with the loge to his left and the screen to his right. The ground had been excavated to subbasement level to include the theater, whose lavish cush-ioned chairs had come from some ancient Hollywood palace. There were five levels of seating for three dozen. He found a rheostat on the wall and turned up the ceiling lights, revealing a curved ceiling of stamped tin in one of Smith's hexagonal designs.

Kendall entered the room. It was like entering a temple of film. He sat in one of the lush chairs replete with cup holder inhaling the rich aroma of the theater.There was a hint of buttered popcorn in the air. The ashtray at his wrist contained a butt. He picked it up. Kent. The screen was framed by Smith's unique stonework proscenium. The stones were a mismatched bunch, varying shades of beige and gray, some with bas relief, some with cuneiforms or hieroglyphs. Certainly, they were not the uniform texture used in the design upstairs. There had to be a reason for that.

Kendall leaned back, the seat tilting with him. It was so comfortable he could have fallen asleep. Maybe he should sleep there.

Kendall heaved himself out of the deep seat and climbed the broad, shallow steps to the rear of the theater where a door led to an old-fashioned projection booth. A digital projector also hung from the ceiling just outside the booth. Kendall went inside and flicked on the lights. There was an ancient control panel with lever lighting not just for the theater, but the entire house. There were four fat cathode-ray closed-circuit television sets. Kendall turned them on one by one. Each showed a grainy black and white live view of different sections of the property: the front alcove, the courtyard, the kitchen, the dining room. Kendall found he could switch from camera to camera and even affect a split screen getting four feeds at once.

Peculiar. Why build a communications center in the basement unless you were a military installation or expecting to be bombed? Maybe Wallanda had been an early zombie-adapter. Geek heaven. Who didn't want their own home theater? The room contained both 35 and 8 mm projectors, VHS players, and a DVD player.

No computers. Wallanda had died before the boom.

Kendall knew quite a few comic creators in the LA area. It would be a blast to invite them to a night at the movies. *Galaxy Quest* or *Mystery Men*. Geek heaven.

Exiting the theater, he followed the corridor counter clockwise. The next room lay beneath the entrance foyer and contained the furnace and the water heater. Both were in good condition. He pulled out the furnace filter. Brand new. Someone was on the ball. A sticker stated that the furnace had been serviced one month prior to Kendall's arrival. He shut the door and moved on. He was now on the west side of the building, beneath the master bedroom and the den, now his office.

The first door opened on a cedar-lined wine cellar, two walls of racks, every slot filled. Dim light poured in from one of the window wells. Just inside the door were controls for temperature and humidity. He pulled a bottle out. Château Mouton-Rothschild.

Ho. Ly. Shit.

Kendall didn't know wine. H was a beer drinker. But the profit potential was not lost on him. There had to be several hundred bottles. If they were intact, they might bring a fortune at auction. Who would know about such things? Nate? Possibly. Being a movie exec required extensive knowledge of wine, guns, and polo. He tucked the bottle under his arm.

The next room was fourteen by twenty, cedar-lined, and filled with costumes from every era. It too had a window well. Kendall spotted a *Star Wars* uniform on a dummy, a red shirt, and a costume from *The Age of Innocence*. He wandered among them, inhaling the rich scent of cedar, sawdust, makeup, and wool, touching the garments. Two layers of shelf—above the racks—contained hat after hat: trilbies, fedoras, bowlers, pork pies, ladies' sun bonnets, Revolutionary tri-corns. A stack of two large plastic boxes with translucent sides interrupted the march of hats.

Standing on a foot stool, Kendall wrestled the top box out and set it on the concrete floor. He opened it up. It was jammed with photographs. He picked up a pale Polaroid from the seventies: a tall, dapper man posing next to his E-type Jag convertible. Frank Wallanda. Other photos showed Wallanda with various stars and personalities: Wyrick, John Wayne, Gina Lollobrigida, Peter Sellers, Elizabeth Taylor, MC Hammer. Other photos showed him posing with a fixed smile with his wife and daughter, the latter a coltish gamin with a goofy grin and silver filigree earrings. The box was a jumble. Digging down, his hands fell on smooth metal. He pulled out an Academy Award. Best Picture for *Dagnabbit Hits the Comeback Trail*. Kendall couldn't believe it. He set the Oscar on the concrete, carefully pressed the lid back on the box, and slid it back on top of the other box on the shelf.

Had Wallanda left a will? Why hadn't his wife, who was still alive, retrieved these precious family mementos?

Why had no one auctioned the contents? Surely Wallanda had heirs, had left a will. Kendall didn't know law, but he had friends who did. He'd heard possession was nine tenths of the law.

On to the next room. Steel door locked shut with an enormous Schrage with a barrel keyhole. Kendall searched among his keys knowing he didn't have it. Who knew what lay beyond? He'd have to get a bolt cutter.

Finally, he came to the garage door. No wonder he couldn't get it open. An ancient roll top desk had been shoved against the door. Kendall could barely budge it. He'd have to get help. He thought of Tommy.

He completed his loop and went upstairs gripping the Oscar and thinking how best to market the wine.

SIXTEEN
FIRST AND LAST DATES

Kendall suggested they go to the Getty Center, Jennifer countered with lunch at Papillion in Santa Monica. Kendall was outside leaning on the rail when Jennifer approached wearing a straw hat, Oakleys, dazzling white teeth, hair blowing in the sea breeze.

"Hi!" she said giving him a peck on the cheek. "Let's go out on the deck, shall we?"

Kendall slipped the maître d' a twenty. The knife-thin, olive-hued young man led them through the dining room out onto the deck overlooking the beach. The scent of diesel and rotten fish mingled with the smell of the sea. Jennifer ordered a Mimosa. Kendall ordered a Pacifica.

Jennifer shook her hair with a practiced maneuver. "Was that party wild or what? I didn't get out of there until two! Fortunately, I went with a girlfriend who drove me home. How you doing?"

"Good. I'm still getting oriented. Haven't finished unpacking."

Jennifer laid her elegant fingers on his wrist. "I heard you bought a Roark Dexter Smith design. Is that true?"

"Yes. It was built by the producer Frank Wallanda ... you know ... *Stylin'*, *The Quinceañera*, *Prom Queen*?"

"I love those movies!" Jennifer said leaning forward, giving Kendall a good view of her cleavage. She wore a V-necked blouse and sharp-creased twill trou. Her small but shapely breasts roamed free. "I hear Nate's got a couple like that in the hopper. What are you working on?"

The red tide rose out of Kendall's tan Tori Richards shirt. He took a slug of water and rubbed his throat. "I, uh, signed a non-disclosure agreement."

Jennifer sat back with a coquettish tilt. "Oh, come on. You can tell me!"

"It's about a cut-rate assassin named Cheap Shot."

Jennifer's jaw hung in a soundless guffaw. "That sounds real bitchin'. Who's in it?"

Kendall winked and held a finger to his mouth.

Jennifer pouted. "You're no fun. Anyhow, I have a shot at a speaking part in Sophia Coppola's next movie. It's a black comedy about a dysfunctional family getting together for a family reunion."

"Break a leg," Kendall said.

Jennifer frowned. "That's not very nice."

The waiter brought their drinks. "Have you had an opportunity to look at the menu?"

"Oh, I know what I want," Jennifer said. "I'll have the Kobe beef sliders."

Kendall ordered a club sandwich. "Break a leg is a traditional theatrical salutation meaning good luck."

"I did not know that," Jennifer said. They made small talk. She'd never heard of the Marx Brothers. She'd never seen *Casablanca*, *Gone with the Wind*, or *The Maltese Falcon*. Her favorite singer was Ke$ha. She thought she could sing and planned to model her career after J. Lo: the songs, the films, the game shows. She worked out every day at Gold's. She had a personal trainer, a manager, and an agent. She'd had a walk-on on *NCIS: Los Angeles*.

Their food came. Jennifer ate like a starving dog. Afterward, they went for a walk on the pier. Jennifer took Kendall's hand. When asked about past credits Kendall cited *Dr. Strange.*

"Dr. Strange? Who's that?"

"You've heard of Marvel Comics, right? *Spider-Man, the Avengers*?"

"I almost had a part in that Avengers movie. So you're a producer with Marvel?"

"No. I'm a comic book artist. I just drew Doc Strange for a while. They've been trying to get a Doc Strange movie off the ground forever, but Robert Downey can't play everyone."

Jennifer launched into a gushing tale of meeting Downey at some party.

"Listen!" she said as they walked back. "The Grunions are playing at the Viper Room tonight, and I have two free passes."

Kendall agreed to pick her up at eight.

Jennifer shared a third-floor walk-up built around a court-yard with a tennis court and a swimming pool in West Holly-wood. Kendall parked on the street and took the stairs. Jennifer's roommate, a lissome blond, opened the door.

"Hi! I'm Rebecca. Jennifer will be ready in a minute. Won't you come in?"

The frilly, frothing living room was decorated with stuffed animals, inspirational samplers, glamour photos of Jennifer and Rebecca, and a framed, signed photograph of Johnny Depp.

"Would you like a drink?" Rebecca said.

"No thanks."

"Jennifer tells me you're a producer."

"I'm an artist, actually."

"Well, that too of course."

Jennifer burst from the corridor in a white and yellow strap-less sundress. "Hi!"

The Viper Room had a goth face--black hoodie over a black facade. It looked like a nameless government lab where they conducted unspeakable experiments. There was a line outside.

The bouncer—it may have been Bill Goldberg—greeted Jennifer by name and let them in.

The Grunion was a punked-out death metal quartet that wore razor-sliced jeans, mascara, and enough ink to turn their arms blue. The lead singer had tatted his whole face to look like a Māori war mask. They sported enough body jewelry that a giant magnet would snatch them all up. You could have hung them by the loops in their heads.

The music was industrial sludge, way too loud so that Kendall was left with only a thumping bass line coming through the floor. Jennifer grabbed his hand and forced him to dance, which he hated. He gave it an hour and dragged her out.

Kendall stood on the sidewalk pounding his head with the base of his palm. "I can't hear!"

"They were loud, weren't they?" Jennifer said laughing. She took his arm. "I'd really love to see your place."

"I haven't finished unpacking. It's a mess. But I promise to have you over as soon as I get things sorted away."

"I understand. Let's go back to my place." Kendall had a stiffie since seeing her in front of the restaurant. He parked a half block away, and they walked back hand in hand. The apartment was empty. Rebecca was spending the night with her boyfriend, a stunt man who moonlighted parking cars at the Spanish Whiskers on Melrose.

As soon as Jennifer shut the door, she turned and gave him the full lip-lock. She ground her pelvis into his and purred like a cat. Kendall was all over her.

She pushed him back, breathless. "Give me a minute, okay?"

Kendall sat with his raging hard-on and wondered if he should go through with this. Well, it was Hollywood. It was practically *de rigueur*. This was how his relationship with Shirley began. The girl obviously thought he was some kind of producer.

Kendall stood and went to the bedroom door. "Hey, Jennifer."

"Make yourself a drink. I'll be right out."

"Hey, Jennifer. I'm not a producer."

"Excuse me?"

"I'm a storyboard artist. I have absolutely no power in any production. In fact, I'm struggling to hang on to my job."

Jennifer came to the bedroom door wearing a robe. "Nate said you were a producer."

"Nate was exaggerating."

Jennifer bit her lower lip. "You're not a producer?"

"No."

"You know," she said, "maybe this isn't a very good idea."

SEVENTEEN
THE DESK

Kendall shut off the garage lights, lowered the door and locked it. He walked up the sidewalk, up the Mayan steps to the portcullis. His castle, although it was more Mayan than Saxon. He let himself in through the heavy copper-paneled door and once again smelled that odd mixture of exotica with a faint putrid undertone. Perhaps all it needed was a thorough scrubbing. He'd ask Torrance about a reliable cleaning service, maybe offer the job to Tommy.

The house seemed to exhale as he entered, embracing him in a warm hush. He paused in the foyer and listened. The house was far from silent. It ticked with the heat of the day. He heard the faint thrush of the ventilation, the barely discernible white noise of traffic.

He locked the door and walked back to his studio. It was just past midnight. He couldn't believe he'd listened to that crap. Anything to get laid, huh? And there was the irony. He'd thrown away a guilt-free fuck! Well, who knew? She could be crazier than an orbital rat, turn vindictive like Glen Close in *Fatal Attraction*.

He'd always been a boy scout, old school. Chivalrous. He got it from reading about *King Arthur* as a child and from the evangelical church he'd attended. The Resurrection Fellowship. They'd had meetings on whether to change the name to the Resurrection Personship. It was undecided. His parents had brought him up to respect women. He'd run through dozens of relationships before he met Shirley.

He had a slight buzz from the three drinks he'd consumed. He knew he shouldn't drive, and he'd been lucky. He vowed not to do it again. Tomorrow he would get a dog. A dog would be there to greet him. A dog would announce visitors. A dog would be able to tell him if the voices he heard were real or not.

Kendall had a dog growing up. His name was Shemp, and he was a shaggy collie-type mixed breed. Kendall and his brother Ron would romp for hours with Shemp. The day they had to put Shemp down—he couldn't see, couldn't climb the steps—was the saddest day of Kendall's childhood.

The house was built for a dog. He could leave the dog in the courtyard all day with no fear it would escape. Kendall sat down on the edge of his massive bed—something out of Cecil B. DeMille—and removed his clothes. He brushed his teeth and went to bed but was unable to sleep. Alcohol and anxiety. Anxiety about the voices. At one point, he fell into a shallow sleep and startled himself awake. He thought he'd heard a scream. It took him a minute to realize it was the wind whistling through his nose.

He flopped, he spun like an axle, did not sleep. He drifted in and out of a dream in which he was visiting an artists' co-op in New York, looking at "art" made of detritus, old iron gears welded together in a meaningless and unappealing manner, children's crayon scrawls, each accompanied by a fast-talking artist explaining his or her art.

"It's conceptual, don't you see," said a snotty Brit. It was Desmond. "It's sorta meta if you know what I mean."

Picasso sat in a corner painting.

Kendall opened his eyes. Daylight filtered in through the skylight. He'd passed the night without screams. He got out of bed. He felt like shit. He took a shower.

Sunday morning coming down. Kendall made coffee, toasted a bagel, went into the studio where a blank page stared at him from the drawing board. He grabbed his patented Timberline page stencil and put down the panels.

Cheap Shot on the cover. Comic artists often drew the cover first to gin up interest in the product. He laid out the hulking Cheap Shot standing on a mountain of discarded plastic drinking bottles, a well-endowed girl wrapped around his leg, a nail gun in one hand and a can of wasp repellent in the other fighting off an army of zombies.

The girl. Did he draw the breasts too big? Since the dawn of the Pleistocene comic book aficionados had decried the crass and sexist depiction of women in comics. Why were their figures so exaggerated? Why didn't they look like ordinary women? The conflict would never be resolved. Kendall understood something many people did not. Comics were fantasy. Men drew most of them to entertain other men. Men did not fantasize about skinny chicks with flat chests or the morbidly obese.

Most comic book artists had never taken life drawing and got their knowledge of anatomy from books on how to draw comics. The best of these imparted an excellent working knowledge of the idealized male or female body. The fans didn't want realism. They wanted fantasy.

Kendall had done life drawing. He'd even sold a few portraits and nudes. His women were gorgeous but realistic. Drawing them excited him. He drew this one. He was excited. The doorbell chimed "Beauty's Only Skin Deep."

Kendall got up. Pulling himself off a drawing board made a great sucking noise like pulling up a moist bathmat. His fatigue rushed back in weighing him down. He looked at his watch. Fuck. Almost noon.

Tommy stood in the door grinning, thumbs tucked into the waist of his cargo shorts wearing hi-zoot sneakers. "Torrance said you might need help moving furniture."

Kendall motioned him in. "Thanks. Yeah. I need your help

with an old desk in the basement. We don't have to move it far. It's blocking the door to the garage. You want some coffee?"

"No thanks, man. I drink energy drinks."

Kendall led the way downstairs. They emerged in the corridor.

"Wow," Tommy said. "This is really creepy."

Kendall showed him the roll top. Together, using all their might, they shifted it away from the garage door down the hall and left it against the wall. Kendall opened the garage door inward. He stepped into the garage and turned on the lights. Tommy followed.

Tommy nearly fell to his knees when he saw the Corvette. "Mahalo! Man, that is so fuckin' bitchin'!"

"You surf?" Kendall said.

"Every chance I get. I only been like three times this year, though, 'cause I been so crazy busy."

Kendall walked over to the tall cabinet holding the surfboard. "Take a look at this."

Tommy's eyes saucered and his jaw hung low. "Whoah dude! Look at that fibro!"

"That's a Stan Mouse Silver Surfer."

"The Surfer is totally rad. You interested in selling?"

Had the board been factory stock or with another painting perhaps. But a Stan Mouse Silver Surfer was likely worth a fortune. On the other hand, Kendall could use the money. On the other hand, Tommy wouldn't have it.

"Let me think about that. I might let you take it to the beach."

"I would be so careful, man! That thing is a babelini magnet."

Kendall let Tommy sit in the Corvette. They turned off the lights and reentered the basement.

"Thanks, Tommy. I owe you one."

"No problem, dude."

Kendall walked with Tommy back to the front entrance and said goodbye. The desk was extremely heavy. What was in it?

Kendall went back into the basement. The roll top curled back into the lid with a guttural purr. It took Kendall's eyes a second to adjust to the dim light. The thing broadcast loathing before he even understood at what he was looking. A trap door opened beneath his feet; an instant of vertigo, loss, hollowness. He stepped back, afraid to turn his eyes from the thing on the desk.

The spiked object was a tarantula carcass. A big one, from which protruded a series of pale white horns. The sight of it stampeded his skin. He froze. It was unmoving. It was dead. He recognized it as a form of fungus that attacks tarantulas, growing long horn-like tendrils out of the host's corpse. He had failed to anticipate tarantulas in his multimillion-dollar house.

Kendall returned to the wardrobe room and seized a whisk broom. He used the broom to shove the grotesque corpse onto a dust pan which he upended into a paper bag and deposited in the secure fifty-gallon plastic garbage bin.

The desk contained numerous cubbyholes stuffed with papers, many of them letters. Kendall withdrew an envelope from a cubbyhole, removed the hand-written letter, and began to read.

EIGHTEEN
TAKE A LETTER, MARIA

JUNE 14, 1981

Frank:

As you know, I have not had much luck with men. My stepfather began raping me when I was twelve. I was too frightened to say anything and what good would it do? My mother was a pill-popping alcoholic who never wanted kids in the first place. She often told me that.

My first boyfriend was a hippie who talked about universal love and healing while beating the shit out of me at home. My second got me hooked on blow and tried to talk me into dancing at a topless joint. It took me seven years to crawl out of that hole.

When I met you, I was three years and twenty-seven days clean and sober. Not only did you get me back on blow, you tried to get me to fuck your pals. I'm not saying it was a one-way street. You got me that apartment and paid the rent. We went to some swell parties.

Then you canceled my credit card and kicked me out of my apartment because you found a newer, younger girl to fuck over. Well, I've got news for you, pal. I have photos of you and your friends at some of your private parties. The kind that could kick you to the curb.

So you're going to pay me to go away, Frank. I'm only asking $50,000, chump change to a big player like you. Get it together in hundreds and put it in a gym bag or you won't like what's going to happen next.

Sincerely,
Maria

K endall looked at the envelope. The return address read M. Guzman, 42355 N. Tedesco Blvd., South Los Angeles. He looked at the desk. There were hundreds of letters stuck in cubbyholes. He pulled out a handful. Most of them hadn't even been opened. They all had hand-written addresses, and some still bore the faint scent of perfume.

Taking Maria's letter, he went upstairs.

What did he really know about Frank Wallanda? Not much. Wallanda's public image was that of a brilliant but benign producer/director of insightful teen comedies. Wyrick's squeaky-clean image had rubbed off on him, but apparently Wallanda was not so squeaky clean at home. Certainly, an egomaniac. Kendall went into the library and carefully read through all the titles. There were a lot of books but nothing exclusive to Wallanda. Lesser filmmakers had been biographed.

Kendall would have to wait for Tuesday for the cable people to hook him up. In the meantime, he had no internet. He probably could have piggybacked on the Skaggs's wireless system if they had one, but he'd need the password. It was a relief not to be checking Facebook and Twitter every five minutes. He called the *Times* and ordered the paper. They kept their sub office open on Sundays.

He found *Movie Makers: 50 Iconic Directors From Chaplin to the Coen Brothers*, and flipped through the table of contents. Wallanda had his own chapter. Kendall sat down to read.

Born in Muncie, IN in 1939, Frank Wallanda was the youngest of five children. His father Lawrence worked as a machine operator at MacIntosh Mfg., his mother Violet was a stay-at-home mom. Wallanda graduated from UC Irvine in 1961 with a degree in film studies and went to work as an intern for legendary producer Ian Sullivan.

In 1971 Wallanda landed an independent production deal with Wyrick Studios and wrote, produced, and directed *The Main Drag*, the first of a string of successful teen comedies that captured the zeitgeist of young America. That was also the year he married Wyrick's only daughter Bree. Their daughter Dorothy was born that year. In 1984 Dorothy became pregnant. Wallanda offered ten thousand dollars to whoever could produce the father. Dorothy died, and the child was stillborn. Bree withdrew from public life but that same year gave birth to their second child, Elaine.

While his personal life was tragic, professionally, Wallanda could do no wrong.

He followed *Drag* with *At the Hop, Stylin'*, and *Quinceañera* which made him a household name. In 1980, he became Vice President in charge of production at Wyrick and midwifed a series of wholesome, all-ages entertainment including the wildly successful animated feature, *Ultra Pigeon Returns*. Wallanda died at his Los Feliz home in 2000 survived by his wife of 30 years, the former Bree Hardison.

Bree has been institutionalized since the mysterious disappearance of their daughter Elaine "Lannie" Wallanda, whose car was found with the engine idling at Griffith Observatory on June 5, 1994. She was eight months pregnant at the time, and there was speculation that the father was a famous Hollywood leading man. The mystery has never been solved. The Wallandas were now childless.

Wallanda led a flamboyant personal life which caused friction with Darryl Wyrick who insisted that all Wyrick executives conduct themselves in a manner above reproach. Wyrick is said to have put stock in astrology, Zoroastrianism, and Kabala. Wyrick died in 1997. Wallanda commissioned a house by notorious architect Roark Dexter Smith. Following Bree's institutionalization, there were rumors of Wallanda's wild parties. The coroner's report following Wallanda's death indicated that he had died of asphyxiation. There were rumors that he was engaged in an auto-erotic enterprise.

Well fuck. Why had no one written a full-blown bio on Wallanda? Was that Lannie's Corvette in the garage? How much would that bring at Barrett-Jackson or Gooding? He'd always wanted a Stingray. There was enough wealth squirreled away in the basement for him to finance a complete restoration, although the car appeared to be in excellent condition.

Kendall stared blankly at the open book on his lap. There was something in there. Something that resonated with another book on the shelf. He got up and examined more titles. *Conversations with Dead Movie Stars* caught his eye. He pulled it down, sat in the leather chair, and turned to the index. There were three Wallanda mentions. He looked them up. Each was a footnote to an actor with whom the author, Portia DeManning, had claimed to communicate.

He turned to the author's bio. "Ms. DeManning holds a PhD in Advanced Parapsychology from the Eheart Institute of Parapsychology and is certified by the American Institute of Mediums. She has counseled numerous actors, writers, producers, and directors over the years including Robert Altman, Burt Reynolds, Frank Wallanda ..."

He phoned Rawlins.

NINETEEN
CROWD FUNDING

Of course, I've seen *Stylin'*!" Rawlins said. "I've seen all Wallanda's flicks. Am I not the foremost film authority in the western hemisphere?"

"Well here's the deal, Greg. I've uncovered a treasure trove of personal stuff about Wallanda. Letters from old lovers and who knows whom; hundreds of them. Why has no one written a serious biography of him? I mean, there are a dozen books about David Lynch for jeebus's sake."

"You still can't bring yourself to say 'Christ' can you?"

"Fuck you."

"That's better. I don't know. It's a golden opportunity for sure. Were you thinking of me?"

"That's why I called you."

Kendall heard Greg thinking.

"This is out of my wheelhouse, so to speak, but as a starving writer, I'm obligated to pursue every venture no matter how recondite. Lemme ax my putative agent. Could you send me some of this material?"

"Yeah. I'll scan some and email ya as soon as I get my cable set up."

As soon as Kendall hung up, exhaustion descended like a fire curtain. He staggered to his bedroom, flopped on the bed, and fell asleep instantly. It was early evening when he woke up, room softly lit by concealed lighting in the ceiling.

He woke up refreshed and dream free. Oh, there were dreams. There were always dreams, but these evaporated as soon as he opened his eyes. He went into the kitchen looking for something to eat out of sheer force of habit. Of course, there was nothing. There was a Tokyo Joe's four blocks away. He got takeout and brought it back, set it up in the kitchen. After he ate, he gravitated to the studio where *Cheap Shot* waited. He really should work off a script. He'd thought about asking Greg but didn't want to join the legions of sock monkeys looking for free work. Greg would agree, just as he'd agreed to write scripts on spec for a half dozen projects that never saw fruition.

Kendall was just trying to put some visuals together to attract a publisher. So many artists had declared freedom from writers and were now doing their own stuff. Some of it was good. Some of it was bad but had great visuals.

He'd considered Kickstarter or IndieGoGo. The problem with that was so had everybody else. There were now a thousand crowdstarter projects vying for his attention, many by friends or acquaintances. And they kept track. If you didn't support X's project, he'd unfriend you. The problem was there were 25 other projects just like X's, and they were all keeping track.

Right after he'd received his mother's inheritance, Kendall had contributed to several friends' projects. But if the point was to put together a war chest, why give X $25? He'll only kick back another $25. And $25 X 26 was $650. Kendall had a profile among the comic community. They'd say look at Kendall. He just came into a whole lot of money and moved to Hollywood. Certainly, old Kendall will kick a couple thou into our graphic novel about a group of super-powered animals threatened with extinction who declare war on humanity. Certainly, Kendall will kick into our GN about a family of friendly ear mites who fight monsters. Surely Kendall will kick in to fight the horror of back acne.

What a relief it was to be off the internet for a few days.

He sat at his drawing board and turned on the radio. It was Sunday. Inexplicably, WAVE was broadcasting come-to-Jesus meetings. There sat his flat screen television, no movie screen but still large, unsheathed on the floor. Certainly, in a major market like Los Angeles, he would be able to rope in a stray signal. He found the cord and the remote and plugged it in.

The lazy TV woke up slowly. He guessed it was saving electricity. White storm and noise. He switched on channel 4, and an image with a scroll leaped onto the screen. The image was of a series of sheriff's deputies in day-glo orange vests searching a steep hillside with some emergency vehicles parked above. A talking head popped up lower right, Asian woman, serious glasses.

"Police have found the body of a young woman in a remote canyon off Paradise Road in Ventura County. There is speculation that she may be another victim of the so-called Kardashian Killer. The name of the victim is being withheld pending notification of next of kin."

Kendall turned it off and drew in silence.

TWENTY
NIGHT MOVES

Desmond, Alice, and Nate stood drooling at Kendall's drawing of the protagonist Cal advancing on the bound Muriel with his giant erect penis. Kendall had only drawn it, so who was he to judge? Was it any classier than drawing for Hustler?

Desmond slapped him on the shoulder. "Faboo, mate!"

"Can't wait to see what you'll do with the next one," Alice said. "Can't you just see Lester doing this?"

"I already have, Alice," Desmond said.

Nate beamed.

The next sequence they expected him to draw involved bestiality. He wondered at what point the bourbon took over and he lost all drawing ability. Every artist strove for the master's blend of technical know-how and loosey-goosey ease of rendering. Kendall just happened to be one of those artists who made it look easy, like Alex Toth or Frazetta.

Drawing that sequence had cost him spiritually and physically. He dreaded another session with the bottle, but it was the only way to get it down. If only he had a little blow.

Belay that you fucking moron.

Kendall pasted a shit-eating grin across his face and heard himself say, "Looking forward to it."

His mortgage was $7860.

Desmond looked at his Victorinix Swiss Army watch. "Gotta run. Got a meeting with Sal Berger downtown."

Alice's phone played the latest Jay-Z. She looked at it. "Me too. Gotta go."

Kendall and Nate watched them leave, shutting the door behind them.

"Nate, did you know Wallanda was married to Wyrick's daughter?"

"Sure, Kendall. Everybody knows that."

"And they never found what happened to his daughter? I mean Wallanda's?"

Nate shook his head. "Horrible. That has got to be every parent's nightmare. I don't know how he worked through that."

"Did you know him?"

Nate looked up. "Yes. I met him once when I was just breaking in, and he was still active at the studio. I was working on my first feature, *Bubbler*. He still came into the office back then. But we weren't, like, close. I'd always hoped to be invited to one of his parties just to see the house. He died before that happened."

"You think he killed himself?" Kendall said.

Nate clasped his hands and looked at Kendall. "You know how David Carradine died? Same thing."

"Well you know you're welcome to stop by anytime."

"Speaking of which, I'm dropping my daughter off for a sleepover at a friend's house in your neighborhood Wednesday night. How 'bout then?"

"Why don'tcha? What time? I should have groceries by then."

"Drop her off at five."

"Great. I'll grill something."

Kendall hit an Albertson's on the way home and stocked up on groceries. He decided to grill chicken. It would be a shock to Nate's refined palate. He backed into the garage and unloaded groceries, moving them bag by bag through the basement entrance up the stairs into the kitchen. There had to be a better way. He looked around the kitchen. A chimney stood out from the wall with a sliding metal door. Kendall slid the door up revealing a dumb-waiter. Of course. The bottom was concealed behind a cabinet door.

Once he got the groceries sorted, he took the bag of charcoal into the courtyard. There was a built-in brick grill and a gas grill as well. Kendall grew up in the Midwest. He'd always grilled with charcoal. He considered a dip in the pool. Anything to put off doing his job.

Kendall had never imagined that drawing comics could be onerous. Might as well bite the bullet and get it over with. He'd have a full day to recover. He flipped the first of many Hungry Man meals in the microwave. While it nuked, he slipped into his swim trunks and threw himself into the pool in a shallow dive. The water was bracingly cool and clean.

By the time he dried and changed, his Salisbury steak was ready. He ate it. He took a fresh bottle of Jim Beam and a glass into the studio and went to work. The scene evoked Catherine the Great. Kendall had studied animal anatomy. The scene required him to draw an erect stallion in both senses.

Kendall poured a couple fingers and swilled it down. Once again, he wished he had a bump, despising himself. Thank God he had no connections out here! Certainly, Nate could fix him up, but once he got on that train, there was no getting off short of a full-scale wreck. He switched on the radio. WAVE played Jeffrey Foskett's "Through My Window." If only he had such a window. All the windows in his house looked inward toward the court-yard. He could feel the surf beckoning.

His hands went through the motions. His brain dictated composition and layout. It was a thoroughly professional job. He prayed that the comic community would never learn of it. Fortu-nately, storyboarders seldom signed their work and were not credited.

He had another slug of bourbon.

An hour later he hunched over the page, a line of drool extending from lip to paper. He jerked himself upright in horror. Drooling on his art. He grabbed a tissue and wiped it clean. He looked at what he'd drawn. Magic. He didn't remember drawing, but it was what they wanted. Black magic.

His head tilted forward and hit the board. He began to snore. He had his standard nightmare. He was at a party. Shirley comes up to him and says, "Let's go." What got him wasn't that they were leaving, it was that she was alive. He wanted to shout, *"Hey wait. No fair! You died!"*

Shirley turned and stomped out the door, slamming it behind her. A piercing scream split the air. It woke him up. Kendall jerked his face off the board and looked around wildly.

The last traces of the scream faded away on the radio.

TWENTY-ONE
RESEARCH

The cable guy arrived at ten waking Kendall from a shallow, unrestful sleep. He got up with a groan, temples throbbing. *Congratulations, asshole. Your second hangover since moving out here.*

Kendall pulled on some pants, padded through the house, and opened the front door. A young Hispanic man in his company uniform was looking around the foyer, carrying a tool kit. He smiled revealing perfect teeth.

"Good morning, sir. Linus Perez for Community Cable. Looks like we're going to have to hook you up."

"Come in, Mr. Perez."

Perez stepped into the foyer and looked at the ceiling, walls, and floor. "This is quite a house."

"It's a Roark Dexter Smith design," Kendall said.

"I've heard of him. When they cable-ized the neighborhood in '98, they put in a feeder to your house, but it was never connected. So it's just a matter of finding it and hooking it up. Show me where you want the hook-ups."

Bleary-eyed and dizzy Kendall guided the tech through the house showing him the computer, the library, the bedroom. He had two TVs, in the den and in the bedroom. He'd set the computer up in the den but had only turned it on to print a file.

Perez consulted a clipboard. "Your connection is via the garage."

Kendall led the way down the steps to the garage door, opened it, turned on the lights. Perez stepped inside. He issued a wolf whistle.

"That's some short, Mr. Coffin!" he exclaimed.

"She's a honey, ain't she?" Kendall said.

The tech walked admiringly around the Corvette.

"Go ahead. Have a seat," Kendall said.

Perez slid behind the wheel and made car noises. He got out, located the cable juncture box toward the front. "I'll have to get more cable from the truck. Is that it?"

"There is one more thing," Kendall said, leading the way out of the garage down the hall to the theater. He opened the double doors and turned on the lights. Perez stepped through the doors.

Wolf whistle. "Wow! Look at this place! Looks like that place I saw all the kung fu movies when I was a kid!"

"Can you run it up to the control booth?" Kendall pointed.

Perez followed his finger. "Sure. Got a digital projector? We rent those, but you might be better off just buying one. It will cost less in the long run."

Kendall thanked him and excused himself. He took a hot shower, shaved, and changed his clothes. He made coffee. Perez appeared in the kitchen.

"It's all set up, Mr. Coffin." Perez held out the clipboard. "Please sign where indicated. Your computer is up and running and the TV. There's a brochure in the den explaining everything. It's pretty intuitive. Give us a call if there are any problems."

Kendall took the clipboard. "Thanks."

"Oh! I almost forgot your phone book." Perez reached in the toolbox and withdrew a cinderblock with a yellow cover. Kendall took it and handed over the clipboard.

Perez left. Kendall went into the den and picked up the remote. He'd ordered the extended premium channel package. It was a business necessity. His accountant assured him he would be able to write it off. He ran through 29 channels and turned it off. He returned to his studio and booted up the computer. He'd been periodically weeding his inbox via his smartphone but skipping his usual habitats, the comics news centers, Facebook, et al.

Kendall googled Frank Wallanda. There were dozens of entries from Wikipedia to the tabloids. It was the latter who claimed that the producer had died from auto-erotic asphyxiation, some claiming to have police photographs. Kendall stayed away from those.

A couple items caught his eye. In 1979, Kirk Savage, the hugely popular guitarist for Rising Gorge, blew his brains out in one of the spare bedrooms. The realtor hadn't put that in the listing. Kendall had the first two Rising Gorge records in vinyl.

The other item was about the fate of Wallanda's projects upon his death. According to the site, Salacious.com, Wallanda had been working on a black comedy about a dominatrix who accidentally kills her big shot Hollywood client and must make it appear as if he's alive for four hilarious days. It was called *What's Up With Big Mitch?* The studio quietly killed it.

Kendall had the impression he was getting a lot more than he'd bargained for. Not just the things that had been left behind: the books, the furniture, the reels, but the history of the house itself. He googled Wallanda House. The confluence of Smith and Wallanda provided the most hits. There had been an article in the LA Reader entitled, "Is Wallanda House Cursed?" It cited Savage's death and a rumor that an aspiring starlet had drowned in the pool one night and the whole incident had been hushed up.

What had that to do with him? So people had died there. So had his late wife in the house he'd just sold. People lived and died in houses; that's what happened. Rumors of Satanism had dogged Smith through his career. It hadn't affected the value of his properties.

His eye fell on *Conversations with Dead Movie Stars*. DeManning claimed to have advised countless Hollywood royalty including Wallanda. She'd had a gossip column in the long-defunct Los Angeles *Argus Leader*. Kendall grabbed his brand new phone book and leafed through the pages. There was a Portia DeManning in Venice. Kendall dialed the number. Even over the phone, it sounded like an antique; something with a rotary dial.

It rang five times. Kendall was about to hang up when it was answered, and a whiskey and cigarette-soaked contralto growled, "What?"

"Is this Portia DeManning?"

"Yes."

"Ma'am, my name is Kendall Coffin. I just moved out here from Omaha and ..."

"You bought the Wallanda place."

TWENTY-TWO
PORTIA

Portia agreed to meet him at Spangles, an old Hollywood hangout on West Pico. A blue neon sign over the door flashed SPANGLES. Neon signs in the window advertised Hamm's and Blatz, two beers that were no longer made. Kendall parked on the street and entered the dark, cool den shortly after 7:00 PM. It smelled of cigarette smoke, although smoking was illegal.

It was cigarette smoke. Kendall followed the tendrils to a back booth where he found an old woman with a wild explosion of curly gray hair and too much makeup: crimson lips, rouge on powdered cheeks, eyelashes like palm fronds, and eyebrows like electrician's tape. She had a stack of books on the table as well as an amber ashtray filled with butts.

"Miss DeManning?" Kendall said.

"Call me Portia, honey," she growled. "Slide your skinny ass in here."

Kendall sat opposite. Portia signaled the waiter, a bald old man with a slouch and an off-white apron. "One more, Harry. And get something for my friend. What are you having?"

Kendall ordered a beer. The waiter left. Portia drew on her cigarette—she used an ivory cigarette holder—and blew a ring.

She looked like Cruella de Ville. "So you bought the Wallanda place, huh?"

"Yup."

"Wha'd you say you did?"

"I'm an artist, Portia. I used to draw comic books. I'm story-boarding for Wyrick."

Portia sucked and blew. "Ah, the mighty Wyrick! He whose shit stinketh not."

"I was hoping you could tell me something about Wallanda … and the house."

"Went there once for a party. Not a party girl. I was too old for that back then. No, old Frank thought it would be a good idea to have a palm reader. Once was enough for me. There's something about that house. Felt it the first time I walked in the door. I really didn't want to know too much, so I ignored that part of me and went with the flow. Old Frank sure knew how to throw a party. The Mamas and the Papas sang. Swingersville. That awful Dr. Mandlebaum was there, plastic surgeon to the stars. We called him Manglebaum. And that actor, what's his name? The one who played Shorty Rogers. They loooved to party. It made the Playboy Mansion look like the Temperance Society. I've been to the mansion too. Used to party with Hef before his balls shriveled up."

The elderly waiter brought their drinks. Portia switched like a thirsty fighter jet. "Once that house gets its claws in you, it doesn't let go. I could feel it beckoning to me sometimes late at night, but I chose not to go there. I have made a practice of prana Buddhism and have mastered certain blocking techniques. If I hadn't done that, I would have gone mad years ago and not just from the house."

"What's wrong with the house?" Kendall said.

"Let me see your palm, honey."

Kendall proffered his hand. Portia took it in both of hers—they were dry and warm—held it palm up while tracing the lines with her index finger. The finger paused. Portia's large brown eyes fixed on Kendall.

"What?" he said, a bolus of dread in his gut.

"Don't worry. I can't really read palms. That's just a hustle. But sometimes I get vibes. You suffered a loss recently."

Careful old buddy, he told himself. *You are in the Land of Goniffs.* But it was he who had called her, and there was something sincere in her manner. All the best grifters had it.

"My wife died six months ago. I found her in my bedroom face down on the TV remote. She died from an overdose of Oxycontin and booze."

"Aww, I'm sorry to hear that, honey," Portia said still holding his hand a little too firmly. "And you wouldn't have moved out here if that hadn't happened."

"True. But the reason I called you, I keep hearing screams late at night. Or I think I do. They usually happen at the tail end of sleep. Or maybe they're short-circuiting my sleep and causing me to wake."

"Have you thought about seeing a therapist? Honestly, I wouldn't be here if it weren't for my therapist."

"I don't think it's in my head."

"How do you know?" Portia said. "Has anyone else heard the screams?"

"There hasn't been anyone there. I'm thinking of getting a dog. They're supposed to be sensitive."

"Yes, dogs can be very sensitive, and they can also be mediums. Mutts are best, although personally, I have a cat. Ozymandias. Ozzy I call him. He's my little darling." Portia scooped a feedbag-sized purse onto the wooden table and rummaged inside, retrieving a glossy photo of a languid gray cat chilling on a sofa.

"Very nice."

"You want to know if the house is haunted."

Yes, that's exactly what he wanted to know but had been afraid to say or even visualize. "Yeah."

"I don't do séances."

"But you wrote that book; *Conversations with Dead Movie Stars.*"

"I did a séance in 1969, and a man died."

"Oh," Kendall said. "Do you think that would happen?"

"I don't know, honey. A séance is all about letting your guard down, and when you let down your guard, all sorts of things are waiting to move in."

Kendall was a huge horror buff and had seen them all. He realized the absurdity of his position. "I don't know what I want."

"Well, I would think twice about a séance. There are a lot of fakes out here who will take your money in a heartbeat and tell you anything you want to hear—or just scare the bejeezus out of you for the fun of it. You know; give the rubes their money's worth."

"So you believe a house can be haunted?"

"I've seen some strange things in my life, that's for sure."

"So when you wrote that book you were really communing with the dead?"

Portia smiled, offering a glimpse of what she must have been like back in the day. "Of course, darling! I've beaten every suit they can throw at me. Did you read the book?"

Kendall colored. "Not yet."

"Read it and decide for yourself."

"If it turns out the house is haunted, would you be able to clear it?"

Portia's laughter sounded like glass in a garbage disposal. "Honey, do I look like an exorcist?"

"Well, would you come over sometime and just give me your impressions?"

"Well, I'll tell you what." Portia broke into a paroxysm of coughing. She removed a wrinkled handkerchief from her bag, crumpled it up, and coughed into it. The hacking died out. She took a sip of her gin and tonic. "Let me talk to a few friends of mine, and I'll let you know."

"What about Wallanda?"

Beat. "There's this website."

"What website?"

"Diedinhouse.com. You go there, enter any address, it will search public records, tell you if any deaths occurred there."

Kendall took out a pen and wrote it down on a coaster.

"You should talk to Bree," Portia said. "She's still alive, you know."

On the way home, he bought a new car battery and filled a plastic container with a gallon of gas.

TWENTY-THREE
TAKING STOCK

Wednesday morning Kendall sent PDFs of the finished drawings to Nate. Drawing those sequences had really taken it out of him. The hangovers. The craving for blow. He reached out to other industry contacts in the area seeking less onerous work. Ripon Games, headquartered in Pasadena, needed designers. He made an appointment with them for the following week. He contacted Marvel and DC about doing fill-in issues. He inquired at Oni, Diamond, IDW, and Boom! Nothing doing.

He could always place *Cheap Shot* with Image for a five-issue run, but it paid nothing up front, and he had to make that monthly nut. Sure, there was always a chance that an Image title could blow up like *The Walking Dead*, but he couldn't count on that. He needed steady income now. He had no IRA. He'd had to tap those funds to pay off Shirley's medical and credit card expenses. The house was his retirement plan. Like an original painting by a beloved master, it could only increase in value. At least that was the theory, notwithstanding his own bargain-basement purchase.

He told himself it was because the house was so atypical of Smith. Smith had pioneered "organic architecture" and most of his private dwellings submerged into their landscapes like snipers in ghillie suits. You wouldn't know there was a house until the front door opened.

Wallanda House flew in the face of organic architecture. It was an *Arabian Nights* fantasy, an Aztec pyramid, a Buddhist temple, as unexpected in its surroundings as Machu Picchu must have seemed to Hiram Bingham. It was a gamble, but so was life. Kendall had chosen the freelancer's life understanding that there was no such thing as guaranteed security unless you worked for the government. And even that seemed dicey these days.

He did the circuit, walking around the inner perimeter and checking every room. There were four bedrooms. That left three for visitors. Of these, each had utilized a different color scheme. White, brown, green, and red. Of course, none were so gauche as primary colors. The green room was a gentle aquamarine with matching skylight depicting lily pads in a blue pond. An old queen-sized frame remained with wrought-iron vines. Otherwise, the room was empty. The red room was rose-colored with matching skylight. The white was a sort of ecru.

Kendall descended to the basement with his iPhone and looked up some of the wine in the cellar. He cataloged the first twelve bottles at between 60 and 70 thousand dollars. Maybe he didn't have to draw that shit after all.

But how would he sell the wine? He knew nothing about wine, except that Shirley liked Chard. Call an auction house? Sotheby's? Who did he know who knew wine? Nate would know. Nate was coming over for dinner.

Kendall put the bottles back and went into the wardrobe. According to hand-written labels, some of the costumes had been used in *The Ten Commandments*, *Ben-Hur*, and *Spartacus*. There was a market for that, too. It seemed Kendall had lucked into a fortune in wine and memorabilia.

There was a great deal of lingerie as well as black leather: pants, shirts, jackets, bras, chaps, caps. He could have outfitted the Village People including the hard hat. He shut the door and went into the garage. The Stingray gleamed like an opal. It was potentially worth six figures. Kendall reached inside and popped the hood. The small block V8 looked to be in excellent condition. He got down on his knees and looked under the car. There didn't appear to be any leaks. Of course, he'd just moved it there a few days ago. He walked toward the front and looked under his Avalon. There were some old stains, but what garage didn't have those?

He pulled a tire gauge from the tool rack and checked the Vette's tire pressure. They were still at 34. The rubber was old but still in good condition. He sat behind the wheel and turned the ignition key. Nothing. The battery would have to be replaced, the fluids refilled. He could do that himself. Kendall's father Paul had been the service manager for a Chrysler dealership in Omaha. It was one thing they shared, a love of cars.

Then there was the surfboard. He used his phone to snap several pictures. He pulled it from the cabinet and leaned it against the Corvette. Bitchin'. It was lighter than he'd imagined.

He replaced the surfboard, went upstairs, and uploaded the picture to his Facebook page with the caption, "Found in my new basement." The response was immediate and enthusiastic. Within minutes the damned thing went viral. He surfed the web checking prices for custom surfboards. Another nice piece of change. In the fresh California light, he saw new possibilities. Maybe California really was the land of golden dreams!

He'd been yearning to come since he heard "Surfin' Safari" in the sixth grade. The pot of gold at the end of the rainbow. The fulfillment of manifest destiny. Those songs got inside his head and created a world as real as anything by Edgar Rice Burroughs or Philip Jose Farmer. Fantasies. Kendall made his living from fantasy. Almost everyone in comics did. Perpetual adolescents pursuing a dream that never was.

And yet here he was. Gone West young man. Still hadn't been to the beach. He could hear those songs in his head. Catch a wave, and you're sitting on top of the world. Kendall had never surfed in his life and had not the slightest idea how to go about it. But the idea of it remained with him as it did, he guessed, with everyone who loved surf music.

How ironic that Brian Wilson, the half-deaf genius, should be the only surviving Wilson brother. By all rights, he should have died first. Dennis used to lay an entire gram of pharmaceutical grade blow on the grand piano in Brian's living room to get him to write a song. Brian would hoover it up and write the song. Dennis drowned in 1983, diving off his yacht in search of something he'd thrown away three years earlier. He'd been drinking heavily. Carl died of lung cancer in 1998. Yet Brian kept on, touring with an ever-changing roster of like-minded souls who'd grown up with his music.

Pet Sounds still made Kendall weep, the sense of loss that permeated the album. It vacuumed the guts out of your heart. He couldn't stop listening. Nor could millions of others. Of the making of lists, there is no end, but *Pet Sounds* had ended up in more Top Ten Greatest Rock Records than any record outside the Beatles.

Kendall thought about taking the board to Venice or Malibu and giving it a whirl, but he'd probably end up bashing his brains out on the pier. Besides, he didn't know how to get to the beaches. You couldn't just show up and start surfing. There were gangs. Ridiculous to picture himself hanging ten, or even one. Leave that pipe dream to someone else. Like Tommy.

The Skaggs were good people. Using his newly acquired phone book, he phoned them. Marge answered.

"Marge, this is Kendall next door. I've got a pass to Wyrick World, and I'd like to take you and your family this coming Sunday if you're interested."

"Oh my, that sounds like fun," Marge said. "We get back from church around noon. Let me ask Torrance and Tommy."

Kendall looked up dog shelters in the area. There was a puppy rescue foundation less than two miles away on Vermont Avenue.

Was he ready for a dog? He was a freelancer. He'd be around most of the time. He had the perfect yard for it. He was lonely.

But not yet. He wasn't about to rush down and get a dog before settling in a little bit.

Marge came back. "Honestly, we don't know what we're doing yet. But Tommy is a definite. I'll call you."

He took a nap. When he woke, it was five o'clock.

TWENTY-FOUR
NATE'S THEOREM

Kendall showered, straightened up the kitchen area, and prepared the grill. He marinated the chicken breasts in Italian dressing and made a salad. He threw some Knorr's Red Rice and Beans in a pot.

"Beauty's Only Skin Deep" played throughout the house. It was six o'clock.

Nate stood in the entry notch looking disheveled. Kendall noted the bottle of wine with irony.

"Hi," he said opening the door. "Come on in."

Nate entered doing bobblehead. Ceiling, floor, walls. "Wow. This is some place. And I've seen some places. Here." He thrust the chilled bottle of Chardonnay at Kendall. Kendall led the way back to the kitchen and put it in the refrigerator.

"Want a beer?" he said. "I'm going to have one."

"Sure."

Kendall withdrew two Odell's Myrcenary Ales from the fridge, popped them on a steel bottle opener screwed into the butcher block table, and retrieved two beer glasses from the cupboard. He handed a bottle and glass to Nate who poured it carefully down the side so as not to leave a head.

They clinked.

They drank.

"Who's your little girl?" Kendall said.

"Angie. Light of my life. Liz and I share custody. Angie's fifteen going on thirty. She's already bugging me about getting her parts."

"In movies?"

Nate nodded smiling. "Wants to be a star."

"You get along with your ex?"

Nate drained half his glass and wiped his mouth. "As much as I can. My own stupid fault for marrying the worthless bitch in the first place."

"I hear ya," Kendall said.

"Christ, that must have been rough. I never met her. What was her name? Sally?"

"Shirley. She seemed like a great idea at the time. Gorgeous. Had a job as a legal assistant. That lasted six months. The looks lasted a few years until she gave up. I remember once we were walking into the Rosemont Horizon for the Chicago con and Harlan Ellison fell to his knees when he saw her. 'You are the most beautiful thing I've ever seen!' he said."

"Harlan, huh? Met him once at a party."

"Once she gave up any pretense of working she stopped going to the gym and went on the drinker's diet. I begged her for a year to let me drop the gym membership. Sixty bucks a month; we were having a real hard time. Finally, after an epic shriek fest, she agreed."

"Putting on weight?"

Kendall swallowed at the memory. He was unable to separate his guilt from the knowledge that he had done everything within his power to make his wife happy. Survivor's guilt. "Yeah. Once she outweighed me, I had zero interest in sex. She said, 'If you love somebody their physical appearance shouldn't have anything to do with whether you have sex with them or not.'"

Nate barked. "Yeah right! Let me tell you something. About a million years ago when I first moved out here, I'd fuck anything in a skirt. I shared a third-floor walk-up with an actor/waiter/bartender, and we'd cruise the bars on Sunset looking for cooze. I also responded to personals in the LA Weekly. So one day I see this personal, 'Lively, lovely, fascinating woman looking for love.' Start corresponding with her. We talk on the phone. Finally, we set up a meeting at Balzac's, which used to be on Sunset. The last thing she says to me before we hang up is, 'I hope you don't mind a woman with a little size.'

"So right away I'm thinking uh-oh, this is a date with Shamu. But my better self says, give her a chance, she may just be tall. I walk in the door. There's one customer. She looks like a manatee with butt cancer and a bad weave. Weighed 250 if she weighed a pound. Gets up and says, 'Oh hi! You must be Nathan!' I turned around and walked right outta there."

"Ha," Kendall said.

"This is Hollywood. It's not like there's a lack of beautiful women. Sure they may be shallow, stupid, and possibly psychopathic, but if you can't get laid out here it's because you're an aardvark! So my message to all the manatees looking for love is, go back to Judge Judy! Go back to Walmart! Go back to Alabama! Get your own reality show like *R&B Divas*!

"No man is happy who is married to a hippo. Men don't want to fuck fat women! Oh sure, you got your exceptions. Watch Jerry Springer. But don't get mad at guys because they don't want to fuck fat women. It's biology! We're all animals, most of all when we're having sex. Which brings us to Nate's Theorem."

Nate paused to smile smugly.

"Dish, girlfriend, dish," Kendall said.

"The angle of the dangle is inversely proportional to the mass of the ass."

"Excuse me?"

"The angle of the dangle is inversely proportional to the mass of the ass. It means …"

"I got it."

"What happened with Jennifer?"

"I told her I wasn't really a producer and she booted me."

Nate stared in open-mouthed astonishment. "What the fuck, Kendall? I set you up for a sweet one and you whiff?"

"Nate, you lied to her. I'm not a producer. I couldn't get her any work."

"She didn't have to know that. This is Hollywood! How far do you think you'll get telling the truth? How far do you think anyone gets?"

Kendall sighed. "Want to see the house?"

TWENTY-FIVE

LET IT SLIDE

Nate whistled as they entered the theater. "I heard about this place. Old Frank would hold screenings here of the rankest porn. This was after Bree was institutionalized. Or maybe not. Who the fuck knows?"

"Do you know where she is?"

Nate shrugged. "Shouldn't be hard to find. Why?"

"I'd like to talk to her."

"I hear she lost her mind. Had a reputation for being high-strung. Why would you want to talk to her?"

"To find out more about the house. Follow me. I want to show you something."

Kendall led Nate around the bend to the wine cellar. He opened the door, flicked on the lights, and motioned the producer in. Nate stopped four feet inside, inhaled deeply, and looked around.

"Holy shit! What is this stuff?"

"I was hoping you could tell me."

Nate went to one of the racks and pulled out several bottles one by one. "I don't know wine, but I know this stuff is old and probably rare. What are you gonna do with it?"

"I'm either gonna drink it or sell it. Know anybody who might be interested?"

"Tons. I'll make you a list."

They went upstairs. Kendall grilled in the back yard. Nate said the latest pages were dead on, and he'd have a new assignment within the week.

"I had the whole office in admiring your erect stallion. I had to swear them all to secrecy to keep it from getting out."

"Great," Kendall said. "Just do me a favor. Don't give me credit."

Nate goggled. He'd switched to Scotch. "What?! This is a Dal Lazlo production! Don't be an idiot."

"Nate, I'm serious. I have a certain reputation to maintain in the comic community."

"Fuck the comic community! You're in the movies now!"

A shroud of unease descended on Kendall's shoulders. He was looking forward to the game company interview. He realized Nate was too drunk to drive and decided to invite him to stay the night. It would be good if someone else could confirm or deny the voices.

They sat at a patio table with a round marble top. After dinner, Nate removed a small amber vial from his jacket pocket and shook white powder out on the tabletop. He pulled out a gold AmEx card and wrangled two lines. He pulled out a small gold straw, did a line and held the straw out to Kendall.

"No thanks," Kendall said without thinking about it.

"You ever do blow?" Nate said bending to the second line.

"I wish I had all the money I threw away on that shit. Now just the sight of it gives me the heebie-jeebies."

Nate snorked. "Well you've got to keep it under control, that's for sure. Things ain't changed much out here. The industry still runs on bullshit, blow, and blow jobs." He looked at his watch. "Whoopsie! Promised I'd meet a guy in Malibu. Thanks for din-din, good buddy!"

"Wait a minute," Kendall said. "I've watched you kill a half bottle of Scotch! You sure you can drive? You're welcome to spend the night here."

Nate got to his feet grinning. "Don't worry my friend. I have plenty of experience. The blow tempers the booze. I'm fine to drive."

"There might be a ghost."

Nate peered at Kendall from beneath bushy brows. "What?"

"I've been hearing strange noises at night. Be nice to have somebody else stay here and tell me whether I'm out of my mind or not."

"You're jerkin' my gherkin."

"No. Really. You should stay."

Nate was already headed off the patio. "Fuggedaboudit! I'll call you in a few days, and we'll figure out where we're at. Great work!"

Kendall followed him out the front door and down the steep stair to the street. Nate got in a silver Boxster, lowered the red top, and chirped away waving an arm in the air. Kendall found himself daydreaming. If Nate flipped the Boxster on the express-way, Kendall would be free of his assignment.

Psycho think, Kendall! Thinking like Shirley.

He shook himself and went inside. He'd signed up for the premium cable package and spent two hours flipping through 143 channels. Reality shows. Cooking shows. MMA. Movies.

Maybe if he slept in a different room. No that couldn't be. Either the house was haunted, or it wasn't.

Having spent most of his net worth on the house, he was loath to believe he'd made a terrible mistake. He took two Benadryl and went to bed. When he lay on his back, his own image stared down at him from the ceiling. He tossed and turned, finally got up and took half a Xanax. He brooded. A common theme: Why did he always choose such terrible women? Before Shirley, there had been a long line of boozers and losers. He supposed it was their vulnerability—their availability—which led him to them.

Mostly he just wanted to get laid. It wasn't until the final three years of his marriage he realized he was wasting his time with a woman who didn't give two figs whether he lived or died so long as she had what she needed. Food, booze, drugs. Shirley had no close friends. Oh, sure there were "the girls," a group of longtime "friends" who met to drink and dish.

They were always "there for each other" until they weren't. Many a night Kendall found Shirley weeping. "I have no friends!" He begged her to get help, but the only help she sought was for physical ailments, real or imagined.

Fibromyalgia. Vapors. Panic attacks.

Wherever Shirley found employment, she became locked in a death struggle with some other female who rubbed her the wrong way. So and so was out to get her. Over and over, job after job. One day she called Kendall from her last place of employment, a law firm. Someone had slashed the tires on her car, the Avalon. Kendall drove downtown in his battered old Civic to pick her up. There was no question someone had shoved a shiv in the tires and while Shirley expressed astonishment Kendall had no doubt it was her Female Enemy from the office.

A week later they fired Shirley for poor attendance.

Let it slide, Kendall. She's dead! How long you gonna stay mad at a dead person?

He slid into a shallow sleep and woke to the faint echo of a scream howling down the corridors.

TWENTY-SIX
SHAPIRO

K endall spent Saturday morning putting the rest of his
stuff away. Off to the dog shelter. Furry Friends occupied
a storefront in a run-down strip mall that also contained a Mr.
Money, Papa John's, Shapiro's Taekwondo, and Victory Liquor.
A couple of low-riders confabbed in a corner of the lot when
Kendall arrived. All the stores had accordion metal gates that
had been pulled aside for business.

Kendall entered Furry Friends. A pachuco with a shaved
skull, head and shoulders inked like an 18th century map,
signed papers at the linoleum counter, a pit bull puppy at his
feet. The puppy wore a spiked leather collar. The counter held
several cardboard brochure stands along with a half-gallon jar
filled with money and a bowl of corn chips.

"How would you like to pay the adoption fee, Mr. Hernandez?" the stringy older woman behind the counter said.

Hernandez dipped into his rear pocket and pulled out a
leather wallet the size of a folded map, peeled off six twenties
and laid them on the counter. The woman took the money, made
change and handed Hernandez a pen and a clipboard.

"Just sign there, and he's all yours. What are you going to call
him?"

"Velazquez," the pachuco said. He took his change, papers, and the puppy and left.

The woman turned to Kendall with a smile. "How can I help you today?"

"I think I want to adopt a dog."

"It's not a decision you make lightly. A dog is a living thing that requires a lot of attention and love. Have you ever owned a dog before?"

"When I was a kid."

The woman handed Kendall a brochure: *Raising Your Puppy.* "You might want to read this before continuing."

Kendall put the brochure in his hip pocket. "I'm pretty sure I want to adopt a dog."

The woman stuck out her hand. "Amy Rothgard."

Kendall shook. "Kendall Coffin."

"What do you do for a living, Kendall?"

She was one of those animal lovers who wasn't about to hand her pups out to just anybody. Yet she had just signed a pit bull over to a gang banger.

"I'm a freelance artist, and I work at home. I'll be there most of the time."

"Excellent! What kind of art?"

"Comic books. Have you heard of Dr. Strange?"

"Of course I've heard of Dr. Strange," Amy said. "My boyfriend collects comics."

"That's one of the titles I've drawn."

Kendall saw barriers falling. He was an arteest! He worked at home! Amy raised a hinged section of the counter. "Why don't you come back here and take a look."

She held open a door behind her. Kendall entered a warehouse-like space with a concrete floor smelling of dog shit and bleach. There were six rectangular wire enclosures, each holding a number of puppies. Clipboards hung from each gate. A young woman in cargo pants and a halter top cleaned dog poop in one of the enclosures.

"Celeste, would you go out front?"

"Sure thing, Amy."

Kendall stopped at the first enclosure. Inside were six puppies, all about the same size, of unknown provenance.

"When the puppies come in," Amy explained, "we first isolate them for a few days while we test them. All adoptable puppies are at least six weeks old and have their rabies and distemper shots. That's covered in the adoption fee. You must also agree to spay or neuter your pet within six months and provide us with proof.

"They experience life through their mouths. They're going to chew. If you adopt a dog, you must supply it with quality chewables. You will not believe how much one of these puppies can chew in a day. I advise against buying any products made in China. They're always mixing things up. Rat poison and fiber, for example. Hard rubber, leather, plastic: whatever you think you need, you need twice as much. Else he's going to chew on your shoes and furniture."

The puppies were adorable. Kendall immediately zeroed in on what looked like a border collie/shepherd mix. It was brown with a white blaze on its chest. Amy opened the gate.

"Go on. Feel free to pet them."

Kendall went inside and crouched. The pup came right up to him, stood on its hind legs, and licked whatever it could reach. "Is it a boy or a girl?"

"Let's see," Amy said, picking the pup up and turning it over. "It's a boy."

"Okay. I'll take that one."

The dog yipped and ran around the car all the way home. With the pup tucked under one arm, Kendall entered his house through the basement entrance. He set the dog down on the ground, and it followed him up the steps, scrambling to leap from one to the next. He put the pup in the inner courtyard and filled a plastic bucket with water. He left for supplies.

An hour later Kendall returned from PetSmart with a crate, leash, collar, bag after bag of doggie chews, and several brands of upscale dog food. As Kendall entered the courtyard, the pup yelped with joy and leaped up, its little tail wagging.

Return him? No way.

Kendall hunkered down. "Sit, Shapiro!"

The puppy grinned and lolled its tongue. He spent the rest of the day teaching the puppy to sit, calling it by name, rewarding it with treats. A good start.

There was a disturbance in the force, a whiff of museum. Kendall turned. Tommy had entered the courtyard through the door off the corridor.

"I rang several times, but there was no answer."

Kendall rose. "That's cool."

Tommy's face lit with delight. "Oh wow, man! You got a dog! What's his name?"

"Shapiro."

Tommy went into full coo mode, sitting on his haunches and beckoning. "C'mere Shapiro! Good dog!" Shapiro climbed into his lap and began furiously licking his neck.

"Just got him," Kendall said. "This is his first day."

"You need somebody to check in on him when you're not around let me know."

"Thanks, Tommy. What about Wyrick World? You interested?"

"You bet! But I'm the only one who can make it. Dad's got a gig in Thousand Oaks, and Mom has her book club. If you want to wait until we all can go that's cool."

"No, we'll go. Just you and me. Leave here around eleven tomorrow?"

"Man it's going to be a zoo, but that's cool!"

Kendall put the crate in his room and brought Shapiro in after observing the dog tinkle. His alternative would be to leave Shapiro in the courtyard at night, but when he went into the house and shut the door, the dog commenced such piteous howling that Kendall brought him in. Shapiro had only tinkled on the hardwood floor once, quickly cleaned with Pine Sol and a rag.

He left the crate door open and spread newspaper with training mats on them. Kendall guessed the mats already smelled like piss but not bad enough for humans.

That night there were no screams and Shapiro didn't howl.

TWENTY-SEVEN
WYRICK WORLD

Kendall woke in the morning to Shapiro curled up beneath the covers and a fresh mound of dog shit on the newspaper. He wrapped and tossed the shit, grabbed the mutt, took him outside, and waited until the dog tinkled.

"Good doggie!" He led the way inside, Shapiro at his heels. Kendall vowed to download the paperless drawing program and purchase all the equipment necessary to render his art on computer without ever touching pencil to paper. He didn't want the storyboards in his house. He was afraid to read the *Night Shifts* script, afraid of what they would ask him to draw. He wondered if they were really making a movie or if this was just an elaborate plan to drive him insane. Maybe they were actually filming a secret documentary. Maybe it was part of an NSA experiment.

Kendall revised his résumé and put together packages for several prospective employers. It was one thing to say you were a comic book artist. It was quite another to slap down several copies of a well-known Marvel title. Comics got him his first house. The bank was secretly thrilled to loan to him. He'd been a celebrity at his local bank and comic shop.

The San Diego Con was in two weeks. Kendall hadn't been in years, not since he stopped drawing Doc Strange. The last time he'd been the place was frighteningly overpacked. 125,000 people in one room. The TV and movie people had taken over, pushing the comics to the side. If you fainted in the main hall, you would remain standing.

He missed San Diego. The con not so much.

The doorbell chimed. It was Tommy with a backpack containing sunscreen and water bottles. They took Kendall's car, pulling into the vast Wyrick World parking lot shortly after noon. Wholesome young men and women wearing brightly colored Wyrick livery guided them to a parking spot a hundred yards from the main entrance.

It was a hot, sunny day in late June. Wyrick World glittered like the promise of a better tomorrow with its Rapunzel tower rising from lush oak, the whirr of carnival rides, the laughter and shriek of children, the voice of the hurdy-gurdy man.

A polished Indian youth in a Dagnabbit Rabbit vest approached them in the line. "Sir, would you please open your backpack for me?"

Tommy set the pack on a steel shelf and opened it. The dude poked around, checked the side pockets, affixed a yellow label to the strap and handed it back. "You folks have a nice day."

A sign over the ticket booth showed prices: $125 for an adult one-day pass. $50 for thirteen to twenty-one. Children under twelve were $25. The sweet young thing at the entry style popped her eyes when Kendall showed her his golden pass which he wore on a chain around his neck.

"Yikes! I've never seen one of these before." She read the fine print and waved them through.

"Y'know," Tommy said, "these wouldn't be too difficult to duplicate."

"Don't even think about it," Kendall said heading straight for Dagnabbit Rabbit's Wild Ride. Wyrick World has been around since the seventies, long enough to acquire the patina of an Ivy

League college. Vines grew on many of the buildings, and the old-fashioned Main Street cried out for Mickey Rooney and Judy Garland. As they walked toward the Arabesque stucco housing Dagnabbit Rabbit, they passed happy families of every persuasion. Everybody loved Darryl Wyrick's creations.

There were entertainers dressed as Awesome Possum, Ultra Pigeon, and Dagnabbit Rabbit moving through the crowd, mugging for kids, posing for pictures. Dagnabbit and Awesome squared off as mock boxers. Tommy and Kendall stood in line behind an excited Mexican family of six, dad in front, the littlest kid in back, so they looked like a set of nesting dolls.

It was a different world once through the sliding doors, cool and dark inside with twinkling lights like fairy dust in the walls and ceiling. Another squeaky-clean kid ushered them into their twelve-seat module, the Mexican family, two couples, and Kendall and Tommy.

"Folks, it's a virtual reality ride which means that while you think you're zipping through space and doing loop-the-loops, you're not. It's all done with visuals, sound, vibrations, and magic. Hang on to the bar and don't leave your seats."

The crowd waited breathlessly in the chill of the theater. Dagnabbit Rabbit was a Jim Carrey/Robin Williams on crack sort of character capable of exploding into violent zaniness at the slightest provocation. He had a long-running dispute with Wyatt Wolf who pursued him relentlessly through the decades. Dag's forest was rife with dinosaurs, cauldrons of magma, and wild animals.

The theme music began. Suddenly the car occupants hurtled through the forest, nearly colliding with a surprised black bear. The Dagnabbit's eye-view ride swooped perilously close to the jaws of a Tyrannosaurus, skimmed the waves of a volcano, and swooped through a petrified forest. Wyatt Wolf was on Dag's ass, howling like Little Richard.

The ride was so realistic Kendall gripped the plastic bar white-knuckled and felt a little queasy as Dagnabbit dodged and twisted like a WWI flying ace dodging Wyatt's rocket-powered grenades. By the time the ride was over Kendall felt like he'd survived a combat mission.

They exited into bright sunlight.

"Let's take in something a little less kinetic," Kendall said.

"Let's take a look at the Town of Tomorrow," Tommy said. They headed toward the futuristic pavilion.

A svelte figure appeared before them as if by magic. She wore a shiny blue/black top hat, a black formal jacket with a swallow tail and fishnet stockings which ended in black high heels. She smiled, doffed her top hat, and pulled out a rabbit. She set the rabbit down, and a boy in Wyrick livery picked it up.

The smiling girl put on the hat, produced four tennis balls, and juggled them in ever increasing loops. She was Illeana the Illusionist. Kendall looked beyond the makeup and saw a shining face. She wore a Doc Strange cloisonné pin on her lapel.

"Doc Strange?" Kendall said. "I draw Doc Strange!"

The tennis balls bounced off the bricks.

"You draw the actual Marvel comic?"

"I do! Well, I did."

She stooped to pick them up, cradling them like babies. "Get out! What's your name?"

"Kendall Coffin."

Her mouth formed a perfect 'O.' "You're Kendall Coffin? I love your stuff!"

"What's your name?"

"Ronnie. Ronnie Arnold!" She thrust out a white-gloved hand, and they shook.

"What are you working on now?" Ronnie said.

Tommy's head rotated through a ninety-degree arc as if he were watching a tennis match. Kendall colored. He couldn't tell her what he was really working on.

"I'm preparing my own title. *Cheap Shot!*"

"That sounds great! I'd love to hear more about it. Are you new in town?"

"Yes. I just moved out a week ago."

"Well if you'd like someone to show you around ..."

They headed for the parking lot with Ronnie's phone number.

"Dude," Tommy said. "That was smoooooooooth."

TWENTY-EIGHT
BUILDING BLOCKS

Kendall couldn't believe his ears. "That's not in the script."

Alice churned the air with jazz hands. "It's the director's idea, and we think it's brilliant."

"Nobody has ever filmed anything like this before," Desmond gushed.

Kendall bit his tongue, nodded, swallowed, and sat down. He had an interview Wednesday with a game company in the Valley. Please God let them hire him away from this madness. The three producers cooed and gushed over his stallion scene. Desmond wanted to turn it into a poster.

"Be a sensation!"

"Let me think about that," Kendall said. He was learning. Don't butt heads with these fuckers. Advance by stealth and guile. Nothing they could say could bring him down. They could throw him the most grotesque scene imagined by Charlie Sheen and 2 Live Crew, and it wouldn't phase him.

Nothing phased him since Ronnie raised her raven-tressed head. Was it too soon to phone her? They'd only met yesterday. Of course not! He wasn't a total dope when it came to women.

"Kendall!" Nate yelped.

Kendall snapped back. "Excuse me?"

"Can you have those new pages for us in a week?"

"You bet. Just get me the updated script by today if you can."

"No prob. Hey is that house of yours acting up again? You hear any voices?"

Kendall colored.

"Wot's this?" Desmond pounced.

"Kendall bought the old Frank Wallanda place. It's a Roark Dexter Smith design. Says it's haunted."

Kendall held up a finger. "I said it might be haunted."

"Really?" Alice zeroed in. "Oh, I would love to see that. I would love it if you invited me to a séance."

Kendall grinned and held up his hands. "No séance! We were both drinking, and I said the house might be haunted, that's all! I was joking."

"Did you or did you not hear voices at night?" Nate said. "I wasn't that drunk."

"You know, Nate, it was my fucking radio. I got it used, and every night at eleven thirty it turns itself on to some religious channel. I unplugged it that night. Slept like a baby."

"I know one of the producers on Ghost Hunters," Desmond said. "Want me to hook you up? They pay big bucks."

Kendall smiled and held up his hands. "I'm good."

Nate's secretary stuck her head in the door. "Your two o'clock is here."

On the way back, Kendall stopped at an Ace Hardware and bought an enormous bolt cutter, another padlock, a doggy door, and had two spare house keys made. It was a beautiful sunny day in Southern California. When he got home, he opened the patio door, and Shapiro rushed to greet him, yapping and lapping.

"My little ghost chaser!"

Kendall played with the dog for a few minutes before calling Ronnie.

"Hi!" she said. "I was hoping you'd call."

They made a date for Friday night. She lived in an apartment complex in Santa Monica. He installed the doggie door. It fit in the same tracks as the sliding door. The doorbell rang. A courier hand-delivered the script revisions. They were so hot the studio was afraid to use the internet. Kendall took the script and sat on the patio, Shapiro worrying a tennis ball at his feet. As he read the new sequence his stomach twisted into a Klein bottle.

As a cineaste, Kendall knew that taboos were made to be broken. Films like Ken Russell's *Women in Love* and *The Devils* had prompted church denunciations and reconsideration of the motion pictures rating system. Likewise, Bertolucci's *Last Tango in Paris* and Paul Verhoeven's *Basic Instinct*. But the scenario they were asking him to storyboard went beyond breaking taboo. It wanted to rub the audience's nose in the most filthy, graphic perversions imaginable. Even if the interview went well and the game company hired him, it would be unwise for Kendall to sever ties with the studio.

Darryl Wyrick spun in his grave.

Damned if you do, damned if you don't.

"Beauty's Only Skin Deep" chimed out of every intercom in every room. Kendall went to the door. It was Torrance with a plate of brownies.

"Can't stop her from baking, damn it!" Torrance said. "Thank God you arrived to take some of the burden."

Kendall invited him. "You want some lemonade?"

They took their lemonade out to the patio. Torrance crouched to play with the puppy. "What's his name?"

"Shapiro."

Torrance laughed. "Say, thanks for taking Tommy to Wyrick World. He really got a kick out of it. Sorry I couldn't come."

"I have a lifetime pass, Torrance, until they take it away."

"Why would they take it away?"

Kendall adopted a German accent. "Schwein! You come to my haus drunk undt disorderly? Hand over your pass!"

Torrance laughed. "That's not likely to happen."

Kendall couldn't mention the most likely reason they would strip him of his pass—his failure to turn in storyboards.

"Tommy tells me you met a young woman."

Kendall clasped his hands over his heart. "Illeana the Illusionist! I'm seeing her on Friday."

"Good for you! I remember back in the bad old eighties when we were touring ..." Torrance's gaze separated and drifted. "Oh hey. Tommy says you've got a theater in there. I always heard about that place. Could I take a look?"

"Sure," Kendall said standing.

He led the way down the stairs and up the cold corridor to the theater.

"Nice and cool down here," Torrance said.

Kendall opened the double doors, stepped inside, and turned on the lights. Torrance's head swung around like a weathercock in a storm.

"Wow. What a great place to hold a small, intimate concert. You could really blast it too 'cause the neighbors wouldn't hear! Maybe if we get the band back together ..."

"That's a great idea, Torrance. Anytime."

Torrance headed for the stage, steadying himself on a gold handrail to his right. He took one big step onto the stage itself. Hands on hips, he examined the stone proscenium. Kendall heard him mutter.

"What the fuck?" Torrance said.

"What?" Kendall said.

"Even Solomon in all his glory was not arrayed like one of these."

Torrance sat on the hardwood platform and pointed at the stone blocks which were about eighteen inches square. "This block has hieroglyphs on it. Look. That's Osiris and Isis, and this is obviously the symbol of some Pharaoh, possibly Ramses II."

"How would you know that?"

"We did the whole Middle East thing a couple years ago; before it blew up. And this stone next to it? Completely different composition, different stone, and appears to have Mayan markings. Look at this gray stone here. Doesn't it look like it came from some gloomy castle? These blocks, man, these blocks are from sacred places all over the world! There's probably some law against having them."

Kendall skipped down the steps and crouched where Torrance pointed. There were six blocks that weren't uniform. Torrance was correct about their provenance.

"Jesus. Was he … robbing historic archaeological sites? Why would he do that?"

Torrance shifted, so he was facing the seats. He removed a fat doobie from his vest. "Mind if I smoke this?"

"No. Go ahead."

"This may be Smith's work. Remember. He was a little unhinged. There was a horrible incident at Bluff House, the dream home he built overlooking the Mississippi. It burned down one night killing Smith, his wife, and his builder."

"Seriously?" Kendall said.

Torrance lit the doobie with a Bic, inhaled and exhaled filling the stage with aromatic smoke. "Seriously. You never heard about this?"

"No."

Torrance got to his feet grunting and passed the doobie to Kendall. Kendall inhaled.

"Yeah. You should check it out. I think I got a book on it somewhere. I'd like to take some pictures of those stones."

"Go ahead."

As they headed upstairs, Kendall remembered the crowbar. He handed it over.

"Thanks," Torrance said. "Say, if you don't have any dinner plans come on over. Marge is making some kind of casserole."

"All righty then," Kendall said.

After Torrance left, Kendall went into his studio and turned on the small TV. The police had found another body in a canyon.

TWENTY-NINE
IT LIVES

Kendall brought a bottle of 1985 Aloxe-Corton Domaine Michel Juillot and a 1979 Abreu Vineyards Cabernet Sauvignon. As he walked up the Skaggs's double-concrete strip driveway, Tommy had his head buried in the engine bay of a Subaru WRX.

"Tommy," Kendall said.

Tommy came up for air. "Hey, Kendall! Just go right in. How'd it go with Illeana?"

"Got a date Friday."

Tommy gave him the thumbs up. "Awesome!"

Kendall went into the kitchen where Marge was making a big bowl of salad.

"Hi, Marge. I brought a red and a white." He set the bottles on the counter.

"Great! Torrance is on the patio. He'll make you a drink."

Torrance sat in one of his Adirondacks with a bible on his lap and lemonade on the table next to him. He stood when he saw Kendall. "Scotch?"

"Sure."

Torrance went inside and returned a minute later with a tall glass bearing a slice of lime and a maraschino cherry. They sat in chairs facing the pool.

"Any progress on the reunion?" Kendall said.

"Yeah, the guys seem amenable. We've had a little interest from the Grammy people. A Gearhead reunion would be a real coup, especially now that the kids are into metal. Iron Maiden, Black Sabbath, Creed. We're even talking about recording. I've got more than enough songs although I don't know how the guys feel singing about Jesus."

"Just substitute the word baby," Kendall said.

"There you go."

They convened around the table and bowed their heads while Torrance said grace. Marge cracked the Juillot and poured glasses for Torrance, Kendall, and herself. Torrance sniffed, savored, swilled, and swallowed.

"That's a good wine!" he said.

"Came from my cellar," Kendall said. "Wallanda left a stocked wine cellar."

"You're kidding."

"Know anything about wine? It's quite a collection."

"I don't, but Reggie does."

"Your bass player Reggie?"

Torrance nodded. "He's in town. I'll give him a call."

"Know anything about cars?"

Torrance pointed his fork at Tommy. "He does. What's up?"

"Got a new battery. Gonna try and get that old Stingray running."

After dinner, Tommy followed Kendall back to his garage. Kendall rolled the door up into the ceiling and turned on the blower. He had the replacement battery on a trickle charger. Tommy took a tire gauge off the shelf at the rear and went around the car with a hand pump.

"This rubber's in cherry shape," he said.

"That rubber's older than you are."

While Kendall poured five gallons of premium into the fuel tank, Tommy popped the hood and checked the oil. "Whoa," he said extending the dipstick toward Kendall. "Hard to believe this oil is forty years old. It looks brand new."

Tommy installed the new battery, connecting the ground first and then the hot wires. The old Corvette had a hand-operated choke on the dash.

Kendall sat behind the wheel and turned the key part way. Lights gleamed, and the radio crackled to life: "Caroline, No." A surfer song from the sixties in his sixties Corvette in California. It made the hair on the back of his neck prickle. Kendall turned the radio off and rotated the key the rest of the way.

The starter churned with a low ripping noise, strong and true. With a rifle report, the engine caught and turned over. A surge of exhilaration erupted from the gas pedal up through his foot and calf, and Kendall had to resist the urge to rev it. Those cylinders had been sitting silent for decades. Better let the oil work its way up there before he pushed it. A cloud of blue smoke issued from the twin tailpipes and whisked toward the street.

Tommy was goggle-eyed. "Let's take it for a spin!"

Kendall let the V8 idle. "You want to back the Toyota up and park it on the street? The key's in it."

Tommy practically ran. Kendall worried that the kid would jam the car, but he got it out quickly, expertly and was back at the garage by the time Kendall had backed up to the street. The transmission seemed a little notchy but what could you expect? It was a miracle the thing ran at all.

Tommy popped into the shotgun seat and fastened his seat-belt. "Let's cruise, dude!"

"We're only going around the block. It's not licensed or insured."

"Oh, come on, dude! Don't you want to hear that muscle car roar? Don't you want to lay rubber?"

Kendall smiled. "We'll see."

He backed into the street, shifted into first, and chirped rubber as he let the clutch out. It was grabby from long disuse.

Tommy pumped his fist. "All right!"

The big engine settled into a subterranean burble as it surged down the street. Kendall could practically feel the down strokes of the pistons. Kendall planned to go down to Hillhurst, turn left, and cut through the neighborhood counterclockwise. As they drove past Griffith Boulevard the wheel suddenly leaped in his hands, and the car swerved left. Kendall was so surprised he just hung on and watched in disbelief as the car headed toward Griffith Park. He pulled to the curb and shut the engine off, sweating.

"What the fuck?" Tommy said. "What was that all about?"

"I don't know, but obviously the car needs work."

They made it back to the garage without incident.

THIRTY
OFF THE PIG

F riday seemed a decade off. Kendall spent most of Tuesday working with Shapiro on toilet skills, surreptitiously eyeing him in the house and swooping down like a screeching hawk when the pup lifted a leg or squatted. Snatching Shapiro like a fumbled football and running for the courtyard. Praising him as he relieved himself on the lawn.

Shapiro yapped joyfully and chased a ball, barely getting his little jaws around it.

Kendall went through his list of S. Cal contacts on Facebook and email, sending job queries. He alphabetized his CD collection. He ate leftovers for dinner and slept with the pup. There were no screams.

On Wednesday Kendall drove to Pasadena. Ripon Games was located in a park-like industrial complex between a health billing company and a Harley-Davidson dealer. The building was long and low, built to withstand the Big One. The decor was Danish modern with swooping steel, lots of glass, and a rectangular reflecting pool out front.

Kendall waited in the black marble foyer, the walls decorated with original art from their hit games *Vomitorium*, *Twerk or Die*, and *Las Exorcistas I* through *IV*. He riffled through the magazines: *Gaming World, Internal Correspondence, Geek, Vibe, Nerd, Gutta World, Hit List, Murder Dog, Wired,* and *Outdoors.*

The receptionist gave him a laminated pass to wear around his neck. A young woman in a smart gray pantsuit, her hair done up in a bun, wearing glasses, came forward with her hand outstretched.

"Mr. Coffin? I'm Patty Hansen, Vice President in charge of Design. Shall we?"

He followed Patty through a sliding glass door into a hushed, carpeted hall, also lined with original art. She led him to a conference room looking out on an interior courtyard xeriscape. A kid wearing suspenders over a light blue shirt with a white collar sat at the head of the table tilted back with his feet up. He had wild curly black hair and an olive complexion. He got up when Kendall and Patty entered.

"Mr. Coffin? Ruben Benson. I started Ripon in my garage when I was twelve years old. I'm a big comic fan, and I've always dug your work. Have a seat! You want something to drink? We have tea, lemonade, bottled water. Help yourself to the fruit."

Kendall shook hands. "Pleased to meet you. Please call me Kendall."

"And call me Rube! That whole thing you did with Dormamu—killer."

"Thank you. That was the writer's idea."

"I know. Writers! God love 'em."

"I know! Shmucks with Underwoods, right?"

Rube stared at him.

"Jack Warner said that."

"Who's Jack Warner?" Ruben said.

"Founded Warner Brothers, I believe," Patty said.

"Right! Right. Have a seat. Before we get into specifics, you'll have to sign a non-disclosure agreement."

Kendall sat and read the boilerplate. He signed it, Patty witnessed it, Rube signed it. Rube leaned forward with his elbows on the table.

"We need a head designer on an exciting new game that's going to fucking rule the next two years. We've already cut a deal with Hangman and Crude Blue Crew to provide the soundtrack."

"*Off the Pig*," Patty said.

"You would be in charge of developing the overall look of the game, which will be urban dystopia."

"We're modeling it on Detroit," Patty said.

"You would also design the Crack City police force and vehicles. You would have a hand in hiring character designers. In fact, it's a real stroke of luck you showing up when you did as you must have some wonderful connections."

"What's the game about?" Kendall said.

"It's the most exciting first-person shooter ever. The player can play solo or in conjunction with anyone from one to twelve other players. The player has access to a wide range of weaponry, all rooted in reality from .50 caliber revolvers to portable chain guns."

"But what's it about?" Kendall said.

Rube glanced at Patty. "It's about killing cops," he said.

The room was too cold. Kendall shivered in his T-shirt and jeans. "Surely, I'm not your only applicant."

"Oh no," Rube said. "We have plenty of qualified applicants, but as soon as you contacted us your name went to the top of the list. Loved your work on Bengal Boy, too. Man, I have all those issues! In fact, I hope you won't find this too nerdy, would you mind signing them?"

Rube roped his backpack and set it on the table. He pulled out six comics, each sealed in its own plastic sleeve with acidless backer boards. He carefully peeled the tape and removed the comics one by one. "Just go ahead and sign on the covers. I'm going to have them framed." He handed Kendall a gold felt-tipped marker.

"Would you like me to make these out to you?"

"Oh no, just your name would be fine."

Kendall dutifully signed the covers of each comic trying not to cover his art.

"Let's talk compensation," Rube said. "The job pays $96,000 a year plus you get stock options."

"Forty-hour week?"

Patty held up a hand. "We're trying to avoid too much government entanglement, so we're keeping it at less than thirty. Of course, you're free to work on projects in your own time. We're not looking to take advantage. And we do have a group health plan, but you have to pay your own premiums."

"It's very reasonable," Rube said.

"I have no problem with that," Kendall said. " I'd like to take a day or two to think it over."

"Certainly," Rube said standing. "As long as you're here let me give you the grand tour."

The executive offices were nerd hordes of action figures, limited edition monster statues, original art, posters, toys, swords, and guns. They were dark with drawn shades, the only light coming from computer monitors. The bullpen was as dark as a cave, divided into numerous cubicles. In each a geek. No one looked up. These were true believers. Creating the next generation of first-person shooters was their calling. They watched Big Bang Theory and haunted aintitcoolnews. They were electronic nerd Morlocks.

On the way back, Kendall realized he would be trading one degradation for another. Weren't there any respectable jobs for him? Why couldn't he find comic work? He was better than he'd ever been. Same old same old. It wasn't what you knew but who you knew. And he knew Nate. He'd hesitated to bring up his objections because he needed the work. But Wyrick was huge, and Nate was an old friend. Surely, he'd understand.

Compared to *Night Shifts*, *Off the Pig* didn't seem so bad.

At least the house had stopped screaming.

THIRTY-ONE
COFFEE TABLE BOOK

Thursday was so beautiful Kendall couldn't bring himself to labor in the basement, so the bolt cutter lay on the workbench in the garage. Tommy came over with a set of chock blocks, a creeper, and a tool kit. With Tommy guiding, Kendall drove the front end of the Vette up on the chock blocks and set the parking brake. Tommy jammed two hard rubber stops under the rear wheels and slid under the front end on the creeper.

"You fix it, you can drive it," Kendall said.

"Awesome!"

Kendall went upstairs into the courtyard to work with Shapiro. The dog was amazingly smart and was almost house-trained. That is, there had been no accidents in the past two days. He tossed the ball for Shapiro and made a few calls.

An editor at IDW offered him a title, but the page rate was too low. His calls to Marvel and DC editors went unreturned. The automatic sprinklers went on, sending Shapiro scurrying and yapping. At noon Tommy emerged from the garage smeared with grease.

"Okay! I changed the brake fluid, bled the brakes, changed the power steering fluid, drained the radiator, and replaced that and replaced two hoses. I greased the chassis pivot points and checked out the steering. Should be good to go."

Kendall filled up at a gas station on Vermont. They got on the Hollywood Freeway headed west and hit seventy in the blink of an eye. Bikers and kids in lowered Hondas gave them the thumbs up. Kendall turned around in Universal City and headed back.

As soon as Kendall pulled up in front of the house, Tommy said, "Can I take her for a spin?"

Kendall held his hand out. "Let me see your license."

Tommy handed it over. Everything was in order. "Are you covered for any vehicle you drive?"

"I think so," Tommy said.

"Okay. My word is good so forgive me if I sound like an old fart. This is a very valuable automobile. It's also very fast, and you are very young. Ten minutes. That's all. After that, we'll see. Don't hit anything and don't get any tickets."

Kendall got out, and Tommy took his place behind the wheel. "Thanks, dude! I won't let you down!"

Tommy squealed the tires pulling out. Kendall stayed where he was watching the blue Corvette hurtle down the road. He turned and went up the steps. He hoped he hadn't made a terrible mistake. Fifteen minutes later Tommy appeared with the keys.

"Hey! If I wash it and wax it, can I take it out on a date?"

"Maybe. But not now."

Kendall followed Tommy out the door and down the steps, opened his garage and drove the Corvette in. The Avalon was on the street. He closed the garage door from inside and went up through the basement. Shapiro waited for him at the top of the stairs yapping. More ball.

For dinner, Kendall popped a can of Blue Buffalo for Shapiro and made himself a quasi-bacon sandwich: two pieces of toast, a tomato slice, and a bottle of bacon bits. After dinner, he went into the den, to the big inbuilt bookcase. A series of coffee table books stood at attention on the lower shelf. There were several volumes devoted to Roark Dexter Smith as well as books on expressionism, surrealists, Egon Schiele, and erotic Japanese prints.

He pulled out *The Making of Wyrick World* and sat in the overstuffed leather chair. The book had been published in 1983 and chronicled the construction of the amusement park in black and white and color. The introduction, by Art Samuelson, Architecture Editor for *Movers and Shakers* magazine contained a short biographical essay.

A SINGULAR VISION

Darryl Wyrick was born in Chicago March 3, 1929, at the height of the Great Depression. The third and last child of boatwright Wilmar Wyrick and his wife Adrienne, Darryl grew up in a loving if threadbare home. Wilmar was Chief Foreman for the Great Lakes Boat Company which built freighters. When he was laid off due to lack of orders, he went to work delivering coal.

Darryl's two older sisters, Anna and Louise, spoiled him and delighted in reading to him from the Sunday funny papers. It is believed young Darryl first fell in love with cartoons and entertainment through the funny papers. He was already drawing Li'l Orphan Annie, Krazy Kat, and Buck Rogers by the age of seven.

Darryl created his first character, Ultra Pigeon, in high school. He made a flip book in the margins of his social studies text for which he was promptly sent to the principal's office and given two weeks' detention. The flip book enjoyed wide circulation beneath desk tops.

Darryl dropped out of high school in the twelfth grade to become a cameraman for the Gotham Documentary Company, making a series of work-related documentaries for the New Deal. Only one remains, Preserving Food Through Refrigeration.

Darryl hitchhiked west in 1947 and found work as an animator at Warner Brothers Studios where he worked on Bugs Bunny, Foghorn Leghorn, and others. He shared an office with Chuck Jones for a year. In 1950 Wyrick sold his car to finance his first animated feature, Ultra Pigeon Flies the Coop, *working with a young team of animators, most of whom would go on to join him at Wyrick Studios. They called themselves "The Crazy Eight" and all lived in the same boarding house in Pasadena.*

Shown as a feature prior to MGM's An American In Paris, Ultra Pigeon Flies the Coop *was an enormous success, resulting in Wyrick's opening of his own studio on the MGM lot.*

In 1945 Wyrick married the actress Joan Hardison. A year later she gave birth to their only child, Bree. Wyrick won the first of many Oscars in 1977 for Dagnabbit Hits the Comeback Trail, *a full-length animated feature starring Dagnabbit Rabbit, voiced by Dom DeLuise. As of this writing, Wyrick Studios has racked up over fifty Oscars including several for Best Picture (*Crazy, Weisenheimers, Battlepug*).*

Wyrick broke ground in Anaheim in 1976 for Wyrick World, a theme park devoted to Wyrick's characters and creations. Wyrick World has been a sensation since it opened its doors in August 1979, and is one of Los Angeles's top attractions. It is estimated over seven million people a year pass through its golden gates.

In 1982 Wyrick created the Velva Voom Foundation, pure scientific research dedicated to finding a cure for cancer and prolonging human life.

Kendall ordered two Wyrick bios from Amazon.

THIRTY-TWO
CHEZ FEZ

K endall roamed the house like a high school student who just landed a date with the head cheerleader. He was pretty sure Ronnie had never been a cheerleader. She would have been one of the goth girls or perhaps just a seedling waiting to bloom. In Kendall's experience, the good-looking, popular girls faded quickly while the meek, the geek, and the pale flowered.

He'd made reservations for seven at Chez Fez, a French Moroccan place on Sunset near the Capitol Building. He debated long and hard before deciding to take the Ray. If Tommy said it was fixed, that was good enough for him. He fed the dog, showered, shaved, smacked himself with Aqua, and was good to go.

Ronnie lived in West Hollywood on the third floor of a midseventies apartment building surrounding a courtyard and a pool. He parked on the street and walked up the outside stairs nervous as a teenager.

A pixie-ish blond answered the door. "Oh, hi! You must be Kendall. I'm Connie, Ronnie's roommate. She'll be ready in a minute. You want to come in?"

The living/dining area was decorated with framed French impressionism, Toulouse Lautrec, and magic posters. *Carter Beats the Devil*. Merino the Magnificent. Illeana the Illusionist. A black and white cat sat on the sofa.

"Make yourself at home. There's beer in the fridge. I gotta get ready."

Connie went down a short hallway and disappeared.

Kendall heard faint salsa through the walls. Magazines and comic books lay on the coffee table including his last issue of Dr. Strange. Ronnie came out as he picked it up. Sheepishly he grinned.

"I didn't just buy that," Ronnie said. "I got it the first day it came out."

"That was a year ago."

"I wrote them a letter demanding to know why you'd been taken off the book."

"New editor. It's just like Hollywood. Your project is alive until they fire the producer. Wow. You look fantastic."

Ronnie pirouetted. She wore a pleated mini-skirt, peach leggings, chunky brown shoes, and a black T-shirt. A strand of pearls encircled her throat. Her long, black hair was gathered in a ponytail. "Thanks ever so, I sweated for hours. Where we going?"

"Dinner on Sunset. We'll see who's playing later. Maybe we'll catch some music."

"Lisa Mychols is playing at the Whiskey!"

They went down the stairs. She took his hand when they hit the sidewalk. Kendall walked up to the blue Corvette and opened the passenger door.

"Wow," Ronnie said sliding in. "Wow! What a cool car!"

Kendall got in the driver's seat and started the engine. "It came with the house."

"Really?"

Kendall put the top down. "Yeah. Buying that house was like winning the lottery, it came with so many extras. I don't understand how I did it."

"Right place right time," Ronnie said as they pulled away from the curb.

It was a glorious early evening in Southern California. The offshore winds had blown the smog into the valley, and they could see downtown LA as they got on Santa Monica at Vermont.

"Can I turn on the radio?" Ronnie asked sweetly.

"Of course."

She turned it on. "Catch A Wave" burst from the speakers. WAVE.

"Oh, I love this song!" she said turning it up.

Chez Fez was a Moroccan-looking stucco with arched windows and entrance. Kendall turned the Vette over to the valet. A man wearing a white dinner shirt, black bloomers stuffed into black boots, and a red fez held the door for them. The maître d' seated them on the patio in back, beneath a Cinzano umbrella. Their waiter was a young Moroccan boy with good English.

"Hello! My name is Raul, and I'll be serving you tonight."

Kendall ordered a martini and Ronnie ordered a gin and tonic. They looked around like bobble heads until the drinks came. Ronnie thought she spotted Michael Broderick in one corner.

Kendall proffered his drink. "Cheers."

They clinked. They drank. She did a minxy thing with her mouth that made him want to leap across the table.

"How long have you been a magician?" Kendall said.

"Since high school. I grew up reading *Scary Godmother*, *Harry Potter*, and Tolkien. And *Dr. Strange*! I started practicing illusions in high school. Started going to local talent shows, tried a little comedy, then I got lucky and apprenticed to Stan Merkle. You know Stan Merkle?"

Kendall shook his head.

"He was sixty-five when I came to him. Worked with Mickey Rooney, Bob Hope, did USO tours with Ann-Margret and Joey Heatherton during Vietnam. Had a stage show in Vegas for a while. That was going to be my goal until I got lucky and landed that Wyrick job."

"Izzat full time?"

"Yup, plus overtime for weekends. They do semi-annual employee evaluations, and I keep landing in the top ten percent! What about you? What brings you out here?"

Kendall briefly related the events leading to his arrival. Ronnie expressed concern when he mentioned his late wife's death. He shrugged it off.

"It's no biggie. The marriage died long ago."

"Yeah, I dated a raging alky once. So how do you like working for Wyrick?"

Raul returned. Ronnie ordered stuffed grape leaves. Kendall ordered souvlaka and eggplant parmesan. They re-upped their drinks.

"I'm not crazy about this project they've got me on."

"What is it?"

Kendall shrugged. "Can't discuss. Confidentiality. I'm looking to pick up some game design work. What about you? You have family out here?"

"I was adopted. My dad was a stuntman for Hal Needham. My mom still lives in the Valley, same house I grew up in."

"Siblings?"

"Nope. I was all they could handle."

Kendall left the Vette at Chez Fez, and they walked hand in hand several blocks to the Whiskey where Ronnie knew the doorman who had appeared in several *Sons of Anarchy* episodes.

"Well if it ain't Ronnie the magician. How you doin', Ronnie?"

She reached up behind his ear and handed him a bronze coin featuring Illeana the Illusionist on one side and an outline of the Wyrick Castle on the other. "Fine, Warren. Can we slip by?"

The doorman smiled and lifted the rope.

THIRTY-THREE
PRESTO

Lisa Mychols was a diminutive blond whose music harked back to the Shangri-Las, Chantelles, Ronnie Spector, and dozens of other girl groups of the sixties and seventies. Kendall and Ronnie danced fifty feet from the stage amid several hundred gyrating fans. The crowd was young, polyglot and motley. The scent of marijuana drifted through the air.

Kendall hated dancing. It was something you did to get laid. He hadn't danced in years, but when Ronnie suddenly broke into a smooth sexy snap, he started moving. Couldn't stop himself.

They stood in the corner kissing.

The streets seemed alive with magic as they returned to the restaurant. Lights gleamed like precious stones, all ugliness obscured. A fresh breeze brought the scent of the ocean. The brightest stars peered through the haze of light.

Chez Fez was still busy at eleven thirty. Kendall tipped the valet a buck. They got in and headed north. Ronnie put her hand on Kendall's arm.

"Take me to your house."

Kendall's heart went *boom boom boom*. He could hardly

believe this sweet curvy thing was sitting next to him. Encouraging him!

He pulled up to the curb outside his garage, got out, unlocked and lifted the door. He got back in the car and drove the Corvette into the garage.

"I want to go in through the front entrance," Ronnie said.

They got out, walked outside. Kendall closed the garage and locked it. They went up the steep concrete steps toward the front entrance, a dark tunnel beneath the massive facade.

"This is kind of creepy!" Ronnie said with delight. "Did you know Roark Dexter Smith was a devil-worshipper?"

"Yeah right. And Winston Churchill was a Grand Druid." He unlocked the wrought-iron gate.

Ronnie ran her hand over the ironwork. "This is lovely." She felt the blue glass globes embedded in the copper door. "Can you imagine what workmanship like this would cost today?"

Kendall unlocked the front door. "Ha. Some of these modern movie palaces are just as nice, believe me."

He opened the door, turned on the light and held the door for Ronnie.

"Like?" she said.

Kendall laughed. "I wouldn't know. Oh, wait! I've been to Nate Polis's house. Used to belong to Errol Flynn."

He led the way down the east gallery turning on lights. Shapiro ran through the doggie door, put his paws up on Ronnie's thigh, yapped, and wagged his tail. Ronnie zeroed in like a heat-seeking missile, picking him up and cradling him.

"Oh, isn't he adorable! What's his name?"

"Shapiro."

Shapiro and Ronnie slobbered on each other. Shapiro squirmed loose, dropped, and followed them to the dining/living area at the south end. Ronnie stepped up to the big glass arch overlooking the city. "It's beautiful," she said.

Kendall opened the door to the courtyard. "You should see it from out here."

The view from the back of the courtyard was even more

dramatic, the city spread out before them like a jeweled blanket. Ronnie ran around the courtyard, squealing with delight, Shapiro yapping at her heels. She stared in awe at the pylons which resembled some ancient Mayan stelae. She knelt and dipped her hand into the pool which glowed like a sapphire with lights turned on.

They went back inside. Shapiro sat and yapped. "Oh shit," Kendall said. "I forgot to feed him."

They went into the kitchen where the little dog went berserk as Kendall opened a can of Blue Buffalo. Shapiro almost knocked the bowl out of Kendall's hand. The dog dove into the bowl and snarfed it up in nothing flat.

"I wonder if they even taste the food," Kendall said.

"We had a Dalmatian named Sidney," Ronnie said. "He was the most insane-for-food dog I've ever known. He once jumped up on a table and ate an entire cooked chicken, bones and all, and the foam plastic plate it was sitting on."

"No way," Kendall said.

"He did. I saw the shit."

"Well, there you are."

He showed her the living room with the Steinway baby grand, the massive molding surrounding the fireplace nook.

"It's like something out of *1001 Arabian Nights*!" Ronnie said.

He led her counterclockwise back through the entrance foyer around to the master bedroom. She put her hands to her mouth at the sight of the bed. "Oh, my Gawwwd."

She looked up and saw the mirror.

"That's the way I found it," Kendall said sheepishly.

"I like it!" Ronnie declared pulling him down into a kiss. She molded to him like vac-u-form. She smelled of jasmine. They tumbled onto the bed, Shapiro yapping with excitement. Shoes came off. Shapiro tired and lay down on a huge cushion that got knocked to the floor.

The rest of their clothes came off. Ronnie had a tat on her ass.

"Velva Voom!" Kendall declared as she squealed with

delight. They banged together like magnetic dogs, shifting, grappling, groping.

"Do you have protection?" Kendall whispered huskily.

Ronnie reached up and pulled a cellophane-wrapped Trojan from behind his ear. As he was about to come, Ronnie reached around behind him and drew her finger up his crack.

"I know what guys like," she whispered as he popped and pogoed. The bed was like a rock. It never squeaked.

They made love three more times.

THIRTY-FOUR

RUDE AWAKENING
SATURDAY

R onnie didn't have to be at work until eleven. Kendall drove her back to her place and left her with a kiss and a promise to call. He levitated home. Not even the horrendous backup on Santa Monica could bring him down. He listened to WAVE—they played Explorers Club's "Freedom Wind" all the way through without commercial interruption. Kendall had never heard it before and freaked out. He wrote down the name during the frequent traffic freeze-ups and ordered the CD off Amazon at a stoplight.

His call to Nate went unreturned. At twelve thirty Patty Hansen called from Ripon. "Have you thought about our offer, Kendall?"

"I'll take it," he heard himself say. Patty gushed and hung up. What the hell. Designing urban thuggery was a big step up from the depravity of *Night Shifts*. It was only entertainment. A man had to eat. And this certainly wouldn't hurt his credentials in either the comic or gaming community. He arranged to meet with Ripon on Tuesday.

While at Nebraska State Kendall took a film writing class from Horace Frizell, who'd written for *NYPD Blue* among others. Professor Frizell said, "You make 'em laugh a little bit, you make 'em cry a little bit, you scare the hell out of them, and that's entertainment."

He got home, changed into his trunks and swam in the pool. Shapiro ran around the perimeter barking. Kendall got out, toweled off, and got dressed. It was 3:00 PM. He phoned Ronnie, heart in his throat like a giddy teenager. He left a message.

Five minutes later she called him back. "I was showing some tourists from Iowa a few tricks! I'd love to see you tonight honey, but I can't. I promised Connie I'd go with her to the airport to pick up her parents."

"What about tomorrow?"

"Tomorrow? Sure! Whoops; gotta go. Here comes a busload of Japanese tourists."

Kendall realized he had a hard-on. *I salivate like a Pavlov dog.* He put his trunks back on and went back in the pool. It was only twenty-five feet long, just long enough to swim laps. He did a hundred, pulling himself out exhausted and exhilarated. He knew he would regret it tomorrow, but the workout felt good. It had been too long since he'd extended himself. He'd seen three fitness clubs in the area and a Krav Maga school.

Kendall had several books on game design. He pulled them out. He'd done character design before when he'd worked briefly for an animation company in Omaha, and in preparing *Cheap Shot* as a possible Saturday morning show.

Kendall did not look forward to his weekly meeting with Nate. He wondered if he could hit Ripon up for an advance. He took out a pad and began to list possible talent to fill out his roster. There were plenty of artist friends on the West Coast who would jump at the opportunity.

It occurred to him to register the Corvette. He went through the basement into the garage and turned on the lights. The Corvette gleamed as if freshly polished. He found the registration papers made out to Frank Wallenda in the glove compartment and carried them back upstairs. He'd need a lawyer to get it all sorted out, and in the meantime, he'd been taking a chance driving around without proper registration. But what the hell. They were giving driver's licenses to illegals now.

The house looked and felt different as the afternoon sun cast horizontal light over the ramparts. The stones took on a golden glow reminiscent of an earlier age, the Hollywood that used to be. The bougainvillea and wisteria bloomed impossibly lush as if they'd been infused with flower growth hormone. Kendall fed Shapiro, microwaved lasagna, and found his DVD of *Sunset Boulevard*. He and Shapiro watched it together.

Kendall imagined there were more Norma Desmonds in Los Angeles than most people thought.

After the movie, they watched *Saturday Night Live*. Kendall laughed once when Miley Cyrus twerked the audience. They went to bed, Shapiro sleeping by Kendall's feet. He dreamed again that he was at a party in his old house in Omaha when Shirley walked into the room with a tray of cocktails. A deep sense of betrayal rushed his crown. It wasn't right. It wasn't fair! Shirley was dead! She couldn't force Kendall into servitude and her despair. Not again.

God was at the party somewhere. Kendall set out to find Him. He went from room to room encountering old friends, high school teachers, Val Kilmer. Someone told him God was in the garage. Kendall went out to the garage. God was sitting behind the wheel of Kendall's Stingray. God was a diminutive woman with bleached platinum hair and too much eyeliner.

"What's the deal, God," Kendall said. "Shirley's in the house passing out cocktails. She's supposed to be dead."

God looked up at him. "Give me the car, and I'll take care of it."

Kendall leaned over and yanked the keys from the ignition. "I'm no fool, God!"

Kendall was at the wheel racing down US 1 with the ocean on his right. Shapiro was in the shotgun seat. Kendall wondered briefly where God had gone. He was in the Malibu hills now, racing along Mulholland.

"Well, the last thing I remember, Doc, I started to swerve. And then I saw the Jag slide into the curve."

A metallic chonk echoed dimly through the house, as of a vault door shutting.

Kendall jolted awake with Shapiro standing on his chest licking his face. Sun shone through the tinted skylight. Kendall looked at the clock. Five thirty. He groaned.

"All right, all right," he said, swinging his legs out and wiping his eyes. He walked across the hall into the courtyard and stretched, reaching for the sky and yawning hugely. He stepped back inside. Shapiro bulleted to the rear of the house, leapt up on the glass door to the strip of yard in back, and barked like a maniac, clawing at the glass.

"What?!!" Kendall said staring through the glass. What did the damned dog want? He had to piss something fierce. He worked his dick free of his jockey shorts and pissed on an azalea bush. It was his yard. Nobody could see. A man had the right to piss in his own yard. It was in the Bill of Rights.

Shapiro whined and scratched at the door. Kendall opened it. The dog ran out and around the corner clockwise. The west side of the house faced a hedge of juniper and poplar trees that could withstand an Abrams tank separating Kendall's house from that of his neighbor. Kendall had been meaning to introduce himself. The narrow space between his house and the hedge lay in shadow. Shapiro confronted a window well a third of the way from the back. It appeared to be covered with a heavy black grate that had not been there before. Kendall walked to the window well and looked down.

His heart shriveled, and his eyes spurted blood. A dark hoodie protruded from beneath the iron grate's leg, pinning the body to the rim of the well by its neck. The left arm was flung out like a semaphore, the rest of the body lay in the well. A thin brown hand extended from the heavy blue sleeve. A crowbar lay on the gravel at the bottom of the well next to a twisted Air Jordan.

Kendall stared at the thing for ten seconds, willing it to be a prank or just a pile of discarded clothing. He knelt, tipped back the top of the hoodie and saw the face of a young man, maybe a teenager, frozen in pain, eyes wide open. Dead, dead, dead. Some junkie trying to pry open one of his basement windows. Kendall saw the slot in the stucco wall from where the grate had sprung. He tried to lift the grate off the boy's neck. It was like struggling with a bear trap.

Shapiro barked at the body. Kendall scooped the dog up and hustled him back into the compound, shutting the door behind him. A sense of urgency jolted him. His first instinct was to call the police, but this wasn't Omaha. This was Los Angeles. The press would treat him like some kind of freak. Anybody who purchased a Roark Dexter Smith house was a priori "rich." Who would set a lethal trap for some poor junkie?

A black junkie found in a rich white man's trap.

No, no, no. First would come the suits. Then they'd start digging into his past, the whole thing with Shirley. Then his comic work and the fact that he drew a "comic about the occult." Kendall hyper-ventilated and felt light-headed. He was having a panic attack. He sat on one of the lawn chairs, lowered his head between his knees, and struggled to control his breathing.

There was only one thing to do.

THIRTY-FIVE
BLOODY SUNDAY

It was Sunday. People took it easy on Sundays. They slept late. Not like the Midwest where pious families put on their best to make the eight o'clock service. No. This was laid-back LA where if you had a religion, you likely worshipped a tree or a water sprite or a guy in an armed compound, and you didn't get up before one in the afternoon.

Heart revving like a two-stroke, Kendall threw on pants, shirt, shoes, and grabbed a pair of heavy leather work gloves. Closing Shapiro into the court, he went around back to where the corpse lay pinioned. Bending his knees, using both legs, he was barely able to lift the iron grate an inch off the boy's neck. It felt like it weighed hundreds of pounds. They must have used leaf springs off a Mack truck. Then he saw the lever protruding from a slot in the wall. He pulled the lever, felt a click, and all resistance vanished. He pushed the heavy grate back into the wall where it clanked back into traction, virtually invisible to the casual observer. It looked like an iron surround to the opening, that was all.

Kendall stepped three feet down into the well, tossed out the crowbar and got his arms under the body, which smelled faintly of stale body odor and french fries. The boy couldn't have weighed more than 130 pounds. Kendall set him on the ledge, got out, looked around. He had absolute seclusion. The view toward the street was blocked by the overgrown juniper and gorse, and nobody could see him from the back yard which ended at a drop-off overlooking the city. The wall of evergreen blocked any view from his neighbor.

The kid had a cheap plastic wallet containing fifteen dollars and an obviously fake ID for one DuWayne Heller, a student at UCLA. Yeah right. The kid's pockets also contained a folding knife, a butane lighter, some crumpled cigarettes, and a crushed bindle made of slick white paper with some kind of drug residue. Kendall used the lighter to burn the bindle. He wiped the wallet and lighter off on his pants and put them back. He carried the corpse hurriedly back around his house and into the courtyard. The body was already stiff.

He set the body on a chaise lounge while he reclaimed his breath, Shapiro whining at his feet. He got the corpse over his shoulder, went through the corridor to the kitchen, and opened the door to the basement. Easing down several steps, he prevented Shapiro from following and closed the door behind him. He carried the corpse down the stairs, through the door into the garage, past the gleaming Corvette to where he'd parked the Toyota. Setting the corpse on the hood, he sprung the trunk and placed the corpse inside. He opened the garage door, pulled the car into the street, got out, and shut the garage behind him.

With the utmost care, he pulled out onto Franklin, drove a few blocks, and turned north toward Griffith Park. He passed a couple joggers and people walking their dogs, but there was virtually no traffic in the park as he drove up past the observatory and deep into its farthest recesses, following the twisting park road among the Russian olive and eucalyptus trees until the blacktop turned to earth and he found himself at a remote canyon. He got out, stood on the car roof, and looked around. He was alone. He heard the wind whistling through the trees and the faint noise of traffic on the 5.

He sprung the trunk, hoisted the dead youth onto his shoulder, and sidestepped down into the canyon, his feet nearly shooting out from under him on the shifting sand. He marched crabwise down the slope a hundred feet, depositing the corpse in a shallow depression beneath a creosote bush. He looked around. Sixty feet away a coyote regarded him quizzically from atop a jutting boulder.

"Just wait 'til I'm gone," Kendall muttered.

The body was a tiny dark spot on the landscape. Kendall covered it with twigs and dust until it was nearly indistinguishable from its surroundings. The coyote did not twitch a whisker. On the way up, he checked for footprints, but there was nothing left in the sand and shale. It had been a dry summer. As he neared the top, he looked down for the coyote and saw the tip of its tail disappearing behind a bush as it headed toward the shallow grave.

He shut the trunk, got in the car, and turned around in a narrow defile, heading back the way he'd come. Near the entrance, he passed a string of ten bicyclists decked out in primary-color spandex and teardrop helmets. They didn't give him a second glance.

He was home in ten minutes, heart pounding like a locomotive. He got out, opened the garage door, drove in, shut off the car, got out, and closed the garage door from the inside. He stood in silence for a minute wondering what he'd just done.

Exactly what crimes had he committed? He'd hurt no one. The intruder was an unwanted visitor. It wasn't even a crime scene; just an unfortunate accident. How could he possibly be held liable for the death of some junkie trying to break into his house? Yet he knew he could. He'd heard enough stories.

Step by step, he reviewed his actions since waking less than an hour previously. He'd been discreet. No one had seen him, and if they had, they barely noticed. The corpse would likely go undiscovered for some time.

Safe.

He was safe. He would tell nobody about this ever. He had to dismantle that security system. He had to find somebody discreet. Maybe on Craigslist. Maybe somebody he knew. Maybe Tommy. Torrance boasted that the kid could fix anything.

No! Was he insane? Why even draw attention to the infernal contraption? He'd have to dismantle it himself.

Shapiro waited for him at the top of the stairs. Now that the body was gone Shapiro wanted breakfast. Kendall put on a pot of coffee and opened a can of Blue Buffalo which the dog inhaled in two seconds. Kendall was famished. He found some Jimmy Dean frozen breakfast sausage sandwiches in the freezer and threw two in the microwave. He took his coffee and breakfast out into the courtyard and set it on a wrought-iron table next to one of the chairs. He tossed the last half sandwich to Shapiro who snatched it out of the air. Presto. Maybe Shapiro could work with Ronnie.

Ronnie! The thought of her banished his gray skies and foul mood.

I wish they all could be California girls.

Maybe he would see her later. Maybe he'd cook. He'd done most of the cooking in Omaha out of necessity, but he found he enjoyed it. Enjoyed shopping for fresh ingredients and putting them together in the kitchen with a good ale.

His newspaper service began that day. He took his dishes into the kitchen, rinsed them, went to the front door, carefully shutting it behind him so Shapiro wouldn't follow, halfway down the steep concrete steps to where his *Times* lay curled into a cylinder with a rubber band around it. He tucked the paper under his arm, refilled his coffee in the kitchen, and went back to the courtyard. He slipped off the rubber band and snapped the paper open on his lap.

KARDASHIAN KILLER CLAIMS 4TH VICTIM

A possible fourth victim of the Kardashian Killer, so-called because of his preference for a certain type, has been located in a steep canyon in Puente Hills. A man walking his dog discovered the body at four thirty yesterday afternoon in a remote section of Juan Vasquez State Park. The body appears to be that of a young woman in her twenties with long dark hair. An eyewitness told the Times *that she appeared to have ligature marks around her neck and wrists, but the police have neither confirmed nor denied these reports.*

The victim's identification is being withheld pending notification of next of kin.

Kendall felt a curl of dread in his chest like a termite. The hair at the base of his neck prickled.

Shapiro danced around his feet yapping. He got up, got the leash, and took Shapiro for a walk around the neighborhood. Shapiro took a dump two houses down, but Kendall was prepared with a plastic grocery bag.

They returned to the house. Kendall flopped to take a nap, but Ronnie's scent lingered on the bedclothes, and it was impossible to sleep. He lay on his back with his hands behind his head staring at himself in the mirror. He might have been in one of the better suites of the Titanic or some fin de siècle art nouveau hotel. He drifted and dozed.

Faint, furious yapping intruded. Kendall opened his eyes and listened. It sounded like Shapiro but coming from way far off. Had he gotten out of the house somehow? Kendall got up and walked around the corridor until he came to the kitchen. The basement door was open. The barking came from down there.

Kendall went down the precipitous stairs, noting the change in temperature, the subtle shift in scents, and followed the barking around the corner to where Shapiro crouched before the Mystery Locker, the hair on his neck standing at attention.

THIRTY-SIX
THE TOY BOX

K endall retrieved the bolt cutters from the garage and laid them across the hasp of the Schlage padlock. The bolt cutters' arms extended three feet. Bracing himself against the wall, Kendall struggled to squeeze the ends together. Even with the leverage, it was very difficult, not like a commercial padlock at all but something you'd find in a high-security prison.

Little by little the beak cut through the hasp. Kendall put one handle under his armpit and used both hands on the other end. He squeezed, and he squeezed. His arm muscles filled with lactic acid and caused him pain. At last—with a supreme effort the jaws bit through, and with a loud *spang*—the lock fell to the floor.

Shapiro retreated to the opposite wall hunkering low and growling with his tail between his legs. Kendall grabbed the doorknob and pulled. It didn't give. The door was stuck. Gripping the knob in both hands, he pulled, and the door came open like peeling up a piece of vinyl flooring with a horrendous screeching noise. A puff of makeup, perfume, and a rancid pong hit him in the face. Shapiro whimpered.

Kendall paused regarding the two-foot gap between door and frame, the blackness beyond. It was his home; it wasn't the

Overlook Hotel. There was nothing in the room that could harm him. The high-pitched keening emanating from the dog shredded his nerves. He turned and pointed.

"Go up, Shapiro! Jesus!"

The dog pricked up its ears and hustled down the hall. A minute later Kendall heard him scurry up the stairs. Smart dog. Kendall stepped inside, felt along the wall for a switch, found it. Light emanated from a single sixty-watt bulb hanging from the ceiling by a frayed cord.

Sucker punch to the gut.

His first thought was Nazi torture chamber. An ancient gynecological examination table occupied the center of the room, hideous in its plain metal apparatus. Something loathsome and spiky occupied the center of the table. It took a moment for Kendall to recognize it. A tarantula corpse the size of a biscuit sprouting twisting white antlers. Again. Cordyceps. He'd looked it up. The fungus had limited mind control properties forcing the tarantula to seek a climate most conducive to its growth.

A pegboard on the wall held dildos neatly arranged by size from hot dog to a tapered monstrosity that resembled a high-speed step drill. Handcuffs, leather blindfolds, whips, and quirts hung from the pegboard. Beneath the pegboard was a worktable on which rested amber plastic pill bottles, funnels, a box of condoms.

Most disturbing of all was the left wall. It consisted of floor-to-ceiling metal shelving jammed with film canisters. Faded paper labels could be seen peeking out from the ends. Kendall approached, keeping his eye on the shelf, and slid out the end canister.

Patsy/Velva 10/23/89

It was Super Eight. There was a projector in the theater. The first films dated from the eighties.

A sharp yelp made him levitate. Shapiro had returned. The

dog lowered itself like a '68 Impala in front of the work bench and made a terrible low growling sound in the back of its throat.

Kendall clapped his hands sharply. "Shapiro! Out!" He pointed to the door. Shapiro turned tail and hunkered out. Kendall pulled the door shut with a metallic thud behind him. He felt as if he'd been buried alive. In a near panic, he threw himself against the door and breathed a sigh of relief when it jolted back open. Shapiro sat outside in the dank, dusty hall whimpering. Kendall pointed down the corridor.

"Go outside!"

Whining, Shapiro slunk around the corner. Kendall returned to the room and shut the door. He counted the canisters on the top shelf. Twenty-four with at least as many on the four shelves below. Well over 100 tapes. How many girls? How many still alive? How many dead? Might he know any of them? Were there any famous faces hiding among the reels whose revelation would cause a sensation?

Would the faces in the reels match those of missing persons? If they were missing, where had they gone? Kendall realized he had opened a can of snakes, but it was his can to do with as he pleased. He was free to close the door, weld it shut. But he knew he wouldn't do that.

He knew he should hand them over to the police, but that would only bring unwanted attention. What was that rotten smell? He feared to know. Kendall hunkered down and looked beneath the worktable. The cement was a different color and consistency as the rest of the floor as if someone had done repair work.

The light flickered. The room grew cold. Kendall felt an unearthly presence. He stood and whirled. As he exhaled his breath crystallized and hung in the air. He heard someone breathing in his ear. Suddenly the scent of Chanel No. 5 was overpowering. He turned again facing nothing, followed by the faintest echo of a scream.

He had to get out of there. Grabbing the Velva film, he tried to open the door. It was jammed. Panic fell like a tiger net.

Breathing raggedly, he turned the knob and leaned against the door with all his might. No one would hear him scream. No one would look. With a grunt of frustration and fear, he threw himself against the door.

It lurched open with a horrendous screech.

He stepped out, slammed the door shut, and ran for the stairs still clutching the film canister. Shapiro waited at the top of the stairs, tail thumping, snout between his forepaws. Kendall slammed shut the basement door.

Sunlight poured through the windows. He felt silly. Too many horror movies. Too many comic books. Shapiro at his heels he went into the library, went online and went to diedinhouse.-com. He registered and entered his address.

There were two listings.

Kirk Savage and April Monahan, the actress who'd died in the pool.

Bring in the exorcists. Phone the ghost busters. Call the Discovery Channel. He'd freaked himself out. The house was old, and he'd been raised on a steady diet of horror movies and comic books.

Breathing deeply and feeling foolish, he swiveled away from the computer and flicked on the big flatscreen. It was tuned to KPOW, the local Fox News affiliate. The evening news was on.

The City of Los Angeles had voted a 55-million-dollar bond measure to proceed with the light rail plan to connect San Diego with Fresno.

"And when we come back we'll have an update on what police believe to be the Kardashian Killer's latest victim."

For an instant, Kendall could swear he saw his breath. He stayed in his chair leaning forward through six commercials. A talking head filled the screen, a curvaceous babe with dark hair.

"Police have identified the murder victim found yesterday in Puente Hills. She is twenty-six-year-old Jennifer Harris of West Hollywood, an aspiring actress."

The photo showed his date from the other night.

THIRTY-SEVEN
SET LIST

Torrance stared at the cuneiform images on the screen. It was a near match for one of the square stones forming the proscenium of Kendall's theater. He would need to take pictures to be sure, but he'd always had a remarkable memory. He could look at a sheet of music and play the line instantly. Flip through the pages and know the whole song. There was something about the mismatched stones in the theater that disturbed him.

Since accepting Jesus into his heart, Torrance had developed a keen interest in archaeology, the birthplace of Judaism, Christianity, and Islam, and the cradle of civilization. He had visited Israel twice with Pastor Joe Arnold from the Resurrection Fellowship where he worshipped and played guitar. Torrance had knelt before the Wailing Wall, visited the site of King David's mythic First Temple, crawled through the tunnels and ruins that crisscrossed beneath the Holy City like the veins and arteries of some great beast.

He had climbed the Great Pyramid at Giza and visited the Valley of the Kings where he'd seen wall paintings similar to those in his neighbor's theater. Torrance believed that the proscenium stones were authentic and most likely illegal. No responsible government or museum would part with such things. They'd been acquired through stealth and skulduggery. To what purpose? Why would someone go to the trouble and expense of amassing a collection of rare archaeological artifacts only to hide them away in a basement theater?

Wallanda had a reputation for debauchery which the press had concealed, aided and abetted by a detachment of Wyrick lawyers. You could hide things like that before the internet, hide that JFK was a womanizer and Rock Hudson was gay. No one wanted to hear that one of America's best-loved children's movie makers was a libertine and abuser of women.

Rumors that Roark Dexter Smith was involved in sorcery and devil worship persisted. Smith's involvement ended with design and construction. It wasn't as if he attended the parties. Or had he? Who would know? Who was still alive that had attended Wallanda's parties?

Not important. Coffin hadn't known the stones were there when he'd bought the place, and Torrance wasn't about to blow the whistle on him. Torrance had his hands full orchestrating the reunion. It was like herding cats. Or hummingbirds. His teammates had always been egocentric and eccentric, and they hadn't improved with age. Only Torrance had changed for the better.

"Yeah right!" he growled and laughed at himself. "Pride goes before destruction, a haughty spirit before a fall."

He went on Facebook and saw who was online. Reggie Markwardt, the bass player, had recently moved to town and bought a shack in San Jac. Reggie hadn't changed. He'd become a rocker to score chicks. Reggie began photographing his one-night stands in 1983 and claimed to have scrapbooks with over 800 photos.

Torrance had his man-whore phase, too; but he hadn't kept track. He didn't miss it: the endless touring, the lack of sleep, the willing supply of groupies, the mounds of coke, the bowls of malted milk balls as mandated by their contracts.

But lately, he'd felt like playing before a live audience again.

The weekly sing-alongs at the Resurrection Church didn't cut it. He wanted to get out there on the strip and tear it up old school. He could handle one or two gigs a month.

He'd met Marge on a trip to the Holy Land in '95.

Reggie was online. They arranged to meet at Reggie's place in a week to blow out the cobwebs and work up a play list. The only other surviving member was guitar player Eddie Prey. Torrance had begun looking for a new drummer. Tommy was more than up to the job, but Tommy was going to begin his freshman year at UC Irvinein the fall and would not be available for performing or recording.

"But, Dad! You never went to college! And I'm good enough to go pro, you said so."

"Son, you gots to get that diploma. Make your old man happy. Become the first male in the Skaggs line to graduate college. You can even major in liberal arts."

Torrance wished he'd had half his son's energy and ambition when he was that age. It seemed Tommy was busy every night: jamming with friends, on dates, or working on inventions with other geniuses. Tommy had purchased his Subaru from scholarship money he won with his science projects. Of course, Tommy was not going to study liberal arts. He planned to study engineering. His latest project was a robot drummer that listened to other musicians and adjusted its beat and tones.

Torrance tried to talk him out of that one.

Hell. Maybe they should just wait for the robot. Too many kids relegated Gearhead to the same class as AC/DC, Def Leppard, Mötley Crüe, et al., groups their parents loved that were still cool. A robot drummer would change all that. Of course, it flew in the face of the authenticity Gearhead brought to every gig. They'd always prided themselves on honest instrumentation and lack of electronics. The wah-wah pedal was as advanced as it got.

Torrance played back the song he'd been working on. It was easy enough to record at home, double-track himself. There was bound to be a fight over the play list. Torrance would no longer play songs that were blasphemous, cutting out their number one hit, "The Devil You Say," and several other anthems. Reggie would be particularly vicious since he sang lead. But Reggie needed money. Reggie always needed money. If Reggie made a million a year, he would spend two million. Torrance had heard that Reggie had fallen on lean times and was desperate for a comeback, had been appearing at sleazy heavy metal cons along- side second-tier acts like Umbrella Pluto and Radioactive Scum. Selling autographs for ten bucks a pop.

They'd talked briefly when Reggie had moved back to town, sixty-five miles away as the crow flies. Reggie had texted him several times asking when they were going to get together. He'd been in touch with Eddie who promised to fly out as soon as Torrance had the band, the song list, and the venues nailed down. Eddie lived in Phoenix where he operated a successful landscaping business. Eddie didn't need the gig, but Gearhead was like the IRA: once in, never out. Rock and roll was like hepatitis. Once it got in your blood, it never went away.

It was a lot like hepatitis.

Once you tasted that rock and roll lifestyle, you never wanted to go back. The world seemed a brighter, more fun place when you were on top, and everybody knew your name. Girls lining up to fuck you and producers laying out the blow.

Torrance was fifty-eight. So was Reggie but that hadn't stopped him from acting like a rock star. The last time he'd acted like a rock star he'd been thrown out of a club on Sunset. There'd been a story on TMZ of a drunken Reggie flipping the bird over the cut line, "DON'T YOU KNOW WHO I AM?"

That would have driven any normal person into hiding, but rock stars were like politicians. They were incapable of shame.

Torrance wondered if he could get them to sing some of his religious songs.

Harsh rapping at the patio door in back. Torrance heaved himself up off his multi-gimbaled chair, down the hall into the living room, and saw his neighbor looking in.

Torrance slid open the door. "Come in, man. What's up?"

Coffin was the color of plain yogurt and sweating.

"What the fuck? You look like you saw a ghost."

"Torrance, do you know anyone who might be willing to hold an exorcism?"

THIRTY-EIGHT
CRAZY TALK

T orrance took Kendall by the arm. "What the fuck, man! Sit down. What the hell happened? You need a drink."

Torrance went to the credenza and filled a tumbler with ice and two inches of Scotch. Then he poured ginger ale for himself and carried them back to where Kendall had collapsed on an elongated cloth sofa. Torrance sat and handed the glass to Kendall.

"What's going on?"

Kendall didn't know what to say. He was suddenly reluctant to share the contents of the Toy Box with his neighbor. Not that he'd done anything wrong. Except hide that body and that had nothing to do with the contents of his cellar. He felt invisible walls closing in on all sides. It wasn't his fault. It was the house.

"I feel like there's something in the house, some kind of presence," he said. "I've felt it from the first night. I hear things ..."

"What kind of things?"

"Women screaming."

Torrance took a slug of ginger ale and unhitched his eyes, staring off into the distance. "I wouldn't know where to start man, but you can bet your ass there's somebody around here willing to take your money. Did you check the Yellow Pages?"

"No," Kendall said. "I met this old dame—Portia DeManning. She wrote a book, *Conversations with Dead Movie Stars*. She's a medium."

"Well there you go," Torrance said.

"She said I should talk to Wallanda's widow, Bree."

Torrance arched his woolly eyebrows. "She's still alive?"

"Yeah. She's in a nursing home. If only I could find her."

"Tommy can do that," Torrance said. "Want me to ask him?"

"Sure. But for Chrissake. Sorry. Don't tell him I want to do a séance. It's not something for kids."

Torrance held up a hand. "No prob. I don't think that sort of thing interests him anyway."

Kendall drained his glass. "You know that girl they found, the latest Kardashian Killer's victim?"

"Yeah."

"I went on a date with her a week ago. Friend fixed us up."

Torrance leaned forward with his massive forearms resting on his knees. "Aw, I'm sorry to hear it, man. You gonna tell the cops?"

"I don't see any reason. I just went on one date with her, that's all. Nothing came of it."

"Yeah, well you'd better be prepared. They might want to ask you some questions."

The bottom fell out of Kendall's gut. He hadn't thought of that. Just what he needed, a couple detectives poking around the house. Well, he'd cross that bridge when it came to him. "So, like, if I had a séance, would you attend?"

"Sure," Torrance said. "But why me?"

"You're a man of faith, Torrance. I need someone there who believes in God."

"Don't you?"

Kendall shrugged. "I'm agnostic."

The door to the garage opened and shut. Moments later Tommy appeared in baggy shorts and a Hulk T-shirt, toting his laptop in a backpack. "Whassup?" he said. "Hello Mr. C."

"Tommy," Torrance said, "Kendall would like you to locate a woman in a nursing home."

Tommy went to the refrigerator and withdrew a quart of milk. "Sure. Just give me the data." He pried open the spout and glugged straight from the container. He closed the spout and returned it to the fridge. Torrance gave him the name and Tommy retreated to his lair.

"I know some feng shui experts," Torrance said.

Kendall gazed at the wall. "I think I need an exorcist."

"Well let me ax you. You're an agnostic. What makes you think an exorcist is gonna do any good?"

"Agnostic means willing to learn. I don't know what else to do. I more or less bet my life on this house, I mean I can't exactly turn around and sell it, can I? People will want to know why. I was a little suspicious I got it so cheap. I mean, this is a famous house, right? Famous designer, famous owner. Why didn't they have buyers lined up? Did they know something I don't?"

"Well you know about the deaths, right?" Torrance said.

"Yeah. It's on this website, diedinhouse.com. But so what? My late wife croaked in our bedroom. I didn't hide that fact, and we sold the house in the first week."

"What about the Discovery Channel? Don't they have some series about ghost busters?"

"Publicity's the last thing I want. I just want it gone."

"Well, hey, you know, as long as you brought it up," Torrance said, "I was doing a little research on those stones down in your theater. The Egyptian and Mayan shit."

Kendall looked up sharply. "What about them?"

"First of all, they're illegal. But you probably knew that. Second, there's a theme. I was looking at some stones you got from Egypt and ancient Mesopotamia and they both reference an ancient female deity, near as I can tell."

"What deity?"

"I don't know. They resemble what the Egyptians called Septhet. She represented the moon, the lunar tides, and fertility."

Kendall shook his head. "Never heard of her."

"Most people haven't. The only reason I have is because of the two tours I took of the Middle East with some scholars. I'd like to go back down there and photograph some of those blocks if you don't mind."

"Be my guest."

Tommy reentered carrying his laptop. "Bree Wallanda lives at the Oakdale Assisted Living Facility in Pasadena."

Torrance tossed Kendall a pen. "Write on that magazine."

Kendall picked a copy of *Juxtapoz* off the coffee table and wrote down the contact information including the address and phone number. Bree had been suffering from dementia twenty years ago when she'd been committed. Kendall doubted she would take a phone call. She might not even be able to talk. She might be dead. There was only one way to find out.

Kendall's cell phone beeped and vibrated. He pulled it out of his pocket. It was Ronnie.

THIRTY-NINE
SURPRISE

Kendall stood and headed for the patio, holding up a finger to indicate he'd be back. He went out through the sliding glass door and stood at the edge of the glowing blue pool.

"What's up, Ronnie?"

"Guess what?!" Excitement and peppermints bubbled from the phone. "I'm off! Want me to come over?"

Kendall had a little automatic pilot which frequently guided him through rough patches. "Sure. Come on over. You have dinner?"

"Just some awful jerky."

"I'll make something. How long will it take you to get here?"

"An hour."

Kendall looked at his watch. It was already six thirty. "Great! See you when you get here."

"Should I bring anything?"

"Nope. I've got it all."

He signed off and stood there for a minute gazing out over the backyard toward the city in the distance. Now, why did he do that? Because he couldn't wait to see her, that's why. He already had a stiffy. He swore he could smell her through the phone. He'd kept his libido in check for so long that now that it was loose he didn't know what to do with it.

He went back inside. Tommy was glued to his laptop. He jumped up when Kendall entered. "Come on! I've got it mapquested. We can be there in forty-five minutes. I'll drive."

"I appreciate that, Tommy, but I need to look into this a little more. It's Sunday evening, and Bree's got to be in her midseventies if she's alive. Let me find out if she's still alive."

Torrance stood and went to the bar. "Don't bug the man. He'll do it or he won't. He doesn't need you."

"I found her address!" Tommy piped up, voice cracking.

This was something he had to do alone, Kendall realized. If he went with anybody, it would be Ronnie, to put the old woman at ease.

"What about this DeManning broad?" Torrance said. "You want to set something up?"

"What?" Tommy said. "What's going on?"

"None of your beeswax!" Torrance said. "Go oil your laptop or something."

Tommy folded his laptop and stood. "Fine." He stalked out.

"He's a good kid," Kendall said.

"He's a great kid, but he's still a teenager. Remember when you were a teenager?"

Kendall held a hand up in the stop gesture. "Understood. So if I set something up, you want to participate?"

"Hell yeah!"

"It might be dangerous."

Torrance boomed basso profundo. "Baby, I was a coke addict for fifteen years! It don't scare me. I got the Lord Jesus in my heart and soul. If there's anything there, it should be afraid of us!" He made a motion toward Kendall's empty glass. Kendall nodded. Torrance poured in a couple fingers.

Kendall phoned Portia. She answered on the first ring.

"This is Portia DeManning."

"Portia, it's Kendall Coffin."

"The cartoonist." Her voice sounded like gravel falling into a galvanized truck bed. "What can I do for you, honey?"

"I want to have a séance, see if we can get in touch with whatever the hell's hanging around in my house."

There was a long silence punctuated by a phlegmy cough. "What makes you think there's something there?"

"I told you about the voices. Abrupt changes in temperature, doors that stick then swing open."

"All right. You know you need five people to hold a séance, right?"

Me, Torrance, Portia, Ronnie ...

"I'm one short."

"No minors. I can bring a fifth."

"I'd have to know who it is," Kendall said.

"Stan Merkle. He's had experience with this sort of thing."

The name clocked Kendall between the eyes. Where did he know him from? "Who's Stan Merkle?"

"Old time, stage illusionist. Used to work Vegas, appeared in a couple MGM musicals. He's spent the last fifteen years of his life debunking various demonic possessions, hauntings, what have you."

"Yeah," Kendall said. "But what if it's real?"

"Well, Stan has a little experience with that too."

"Portia, that would be great." He set up a tentative time; sometime next week depending on the availability of the participants. It was possible Ronnie couldn't come due to her job. Kendall racked his brain to come up with a replacement, but all he could think of was Nate. Nate was too busy for nonsense. Of course, Nate had a keen nose for the bizarre and twisted and might get a kick out of it. The séance wouldn't work if Nate were crackin' wise and being sarcastic.

So no Nate. Tommy was out of the question. Just too young. Maybe Marge.

It was just Kendall and Torrance in the big room now, in cool shade as the sun slipped behind the poplars. They sat on the sofa and sipped their drinks.

"Sometime next week," Kendall said. "I'll let you know."

"I heard you talking. If you need a fifth person, we can always ask Eddie."

"I got it covered," Kendall said. "Thanks for the help, man. Gotta go. Somebody's coming over."

"That girl you met at Wyrick World?"

Kendall smiled and let himself out. He was walking past the garage when his cell phone buzzed. It was Ronnie.

"Hi," he said.

"I'm here," she said.

"Where?"

"In your house. I'm waiting for you."

"That was quick."

"Hurry." She hung up.

Kendall quickened his pace. It was that sex thing. It was exciting, and a little bit scary because let's face it. When you had sex, you became a sort of animal for a little while. The reptile brain took over. If the house were on fire, you wouldn't notice. Nature didn't care about good manners or cleanliness. All Nature wanted was propagation of the species by any means necessary.

The ends justify the means.

Give in to your base instincts and worry about it later. Kendall went down to the street, noted Ronnie's Ford Focus snugged to the curb, and went up the long steps to the front door.

Ronnie had left it unlocked. He stepped inside and locked it behind him. The house was dark.

"Ronnie?" he said a little too loud. It didn't sound right, like shouting in a cathedral. He headed back through the dining and living rooms. She wasn't there. He crossed over to the other wing and went into his bedroom.

He froze, torn between screaming animal lust and a huge neon sign that screamed WRONG, WRONG, WRONG. It took a second for the dime to drop.

Ronnie was tied to the side of the bed, her legs splayed: one toward the head, the other tied to the foot, her hands tied behind her. She wore fishnet stockings and a garter belt. She wore a gag ball and a T-shirt. No pants. The Velva on her butt winked at him.

Kendall short-circuited. His blood rushed to his crotch, and he saw and heard white noise.

FORTY
BEST SCREW EVER

Ignoring the Saturn booster in his groin, Kendall rushed to the bed and unhooked the gag ball via a rubber band around the back of her neck.

"Who did this to you?" he said breathing hard.

"Nobody! I did it to myself. Now put the gag ball back and fuck me."

He froze, too stunned to move. Ronnie writhed and twisted her head to look at him.

"Come on. You know you want to."

With electric anticipation, he hooked the gag ball back in her mouth, peeled off his shoes and trousers, and mounted her, cupping her small breasts in his hands. He was pasted to the underside of the canopy looking down. He was standing across the room looking on, looking at himself in coitus with the pale writhing figure beneath him.

As he humped her with his hands on her head, he felt moist breath on the back of his neck, and for an instant, he stopped, hardly daring to breathe. Chanel No. 5 and the hint of rot. Ronnie's thrusts and growls urged him back into action.

He came in a shuddering rush and collapsed to the floor. As he lay there spent, Ronnie wriggled and was free, smiling and reaching for one ankle, then the other. She grabbed him beneath the arms and dragged him up onto the bed, surprising him with her strength. They lay on the bed nose to nose.

"Did you like that?" she said with a mischievous grin.

"My God," Kendall said. "I've never come so hard in my life."

"Oh, there's lots of little tricks I can show you," Ronnie purred laying her leg over his.

Kendall's ticker tossed like a lifeboat in the North Atlantic. What just happened? Even though it was entirely consensual—had not even been his idea—it bothered him. It bothered him that he enjoyed it so much. It bothered him how quickly all rational thought fled the moment he saw her like that. Was he that kind of person? Were all men? Certainly, he was aware of the allure of bondage. He'd seen the Betty Page pics. He saw how sex could take over your life; how you became obsessed with pussy, so that's all you lived for. He'd known guys like that. Guys like Nate. They saw a tight ass and their hearts jammed in their throats. The great national obsession.

Kendall knew a lot of very good artists who turned out pin-up after pin-up as if they were incapable of drawing anything but sexy women. Perhaps they were. You draw what the heart desires.

"Hey," she said after a while. "You were going to cook for me."

Kendall pulled on his pants. "That's right." It was seven thirty. He went into the kitchen and took the chicken breasts out of the refrigerator where they had been marinating in Newman's Own Balsamic Vinaigrette Dressing. He went out to the barbecue pit, swept away the ashes, replacing them with fresh coals.

Ronnie appeared and pulled salad fixings out of the refrigerator, setting them on the counter.

"What's up, baby sweetheart darling?" she said. "Did you create any new monsters today?"

"None that I know of. Hey, are you up for a séance?"

Ronnie stopped what she was doing and looked at him with a half guffaw. "A what?"

"A séance. You know … we hold hands in the dark and commune with the dead."

"Where? Why?"

"Rightchere. With your pal Stan Merkle."

Ronnie did that minxy thing with her mouth. "Stan? Really? What's going on? Who died here?"

"Kirk Savage and April Monahan. He was a rock star, and she was an aspiring actress." Kendall used "quote fingers" over the latter.

"I think I heard something about that. But what's Stan got to do with that? God, I haven't spoken to him in over a year. I should give him a call."

"You might as well. Did you know he did séances?"

"I knew he debunked a lot of shit. He even had a TV show for a couple years. It was local. He'd go into local haunted houses and broker deals with the ghosts."

"Oh, come on," Kendall said leading the way to the courtyard. "It had to be a goof."

Ronnie followed. "It was a goof. It was like *Ghostbusters* for real, only it wasn't. I mean everybody was in on the gag. I remember seeing it when I was a little girl. I should really call Stan."

"Why don't you?"

Kendall cooked while Ronnie retrieved her phone. She stood in a far corner of the courtyard gazing out at the city. She returned still holding phone to ear.

"He'll do it! I told him about you, and he can't wait to meet you. Stan's a huge comic fan." She held out the phone. "Here. He wants to talk to you."

"This is Kendall."

"Mr. Coffin, this is Stan Merkle," said a voice as dry as Paul Harvey. "I'd like to ask you a few questions."

"I appreciate your helping me out, Mr. Merkle. What do you want to know?"

"Have you been experiencing any inexplicable phenomena? Strange sounds, doors opening, and closing by themselves, that sort of thing."

"I hear a woman screaming, sometimes, when I'm asleep."

"Do you hear her when you're awake?"

"That's the thing, Mr. Merkle. I wake up, and it's like I catch just the tail end of the scream fading away. So I don't know for sure. I got a dog the other day, and the screams seemed to have stopped."

"I happen to be somewhat familiar with your house, Mr. Coffin. I played a gig there for the late Frank Wallanda in 1988. I could tell at the time that things weren't quite right with the house, but it wasn't my place to bring it up. You know sometimes it's better to just let things slide."

"I was hoping you could stop whatever it is. Exorcise it. You know. Make it leave."

"I don't know if I can do that, but I would certainly like to learn what's there."

They agreed on a tentative date. Kendall told Merkle the personnel. It was set for the following Friday. Kendall would lay out a light buffet.

They ate outside at the wrought-iron table, Shapiro moving hopefully from foot to foot.

After dinner, they made love again in a more conventional manner then chilled back in the massive master bed and watched television. Ronnie propped herself up on Kendall's armpit. "I feel like I'm on some huge luxury liner in the thirties."

They watched the new *Agents of SHIELD*. Kendall switched to KPOW for the ten o'clock news. There was a bit about the upcoming San Diego Con.

"You going?" Ronnie said.

"Not this year. I went thirteen years in a row."

Back to the stern-visaged Hispanic anchorette. "Concern about the Kardashian Killer has caused an unprecedented surge in firearms and home security sales. Chief Orin Patterson has announced the formation of a task force to find the rapist/murderer."

A somber-looking black man with a white mustache appeared on-screen. "The Mayor has instructed me to form a task force in order to catch the so-called Kardashian Killer. I want to assure the people of Los Angeles that we are working to apprehend this killer to the best of our ability. In the meantime, we advise young women not to jog after dark, or to buddy up. In fact, it's best to buddy up every time you go out."

"What's wrong?" Ronnie said. "You're rigid as a plank."

Kendall switched off the television. "Nothing. Maybe you should be more careful."

Ronnie grinned. "Don't worry about me. I can take care of myself."

He hardly slept, but at least there were no screams.

FORTY-ONE
BREE

Ronnie was gone when Kendall woke, her scent all over the bedclothes. She left a note: "Call me." Kendall fed Shapiro, showered, dressed, had breakfast, and cleaned up dog shit. Today he intended to visit Oakdale Assisted Living and talk to Bree Wallanda. He had no idea how he was going to do that, but he hoped to have a plan shortly. He decided on the old clipboard trick. A man in a uniform with a clipboard could go anywhere.

He went into the basement, passed the cursed door without looking, and went into the wardrobe room. The junkie had died outside this room, the deep window well casting dim light on the rows of costumes. Kendall flipped on the overhead fluorescents and went through the wardrobes until he found what he needed, a gray, two-piece heavy cotton uniform with Poole Heating & Cooling/Tony in red script on the breast. Inside a brown tag had been affixed to the collar with a safety pin. "Property of Wyrick Studios; *Flakes*/Director Wallanda."

He tried it on. Perfect. As if made for him. At ten he left home in the Toyota and drove to Pasadena. Oakdale was on Fern Avenue, a long low blond-brick building in a park-like setting off Los Robles. Kendall found parking in a commercial lot, grabbed his clipboard, and walked a couple blocks to the nursing home. A handicapped van unloaded a wheelchair out front, and he was able to walk right in. He paused in front of the curving front desk.

"Sir," a middle-aged woman with silver hair said to him. "You have to sign in."

Kendall smiled at her. "Where's the furnace?"

"Take the elevator to the basement. It's at the north end."

Kendall signed Tony Dickens and went to the elevator. He took the elevator to the basement and exited into a long concrete corridor with a series of wide white doors. Some of the doors were open, and he could hear the sounds of food preparation and smell the food. Mexican. He spotted a Latino woman in a maid's uniform wheeling a hamper of laundry down the corridor.

"Ma'am," he said consulting his clipboard. "Do you know where I can find Bree Wallanda's room? We have a complaint about the heat."

The woman paused. There was sweat on her brow. "She on the third floor, I think, down at the end. She has Awesome Possum next to her door."

"Thank you."

Kendall turned on point and headed for the stairs, taking them two at a time all the way to the third floor. He walked quickly from door to door consulting his chart until he came to the end. Not only was Awesome Possum on the door, there was a soft plastic doll of Velva Voom on the side credenza. The door was open, and a middle-aged black woman was inside changing the sheets. Kendall cleared his throat.

The woman turned. "Yes?"

"Looking for Mrs. Wallanda."

The housekeeper nodded toward the windows. "She's down on the patio."

"Thank you." Kendall took the stairs back down to the first floor and exited into the rear, a broad meandering patio built around a pond with a fountain. Fat gold koi swam in the pond. Locust and sycamore shaded the patches of verdant lawn. Perhaps a dozen residents were in the back creeping along with walkers, seated on the benches or in wheelchairs. An attendant watched carefully while a resident washed down some pills with a little paper cup. Kendall kept his purposeful stride and his eyes down as if looking for a valve set in the ground, surreptitiously eyeing the inhabitants.

She would be very old and most likely immobile. Toward the rear, demarcated by a brick fence topped with concertina wire (as if the residents were planning a mass escape) he found a very old woman wrapped in a shawl and a brightly colored blanket bearing Illeana the Illusionist. A crenellated neck—the color of parchment—held up a wizened face partially hidden by massive wrap-around sunglasses. Kendall thought of a turtle. The old woman gazed at the pond. Kendall sat on a bench next to her.

"Mrs. Wallanda?" he said softly. He heard children shrieking, a dog barking.

She nodded minutely and looked at him carrying the overwhelming scent of violets. "Who are you?"

"I'm Kendall Coffin, ma'am. I bought your old house."

Her head went back, chin compressing into her neck like a dubious poodle. "What?"

"I said I bought your old house in Los Feliz. I wonder if you'd mind answering a few questions about it?"

"I was perfectly happy with the old house. I told him I didn't want to move but would he listen to me?"

"What house do you mean?"

"The one we lived in when Lannie was born. A very nice seven-bedroom hacienda up in the hills. I did not like that man Smith. He reminded me of a shark. You couldn't get a word in edgewise when Smith was around. And you know who was even worse? Dr. Mandlebaum. I would never let that man touch me. You'd have to be crazy to let him work on your face."

"Did Lannie's birth have anything to do with the move?"

"No. Frank didn't really want to be a father. He didn't want to be married. Ha!" she barked mirthlessly. "I was just a stupid young girl. How was I to know? Frank was not the man I thought he was."

"How so?"

"Frank only loved himself. He had a sick fixation on that cartoon character, Vulva."

"Velva Voom?"

She peered at him with intense blue eyes. "Velva had only one weakness, you know."

"What's that, Mrs. Wallanda?"

She looked at him with startling lucidity. "I'm sorry, what is your name?"

"Kendall Coffin."

Her rouged lips formed a slit. "That's an unusual name."

"Actually, it's fairly common."

"And you now live in the Smith house?"

"Yes," Kendall said. "The reason I'm here, I've been hearing screams at night ..."

Her hand shot out and gripped his wrist like barbed wire. "Do you know what a nedrebo is?" she said in a voice like a rasp. Her eyes were barely visible behind the curved black plastic.

"A what?"

"I'm sorry, what is your name?"

"Kendall Coffin. Do you know of anybody who died in your house?"

"You've heard screams you say?"

"Yes. I know of two deaths that occurred there, Kirk Savage and April Monahan. Are you aware of those?"

Her hand slipped off his wrist, and her gaze wandered. He wondered if he'd lost her. "I wasn't there for either of those parties, young man. By then I'd finally figured out to whom I was married. He had me declared insane and locked up, did you know that?"

"I'm very sorry to hear it. Do you know anything about the basement?"

The old lady looked around, paranoid. "Don't go in the base-ment," she hissed.

Kendall leaned forward, framing his words soothingly. "Why not? What went on in the basement?"

"Don't go in the basement," she hissed again showing yellow teeth. Kendall looked up. Two beefy security guards in navy blue trou and sky-blue shirts rolled his way.

"Thank you for your help, ma'am. I wonder if I can come back and ask you some more questions?"

"I'm sorry, what is your name?"

The guards were there, one black, one Mexican. The black man said, "Sir, may we see some identification?"

Kendall stood. "I was just leaving."

FORTY-TWO

PHILOSOPHER'S STONES

N ate stared at him in disbelief. "You're what?"

"I'm sorry, man. I can't do it anymore. I feel like I need a shower every time I draw a page."

Nate came around from behind his desk and chopped air. "Are you out of your mind? Do you know how many people would kill to have your job? I put a great deal of my personal credibility on the line to get you this gig. Moreover, everybody thinks you're doing a bang-up job! What is this prude bullshit? What, you suddenly found Jesus Christ or something?"

"No, Nate. I'm just not comfortable drawing this material."

"Why not? Give you a woody? It's supposed to! Fuck! The entire industry is designed to give you a woody! I know you, man. You're not some uptight fundamentalist. We both banged the same girl! Remember that? What's her name, Rhonda."

"It was Rhoda."

"Whatever! Dude, I have to level with you. If you walk out on this, it's likely all the other Wyrick jobs are gonna dry up and blow away."

Kendall smiled. "Nick, I've accepted a position with Ripon Games. I'll do fine. And I want you to know I appreciate everything you've done for me. I mean it. And I won't forget when they decide to make a movie of one of my characters. I want you to produce."

Nick made a what-me-worry gesture and guffawed. "Christ I love to listen to my own bullshit. All right. All right. Desmond and Alice will be livid, but I can handle that. I've already got some guys lined up. Listen. I'm having another little get-together in a week. I'll have you up, see if I can get you laid again."

"Did you hear about Jennifer?"

"No. Don't tell me you two are an item?"

"She was murdered last week by the Kardashian Killer."

Nate's eyes and mouth went round. "You're shitting me."

"I'm not. Where have you been hiding? It's all over the news."

Nate slumped in his chair. "That's terrible! I mean, I hardly knew the girl but still! Have they had the funeral?"

"I don't know."

Nate thumbed the intercom. "Judy, find out where they're holding Jennifer ..." He looked at Kendall.

"Harris."

"Find out where they're holding Jennifer Harris's funeral and send some flowers with my name on it. Spend a hundred bucks."

"Okay boss," Judy replied.

Nate swiveled to the fridge, withdrew an Icelandic bottled water, turned to Kendall. "Want one?" He tossed the plastic bottle, and Kendall caught it with the sound of a ball hitting a glove.

Nate twisted one off. "How's the new house working out? Man, that is some place."

"I don't know how you ever made it home in one piece," Kendall said.

Nate snorted. "I know how to hold my liquor. I was thinking. You ought to hold a murder mystery weekend there. Folks'd go crazy."

"Not me, Nate. I'm a private kind of guy."

"Just a thought. I know a gal puts those things on, she's very good."

The intercom buzzed. "Your two o'clock's here," Judy said.

Kendall excused himself and retrieved his car from the studio lot. It had gone better than he'd hoped, but the Ripon job had to work out now because there was no going back. Kendall knew how things worked. Nate would be lucky to still have his job at the end of the year. One of the barracudas, Krout or Summers, was looking to replace him.

He drove home tuned to the news channel just waiting for the other shoe to drop. Thus far there hadn't been a word about the dead junkie he'd left in the canyon. Maybe the cops knew about it and didn't consider it newsworthy. Maybe it wasn't newsworthy. Three hundred and ninety died from homicide every day in Los Angeles, up considerably from the nineties. Still. And those were only the ones that were reported. Who knew how many undetected homicides occurred?

He could still smell that graphite odor in his nose.

When he got home, Kendall shed his clothes in the hall and threw himself into the pool. He had complete privacy in the courtyard as Smith intended. He swam laps while Shapiro ran around the perimeter barking until they were both too tired to continue. Kendall hauled himself out, dried himself off, and changed into sneakers and jeans.

The doorbell chimed. Torrance with a fancy-ass digital camera.

"I'd like to photograph those proscenium stones if you don't mind."

Kendall beckoned him in. "Sure. Be my guest." He led the way into the basement wondering if he should show his neighbor the Toy Box. He decided against it. He didn't know what to make of it himself, and he felt he was being bombarded with too much stimuli. First the Toy Box then Ronnie's startling performance.

Kendall wasn't one of those guys who defined himself by sex. A lot of those Hollywood types were. Guys who boasted about their conquests: Wilt Chamberlain, Gene Simmons, Errol Flynn. Always guys. You never heard women boasting about their sexual conquests. Well, maybe Madonna.

One thousand, two thousand, when did they cease to become human beings and just become statistics?

Kendall opened the door to the theater and turned on the lights. As always, he was surprised anew by this golden age movie palace hidden beneath his house. Whoda thunk it? It was cool. Maybe the world's coolest room.

Torrance paused next to him as if he too were overcome with awe.

"This is what Howard Carter must have felt when he broke into King Tut's tomb."

"Yeah," Kendall said. "I can barely believe it's here."

Torrance went down the broad hardwood stairs to the front and stepped up on the one-foot stage. He knelt before the right proscenium and lined up shots. The camera flashed sporadically. Torrance rose with his subject matter. He did the other side.

"All right," he said, turning toward Kendall. "There are sixteen blocks here that look like they're from ancient archaeological sites. You got a couple Amerindian stones. You look at this one here?" He indicated a stone about three feet above the floor on the left side.

"See how it depicts Spanish invaders? Rattlesnakes and scorpions? This is Amerindian off the Colorado Plateau, no question about it. That one's a Russian icon. A couple of these look Mayan. They can take a spectrograph off the stone and use that with satellite technology to match it up with ruins in the jungle."

"Sounds expensive," Kendall said.

"We're not going to do that. Just sayin'. Okay. I'll see what I can find about these stones. They may have some bearing on your séance. Any more word on that?"

"This Friday, hopefully, if we can line everybody up. You, me, Ronnie, Portia DeManning, and Stan Merkle."

"Who's Ronnie?"

"She's my girlfriend."

Torrance grinned and biffed him in the shoulder. "Dude! This the girl from Wyrick World?"

"Yeah. She's an illusionist."

"You mentioned this DeManning broad, but who's Merkle?"

Kendall filled him in.

They headed for the stairs. "You want to come over for dinner?" Torrance said.

"No thanks. Got too much to do," Kendall said.

They entered the kitchen. Shapiro sat there with a hang-dog expression next to a pile of feces.

FORTY-THREE
BURN THE FILMS

F uck," Kendall said. "He knows better than that! There's a
dog door, dummie."

Torrance left while Kendall cleaned up the dog shit. Shapiro
whined.

"Don't worry about it, Shap," Kendall said. "I'll give you a
treat."

He irradiated some canned chili and watched the hour-long
evening news. No progress with the Kardashian Killer. The
police asked all responsible citizens to keep their eyes open for a
young white male.

There was nothing left to do but look at the films. He didn't
want to, but he had no choice. He had to know what lay in his
own house. He took the canister into the basement, into the
theater's projection booth, and threaded it through the Super
Eight projector. He shut off the house lights, started the film,
went out, down to the front row, and sprawled in the catbird seat
which contained a control panel linked to the projection booth.

White flickers and white noise gave way to two hands
holding a black and white clapper: "Velva Visits Uranus."

A young woman, her black hair done in Velva's bouffant
style, pranced in front of the camera in front of a Murphy bed. A

naked man wearing a dog mask and carrying a whip entered the picture. They did a Snidely Whiplash routine with the man brandishing the whip before forcing Velva face down on the bed.

Kendall turned it off. A pit of acid settled in his stomach. He felt covered in a greasy film.

He thought about destroying the film, but how would he do it? Burning it would attract too much attention. Even if he carted it all up into the hills—and there had to be several hundred pounds of canisters—the flames would attract the authorities. He could put it in his garbage, but that would not protect him from the garbage police, which routinely reported errors in recycling, or those who picked through garbage dumps for that matter.

He could leave it where it was, but it was like leaving a cancerous tumor in the body. Just having it under the same roof disturbed him. It made him feel dirty, his mind at war with his cock.

He saw how it was, how a man could become so fixated on sex that it dominated his every conscious thought to the exclusion of all else. Ted Bundy, the Hillside Stranglers, Ariel Castro had all killed for sex. Thrown their lives away for sex. Sex made the world go round. They used it to sell everything from perfume to Porsches. Whole societies—whole religions were built around sex.

What was Islam if not sexual pathology? An entire religion based on morbid fear of human sexuality and the female body. Over a billion Muslims. And the Mennonites! Well, what about Christianity?

None of it was solid.

He returned to the projection booth and examined the spines of two feet of DVDs. He pulled Velva Visits Venus, the cartoon that had inspired Wallanda's obscenity. Fleeing a barking dog, Velva stows aboard a green rocket shaped like a wine bottle that takes her to Venus, a lush, garden-like planet reminiscent of the courtyard upstairs. She finds a fountain spouting red wine, dives in it like a porpoise, splashes so that it hits her on the head, and floats on her back, eyes shut in bliss. The soundtrack sounded like the Spike Jones Orchestra.

He couldn't wait to get out of there. He ran upstairs and went into his garden and sat in an Adirondack. Shapiro lay down with his snout on Kendall's foot. The lowering sun lit the lush vegetation creeping up the west-facing inner wall: bougainvillea, wisteria, hibiscus, hollyhocks, and night blooming jasmine in almost comical profusion.

"Night blooming jasmine, its smell comes creeping 'round my window," Brian Wilson sang on "Rio Grande." Kendall heard it in his head. The blooms were on the verge of rioting they were so thick. The motley vegetation seemed both vibrantly healthy and on the verge of decay like an aging Hollywood beauty who has mastered the art of makeup. But makeup can only take you so far. Come the dawn and the lines begin to show.

The vegetation surrounded the sliding glass doors and big windows facing inward.

Kendall saw a streak and simultaneously heard a loud whump to his left. It took him a second to register the tiny bird twitching on the flagstone beneath the window. He got up and walked over. A heart the size of a pencil eraser lay beside the bird, pulsed twice, and went still. He scooped it up and put it in the garbage.

Kendall knew he had to destroy the films and the tapes. But how? He could burn them. Use a portable fire pit in the center of his courtyard. But the flames were sure to excite some of his neighbors who would no doubt report him to the environmental gestapo. Store them in a shed? He had a nightmare scenario of two beefy guys on Storage Wars rolling up the door and seeing the stacked canisters.

Of course, that wouldn't happen if he paid his fees on time. He might even broker a lifetime one sum deal. But he did not want to be associated with the tapes in any shape, manner, or form, alive or dead. Storage was out.

They must cease to exist.

He could rent a truck, drive to Nevada, and dump them down an abandoned mineshaft, but even that wouldn't guarantee their loss.

No, he had to destroy them physically. But how?

You idiot, said his inner demon. *Do you know what those tapes are worth?*

SHUT UP, SHUT UP, SHUT UP.

Shapiro laid his nose on Kendall's knee and yipped. He'd been emitting a high-pitched whine, and his eyes were screwed shut. Kendall shook himself and scratched Shapiro behind the ears.

"Sorry! Sorry. I know how sensitive you are."

He went into the studio, went online and googled nedrebo. Nada. The closest he came was a clothing store in Wisconsin. There was nothing close in Latin. He wondered if he'd misunderstood her.

He went in the house, found his Brian Wilson CD, slipped it in, cranked it, and took a shower. "Rio Grande" played through the shower speakers.

FORTY-FOUR
DOLLAR TOUR

Kendall arrived at Ripon at 9:00 AM on Wednesday morning. Patty embraced him in the foyer and showed him to his corner office looking out on a busy commercial avenue. Several wall posters advertised Ripon games including *Spartacus* and *Off the Pig*.

"You have to supply your own toys," Patty said. "Meeting at ten."

She left Kendall alone in the spacious office with windows on two perpendicular walls. The sign of success. A corner office. He wished his folks could see him now.

He filled out paperwork, both analog and digital.

The meeting room was industrial chic with exposed beams and girders, railroad timber wood floor, and a conference table made of reclaimed barn wood. Ruben sat at the head like Richie Rich with his Crocs up on the table. Two kids in their twenties sat at the table with laptops. One had his foot on a skateboard. Ruben introduced them as Wayne Barkley and Mick Runge. Wayne was black. Mick was white.

"Wayne and Mick will be working under you developing *Off the Pig*."

"Far out, dude," Wayne said stretching to shake. "Love your work on Doc Strange."

Mick stood to shake Kendall's hand. "I've loved your work ever since I was a little kid."

"You're still a kid," Kendall said.

Ruben used a PowerPoint presentation to run through *Off the Pig*. "I would like to see character designs for the nine principles on Monday," he said. "Can do?"

Kendall looked at Wayne and Mick. Wayne looked like Paul Bunyan, six six. Mick looked like a board rat with sleeved tats and faux bone ear piercings big enough to pass a dime. They looked up, happy and confident.

"Can do. Boys, we'll meet in my office when this is over."

Ruben's feet hit the floor. "It's over."

Kendall assigned four characters to Wayne and four characters to Mick. Kendall would design the main character himself. Grange was a Rambo/John McLane/Jason Bourne mash-up, an honorable cop cashiered on trumped-up charges who vows to rid Crack City of corruption. Crack City was Bucktown.

Mick sheepishly pulled a bagged and boarded copy of *Dr. Strange: Nightmare in Eden #1* from his backpack. "Would you sign this? Just make it out to Mick."

Kendall removed the comic from its crypt and signed on the splash page, the letter 'K' inside a coffin outline. He spent the next several hours familiarizing himself with the game and making a few preliminary sketches on bristol board. It was now possible to create stunning comic book art without ever touching a pencil. Artists used a stylus to draw directly on a screen. You could draw, ink, and color all in one sitting.

Kendall could never do that. He'd been born with a #2 pencil in his hand. At 3:30 PM Stan Merkle phoned on Kendall's private line. He wanted to case the joint that night if that was all right. Kendall promised to meet him at the house at six.

He called Ronnie and asked her to join them.

"Oh, I'd love to!" she wailed. "But I can't! We've got our book club tonight! We're all going to get drunk and discuss *50 Shades of Grey.*"

"I love that you have a book club," Kendall said. They made plans to meet on Thursday. Kendall left Pasadena at five. He parked in front of his house just after six. As he retrieved his backpack from the car, a Yellow Cab pulled up. The rear door opened and a little old man in a trilby and a black leather sports jacket got out. He had glasses the size of a Chrysler windshield and carried a leather bag.

"Mr. Merkle?" Kendall said.

"Call me Sid," he replied. Kendall grinned. Paul Harvey.

Kendall led the way up the steps, Merkle at his heels. The magician could have been anywhere from sixty to ninety. The magician didn't speak until they were inside the house. Shapiro ran up to the old man and stood on his hind legs. Merkle hunkered down to administer a brief head massage.

"What's his name?"

"Shapiro."

"Damned interesting."

"Let me give you the dollar tour."

Merkle held a hand up. "Just a minute. Let me just absorb this for a minute." They stood in an awkward silence.

Merkle nodded once to himself. "Lead on, MacDuff! And cursed be he who first cries, hold, enough!"

Kendall led him clockwise around the perimeter, Shapiro following. They stopped in the living room. Merkle clapped his hands and looked around. "So. The infamous party room. I was here once. I have heard many tales over the years, young man."

"Such as?"

"'Twas here Brent Colfax contracted herpes from Gwen Haspill," he said citing the director and star of *Ahoy the Shore.*

"Well are you, like, getting any vibes off the room?" Kendall said. "Are you psychic?"

"I am not psychic, young man. My dear friend Portia has the Gift. I'm just very good at using the five senses I have. Now I would like for you to describe for me in detail what it is that makes you think the place may be haunted." He sat down on the sofa. Shapiro immediately leaped up and laid his snout on the magician's knee.

Kendall told him about the screams, but not about the basement.

"After I got Shapiro the screams stopped."

"Ah," Merkle said, stroking the dog. "Dogs are hypersensitive."

"Yeah, well, if he's so hypersensitive, why didn't he notice the screams?"

Merkle looked up from beneath shaggy brows. "Perhaps the entity—if there is an entity—senses him and does not wish to arouse further suspicion. If you please, I would like a few minutes by myself in this room."

"With or without Shapiro?"

"Take the dog with you."

Kendall whistled. Shapiro followed him into the hall where he shut the door on the living room. He opened the sliding glass door to the court, and they went outside. The sun slanted in over the roof highlighting the wall of riotous vegetation. The explosion of floral life reminded Kendall of cancer cells. They just weren't natural. The blood red hibiscuses were the size of hats. The bougainvillea resembled a fireworks display in freeze frame.

The lawn was overgrown. He had a lawnmower in the garage. Time to haul it out and see if it worked. He knelt and dug out the lone dandelion. The corridor opened, and Merkle emerged.

"Shall we continue?"

They continued their circumnavigation, Kendall answering the magician's questions. Finally, they arrived back at the front entrance.

"What about the basement?" Merkle said.

"Is that really necessary?"

Merkle stared at Kendall until his shoulders slumped and he

turned. Kendall was careful to keep Shapiro out of the basement. He led Merkle to the theater and turned on the lights. The magician stood with his cap in hand gazing at every part: the walls, the ceiling, the floors, the stage, and proscenium. He went down the broad, shallow steps and up on the stage.

"They had live performances here as well as films," he said running his fingers over the stones. "Quite a collection. I'm sure there are some national historical societies who would be interested in these."

"I have no idea what they are," Kendall said. "They were here when I bought the place."

"Well, I certainly have no intention of mentioning them to anyone. I appreciate that you have come to me seeking assistance."

Merkle spent ten minutes in the theater inspecting the projection booth, sitting in the seats, and going up and down the aisles. Kendall showed him the furnace and hot water unit followed by the wardrobe room. Merkle stood in the middle of the room slowly inhaling like a wine taster.

"Ah, the smell of movies! Who does not love the movies? My first movie was *White Heat*. Cost a quarter to get in." He went down the aisles pulling out costumes, clucking, and grunting.

"You'll not want for costumes on Halloween."

Next stop, the wine cellar. The old man emitted a low wolf whistle. He went from rack to rack pulling out bottles and inspecting the labels.

"Are you shitting me?" he said. "This is worth a fortune!"

"I know."

Finally, he was finished. "What else?"

"That's it," Kendall lied. They went past the Toy Box, once again locked.

"What's in here?"

"I haven't gone in there yet." He cast his eyes down.

Merkle made an indecipherable noise. They went upstairs.

"Thank you, Mr. Coffin. I believe I have what I need to make a determination. I will be in touch. Now if you would be so kind as to call me a cab?"

"Mr. Merkle, do you know what a nedrebo is?"

Merkle tasted the word. "Nedrebo. I do not. What is it?"

"No idea. I'll call you that cab."

FORTY-FIVE

KILLER ON THE STRIP

The killer cruised the Strip looking for a certain type. Long, dark hair, voluptuous figure, not too tall. He relished the moniker bestowed on him by the media. There was no shame in liking Kardashians. There was no shame in attraction to any nubile female between the ages of fifteen and forty. The shame was in attraction to children. Or other men. These were abominations he could not abide, but as of yet, no one had connected him with the disappearance of several young, male hustlers.

They hadn't even found all the bodies.

He pulled off Sunset onto Marriotte next to Ramblin' Pam's, Johnny Depp's new nightclub, and a line that stretched around the corner. Every time he drove by it was a target-rich environment. They were so gullible! They looked like seasoned sirens of the silver screen, but many were fresh fish off the Greyhound. The killer drove by the line a half block to the John C. Macy Parking Ramp and entered, taking a ticket from the kiosk. He parked in shadow on Level 2 where he wouldn't be noticed, got out of the car, beeped it locked and went down the stairs to the street.

He passed a darkened jewelry store window. Lookin' sharp in crisply creased khakis, red Keds, black silk T, and black cotton sports jacket, grey trilby holding down his long, Thor-like locks. Neat Van Dyke tied into a mustache, none of that stupid billy goat fuzz that seemed to be the norm. He walked in his own little cloud of Paco Raban, having learned long ago the importance of scent on the female form.

He casually joined the end of the line. It was fifteen minutes before he was admitted, during which time he practiced on a couple of drag queens who found him irresistible. Once in, he gravitated to the horseshoe-shaped bar and ordered a tonic water with a slice of lime. The killer never drank. He feared the loss of control. Casually he surveyed the audience until he found what he was looking for, two attractive women in their early twenties dancing together. One was tall and angular with a tight cap of red hair. The other was Latino, buxom with glossy black hair to her ass.

The killer floated their way, spying their purses next to them at a little round table, and when they sat down flushed and laughing, he made his move.

"Hi!" he said from a safe distance. "You do the monkey really well." This to the buxom black-haired babe.

"Thanks," she said in the first blush of excitement.

He looked at the redhead. "You too!"

Redhead made a brushing motion with her fingers but smiled.

"I'm Jessie," he declared holding out his hand, shaking each in turn. "Haven't seen you in here before."

"First time," redhead said.

"Do you want to sit down?" said his target. "I'm Kathleen, and this is Suzy."

The killer set down his drink. "Let me buy you two ladies a drink. What are you having?"

"Piña Colada," Kathleen said.

"Cuba Libre," Suzy said.

The killer smiled and went to the bar. It was child's play to load the drinks on the way back with ecstasy for Kathleen, ketamine for Suzy. They were dancing when he returned, so he set the drinks on the table and joined them in a non-threatening way. It was an old-school jam—something by SOS—and when it ended they all laughed and sat down. The girls surveyed the room turret-like in search of celebrities.

"Is that Paris Hilton?" Suzy said.

Kathleen popped up and sat down. "No."

"I saw Johnny Depp in here last week," the killer said.

"You sound British," Suzy said.

"That's because I am British. Cornish to be precise."

"Where's Cornish?"

"Cornwall, eckshually. What do you ladies do?"

Suzy was a hairdresser. Kathleen was an aspiring singer/actress who worked as a waiter. Perfect.

"What do you do, Jessie?" Kathleen said brushing his wrist with her fingers.

"I'm a vampire."

Both girls held their mouths open waiting for a punch line. The killer grinned.

"I've been cast as nefarious Count Quirmbach in an upcoming vampire drama on CW. It's called *Stakes*."

The girls goggled. "Really?" Kathleen gushed, eyes huge.

"Yeah. So I'm sort of celebrating. The show doesn't start until February, but we're shooting right now. It's really good. It's based on a comic book by Todd Jones and Felipe Echevarria."

"Who else is in it?" Suzy said. "Anyone we might know?"

"Not yet, although they're talking to Lance Henriksen about a guest shot."

The girls were agog, draining their drinks in record time. Soon they had to go to the ladies' room. When they returned Suzy was tripping, and Kathleen was stumbling. The killer rose and helped Kathleen into her chair. Suzy stared at the bubbling plasma lights radiating from the floor across the room.

"Hold on," she said. "I have to see these." She pranced off.

Kathleen put a hand to her head. "Wow! I feel woozy all of a sudden."

"Little fresh air? Come on." She didn't protest as he helped her to her feet and walked her out of the club.

Halfway to the parking garage, she said, "Wait. Where are we going?"

But by then it was too late.

FORTY-SIX
BONFIRE
WEDNESDAY NIGHT/THURSDAY MORNING

T he films filled the Avalon to the gunwales and caused it to sink low on its suspension. Kendall just managed to squeeze every Super Eight canister and all the DVDs into the car's cavernous trunk and interior. He'd stuck several cans of lighter fluid in the few nooks left.

The plan was risky. But it was the only way. He had to make certain the films were utterly destroyed, and there was no chance anyone would ever look at them again. He'd pulled the Avalon into the garage to load it safe from prying eyes. It was one thirty in the morning.

He went back into the house, into the den, into the safe hidden behind the Picasso, and removed his father's 1911 Colt .45 which his dad had carried with him throughout Vietnam. Kendall hadn't fired it in years. He wasn't a gun nut, but he wasn't against them either, and the Colt was a family heirloom. Kendall had taken a gun safety class in the Boy Scouts back before they were outlawed and knew how to handle a weapon.

Always assume the weapon is loaded.

Do not point the weapon at another living thing unless you intend to do harm.

Then there was John Bernard Brooks in *The Shootist*: "First of all, friend, there's no one up there shooting back at you. Second, I found most men aren't willing, they bat an eye, or draw a breath before they shoot. I won't."

Like most who labored in pop culture, Kendall had absorbed the films of John Wayne as an essay on manhood. Kendall was not a bully or aggressive, but neither was he a coward. In the words of John Bernard Brooks, "I won't be wronged. I won't be insulted. I won't be laid a-hand on. I don't do these things to other people, and I require the same from them."

He'd also done countless tours on *Call of Duty* and *Tom Clancy's Rainbow 6*. Kendall had wrestled at 170 in high school and had gone to the state championships four years in a row. He was no coward.

He reminded himself of that as he shoved the clip into the pistol's butt and rammed it home. His plan verged on insane, but it was the only solution to getting rid of the tapes without attracting undue attention. He jammed the heavy pistol into the pocket of his nylon windbreaker where it sank like an anchor. The windbreaker was black, XXXL, and had a stand-up collar. He wore a black turtleneck and a black knit cap.

He returned to the garage, opened the door with an annoying squeak, backed out into the street, closed the garage door, and headed for downtown Los Angeles. He drove to where the 101 crossed the 110, one of the biggest freeway interchanges in the world. The concrete aprons crisscrossed above a grimy no man's land inhabited by drug addicts, runaway teens, and the homeless. Night after night they stood around a series of fifty-gallon barrels burning with the discarded detritus of the city, invisible to the world.

Kendall took the North Figueroa exit to the frontage road that ran below the massive struts. The Avalon's wheels crunched over decades of broken glass, the burning barrels casting an eerie light on the underside of the freeway which thrummed like a high-tension wire. Graffiti covered every cement surface to a depth of twelve messages. One immense sloping slab, easily fifty by sixty feet, looked like Jackson Pollack with words. Something

Vanity Fair would use for a fashion shoot if you took away the needles, broken glass, and used condoms. The tag "Shred Husl" appeared over all in red stylized cursive. Kendall stuck the pistol in his waist.

Cesar Chavez, Tupac, and Trayvon Martin marched arm in arm.

A dozen zombies eyed the encroaching automobile with a mixture of fear and excitement. In the eerie flickering light, they looked like extras from *The Walking Dead*, gaunt and clothed in rags. Kendall stopped ten feet from the nearest barrel, blazing brightly. The six men surrounding the barrel riveted him in their gaze. He put on a pair of mirrored gargoyles, pulled the knit cap low on his forehead, and rolled the turtleneck up over his chin and mouth.

Who knows what evil lurks in the hearts of men?

The Shadow knows!

He got out of the car, opened the rear door, and removed a stack of canisters. Two men stepped aside to let him through.

He set the canisters on the ground next to the barrel and opened one, spilling the coiled film into the barrel where it blazed and snapped like a snake of fire.

A tall man wearing a red, green, and yellow knit cap bulging with coiled hair and a ragged trench coat fronted him.

"Fuck you doin'?"

Kendall ignored him, opened another can and poured in the film. The zombie put a hand on his shoulder.

"I axed you sumpin, sucker!"

Kendall whipped the arm off with a circular gesture, stepped back and let his windbreaker fall open to reveal the butt of the .45 sticking out of his waist. His hand hovered.

The zombie made a placating gesture with his hands and backed away. "Yeah. Okay. Do whatcha gotta."

Kendall gave him a hard gaze before returning to his task. As a comic book illustrator, he understood the value of symbolism. Now he had an audience. They formed a circle ten feet around the barrel and watched while he methodically emptied every canister. When he went back for more, several of them helped carry stacks and cartridges to the burning barrel. They nudged each other murmuring and passed bottles. Although they mumbled, Kendall heard them with an almost hallucinatory acuity.

"Dude's an actor. He destroyin' his own masterpiece 'cause the studio cut it wrong."

"He gettin' rid that shit for somebody else. Man on a mission."

A cry of madness issued from fifty yards away where other denizens of the dark were oblivious to everything but their own private hells. It took him forty-five minutes to burn all the tapes and toss the video tapes in on top. He didn't need the lighter fluid. The film was highly flammable. It was incandescent. Boy Scouts could have used it to light fires.

He searched the car. He'd done it. Every fucking tape. He got in the car and drove away, tires crunching on broken glass.

FORTY-SEVEN
ORBIT

Kendall woke at the tongue, a hungry Shapiro vigorously licking his face. He glanced at the clock. It was ten thirty. He'd arrived home late last night and had trouble sleeping. Haunted by his dead wife.

He pushed the dog away and swung his legs out of bed. "Easy, big fella. Breakfast is coming."

He splashed water on his face, thought about throwing himself into the pool but decided to wait. Shapiro preceded him to the kitchen looking anxiously over his shoulder, following from in front. Once in the kitchen, the dog danced around and leaped up with his forepaws on his master's thighs while Kendall opened a can of Science Diet. Shapiro was growing fast. It never failed to amaze Kendall how ravenous the dog was. Shapiro was well fed; no ribs protruded. You could barely feel them when you ran your hands down his torso. Yet, the dog never seemed to get enough. Just as an experiment Kendall laid out the entire can; twice what the can recommended according to Shapiro's weight.

Shapiro wolfed it down then sat back tail wagging with quizzical eyes.

Please, sir, may I have some more?

"No, you can't have more, you slathering beast! Jeebus! You'd be big as a house."

As project director on *Off the Pig*, he had the luxury of deciding his office hours or working at home. Ripon Games was born of nerd and geek culture and understood the importance of maximum personal freedom within the parameters of the job.

He put some coffee on and headed out front for the *Times*. He laid the paper flat on his wooden breakfast table while he nuked a couple Jimmy Dean Pork Sausage Breakfast Biscuits. He sat at the table and read the paper while he ate. Iran had blocked UN inspectors from its enriched uranium facilities. Islamic extremists slaughtered 89 people at a mall in Mozambique. California was proceeding with a light rail line from Los Angeles to Sacramento that nobody wanted. The Dodgers had slipped to sixth place in the Western Division.

He turned to the comic section with a mixture of nostalgia and dread. As a comic book artist, he was also a fan of the comic strips which preceded and gave birth to the comic book. The first comic books were just collections of newspaper strips. Some of the greatest masters of the form plied their art in the Sunday funnies. Alex Raymond, Hal Foster, Chester Gould, Winsor McCay. Now the strips were dying as the newspapers were dying. The strips had been dying long before the papers themselves saw the handwriting on the wall. As papers became more and more dependent on advertising revenue, they reduced the size of the comic strips so that they were now mere shadows of their former selves. There was an entirely new class of humorless humor strips based on attitude. Sarcasm had replaced wit. Many of the new strips consisted of only one crudely drawn panel as if the creator couldn't be bothered.

Kendall perused the offerings. The syndicate recycled a number of popular strips such as *Peanuts* and *Smoky Stover* because it could generate revenue without actually paying an artist.

At least the Sunday edition carried the new *Prince Valiant*, written and drawn by friends of his. Disgusted, he turned the page.

Obituaries. Like a single red cardinal in a white winter landscape, the black and white photograph of the grimly elegant woman drew his eye.

Bree Wallanda Wyrick, July 15, 1952–July 22, 2018.

Bree Wallanda Wyrick passed away today at Oakdale Assisted Living Facility in Pasadena, where she had lived since 1985. Bree Wallanda was born to animation pioneer and producer Darryl Wyrick and his wife Dorothy in July 1946 and grew up an only child in a loving environment not all that different from the scenes depicted in Wyrick's movies.

Interested at a young age in the theater, Bree appeared in numerous high school productions including Our Town *and* The Taming of the Shrew. *She also participated in summer theater.*

In March 1970, Bree auditioned for a part in the Hal Wordsworth production of Cats on a String, *a comedy starring Farley Granger and Ann Miller. There she met the young Frank Wallanda, then assisting Art Director Hal Pereira. They began dating and were married in 1971. Shortly thereafter Wyrick began his meteoric rise.*

Bree starred in three Darryl Wyrick productions: The Main Man, Dogs on Broadway, *and Oscar-winning Best Picture* Weasels Ripped My Flesh *for which she was nominated Best Supporting Actress. She played a childless pain-in-the-ass named Emily married to a self-pitying writer named Elliot. Variety declared her the new Judy Holliday. Bree gave birth to daughter Dorothy on Jan. 1, 1980. In September 1996, Dorothy was involved in a fatal automobile accident while riding as a passenger in what police later determined to be a "drag race" between two young men. She was three months' pregnant.*

The young man who was driving Dorothy's vehicle died in the crash, and she was severely injured. She was taken to St. Mary's Hospital where she slipped into a coma. Two weeks later, the Wallandas had Dorothy taken off life support.

Bree became pregnant that year and gave birth to their second daughter, Elaine, or "Lannie," as she came to be known. Dorothy's death triggered bouts of depression in Bree who gradually withdrew from public life and entered Oakdale in 1988.

Lannie showed an interest in movie-making and acting at an early age and appeared in numerous commercials as a baby. She made her big-screen debut as the irrepressible Midge in the classic Wyrick comedy, No Snoozing. *She was set to star in the first* Marigold *when tragedy struck. On the night of June 5, 1994, Lannie's Corvette was found with the engine idling at Griffith Observatory. Lannie was never seen again.*

Bree is survived by many friends from the industry which she loved. Memorial Services will be held July 25 at St. Vincent's Church in Pasadena at 10:00 AM.

Kendall's throat went dry. His hand slipped, and the newspaper fell to the floor. He couldn't help but ask himself, would she have lived if he hadn't visited?

That was nonsense. He had nothing to do with her death. Her time was up.

But damn!

He'd wanted to ask her more questions, and now he'd never get the chance. Sunlight poured through the windows and skylight yet his heart remained cold. Whatever secrets Wallanda held he would have to learn by other means.

He called the realtor. She was cruising to Santa Monica to show off a property.

"What can I do for you, Kendall?"

"Maureen, would it be possible to contact the previous renters? I'd like to ask them some questions."

He could practically hear her biting her lip. "Listen, I'm on the road right now. Let me get back to you after I get back to my office, which should be by three."

"Sure."

His phone beeped. It was Ronnie and just like that the needle swung from red to black. "Hi!" he said. "You coming over after work?"

At the same time, she said, "Can I come over after work?"
They both laughed.
He already had a hard-on.

FORTY-EIGHT
DATE NIGHT

After he got off the phone, Kendall checked the cabinet of DVDs that occupied a part of the media wall and found copies of *The Main Man, Dogs on Broadway,* and *Weasels Ripped My Flesh.* He wondered if he could talk Ronnie into watching one.

He hit the drawing board and did a dozen studies for Grange Brockton, *Off the Pig's* protagonist, a tough-as-nails former cop whose entire family was wiped out by a pair of crooked cops because they had inadvertently witnessed the cops snuff a prosecution witness. The game itself was completely amoral. Kendall didn't think about that. He thought about who would play Grange in the movie.

Who else but Michael Jai White? Ripon was experimenting with themes, offering versions with Black, Asian, and Hispanic protagonists. They did not offer a version with white protagonists. Not his concern. He went to work and in the next couple of hours turned out almost two dozen studies of Grange wearing everything from a tux to combat fatigues, holding everything from a Beretta to an M-50.

"Deadman's Curve" burst from the radio like a machine gun blast causing Kendall to jump in his chair. He stared at the Sony he'd had for over a decade. It had never done that before. The radio was tuned to WAVE. He got up and turned it down but left it on. He loved surf music. He still hadn't been to the beach!

He wondered if Ronnie knew anything about surfing. He could buy a rack and put the board on top of the Avalon, or stick it through the back-seat side windows. They could go to Santa Monica or Malibu and paddle around.

The radio station broke for the news, and Kendall realized it was six o'clock. Ronnie got off at six, but it would take her at least an hour to get to his house. He pushed himself away from the drawing board and headed for the kitchen, Shapiro following from the front, performing loop-de-loops and wagging his little tail.

He fed Shapiro, hopped in the Avalon, and drove to a nearby Albertson's where he purchased a pork loin, a can of frozen orange juice, some sesame oil, brown sugar, and salad fixings. Standing in the checkout line, he saw a number of magazines in a rack including *Cosmopolitan*.

"SEXATHON: Do It All Night Long" topped the cover. Babs and James Brolin were embroiled in divorce hell. Tori Spelling peddled her sex tape. Kendall paid for his groceries and got the hell out.

At home, he let the orange juice melt then made a marinade of the OJ, sesame oil, brown sugar, and a little garlic. He tossed it in a plastic container with the tenderloin. Everything was ready by the time Ronnie arrived in her nine-year-old Focus at seven fifteen and let herself in with the key he'd given her.

Shapiro announced her arrival by preceding her yelping. She stepped into the kitchen, dropped her purse, and came into Kendall's arms. Long kiss.

"I need a drink!" Ronnie said. "There was a creep at work today. Kept following me around wanting to know if he could 'show me his set.' I had to call security."

Kendall looked at her with concern. "Did you get a good look at him? Do you know who he is?"

She did the minx thing with her mouth. "Some tourist from

Iowa. Who the fuck cares? He knows nothing about me! I didn't just fall off the turnip truck y'know."

"Well, you can't be too careful. You might think about dying your hair blond or red."

Ronnie vogued into exaggerated disbelief. "What?!"

"Until they catch this Kardashian Killer."

She laughed silver coins. "Don't worry about Ronnie! Ronnie can take care of herself."

"You got a gun?"

The minx thing. She reached into her backpack and pulled out an ice pick. "How you like them apples? Huh?"

"Ouch."

He thought about telling her about Jennifer. *Not a good idea.*

Kendall made them both gin and tonics, and they took them out to the courtyard which lingered in a warm violet glow from the lowering sun, horizontal rays lighting up the hibiscus and azalea like a tropical jungle. The scent of flowers reminded Kendall of Portia and the women at the nursing home.

"Your garden is so lush," Ronnie said. "How do you do it? I have a black thumb."

"I didn't do a thing but water it. That's just the way it is."

They ate outside. After dinner, Ronnie helped carry the dishes inside.

"Want to watch a movie? *Weasels Ripped My Flesh* starring Bree Wyrick. Supposed to be her best performance."

Ronnie threw her arms around his neck. "Sure. But don't you, you know ... want to fool around first?"

Kendall cupped her ass in his hands. "Sure."

"Do you want to tie me up?"

"Uh, not really, Ron. That's not really my thing."

"I thought all guys liked to see women tied up."

Kendall let her go and turned to the dishes. "Why would you think that?"

"A boyfriend told me."

"He was full of shit."

"Okay, okay. You don't have to."

Kendall turned back and smiled. "Sorry. It's just not my thing, is all."

"No problem. What about my suggestion?"

Kendall threw the dish towel on the counter and smacked Ronnie on the butt. "Let's go, hot stuff."

In the bedroom Ronnie stripped in seconds, turning her back, bending over the bed and pouting over her shoulder, her tramp stamp on full display.

Later they watched *Weasels Ripped My Flesh*, a black comedy about a dysfunctional family reunion. Bree Wyrick played a JAP who burned all her sheets by smoking in bed. Charles Grodin was her writer husband during a troubled weekend they spent with her family in Wisconsin. Bree was very good but so were a thousand other perfectly competent, comely actresses who flashed for a split second and were gone.

FORTY-NINE
SÉANCE

K endall arrived at Ripon early and was at his drawing
board by eight o'clock. Ronnie had the day off and
offered to do the shopping and cooking. He couldn't very well
ask these people to conduct a séance without feeding them.

At ten he met with Wayne and Mick to review their preliminary designs. All was copacetic. Wayne was in charge of pigs.
Mick was in charge of offers. The pigs were all white.

"Wayne, ohmina have to ask you to mix it up a little here, I
want at least one black cop, an Asian, and a Hispanic."

Wayne grinned displaying dazzling white teeth. "You got it,
chief."

Mick made a fist. "Diversity!" He and Wayne high-fived.

Alone in his office, Kendall reviewed the environment
designs. At two he met with the three other designers working
on the settings. It was a downscale, urban environment
patterned off South Los Angeles. There were barrios and block
parties. The pigs drove menacing Chryslers. The playas drove
low-riders.

His cell chimed. It was Maureen, the realtor.

"Hi, Maureen."

"Hello, Mr. Coffin. You asked about the previous renters. I

had to track them down as I inherited the listing from a man who retired, and all he could give me was their names. Mr. and Mrs. Ronald Hudspeth. They left no forwarding address, and there's no record of how to contact them at the company. I find this very surprising. I really wouldn't know how to get in touch with them."

Kendall wrote down their names. "Thanks, Maureen. Did you know that before that, the last owner killed his wife?"

Silence.

"I think I may have heard something like that. But I don't think it was in the house."

"It wasn't."

"Is there anything I can help you with? How are you enjoying the new house?"

"It's great," Kendall said.

He did a Google search for Ronald Hudspeth. He went on Facebook. Nothing.

When he got home at six thirty the house smelled deliciously of pot roast. Ronnie whirled about the kitchen with Shapiro at her heels. The dining room table was laid for five with the mismatched place settings Kendall had brought from Nebraska. Two bottles of merlot from the wine cellar breathed on the sideboard.

Torrance arrived at seven with another bottle of merlot.

"Coals to Newcastle!" Kendall exclaimed accepting the bottle. As they were about to head back, the doorbell chimed. Merkle and Portia arrived together sharing a cab. Portia carried a stuffed Gladstone over one shoulder and a nimbus of cigarette smoke. Kendall took their coats and led the way to the dining room where Ronnie threw up her arms and embraced the old magician.

"Stan! I'm so glad you could come."

"Hello, little girl. What's going on with you?"

Ronnie brought Merkle up to speed while Kendall poured wine. They finished dinner by eight and transferred to the living room.

"We will need to sit next to each other so that we can hold hands," Portia said in a pantherish growl. "This will be necessary to protect us should the spirits of the dead seek to enter our bodies. Kendall, turn down the lights."

They sat in a circle.

"I'd like to say something," Torrance said. "The Spirit clearly says that in later times some will abandon the faith and follow deceiving spirits and things taught by demons. Such teachings come through hypocritical liars, whose consciences have been seared as with a hot iron."

"Amen," Kendall said.

Portia sat in a winged chair upholstered with a cubist design and opened the Gladstone at her feet, removing three brass candleholders and three white tapers. She set these on the low coffee table around which they gathered. Kendall and Ronnie sat side by side on the leather sofa at six o'clock. Merkle sat at nine, Portia at twelve, and Torrance at three. Portia lit the candles with a match. Shapiro curled up beneath her chair.

"Kendall, tell us why you think a séance is necessary."

Kendall cleared his throat. He felt nervous. He took a sip of the merlot. "Okay. Well as you all know this is a Roark Dexter Smith house, and he was supposed to be some kind of sorcerer. Or not. I've been hearing strange sounds at night, and I sometimes get the feeling I'm not alone when I know damn well I'm the only one here."

"What kind of sounds?" Merkle said.

"A woman screaming just when I wake up. Two people died in this house that I know of. The rocker Kirk Savage and an aspiring actress named April Monahan. Savage shot himself, and Monahan drowned in the pool."

"Are they the only ones?" Merkle said.

"Stan!" Ronnie barked. "How many people do you think die in a house? I mean we've all been in a zillion houses. How many of them were houses where people died while actually being in the house?"

"There are some places," Portia said, "that serve as spiritual sinkholes. You've all seen retail space that can't seem to hold a business. First, it's a restaurant then a month later it's discount tires then a month later it's medical marijuana. It may not be the business. It may be the place."

She broke into a paroxysm of coughing, and they waited politely while she got it under control. "Sorry about that," she said in a phlegmy voice. "Nobody knows why but it may be that the spirits of the dead linger where they were murdered and that their tortured souls can affect those of a sensitive nature."

"Yeah, but Savage killed himself and Monahan drowned. They weren't murdered."

"Probably not. All right. Let's see what we can see. I'd like us to all join hands, relax and let yourselves be open to whatever happens."

"I'd like to say the Invocation of Perigamas if you don't mind," Merkle said, pulling out a small recording device. "And I'd like to record this if no one objects."

"Go on Stan," Portia said.

They all joined hands. Merkle lowered his head and spoke in his radio announcer's voice. The words were unintelligible, guttural, not of this continent.

There was a minute of silence, and then Portia began. "If there are any spirits in this house let them show themselves."

Night lowered over the house like a shroud. Kendall could hear the distant murmur of traffic and Portia's wheeze. He looked up. The others all had their heads bowed. He bowed, gripping Ronnie's hand tightly.

This was fun! For a comic and horror fan like Kendall, this was what a Friday evening ought to be. He wondered if Portia were putting them all on. He wondered if Merkle was in on it. Maybe it was a stupid idea, but it made for an entertaining evening.

Was he supposed to tip them when it was over?

Portia inhaled sharply. Torrance and Merkle winced. Kendall looked down and realized the old woman was squeezing their hands white.

"Who are you?" she hissed.

The hair stood on Kendall's neck.

"Where I'm at?" Portia said. But not in Portia's voice. It was the voice of a young black man. "Fuck is this place?"

"Tell us your name," Merkle said in his dry announcer's voice.

"Powa pLaya," the man said. "That my street handle. My real name DuWayne. DuWayne Heller. I want to go home."

Barbed wire lodged in Kendall's chest. He looked around frantically and surreptitiously, but no one was taking notes. They were afraid to release their grips and break the spell. But the recorder.

"What happened to you, Mr. Heller?" Merkle said.

"Didn't think nobody lived here …" His voice trailed off. Portia's head slumped, chin on ample breast.

The candles flickered.

"Someone else," Portia said in her own voice. "Someone new. Tell us your name."

"Crystal," Portia said. Only it wasn't Portia. She spoke in the voice of a young woman who had never smoked. No phlegm, no hacking, clear tones with a fillip of query.

"I prayed for this to stop," Crystal said. "I never wanted any of it to happen, but she keeps us here and won't let go."

"Who keeps you here?" Merkle asked.

"She has many names. We call her Clea."

"How many of you are there?" Merkle said as if he were interviewing a senator.

"I don't know. They come and go."

"What's your full name, my dear?" Merkle continued.

"Crystal Feathers. I'm from Brookings, South Dakota."

"What are you doing in this house?" Merkle said.

"Frank invited me. I used to date Frank. He said he could get me in a Bruce Willis movie." She started to sob. Emotionally devastating cries issued from the old woman's face. She wailed.

"That's the sound!" Kendall said. The others watched Portia writhe in horror, unable to release their grips. Tears ran down her cheeks and dripped onto the chair. They waited for the tears to subside.

"It's all right," Merkle said in a kindly voice. "Crystal, we're going to get you out of here. Can you tell us who else is in there with you?"

"Ask Mr. Wyrick. He's waiting for you."

"Where is Mr. Wyrick?" Merkle said.

"In his castle. I have to go," Crystal said with a quickening of fear. "She's coming."

"Who's coming?" Merkle said. He thrust his head forward, cords standing out on his neck.

Merkle released his grip and stood bolt upright like a galvanized frog leg, eyes and mouth wide open, and a harsh gurgling noise came from his throat. He flexed and spun like a Daffy Duck cartoon speeded up and fell to the ground with a thump, his sightless eyes staring at the ceiling.

FIFTY
THE COPS

R onnie flew off the sofa and knelt next to her teacher, taking his head in her hands. "Stan! Stan! Oh no! Oh God no! Somebody do something!"

Kendall got down next to her. "Look out." He took Stan's head, tilted it back, opened Stan's mouth, shoved the tongue out of the way with his thumb, and began mouth to mouth, but he knew it was a non-starter. He could tell by the magician's sightless eyes that Stan was dead. Nevertheless, he kept at it for what seemed like an eternity, carefully pacing his breaths, watching the magician's lungs artificially inflate.

He'd done the same thing with Shirley with the same results.

"Dear Lord in heaven," Torrance said. "There's a reason God took this man at this time. He's trying to send us a message."

"Shut up with that shit!" Ronnie snapped with surprising vehemence. "Stan was an atheist! Don't you know anything?"

Torrance looked stunned.

Kendall looked up from his fruitless effort. "Ronnie, it's okay. I don't think Mr. Merkle is coming back."

"We have to call 911," Torrance said.

A monstrous hand crushed Kendall's heart into crumpled aluminum foil. He looked up in despair at the recording device on the table. Torrance pulled out his cell. All eyes were on him. Kendall pocketed the recorder.

"This is Torrance Skaggs," Torrance said into the phone. "I'm at my neighbor's house at 5121 Franklin Avenue. There's been a death here …"

The cops would open Kendall to unwanted scrutiny. What if the others remembered the first voice and told the police? Would it register? Would the police begin a search for DuWayne Heller? It was unthinkable. They would have to explain they were holding a séance.

Torrance spoke briefly into the phone and hung up. "They're on their way."

"Mr. Merkle is gone," Kendall said. "He had a heart attack. That's all. If we tell them we were holding a séance …"

"I don't see any harm in that, Kendall," his neighbor said. "As long as we don't insist what we heard was real." He looked at Portia.

"What?" she said coughing. She heaved herself from her chair. "I need a smoke." She headed for the courtyard and slid open the sliding glass door. Kendall followed her outside.

"You're not gonna tell them that shit about the ghosts, are you?" Kendall said anxiously.

Portia put an American Spirit to her lips and lit it. "Trust me. They're not interested in that, but I'm not going to lie. This is Hollyweird. A séance is all in a day's work to them."

Ronnie came out and took Kendall's arm. "Poor Stan."

Kendall held her. "I'm so sorry. How old was he anyway?"

"He was in his eighties, but he was in good health."

Portia put a hand on Ronnie's shoulder. "Maybe it's for the best, honey. There are worse ways to go. Living on life support in some smelly nursing home …"

Torrance stuck his head out. "The cops are here."

Kendall looked through the glass at two uniformed policemen followed by two EMTs in white carrying a fold-up stretcher. The EMTs opened the folder and knelt next to Merkle's body. One checked vital signs while the other eased out the old man's wallet. The two cops came outside. A black man the size of a refrigerator and a Latino, slim as a rake.

"I'm Officer Upchurch," the refrigerator said. "This is Officer Gomez. Whose house is this?"

Kendall raised his hand.

"May I see some identification, sir?"

Kendall handed the cop his driver's license. Gomez checked Portia and Ronnie.

"Okay," Upchurch said. "What happened?"

"We were holding a séance," Kendall said. "And suddenly Mr. Merkle stood up real stiff like and keeled over."

The two cops glanced at each other. They'd seen it all. As ethnic cops in a toney white district, they had learned to tread softly.

"Okay," Upchurch said. "We'd like to get your statements one at a time. I'll start with Mr. Coffin. Can we go up there?" He gestured to the other end of the courtyard and the patio where they would have some privacy.

They walked over and sat out of hearing from the others. Upchurch pulled out a spiral pad and a pen. "What about this séance?"

"I just moved in. This is a famous house. It was designed by Roark Dexter Smith for Frank Wallanda, the Wyrick executive. I've been hearing strange things since I moved in. Listen, officer, I write comic books for a living. I'm a pop culture and horror nut. I drew Doc Strange for Marvel. A séance to us is like a video game. We really didn't expect to find anything, you know?"

Upchurch looked up with piercing brown eyes. "Did you find anything?"

"No."

"You drew Doc Strange, huh?"

"Yes, sir."

"These people, what's their relationship to you?"

"Torrance is my neighbor. Ronnie's my girlfriend. Portia and Merkle, we brought in because they said they could do a séance."

Through the windows, Kendall watched the EMTs strap Merkle to the stretcher and carry him out. Two more cops arrived. Gomez questioned Portia. Upchurch excused himself and left the house to run their names through the system.

The last cop left at ten fifteen. Torrance offered to drive Portia home. Kendall and Ronnie were alone on the sofa. He put his arms around her, and she bawled. He held her against his chest feeling her tears through his shirt for a long time. Gradually the sobbing subsided and changed over to hiccoughs.

Kendall turned away then whipped back at her with his thumbs in his ears, hands spread wide, cross-eyed. "BOO!"

Ronnie gasped and *eeped*. She stared at him red-faced for long seconds.

"Hiccough gone?" Kendall said.

Ronnie laughed. "Yeah, thanks a lot. I'm sorry. Stan taught me so much. He was like a father to me."

"I know. I'm so sorry."

"What really happened, baby? Tell me what you saw."

Kendall told her what he saw, leaving out the recorder.

"That's what I saw too," Ronnie said. "Maybe it wasn't a heart attack. Maybe somebody pushed."

"So we're talking ghosts, right?" Kendall said. "'Cause I didn't think it would come to this, but I guess I always knew it would. We're talking fucking spirits of the dead, supernatural phenomena, the whole nine yards. Wow."

Ronnie grabbed his hand. "What else?"

"We don't know. We don't know what it was. It's this damn house!"

"This is Hollywood. You can find exorcists in the Yellow Pages under ghost busters."

"Do you think Portia was faking?" Kendall said.

Minx face. "I don't think so. When she started talking as that black man, it really creeped me out."

She snuggled in. Kendall held her.

"How many people have died in this house anyway?"

"There are only two of whom I know. The rocker and the

actress. He shot himself. She was probably on drugs. Frank Wallanda was what they used to call a libertine. The last owner killed his wife. Not here, at a restaurant."

"But what about that guy and that girl? We have to look into that, Kendall. We have to find out who those people are and what happened to them! Crystal Feathers and DuWayne Heller. Write it down. Where's that recorder?"

"I've got it."

"Why didn't you give it to the cops? You could get in trouble for that."

"I don't know. I'll give it to them. I'll tell them we were so freaked out we forgot about it."

Ronnie grabbed her backpack and pulled out her laptop. She opened it, opened a file, and wrote down the names.

"What are you going to do? Hire a detective?" Kendall laughed mirthlessly. "That's all this needs."

"I know some private investigators."

"It's my house, I'll do it."

Ronnie gave him a funny look. "Don't you want to know?"

"Of course, I do. What did she mean, Wyrick was waiting for us in his castle?"

"Wyrick World. The castle. I've never been down there, but the R&D department is supposed to be in the basement. They call it the Dungeon."

FIFTY-ONE

THE DUNGEON

Ronnie set off for her job at Wyrick World while Kendall did the same for Ripon. Characters and environments were on track, and it looked as if they would easily hit their target date. Ripon planned a big roll-out including television ads on Fox, USA, and TNT. Kendall was at his desk when he received a peculiar phone call.

"Mr. Coffin, my name is Randy Blix with *Groovy News*. Could I ask you a few questions about *Off the Pig*?"

"How do you know about *Off the Pig*? We haven't made any announcements."

"We have our ear to the ground. *Groovy News* is all about pop culture. Can you tell me how this game came to be?"

"I'm sorry, Mr. Blix, but I'm not at liberty to discuss this. I suggest you direct your inquiries to our Vice President Patty Hansen." He hung up.

Alone in his office, he googled Crystal Feathers. A picture of a pretty young woman with blond bangs appeared on the screen.

Wikipedia: Crystal Feathers—The Soiled Dove Murder. Crystal Feathers was an aspiring actress from Brookings, South Dakota, who was found murdered in a vacant lot in Los Angeles on July 19, 1990, by two boys riding skateboards. Ms. Feathers's body had been cut in

half, her internal organs removed, and she had been grossly mutilated.
Known as "The Soiled Dove" because her single screen credit was as a
bit actor in the Return to Lonesome Dove *television series. Feathers's*
murder remains unsolved to this day.

Poor girl. Didn't even get in on the original.

With an imploding sensation in his gut, Kendall knew where
the murder had taken place. He forced himself to set it aside.
He'd always been good at compartmentalizing. It's how he'd
survived his marriage.

Kendall had lunch with Wayne and Mick at a Mexican place.
Geek exploded. Both Wayne and Mick were huge comic fans and
loved Kendall's work on Doc Strange, although Wayne leaned
toward Django, Luke Cage, and the Black Panther.

"Think you'll ever draw comics again?" Wayne said.

"I don't know. I make a lot more money designing games."

"I hear ya," Wayne said, "but I still go to San Diego every
year and show them my portfolio. You going?"

Kendall drummed his fingers on the table. "I doubt it. I have
no incentive to go on my own and the last couple times I was
there it was no fun. Imagine 125,000 people in one room. If you
passed out, your head would never hit the floor. You would just
drift randomly around the convention hall held up by the
crush."

Kendall left at five and drove to Anaheim on the 605 and the
5. Traffic was glacial. The radio played the Sunchymes. Ninety-
five minutes later he turned into the massive Wyrick World
parking block and parked on the fourth tier, grabbing his
sketchpad before shutting the door. The throngs milling on both
side of the busy highway reminded him of SDCC. Four cops
directed traffic. At the blast of a whistle, Kendall joined the mob
heading over. He went directly to the VIP gate and showed his
pass.

It was seven by the time he met Ronnie outside the Silver
Grill Saloon in the Old West. Ronnie wore her Illeana gear

including the black satin split tail jacket and top hat. They went inside and got a booth by the window looking out on a cobble-stone Main Street as several actors enacted a gunfight and Japanese tourists took pictures. An authentic Main Street would have been a mix of mud and horse shit.

"We'll head over after dinner," Ronnie said. "I know a main-tenance tunnel that should take us there."

"How are we going to get past security?" Kendall said.

"Don't worry. I've got it all figured out. The guy in charge is a huge comic geek."

The waitress took their order.

The sky glowed magenta when they left the restaurant and walked behind the row of faux nineteenth century storefronts. In back of the Pickle Brothers General Store was a cement loading dock and next to it was a stairway descending to a locked steel door that said EMPLOYEES ONLY. A chain barred the entrance. Ronnie unhooked the chain and hooked it again behind them. They went down to the door which crouched in a concrete foxhole. Ronnie drew a key ring from her black magician's bag, tried several keys before the door unlocked.

They stepped into a dimly lit concrete corridor.

"Where'd you get the key?" Kendall said.

"Don't worry about the key," Ronnie said taking his hand and leading him down the corridor. They rounded a bend, went down several more steps and through another door into a larger corridor through which techs wheeled equipment on dollies. A man in a gray jumpsuit rumbled by pushing a giant fiberglass Ultra Pigeon head. A metal door with a round window was marked with Ultra Pigeon dressed like the Rocketeer. R&D it said. There was a keycard box and screen on the wall. Ronnie put her hat on, dipped into her bag of tricks, withdrew a card, and slid it into the slot. She passed her palm over the screen. The door clicked open.

They entered a brightly lit foyer with a faux parquet floor, a couple of leather sofas, ferns, two tables loaded with Wyrick publications, a coffee machine, and a young man in a light blue

Wyrick Security uniform sitting behind a desk reading *Badger*. Behind him, another locked door led to the laboratories. The guard put down the comic and looked up with a smile which stretched wider at the sight of visitors.

"Hello, Ronnie! What brings you to the dungeons?"

"Hi, Mark. This is my friend Kendall Coffin."

Mark stood and thrust out is hand. "Kendall Coffin the comic book artist? Love your stuff man!"

Kendall shook. "What are you reading?"

Mark handed Kendall the *Badger*, which showed Badger and Elvis Presley squaring off on the cover.

"Great stuff," Kendall said.

"Would you mind if we took a look around?" Ronnie said.

A wrinkle of distress appeared on Mark's brow. "I don't know. R&D is off-limits except to red card holders."

"Oh puleeeeeze! We won't touch anything, and we won't bother anyone. There's nobody back there. It's Saturday night! Kendall will do a sketch for you, won't you Kendall?"

"Sure."

Greed gleamed in Mark's eyes. He reached beneath the desk and withdrew two red visitor badges on lanyards. "Wear these."

"Thanks, Markie!" Ronnie squeaked.

Mark hit a button. The door clicked. They stood on a platform overlooking a long, high-ceilinged rectangular room divided into cubicles and meeting spaces, not unlike Ripon Games. Doors radiated from the three sides they could see. The lighting was dim, provided by floor-mounted theater lights. Some of the cubicles glowed softly from monitors, and each was marked with pop paraphernalia: a poster of Kid Creole, plastic robots, Godzilla, LOTR, the Flash. Just like Ripon.

"This was all here from the very beginning," Ronnie said in hushed tones. "Wyrick planned ahead."

They went down steel steps to the carpeted main floor. An electronic hush filled the room, a low-level buzzing more felt than heard. Wyrick characters decorated each door along with a word balloon. "CGI." "Animatronics." "Artificial Intelligence."

"Whoa," Kendall said. "That's a scary thought."

At the far end of the room was an unmarked fortified door with a keyboard, screen, and card swipe. Kendall looked up. Smoky hemispheres adhered to the ceiling in two rows. They were being watched and recorded. What if this cost Ronnie her job?

Kendall looked at the door. "No way."

Ronnie elbowed him in the ribs. "Stand aside."

He watched while she inserted a key card with one hand and passed her other hand over the screen as if she were polishing a car. Wax on, wax off. A second later, the door popped open. They stepped through into a chilled corridor lit by fluorescent bulbs in hooded metal shades.

"How did you do that?" Kendall said.

Ronnie winked at him. "Magic."

Fifty feet on, they turned right encountering a sealed door which resembled an airlock on a nuclear submarine. This one also had a screen and a card swipe. Ronnie polished the car. The door popped open.

Inside was a deep room with what appeared to be a series of glass and steel pods lying horizontally, side by side, two on one side, two on the other. It was so cold in the room they could see their breath. Kendall hugged himself. At the far end was a slate-topped counter with a sink beneath a wall-wide cabinet.

"Jeebus! It's freezing!"

Ronnie took his hand. "Come on. Let's find Darryl."

FIFTY-TWO
DARRYL

K endall followed Ronnie down the steps. Each pod was hooked to a monitor on which scrolled colored lines of data. There were also clipboards resting on the feet. Kendall peered into the frosted face shield and beheld a wizened homunculus who might have been a man-sized ginseng root. Behind the heads was a wall of metal cabinetry displaying analog gauges, ancient magnetic recording tape, and a series of levers that could have come from *Colossus: The Forbin Project*.

"Here he is!" Ronnie hissed, her words forming a cumulus cloud. Kendall went over. It was the end pod on the left. He peered through the frosted glass and beheld the still pink face of the man who had shaped so much American culture. Darryl Wyrick looked no worse off than Lenin.

No way a man could lie frozen for forty years and wake up. No way. You could freeze chicken once, but once you thawed it out, you couldn't freeze it again. Even if they could somehow wake him up, they would be sentencing him to death if he tried to hibernate again. Just waking him up might kill him.

Why were there no klaxons and flashing lights? Wouldn't the man who founded Wyrick World rate world-class security? But Wyrick was no Einstein. He was no great scientist or world leader. He was an entertainer! Kendall heard a high keening buzz at the very edge of his range. It was either the electronics or his brain frying. Ronnie studied the flow of data for a minute then delicately began to press the keys.

"What are you doing?"

"I'm waking him up! Isn't that why we're here?"

"How the fuck do you know how to work that thing? What if we kill him?"

Ronnie looked up at him with piercing green eyes. "I researched it online. Don't worry! I know what I'm doing."

A series of red lights began to blink sequentially. The monitor flashed red with a big black WARNING. Ronnie stroked the keys, and the image morphed into a series of colored graphs rolling left to right like the breakers off Malibu Point. The pod emitted a low humming sound, and the frost in the face shield retreated until it was crystal clear.

Ronnie put a hand on Kendall's shoulder. "Go down to that sink. Find a cup or something and a straw and fill it with water."

Kendall did as he was told. He found a stack of red sippee cups in the cabinet and a box of straws. He filled the cup with water and straw and brought it back to the pod. Lights went on in the chamber. The old man's skin flushed a healthy pink as if warm water suddenly flowed through his veins. He opened his eyes. Kendall shouted *"Eep!"* and lurched back, nearly spilling the water.

Ronnie rounded on him angrily. *"SHHH!"* she shushed. She turned back to the keyboard. She touched a button on the pod itself, and it hissed. She crouched and turned a crank at knee level. The pod rotated on its equator to a 45-degree angle.

Ronnie released two latches on either side of the curving faceplate, and it opened with a hiss. She took the cup and held it so that the straw was at Wyrick's mouth. His lips went around the straw, and he sucked. Wyrick had been 86 when he "died," but the man sucking at the straw appeared to be in his sixties. How was it possible? Had he been aging backward like Merlin? Wyrick wore a three-piece suit of fine gray worsted with a subtle blue stripe. A pale blue button-down shirt and a bright red tie. A discreet wire ran from a gray, plastic pod on his forehead and down his collar. There was also a disc-shaped device attached to his forehead.

The tycoon blinked, cleared his throat, and said, "More."

Ronnie handed Kendall the cup, and he refilled it. Wyrick drained the second cup.

For a long time, he lay there looking off into the distance. Abruptly his eyes focused on Ronnie.

"Who are you?" he croaked.

"Ronnie Arnold, Mr. Wyrick. I work at Wyrick World."

"Thought you looked familiar. Are you Illeana?"

"Yes, sir."

"What year is this?"

She told him.

"So soon?" he said. His eyes focused on Kendall. "You?"

"Kendall Coffin, sir. I'm a comic book illustrator."

"Why did you wake me?"

"We have some questions," Ronnie said. "We hope you don't mind."

"Does the organization know? Family?"

"No," Ronnie said.

"Do you mean to tell me you took it upon yourselves to revive me?"

"We did, sir. We hope you're not angry."

"No, this is good. I'd hoped for something like this, but I never dreamed it would happen this way. In fact, I left strict instructions to be revived in the year 2001, but since that never happened, I am in your debt. Who else knows I'm back?"

"Nobody," Ronnie said.

"Keep it that way. What do you want to know?"

Ronnie looked at Kendall.

"Sir, I spoke to Bree."

"She is still alive?"

"I'm very sorry to tell you she passed away this week. She was eighty-six."

The old man's eyes misted over. "I warned her not to marry that shmuck."

"It's about Frank Wallanda I wish to ask," Kendall said. "I'm living in the house he built with Roark Dexter Smith."

"I never liked that house. Those two were crazy. They wanted to make a movie. A haunted house movie with unbelievable gore and all sorts of sadomasochistic nonsense. I told them not in my lifetime."

"Sir, are you aware of any deaths that took place in that house?"

Wyrick looked puzzled. "I knew Frank used it for a party palace. I warned him not to endanger his image. Your reputation is all you've got. But no, I'm not aware of any deaths. Why do you ask?"

"I've been hearing screams at night. When I spoke to Bree last week, she warned me about something called a nedrebo. Do you know what that is?"

Wyrick stiffened, unable to conceal a wave of revulsion. "Frank Wallanda was a filthy, decadent, and yes, evil man! I would not have put up with him except that he seduced my darling daughter and turned her against me. And his movies were good. I have to give him that. His films made money. I went to his house once for a party. It was obvious to me he'd hired prostitutes to service his guests. And he couldn't hold his liquor. He'd get stewed and tell the filthiest stories. I watched him for a while talking to that architect, Smith. Frank starts laughing. Gets up and comes over to me. 'Roark just told me the funniest story!' he says. 'Do you know what a nedrebo is?' I walked away. I never did find out. I don't want to know. The next day he called me all apologies. 'I hope I didn't make too much of a fool of myself last night.'"

Wyrick cleared his throat.

"Please bring me another glass of water."

Kendall did so. The old man drained it.

"Are there any more questions?"

"Did you know a Crystal Feathers?"

"No. Not sure how good my memory is, but it used to be pretty good."

Ronnie and Kendall looked at one another.

"Sir, I don't know much about medicine," Kendall said, "but I believe your revival is some kind of scientific miracle. How did you do it?"

Wyrick winked at him. "If there are no more questions you may leave me now. Please do not mention our encounter. You were never here, understand?"

"Will you be all right?" Ronnie said.

"I'm fine."

"How can you even move?" Kendall said. "Your muscles have been dormant for forty years."

"Go."

FIFTY-THREE
MEMORIAL SERVICE
SATURDAY THROUGH MONDAY

On the way out, Kendall paused to sketch Doc Strange for Mark, wondering why they hadn't been swarmed with security. Surely there were cameras in that vault. No one stopped them. It was 1:00 AM by the time they returned to Wallanda House. They could hear Shapiro yapping as they went up the stairs. They were too excited to sleep. They made love, finally drifting off toward dawn.

On Sunday, they slept in. Ronnie learned from her Facebook page that there was a memorial for Stanley Merkle at The Magic Castle in Pasadena at 7:00 PM on Monday.

"I'll come over, and we'll go together, okay?"

Ronnie left at one and Kendall spent the rest of the day working on character designs and coordinating with his team. At six fifteen, Ruben Benson called to tell Kendall how pleased he was with their progress.

Kendall knocked off at seven, nuked a lasagna, and fed the dog. He watched most of *Once Upon a Time in the West* and went to sleep. He was blasted out of bed at six fifteen Monday morning by Dick Dale's "Let's Go Trippin'" at top volume. His Sony with remote that he'd never learned how to program. Well, he told himself, it could have been worse. It could have been rap.

He got up, padded into the den, and turned it off.

Kendall showered, shaved, fed the dog, and drove to Ripon. On his lunch break, he phoned Torrance and suggested they go together to the memorial. The Magic Castle was five miles east on Franklin Avenue. Kendall parked on the street behind Ronnie's car. His front door was unlocked, Shapiro running around the pool yapping while Ronnie swam laps. She got out wearing an iridescent blue one piece, gave him a cold kiss, and headed for the showers, the sun gleaming off her metallic ass.

Torrance came over at six thirty wearing a silvery suit and a blazingly white dress shirt open at the collar. Ronnie emerged from the bathroom in a little black cocktail dress more suitable to a lounge than a wake. Torrance couldn't suppress a whistle and a grin.

"You might wake the dead in that outfit, little lady," he said. "Kendall, I found out some interesting stuff about those stones in your proscenium."

"Like what?"

"I'll show you later."

Kendall put on a blue blazer with gold buttons and beige khakis. They went in his car. Liveried attendants directed guests through the foyer, up the Grand Staircase to the Palace of Mystery. It was just before seven when they copped three of the few remaining seats in the back row. Merkle had been popular and influential. Actors, producers, writers, and musicians filled the sixty-seat theater to capacity. There was a simple card table set up on the stage with a top hat on it as well as an oak dais. A hum of conversation hung over the room like a layer of smog. No matter what the occasion, it was all right to deal.

A man stepped out of the wings wearing a black suit, white shirt, and red tie. He was tall and imposing with puffy cheeks. He took his place behind the dais and the conversation immediately dissipated.

"Good evening, folks, and thank you for coming. I'm Mark Travanier, and I had the pleasure of working with Stan on several animated projects in the eighties. Many of you don't know this, but Stan was also a gifted voice actor and was the voice behind Awesome Possum, the Red Lobster, and many other popular kids' characters. I'd like to say a few words, and then I'm going to turn the mic over to whoever wants to remember Stan.

"I first met Stan at Hanna-Barbera in the early eighties where we worked on *Scooby-Doo*. I wasn't aware he was a magician until one day I was looking for my pen and Stan pulled it out of my ear. He was old then. It's really quite a miracle he lasted as long as he did, and I really can't think of a better way to go than during a séance.

"Stan was born in 1929 in Florence, Nebraska, and moved to Los Angeles with his family when he was five. His father Winston was a plumber but somehow became a set designer at the old MGM where Stan began hanging around, age ten, bothering stars like Spencer Tracy, Katherine Hepburn, and Edward G. Robinson. At age twelve he saw a performance by the legendary Robin Hyatt and from that moment wanted nothing more than to be a stage magician.

"Stan appeared in more than 115 films and performed countless times all over the country. He outlived four wives. He has only one living descendant, great grandson Robert, currently serving with the Marines in Afghanistan. I feel privileged to have known him. I see Myron Beckel has something to say. Myron?"

As speakers took turns, Kendall looked around. David Copperfield and Gillette Penn sat in the front row. Penn gave a ten-minute eulogy. Travanier took the stage.

"Anyone else?"

Coughing exploded from the other side of the room. Portia stood pounding her chest. "I'd like to say a few words," she growled making her way to the lectern. She struggled to make the podium. Travanier helped her.

"I know you're all dying to get to the pub, so I'll make this brief. Stan was one of the first persons I met when I came to Hollywood in the sixties. He came in for a palm reading. I looked at his hand and said, 'Mr. Merkle, you've been a bad boy!' He winked at me and said, 'Honey, you don't know the half of it!'"

The audience roared its delight.

"Stan helped me get work. He's the one that got me a gig on *The Tonight Show*. Johnny Carson always said I was the inspiration for Karnak the Magnificent, but it was actually Stan."

Kendall wondered if she was making it up as she went along. Portia closed the show and most of the attendees repaired to the Hat & Hare Pub in the basement to drink and tell stories.

Portia stood chatting outside the lecture hall as Kendall and Ronnie left. He touched Portia on the arm. "I'll call you later."

"Please," Portia said.

Torrance told them to go on without him. He'd never been to the Magic Castle and wanted to talk to some of the regulars. "Say, Kendall," he said. "I need to talk to you about those stones in your theater. I'll catch you tomorrow, hey?"

"Sounds good."

Kendall retrieved his car, and he and Ronnie drove home.

FIFTY-FOUR
WORRY

Ronnie let her left hand trail along Kendall's thigh. He kept putting it back in her lap, and she kept coming back like a stray cat. By the time they got home, he was hotter than a nine-dollar toaster. They parked in front. Kendall fumbled with the keys and stumbled inside. They made their way to the bedroom. Twenty minutes later it was all over.

"I'm famished," Ronnie declared.

Kendall swung his legs over and put on his pants. "Let me see what I've got."

He went into the kitchen and opened the refrigerator. Bacon, smoked sausage, beer, eggs, a box of baking soda, and some three-day-old lasagna. He opened the vegetable crisper and found a head of lettuce, a red onion, and some Roma tomatoes.

The freezer contained four packages of frozen lasagna. He looked in the cupboard and found a box of rice and beans.

Kendall switched on the counter-top television while he prepared the salad. He shredded the lettuce leaving out the spines, put it in his salad spinner and spun. He added onion and sliced tomatoes. He found cans of peas and chickpeas in the cupboard.

A slick little fanfare announced the ten o'clock news. A beautiful Indian woman related the day's events beginning with the latest health insurance cock-ups. Spider-Man and Batman got into another brawl in front of Grauman's Chinese Theater. The mayor promised that the new light rail system, which nobody wanted, would be up and running by November.

Dealin' Doug screamed Dodge deals. Kendall added the peas and chickpeas.

Kendall's head snapped.

"... believed to be the Kardashian Killer's next victim. A jogger found the body this morning at a remote arroyo in Griffith Park. Then the story turns bizarre. A detective who did not wish to be identified confirmed the existence of another body nearby but offered no further information. Police say they may have found a serial killer's dumping ground."

"What's wrong?" Ronnie said.

Kendall snapped toward her. "Nothing. Why?"

"You looked like you were having a stroke! Your neck muscles were standing out."

"They found another body."

"I wish they'd find that guy!" Ronnie said, coming up behind Kendall and putting her hands around him. Kendall picked up the remote and turned off the television. He went into the den where he stored his CDs, returned with *Pet Sounds* and put it in the counter Sony.

Ronnie chattered as Kendall cooked, oblivious to his gloom. He had no doubt that the second body was the one he'd dumped. He frantically tried to remember if he'd left any sign of himself. They said that a killer invariably leaves some sign of himself with a victim, but that was a crock. What about drone pilots? They dropped bombs in Afghanistan from bunkers in Arizona.

Kendall had been very careful. His fingerprints wouldn't adhere to the junkie's clothes. What else was there? Tire tracks? It had rained since then. Nevertheless, the strain of not knowing descended on him like heavy chains. He was glad they'd made love before he learned the news. He doubted he would be able to function for the rest of the night. He would just have to gut it out, waiting for that knock at the door, hoping it never came. Maybe in a month or a year, the chains would lift. By then they'd stop looking. Who cared about some junkie?

He'd put the dude's wallet back. DuWayne Heller. Student at UCLA. A mathematics major no doubt. Probably wasn't his real name, and if that kid had been a student at UCLA, Kendall was the President.

Finally, Ronnie looked up from her nearly empty bowl. "What?"

"What, what?"

"You're obsessing about something. I can tell. You've done nothing but grunt throughout dinner."

"Sorry. I was thinking about work."

"How's that going?"

"Great," Kendall said. "*Off the Pig* will be a big hit."

Ronnie looked at him funny. "You don't really like it, do you?"

Kendall smiled. "Beats drawing women getting fucked by horses!"

Ronnie's mouth made a half shocked, half-delighted oval. "What?"

"Oh, yeah. I had to quit that Wyrick job because they wanted me to draw scenes that would gag a dog off a gut wagon. So now I'm constructing a universe in which young thugs see how many cops they can kill. Of course, the cops are all crooked. They were all white too until I made a few suggestions. I'm not complaining. I feel privileged to make a living doing what I love."

Ronnie got up, went behind him, and began kneading his shoulders. "Why don't you go back to drawing comics?"

"Doesn't pay enough! I have a house and a dog to support."

"Leave the dishes," Ronnie said. "I'll take care of them in the morning. Come on to bed."

Kendall groaned. "You're gonna have to give me some recharge time."

"We don't have to make love constantly, silly! I just like watching television in bed."

As soon as they got on the bed, Shapiro jumped up and insinuated himself between them. Ronnie commandeered the remote and flipped through stations.

"Ooh!" she cooed. "*Catwoman* is on! It's so awful we have to watch it."

Ronnie conked out before Kendall, and a half hour later he turned off the television and the light.

He dreamt of Ronnie in a Catwoman suit. He reached to embrace her, and she slashed him across the face and chest.

He woke up with a gasp and felt a searing pain, but by the time his hand moved to his face, it was gone.

FIFTY-FIVE

LATE NIGHT PHONE CALL

Torrance dropped Portia off via taxi at her bungalow at eleven thirty. She'd laughed so hard her sides ached. Torrance walked her to the door of her tiny American Craftsman bungalow which she'd purchased for eighty thousand in 1969. It was a neighborhood of well-preserved bungalows stuck between a block of tacky plywood apartments and a newly gentrified district of slightly larger bungalows and renovated office buildings.

Diffuse light from streetlights and the city itself permeated the night, creating a soft glow. Portia's cat Ozymandias mewed from the little bay window.

"That was swell, Torrance," Portia growled, putting a hand on his arm. "We must do that again sometime."

"Sure 'nuff. We sure had 'em going!"

She laughed in memory, unlocked the door, and went inside. She thought briefly of inviting him inside but what was the point? She was too old for sex, and she was all talked out. She locked the door and turned on the hall light. Ozymandias wound between her legs purring.

"Ozzy," she said going into the living room and collapsing into an overstuffed chair upholstered with pink paisleys. Ozzy leapt up and settled into her lap. Portia reached for the package of Camels on the table, shook one out and lit it with a match.

She didn't believe Stan's death was a coincidence. He'd always seemed indestructible and had never been sick a day in his life, or so he claimed. He bragged that his doctor told him he was on track to hit the century mark.

There was something in the house. Some unclean spirit that wanted blood. Portia had always had the Gift, since she was a child in her parents' home in Minneapolis in the fifties. She could predict the Saturday morning cartoon shows. Whenever Looney Tunes or Merrie Melodies blasted their fanfares, she would know without question which cartoon would appear: "What's Opera, Doc?", "Marvin the Martian," Boris and Natasha.

Her father Lester was a forklift mechanic. Her mother Edith worked at the cosmetics counter for Sears. She had two sisters and three brothers, and there never seemed to be enough food around the house. She noticed when visiting her friends that their homes didn't smell funny like hers: a sour mash of dead skin, fried liver, and pine soap.

One day—when she was ten—there was a phone call, and her mother started screaming. Her brother Paul had been killed drag-racing. The car burst into flames, and there wasn't enough left to fill a shoebox. She thought she saw secret relief in her father's eyes: one less mouth to feed. Her brother Ned joined the Navy as soon as he turned eighteen. He couldn't wait to get out of there.

Older sister Kathy got pregnant at sixteen and dropped out of high school. She started turning tricks at age eighteen, leaving little Joshua with Edith and Portia.

Portia first imagined a life in showbiz in high school where she acted in *Our Town* and *A Christmas Carol*. She knew she didn't have the looks to be a leading lady, but maybe one of those character actors like Carol Burnett or Audrey Meadows. When she was sixteen, she went with two friends to the Bixby Traveling Carnival and Circus in the tiny town of Allenton, an annual event honoring Allenton Days. By night the dizzying neon of the Tilt-A-Whirl, Wild Mouse, and Ferris Wheel beckoned and cajoled, a magic kingdom of seedy fun, that dangerous undertow of sin and degradation lurking in the shadows. Rita's older brother got them a bottle of sloe gin.

The carnies were hard men with pocked faces, dark mustaches, tattoos, and cigarettes dangling from their lower lips, murmuring casual obscenities at the more attractive women. The cry of the carnival barker sounded like the muezzins of the faithful. "Step right up!" "Try your luck!" "You there, soldier boy! How'd you like to give the little lady something to remember?"

Portia and her friends held hands and grinned at one another. Ahead lay the eerie facade of the gypsy palm reader, an old woman the texture of a stewed prune wearing gypsy rags and a scarf. A half dozen cut glass necklaces dangled from her wattled neck. Her marquee featured a lurid painting of the Masonic eye gazing sternly over a convoy of Amish accompanied by sheep and cattle. They looked scared. Buzzed on gin, the girls goaded each other into paying the two bucks for a palm reading.

The old woman sat in a garishly painted booth beneath a sign that said MADAME EUGENIE in lurid red script, outlined with yellow. Skeletons, mystics, a genie from a bottle, a flying eye, and other symbols decorated the front of the booth. Madame Eugenie herself stank of gin and had bulging yellow eyes.

Rita, the prettiest, went first. Madame slurred her words as she spun a fairy tale of success in love and life. Next up was Alice, a fat, plain-featured girl. Her fate was even more glorious than Rita's, involving a Nordic prince and riding through the snow wrapped in wolf skins drawn by two white stallions.

Finally, it was Portia's turn. She took her place on the chipped kitchen chair and placed her hand palm up on the scarred wood counter. Numerous wags had carved their initials in it when the booth was shut down. Madame Eugenie pressed her fingers into the palm and looked down. She looked up, startled.

"You have the Gift," she hissed with a hint of garlic. She

handed Portia back her two bucks. "No can read this. Good night." She stood and lowered the wood shingle covering the access.

"What did she say?!" Rita demanded.

Portia forced a smile. "Bor-ing! I'm going to marry a nice boy and raise two kids."

Portia didn't sleep that night, tossing in a bouillabaisse of anxiety and excitement. By dawn, she'd figured it out. Portia moved out of the house at eighteen, took a job as a hostess at a local supper club, saving her money to move to Hollywood. One morning she woke up in her rented room above a hardware store and knew with terrible certainty that her brother Ned had been killed in a training accident. She raced home on her bicycle and arrived just in time to see an olive-green Ford pull up in front of her parents' house and a uniformed officer get out.

She made the move when she was twenty, renting a cheap apartment with two girls she met at a casting agency. She made the rounds, got a few bit parts in Universal productions, once on *Maverick*, all the while refining her fortune-telling shtick. She practiced on her roommates. She freaked them out. The evening of November 21, 1963, she told her roommates, "Tomorrow the President will die."

Two days later one of her roommates moved back to Iowa.

Same thing the night before Martin Luther King was shot.

And John Lennon.

Portia was unaware, during the séance, of those who spoke through her. Coffin's house filled her with a vague dread, half-glimpsed abominations and the lingering odor of death. An adumbration of disaster descended on her as she walked up the steps, but she'd ignored her instincts and gone anyway.

Now, with Ozzy purring on her ample breast, it seemed a distant memory. Stan got her jobs at industry parties, then at the Comedy Club and other venues. In 1965 the *Los Angeles Courier* offered her a weekly column. People wrote in from around the world with their questions. They sent pictures, money, small articles of clothing. Sometimes Portia got vibes, sometimes not.

Portia knew things about Stan she dared not say. He'd told her that when he'd first arrived in Hollywood in the forties, he'd worked as a pimp. A beating by an angry john convinced him to seek another line of work. He'd always gambled, always done card tricks, was a gifted prestidigitator. He'd taught Portia many a trick. Stan was one of the few people she knew who had substantially changed for the better over the years and confided in her how he regretted what he'd done to women.

She couldn't help but wonder if his past had anything to do with his death.

Ozzy sank his claws into her bosom and hissed rank in her face. She saw a flash of white, a sheet of foolscap whipped before her eyes.

The pink princess phone on the end table rang. She stared at it with dread. It rang again. She picked it up.

"Hello," she croaked.

A hiss of white noise.

Portia held her breath.

"Hello, Portia." The voice was feminine, sensual, mocking.

"Who is this?" Portia said.

"You know who this is. You were in my house. It won't end well for you and your friends. You know that. Why did you come into my house? Wasn't once enough?"

"Tell me your name," Portia said, seeing her breath freeze.

"How's that old pussy of yours? It's seen enough action, must look like a wizard's sleeve by now."

"What do you want?"

A low, sexy chortle. "I want you to come back to this house where you pulled a train for Frank Wallanda and do it again for my friends and me. Then I want you to die."

FIFTY-SIX

ON THE PROWL

On a scale of one to ten, the killer gave her a twelve. The moment he laid eyes on the petite, curvaceous brunette, she was doomed. Never had he beheld a female who so completely fulfilled his fantasies. He began his patient seduction. He friended her on Facebook under false pretenses. Said he'd seen her perform and was a fan of the genre. He used his Norman Drago persona with a photo he snagged off an obscure corner of the internet.

Norman Drago was an SFX wizard who had worked for both Wyrick and Pixar. Norman Drago was an honorably discharged veteran who had served in the Iraq War under Bush the Second. Norman Drago was an avid surfer and scuba diver. Norman Drago was in a happy relationship with aspiring actress Felicity Gonzalez. Norman Drago had worked on *The Incredibles*, *Troy*, and *Saving Private Ryan*.

Norman Drago lived in Century City and drove a Porsche. He had been a close personal friend of the late Paul Walker. He'd instant-messaged her, but she was coy and seldom replied. Nevertheless, he adduced her hidden desire for abuse and death at his hands, and he watched her from afar.

Unfortunately, his many responsibilities prevented him from

making it a full-time job, and he was forced to catch snatches when and where he could, usually on weekends or at night. He'd only just managed to attend the memorial service for some old hack magician. He attended as Norman Drago. They never even asked for his Magic Castle membership card. A face like his opened doors.

The killer kept a file. Not on his computer; he wasn't that stupid. A real, old-fashioned file filled with press clippings gleaned from the dailies, weeklies, and trade publications. The Perfect Girl was not a major player. If she were to live it was possible, but Tinseltown was bursting with beautiful, young, talented things. The odds were stacked against you. The killer knew this better than anyone considering his own early struggles, how far he'd come, and how much of it was based on dumb luck.

He kept a map in his head where he dropped the bodies. Steep canyons were best, where the coyote and carrion birds could get at them. The police had only been able to identify two of his victims by dental records, and they had the numbers wrong. In the two years he'd campaigned, the killer had disposed of six bodies. It went without saying he kept a file on himself as well. He planned to write his autobiography but couldn't figure out a way to get paid without revealing himself.

Every couple of weeks or so he would drop by Wyrick World and watch her from afar. Once he used a telephoto lens to film her but had to quit when a security guard came his way. It was a simple matter to learn where she lived, but his work prevented him from giving her the attention she deserved. He monitored her Facebook and Twitter accounts when he had the time.

He read up on other serial killers and saw all the films. *The Hillside Stranglers* were his favorites. He'd begun preparing his defense years ago.

Your honor, the defendant first encountered violent online porn when he was nine years old. He came from a dysfunctional family and his father often boasted of his many conquests.

The killer's eyes automatically swept the perimeter. He

looked in the rearview. Ho shit. An LA squad car grooving up slowly. It was dark, and they had not yet seen him due to the headrest. The killer slunk low in his seat and held his breath as the cruiser slowly passed. He hunkered for twenty seconds before sticking his head up cautiously like a groundhog emerging from hibernation. The cruiser was on the next block, shining its spotlight at a house on the opposite side of the street.

The killer exhaled. It was endorphin city every time he outwitted the cops or had a close call. What was life but a series of highs? The killer viewed with contempt the little people who lived in the valley, drove Kias, whose weekly highlights included getting shit-faced, watching the Dodgers and the Rams, and porking the old lady.

He decided he would have been happier in the age of Genghis Kahn. He was a primordial man. Food, sex, power.

Fucking house. You couldn't tell a thing by looking at it. You couldn't see the front door, and the lone exterior window glowed a perpetual soft pink, so you didn't know if anyone was home. He knew they were home. Her car was parked on the street. Piece of shit Ford. His own car was far from conspicuous.

His mind drifted to the last bitch he'd raped and murdered. He smiled at the thought. She begged and pleaded and that only made it more fun. She went down kicking and squirming with him inside her. Of course, he used a rubber to avoid leaving DNA, and even if they found some lotsa luck matching it up. He had a clean record. Nowhere was his DNA on file. He was so far from the standard serial killer profile they would never think of anyone like him.

He slipped on the ear buds and brought his favorite song up on his iPod. "Midnight Rambler" by the Rolling Stones. He hunkered low in the seat, shoulders bopping.

Ho shit! Here they came again, shining their spotlights on license plates. WTF?! It wasn't Compton! For whom could they possibly be looking? The killer had no choice but to scrunch down once again and pray they didn't notice. He took extraordinary pains to remain unnoticeable. He heard the crunch of the cop car's tires on the asphalt through the open window. He shut off his iPod and lay in a state of terror and excitement, breathing shallowly.

The crunching stopped. The searchlight swept over the windshield and then canted low. He held his breath. The cop car moved on. The killer reached up and tilted the rearview so he could follow the cops' progress. They drove down the block and then turned off onto a side street.

The killer felt that special elation that only came from outwitting the cops. It was time to get the hell out of Dodge.

FIFTY-SEVEN

PUNCH THE GUT
TUESDAY MORNING

Kendall and Ronnie showered together in the enormous high-zoot shower. Ronnie rubbed herself against him. Kendall turned away.

"You're no fun," Ronnie pouted.

"My day is like a mullet. Business in front, party at the end. What time do you get off work?"

Ronnie made plans to return that evening. Shapiro hounded them down the hall until Kendall unloaded a tin of Science Diet in his bowl.

"Are you sure you're feeding him enough?" Ronnie said.

Kendall regarded the dog. Shapiro had put on weight. No telling how big he would get. The dog sat at his feet with pleading eyes, tail thumping.

"Oh, what the hell," Kendall said and opened up another tin.

"They say you shouldn't be able to see his ribs, but you should be able to feel them," Ronnie said.

Shapiro's ribs were slightly visible as he pushed his bowl around the floor. "He's only ten weeks old," Kendall said.

He put two bowls on the kitchen table and three boxes of cereal: Rice Crispies, Post Raisin Bran, and Kellogg's Frosted

Flakes with Tony the Tiger. Ronnie grinned as she went for the Frosted Flakes.

Sunlight poured through the windows and skylight casting a golden patina, an NC Wyeth painting.

Kendall brewed coffee and handed Ronnie a Doc Strange mug. He took his in a bone mug. Ronnie turned on the countertop TV. A public service ad told them how to be a good father. "You don't have to be perfect to be a perfect dad."

Back to the news featuring a singer/actress/model who'd lucked out. She was a Latina beauty wearing horn-rimmed glasses.

Just the killer's type, Kendall thought.

"There's been an update on those two bodies found in Griffith Park. Police Chief Harold Page will hold a press conference this morning at 10:00 AM. It is believed he will report on the special task force formed to hunt the so-called Kardashian Killer. Thus far there is no evidence that the two bodies located in a remote canyon in the park are in any way related."

Kendall looked at Ronnie shoveling cornflakes.

"Do you have a gun?"

Ronnie looked at him with a silent guffaw. "A what?"

"A gun. It's not safe out there for anyone, particularly someone who looks like you."

"What do I look like?"

"You look like those girls the Kardashian Killer killed."

"You think I look like a Kardashian?"

"You know what I mean."

"No, I don't have a gun. It's impossible to get one anyway, even if I wanted one, which I don't. Don't worry about me. I can handle myself."

Kendall dropped it. There was nothing he could do. She didn't want a gun, wasn't about to take a gun safety class and start packing even if she were able to get one. He didn't doubt guns were readily available. Just not through legal channels. He could always borrow one from Spielberg who was reputed to have one of the world's largest collections.

"Do you have any pepper spray or something? Brass knuckles?"

Ronnie laughed. "Stop worrying! I'll be fine. I've got an ice pick."

Kendall turned back to the TV. Spider-Man and Batman were fighting again over turf in front of Grauman's. The I-5 was backed up due to a rollover. Heavy clouds were moving in from a low-pressure area in the Pacific. Angelenos could expect a little rain.

Shot of the mob outside the San Diego Convention Center from last year. "Publishers, vendors, and production companies have already begun setting up for this year's San Diego Comic-Con, the West Coast phenomenon that began as a small fan cele-bration in the basement of the US Grant and has since burgeoned into one of the largest entertainment trade shows in the world," said the nerd/glam young man standing in front of a line of cosplayers.

"Are you going to San Diego?" Ronnie asked.

"Not this year. Got no reason. Too late to even book a hotel room. It's probably too late to book a hotel room for next year. The only hope I ever have of going to San Diego is if they make me a guest, which is doubtful."

"I went last year," Ronnie said. "Just for a day with a friend of mine. It was so packed inside you couldn't move."

"I know. It's no fun anymore."

Even through the thick walls, they heard the screech of tires and the sickening impact of metal on flesh. Kendall looked for Shapiro. A woman screamed. Kendall ran toward the front door leaving a bewildered Ronnie at the kitchen table. The front door was open.

He ran out of the alcove taking the front steps three at a time. A perfectly restored British Racing Green XKE was stopped at an angle in the middle of the street, driver's door open. The driver knelt in front of the car examining an inert mound of fur while a woman with a yapping Chihuahua on a leash stood on the oppo-site side sobbing.

Kendall ran out into the street and knelt next to his dead dog. He looked up in grief into the shocked face of Desmond Krout.

FIFTY-EIGHT

MIND OF ITS OWN

K rout was in tears. "I am so sorry. I am so sorry." He did a slow double take. "Kender?"

"Kendall," Kendall said, in a state of shock. He felt Shapiro, but the dog was dead, tongue protruding, eyes open. An augur of ice burrowed into his chest. He gathered the inert mound of fur to him, and the floodgates opened. Even as he was gasping and heaving, he wondered where it came from. He'd only had the dog a couple weeks and yet here he was crying as he never had over the death of his wife.

Maybe that was it. Maybe this was the big delayed reaction, but when he searched within himself for that feeling for Shirley it wasn't there. The grief was real. He'd loved the fucking dog more than his dead wife. Was that wrong?

He felt a warm arm around his shoulders, and Ronnie was there, hugging him. Kendall didn't know what to do. What was the protocol? Did you call the police for something like this?

"I was just passing through," Desmond said. "He ran out between the cars so fast I didn't see him until it was too late! I tried to stop."

Kendall looked at Krout through tear-blurred eyes. Krout's gold earring caught the morning light and twinkled. Krout had jutting teeth and a big bony jaw like a horse. He was handsome until he showed his teeth.

"Dude," the producer said. "I want to make this right. There's no need to get the cops involved. Whatever it takes. You take a few days to think about it and then get back to me, okay? You have my card."

Kendall stared uncomprehendingly. He looked up as an LAPD Crown Vic pulled up, its grill facing the front of the Jag. Desmond quailed, teeth jutting like a chimp's. A burly cop got out of the driver's seat, his smaller Latino companion from the other side. Upchurch and Gomez.

"What happened?" Upchurch said.

Desmond stood. "Officer, the dog ran out in front of me without any warning. I didn't have time to stop."

The cop looked at the dog then at Kendall. "Your dog?"

Kendall could only nod.

"You've been having a tough time. Did anybody see it happen?"

"I did," said the woman with the Chihuahua. "I was walking Maxie when this gentleman passed me. I heard the tires screech and then a yelp."

"Did you actually see him strike the dog, ma'am?" Upchurch asked.

"Well, no …"

"How fast was he going?"

The woman looked timidly from cop to Desmond and back. "About the speed limit."

"And what is the speed limit?" the cop said.

"About thirty-five," the woman answered.

"It's twenty-five, ma'am," Upchurch said. The woman looked abashed.

When Kendall looked at Desmond, the producer was casting sideways glances at Ronnie with hooded eyes. The cops declined to press charges.

Gomez knelt next to Kendall. "Sorry for your loss."

Kendall could only shake his head. Gomez put a hand on his shoulder and stood.

"Watch your speed out here," the big cop said. "It's twenty-five in all residential areas unless otherwise noted."

"Yes sir," Desmond replied.

"Mr. Coffin, will you take care of your pet's body?"

Kendall nodded, picking up Shapiro and cradling him in his arms. What was he supposed to do with the body?

"Please clear the street," Upchurch said. Both cops turned in unison and returned to their vehicle. Eight cars had come to a standstill behind the audience. The only thing that prevented the drivers from screaming, uttering dire threats, and exchanging gunfire was the police presence. They politely waited until Desmond had pulled over before cautiously proceeding.

Desmond got out and chased after Kendall who carried his dead dog up the steps.

"Kendall! You'll call me, right?"

Kendall looked at him with dead eyes. "I'll call."

Kendall carried his dead dog through the house and out onto the terrace, laying him in the grass. "What do I do with him?"

"Any veterinarian can dispose of the body, or the local pet shelter; costs about a buck a pound. You can't swing a dead cat out here without hitting an animal hospital or shelter."

She saw the look on his face. "I'm sorry. I didn't mean that."

Kendall broke down in sobs. Ronnie put her arm around him. "Poor baby! Do you want me to stay with you? I could call in sick."

Kendall got hold of himself and straightened his shoulders. "No, you go to work. I'll take care of it. There's a pet shelter on the way to work."

Ronnie looked at her Illeana watch. "Oh, I'd better get going. Traffic's gonna be a bitch."

Kendall kissed her goodbye. He sat in a lawn chair over Shapiro's body for an hour, his mind a ball of confusion. What had Desmond been doing driving through his neighborhood in the morning? The producer had told Kendall he lived in Holmby

Hills. Just a bizarre coincidence? Kendall prayed it was so. An anemone of dread insinuated itself in the back of his medulla-- the possibility that with Shapiro dead the screams would return.

He couldn't wait around and see. He'd fallen a couple days behind schedule on *Off the Pig*, and there was an eleven o'clock meeting. Stopping by the shelter would delay his arrival, but there was no help for it. He couldn't very well leave the carcass in the sun all day.

Kendall heaved himself to his feet, went in the house, and retrieved a plastic garbage bag. He wrestled the carcass into the bag and carried it down to his car, which he'd parked several places up on the street. He popped the trunk and gently laid his pet's body inside.

He went back into the house and checked himself in the mirror. He needed a shave, but there was no time. They loved the scruffy look at Ripon. He grabbed his laptop and a sports jacket and left the house, locking the door behind him.

How had the door become open? He was certain he'd locked it after Ronnie's arrival the previous evening. He wondered if Ronnie had left it open. But she would have had to make a special trip to do that. It made no sense!

He beeped open the Avalon and got in. He turned the key. The engine whined for long seconds but refused to start. *What the fuck?!* He had a half tank of gas, and the damned thing used fuel injection. He tried again. And again. The starter motor whined and slowed. If he continued, he would burn the battery.

He'd have to take the Corvette. It lacked registration or insur- ance, but he had no choice. There were thousands if not millions of similarly unregistered, uninsured vehicles roaming the high- ways and byways of Southern California. The cops couldn't take notice of them all. It was a calculated risk like sneaking into the country. Wearily, he got out of the car, popped the trunk, and picked up his dog. He walked up the sidewalk to his garage, laid the body on the brick retaining wall, unlocked the garage, and pushed the door up into the roof. He went inside. It was bright enough he did not have to turn on the lights. He took the keys out of the Vette's ignition and unlocked the trunk. He went outside, hefted the carcass, and put it in the Corvette's trunk leaving enough room for a shot glass and a cue ball.

He got in the Vette and turned the key. The small block V8 roared to life, glass packs rattling. He backed carefully into the street and left it in idle while he got out and closed the garage door. He made a U-turn intending to hit the 101 off Vermont. The stoplight at Franklin and Vermont turned yellow as he approached, and he slowed down and occupied the center lane. He could see cross-traffic inching ahead.

As soon as the light turned red the Corvette roared, leaped forward, and veered to the right heading north, leaving angry commuters cursing and honking. Kendall automatically seized the wheel and tried to pull the stick out of first. The car surged forward, the transmission jerking in his hand as it shifted into second. He stood on the brakes. There was no response. The car accelerated shifting from third to fourth, the terrorized driver hanging on for dear life.

FIFTY-NINE
WHAT'S ONE MORE

The Stingray turned right on Los Feliz hard enough to lift its inside front wheel, narrowly missing several parked cars. Kendall gripped the wheel simply to have something to hold. Did the car intend to murder him? He giggled maniacally at the absurdity. Cars didn't intend! They were inanimate objects.

The Vette squirted into Griffith Park. Where were the cops when you needed them? Not that they could have done anything except shoot out the tires or lay down a strip of nails. He passed a jogger who flipped him the bird and yelled something lost in the car's bellow. He looked at the speedo—eighty freakin' mph in Griffith Park! Any second the car would catapult off one of those hairpin curves and kill them both.

Kendall and the car.

They roared by the observatory, lot half full including several yellow school buses. Some kids in the parking lot leaning against the parapet pointed and cheered. The car took the twisting path north through the hills, spraying gravel on the hairpin curves. It abruptly nosed off the asphalt onto a dirt fire road that ended with a stout chain supporting a red sign stretching between two steel stanchions buried in the ground. Kendall hunkered low in the seat pulling the ancient, lap-only seatbelt as tight as he could across his pelvis and braced for the impact.

The Vette snapped the chain. Kendall heard a sharp *ping*! And watched a glinting shard fly toward the sun. The Stingray scrambled down a harsh washboard surface churning up a cloud of dust. The air smelled of dust, eucalyptus, and pine. On it drove until they reached one of the most remote sections of the park somewhere northwest of the observatory but short of Griffith Park Drive. The car downshifted: four to three to two to one, each shift double-clutched and accompanied by a symphonic arpeggio from the engine, pedals pumping beneath his feet.

It pulled up to a precipice overlooking a wild canyon, home to coyote, feral pigs, wolves, and snakes. Kendall still gripped the wheel, his breath rasping fast and shallow. His heart redlined. The back of his shirt stuck to the leather. He felt sweat run down his forehead and drip onto his shirt, his breathing a ragged wheeze. Tentatively he pulled his right hand off the wheel and turned off the ignition. The engine died.

He jerked the parking brake with all his might, opened the door, swung out his legs, and sat with his head between his knees.

The fuck just happened?

Would anyone believe him?

He listened for the wail of sirens, but all he heard was the distant susurrus of the city, traffic zooming on the I-5. His phone was in his pocket. *Hello, I've just been kidnapped by my car. I'm being held prisoner in Griffith Park.*

He sprung the hood and got out. The engine was clean enough to eat. There were no strange contraptions anywhere in the engine well as far as he could tell. He looked up. The canyon sloped away precipitously from where he stood, protected only by a low wood barrier. The place was clean, unlittered. At this hour of the morning, the overcast sky threw dim light into the canyon. Kendall stepped over the barrier and looked down: the usual collection of scrub brush, cacti, eucalyptus, and rocks burnt to a high sienna.

They'd found so many bodies in Griffith Park over the years, what was one more? Burbank gleamed in the morning sun. With an enormous sigh, Kendall returned to the Vette and gathered Shapiro into his arms. Underneath lay a folded Army spade. He'd never seen it before, but he'd never really looked in the trunk before.

Great. Maybe the car just wanted him to bury his dog out here. Kendall stepped carefully over the barrier and looked for a way down. He spotted a narrow switchback created by deer or hikers and carefully picked his way down the slope, stepping sideways in his waffle stompers. Looking for a place he wouldn't be visible to anyone above. He'd descended approximately two hundred feet when he found what he was looking for, a ledge which penetrated back into the hill creating a shallow cave, almost completely overrun with wild juniper. He gently set the bag down in the shallow cave out of the sun and returned to the car for the spade.

His second body in two weeks.

He couldn't but reflect on the two other bodies found in the park: the dead junkie and the murder victim. How many undiscovered bodies still lurked in Griffith Park?

Kendall crab-walked down the slope to Shapiro's burial plot. The gorse and juniper were a springy mass of wires through which he could not dig. He attacked the juniper at the base with the spade. Sweat poured down his forehead into his eyes blinding him. It was a hot day despite the overcast sky, and the humidity promised righteous rain. By the time he'd excavated the stubborn little plant's root ball his shirt was soaked through, and it was ten thirty. He tried to get a signal on his phone, but it was no good deep in the canyon.

Fuck it. He'd stay late if he had to. They'd understand when he explained.

Bending his knees, he pulled on the juniper. It resisted. Getting a better grip, he strained, feeling it begin to loosen. He worked it back and forth like a dog with a rag until it suddenly popped loose, propelling him backward off the precarious ledge.

The thought flashed through his mind that now they would find his body in the park.

He rolled over rocky protrusions like a tumbleweed until he came to rest against the trunk of a spongy gorse bush that halted his downward spiral.

He sat up, feeling his body pull at him in a half dozen places. His shirt was torn, and he bled from his elbows and knees. He sat there for a minute. It had been a hell of a morning and the day was young.

Down here not even the sound of the nearby freeway was audible. Kendall got to one knee and stared at something in the ground. A white tip. It didn't belong. He slowly extended his hand and seized the tip which protruded perhaps a half inch. He gently pulled. It was attached to something. He worked back and forth as he had the bush using his other hand to clear away the dirt. He saw it for what it was.

A distal phalange.

SIXTY
WHAT THE CAR KNEW

A s an artist, Kendall knew every bone in the human body. He pulled out his penknife and dug around. The phalange was attached to a hand, small enough to be that of a child's or a woman's. He sat stunned for a minute, mind blank.

He knew he had an immediate duty to report it to the police. They would ask what he was doing there. It was illegal to bury your dog in Griffith Park.

Then he would be on their radar. They'd note the accident that morning, Merkle's death last week, the house itself, its strange history. He didn't need that. He'd have to think about it. Figure out where the hell he was and take notes. Too bad there wasn't a GPS in the car.

Maybe later he'd make an anonymous call. But then they'd almost certainly find Shapiro. He'd come with a chip from the shelter. They'd trace it back to him. Same problem. He'd be better off just covering it up and forgetting it.

Unless the bones were the reason the car drove here.

Kendall laughed until tears ran down his cheeks. He gradually petered out and looked around self-consciously to see if anyone heard. He was alone.

He knew he couldn't just leave it. It really was the reason the car had driven him here. The house was trying to tell him something through the car, something he probably didn't want to hear.

He had no choice. Kendall got slowly to his feet feeling bruises on his thighs, arms, and chest and carefully picked his way back up the inhospitable slope. He grabbed the spade and headed back down, sliding halfway on his ass.

He reached the site. He was thirsty, but there was nothing. Kendall attacked the skeleton delicately, chipping away around the fingers with his penknife, brushing out the dirt with his fingers. He got down to mid-palm before picking up the spade.

He did not know for what he was looking. All he knew was that he had to uncover some secret, some sign of who this person was. Judging from the way the skeleton was embedded in the hard earth, it had been there a long time, possibly decades. He planted the pointed blade of the olive-green spade a foot from the hand and jumped on top, driving it two inches into the earth. Crouching, he rocked back and forth working the blade side to side until it sank another four inches. Very carefully he pried up the sandy, loam and set it aside. The canyon gave its flesh to the shovel. Little by little, he dug down and inward until he encountered ribs. The body appeared to be lying on its side with its knees drawn up. Perhaps he had stumbled upon something far older than the observatory, a Native American.

A flap of bleached pink fabric showed. He gently tugged but the earth wouldn't give it up, and he went back to the penknife. It took twenty minutes to finally expose the skull, wispy blond hair still attached. This was no Native American. He gently dug around with the penknife to free the skull, and when he finally exposed the teeth, they were perfect save for one gold filling.

Now what? The skeleton lay there surrounded by wisps of fabric. A cascade of dirt tumbled from the side of the excavation and fell on the skull. Kendall brushed it away and felt something sharp and hard. He sifted through the pile of dirt and retrieved what at first looked like a rusted screen fragment, but when he held it close he realized it was jewelry; a silver snowflake with a tiny silver loop at the top that might at one time have been an earring.

He slipped the fragment into his pocket, piled the dirt back over the skeleton so that it was completely concealed and went to bury his dead dog.

SIXTY-ONE
THE DETONATOR

Kendall phoned Ripon as soon as he reached the heights. He told the receptionist he'd had car trouble and would be in within the hour. Filthy, bleeding, and thirsty he got in his Corvette and stared at the key.

He turned the key. The engine started and settled down to idle. The gears and pedals worked as intended. He'd wasted enough time. Rather than return home to shower and dress he headed straight toward Pasadena. He could shower in the men's locker room and get a fresh T-shirt advertising Ripon games such as *Task Force* and *Battle Ax*. Nobody cared about dirty, torn jeans. He pulled into Ripon shortly before one, having endured a particularly glacial episode on the I-5.

He entered via the parking lot, heading for his office to drop off his laptop when Mick entered from the other end and stopped.

"Dude! What happened to you?"

"I tripped running in the hills. I'm fine. Is that meeting still going on?"

"Yeah, man. Ruben's meetings are like forever."

"Do me a favor. Grab me a fresh large T-shirt from that box in the storeroom, any design, and leave it on my desk."

Mick saluted. "Will do."

Kendall went into the locker room, stripped, and took a shower. As he dried off, he noticed a scrape along his jaw which made it look as if he'd been in a fight. Hair still damp, he went to the conference room and entered.

Six pairs of eyes turned toward him: Ruben, Patty Hansen, Wayne, Mick, and two kids he didn't recognize.

Ruben stood wide-eyed. "Are you all right? Judy from reception told us you'd had an accident!"

"It was no big deal. I fell down a cliff. Obviously, I wasn't seriously hurt. Very sorry I'm late, it won't happen again." He took a seat down the table next to one of the kids, a slim young woman with a tight cap of curly black hair and an Egyptian profile.

"Tonya, that's Kendall Coffin who's heading up *Off the Pig*. Kendall, Tonya, Ralph."

Nods all around.

"Love your stuff, man," Ralph said. "Big fan."

"To recap," Ruben said, "we are on schedule with *Off the Pig*. In August, we're going to start *The Detonator*."

Wayne clapped his hands.

"Far out!" Ralph said.

The Detonator was a movie franchise starring the late Gabe Winner who'd died hiking in the Colorado Rockies. The Detonator was Ayrton Rawls, an ex-Delta Forces merc now working for the government in a special capacity. He was Rambo, James Bond, and John McClane. Now that people no longer trusted the government, he'd gone rogue. A new Detonator was in the works starring Ryan Gosling.

"Kendall, you're going to head up this project."

Kendall looked at him startled.

Ruben peered. "Are you all right?"

"I'm sorry," Kendall said. "I lost my dog this morning. He got run over. That's why I'm so late."

The mood around the table morphed into cooing compassion. Tonya put her hand on his arm.

"Oh, you poor thing!"

"I'm so sorry!" Patty Hansen said.

"Dude, that sucks," said Ralph.

Kendall's eyes brimmed. He sniffed and reached for a tissue from a box on the credenza behind him.

"That really sucks, man," said Mick.

They'd all seen the pictures he'd posted on Facebook. They posted pictures of their own pets and in the rare case, children.

Kendall waved his arms. "It's all right. The show must go on. I'll cry later. Please carry on."

"You all know the Detonator! The studio shipped us a crate of DVDs so grab one and watch all the movies again. Kendall, can you come up with a scenario pitting Detonator against Islamic terrorists?"

"I don't know if that's going to fly, Rube."

Ruben placed his palms flat on the table and went bug-eyed. "What?! They're like the fuckin' Nazis in WWII! Who's going to object?"

Kendall couldn't believe Ruben was so naive. "CAIR, MSNBC, and probably most of the alphabet networks. They'll call it stereotyping. No prob. I'm an expert at these kinds of trade-offs. I worked in comics, remember? They could be right-wing fundamentalists."

"Not if they're Christian," Patty said.

"They could be right-wing, fundamentalist atheists, or some weird sect like Scientology. They want to blow up the world so they can come back, having survived in their specially shielded subterranean shelters and take over. They want to breed a new race of humans free of the flaws of the past."

Ruben snapped his fingers and pointed. "Now you're talking. Can you have scenarios for me next week?"

"Sure, boss, sure."

"You want help with the scenarios?" Wayne said.

"Sure. Keep it short."

Ralph waved his hand like a schoolboy. "I want to design Mose! Can I design Mose?"

Mose was the Detonator's trusty tech-wise sidekick, a six-foot-eight black man built like a Mack truck.

"We'll meet about it next week," Kendall said. "But if you want to shoot me some sketches that's fine."

Ruben rubbed his hands together in satisfaction. "Break out the champagne, Patty."

A smiling Patty stood and left the room.

"What's going on?" Wayne said.

"We'll wait for the champagne," Ruben said, opening the sideboard behind him and handing out clear plastic party glasses.

Patty returned with two bottles of Moet and set them on the table. Ruben opened them using a Western bandanna. The cork popped loudly. He filled the glasses and handed them out until everyone had one.

"Ready? Wayfarer Studios is having a huge Detonator exhibit at San Diego this weekend, and we're invited."

Ralph goggled. "All of us?"

"Well here's the deal," Ruben said. "I can't pay for all of you, but I can promise you free admittance, and I'll buy you dinner. Kendall, you and Patty are fully comped."

Mick pumped his fist in the air. "I can't believe it! We're going to San Diego!"

SIXTY-TWO
A STARTLING DISCOVERY

It was seven thirty by the time Kendall got home. Ronnie's car was parked behind his inert Avalon. He put the Stingray in the garage and went upstairs with a heavy heart. Something had gone out of him that morning. He'd grown used to having a happy puppy greeting.

Ronnie made up for it. She was waiting for him at the top of the stairs and gave him a big hug.

"How'd it go?" she said.

"All right. I'm going to San Diego. Ripon just got a platform with Wayfarer. We're doing the Detonator game."

"Ooooh! Can I come?"

"Sure. I'm going down Thursday night."

"I'll have to check. I may only be able to make it on Saturday. Were you all right with Shapiro?"

Kendall nodded.

"What did you do with him?"

"I took him to the shelter. Buck a pound to incinerate him and spread his ashes in the Sierra Nevada." Cringe of shame. He'd become adept at lying with Shirley.

"Why are you all banged up?"

"It's nothing. Let me change clothes. I'll be right back."

He went into his bedroom and stripped. He took the silver filigree from the grave in Griffith Park and put it in the change pocket of fresh blue jeans. He looked at himself in the mirror and couldn't come up with a decent lie to explain the scrape on his chin. Enticing aromas emanated from the kitchen.

"What's cookin'?" he shouted.

"Meatloaf. Baked potatoes. Salad. Would you pour me a couple fingers of Scotch over rocks?"

Kendall put on fresh clothes, went into the kitchen, stuck two tumblers under the icer, and filled them with ice. He went into the dining room and poured a couple fingers of Glenlivet in each glass and carried them into the kitchen. Ronnie had the counter-top TV on. Kendall turned it off and slipped the new Explorers Club into the counter-top CD player. He sat at the kitchen table and watched Ronnie cook and gradually the emptiness of the morning leached away replaced by love of a warm woman.

Kendall tended to give his heart away too easily. But this time, this time it would be different. Even after knowing her for a few short weeks, he saw she was a woman comfortable in her own skin, not a user nor a psychotic. He always knew those women were out there, but he'd had little personal experience.

He'd lived with Shirley for a year before she got up unsmiling one morning and said, "Either we get married, or I'm out of here."

That was the past. Hopefully, he'd learned. He wasn't about to pop the question just yet. He wasn't crazy. He was in his early forties and gun-shy. He'd thought Shirley was the bee's knees.

Ronnie was as different from Shirley as she was from every other woman on the planet.

Ronnie bopped to the music. "That's nice. Sounds like the Beach Boys."

"It's Explorers Club," Kendall said. "How long 'til dinner?"

"Fifteen minutes."

Kendall fingered the silver remnant in his pocket. "I'll be right back."

"Where you going?"

"Basement. I'm just going to dig out a suitcase."

He opened the basement door and turned on the lights. The steps descended into gloom. Down he went, eyes adjusting to the feeble light of a bare bulb encased in a cage. He went to the wardrobe room and turned on the light. A dozen suitcases stood shoulder to shoulder against one wall. Who knew what they contained? But that wasn't why he'd come. He went over to where the photo bins lay on a shelf and stood on a stool to slide off the top box. He carried the heavy box over to a makeup desk, replete with a big mirror surrounded by bulbs. He set the box down on the desk and turned on the mirror lights.

He took out the silver filigree. The photo box covered the entire desktop, but the desk had two slide-out shelves on either side. Kendall pulled one out and laid the earring on it. He pried the lid off the photo box and began going through the pictures. There were so many. One of a child in a Daniel Boone hat riding a tricycle, the pale colors of the fifties. Probably Wallanda. Photos of Wallanda as a college kid in blinding whites on the tennis court. The proud fraternity, the boys grinning with slicked-down hair in cardigans and ties.

One six-by-eight color photo showed Wallanda and Bree at their wedding—he in white tie and tails, she in a stunning white strapless gown—looking deliriously happy in front of swaying palm trees, white beach, and azure sea. Other photos showed the wedding party, young, tanned, beautiful, and fit. Wallanda doing the limbo rock beneath a bamboo pole held by two shrieking young women.

A photo of the buffet featuring an entire roast pig. Kendall figured Hawaii. Bride and groom at the helm of a dazzling white sailboat in a Caribbean chop. Dancing in a gazebo to a band that included ukulele and steel drum.

The next picture showed Wallanda grinning in front of an excavation, a backhoe visible in the background, with his hand on the shoulder of a slight, smaller, older man with a full head of white hair wearing a three-piece suit. The other man was not smiling, and it took Kendall a slow minute to realize that it was

Roark Dexter Smith—the architect—and that this was the house in which he now stood.

A six-by-ten color glossy, obviously out of sequence, taken at one of Wallanda's parties. A man sat on the sofa with his arm around the waist of a laughing young woman who wore nothing but a skirt. The man wore a severe black suit and tie, but the collar was open and the tie undone. His mouth was set as if he had a stick up his ass. He had slicked-back, black hair like a forties film villain, and wore round, black-rimmed glasses. Mandlebaum, plastic surgeon to the stars. Behind him, Wallanda and his date grinned at the camera. The young lady looked familiar. It was Crystal Feathers.

Kendall pulled out the chair and sat down. The photos showed a time-lapse of the house under construction: concrete foundation, wood framing, the walls rising in stucco.

The finished house. Wallanda and Bree posing in the art deco living room. The baby. The little girl. Dorothy on the same tricycle young Frank rode. Dorothy on her first two-wheeler. Dorothy on a horse with an English saddle, wearing one of those little leather jockey caps. Dorothy posing with her horse and a blue ribbon.

No photos of Dorothy past high school. She was replaced by Lannie. Lannie in pig tails and a party dress at her third birthday party. A coltish Lannie diving off the high board at summer camp.

Lannie and a gawkish young man with long dark hair and glasses posing in their prom duds. Lannie wore silver earrings.

"Kendall!" Ronnie called from the top of the stairs, her voice a distant echo. "Soup's on!"

"BE RIGHT UP!" Kendall bellowed bringing the photo close to his face. He picked up the artifact from the park. They were the same.

SIXTY-THREE

THE STONES

K endall put the photo back in the box, left it on the desk, and went upstairs. He had just solved one of Tinseltown's enduring mysteries.What happened to Lannie Wallanda. If he told the police, he'd have to explain what he'd been doing in Griffith Park, and that would bring scrutiny.

Scrutiny, scrutiny, scrutiny. He wanted to scream.

He was under intense pressure from previous secrets and feared that adding one more would blow the balloon, like the fat man in Monty Python's *Meaning of Life*. All through dinner he felt the need to tell Ronnie his secrets, but experience held him back. He'd learned not to do that with Shirley. Not that Ronnie was anything like Shirley, but a secret was a secret. Letting it out could cause more anxiety than holding it in.

Ronnie served dinner. Kendall accidentally knocked a slice of tomato on the floor and was surprised when Shapiro didn't clean it up. He turned away to hide his gut punch.

"You haven't heard anything about Mr. Wyrick, have you?" he asked.

"No," Ronnie said. "You'd think they'd notice him missing."

She looked into the distance.

"Unless he did something to make them think everything was fine. You really couldn't see into those tubes when they were powered up, and nobody's supposed to be in there."

"And nobody saw us go in? They had cameras up the yib-yob."

"I know," Ronnie said. "It's odd. They must have over a thousand cameras at Wyrick World. You can't expect someone to sit down and watch every second of everything being recorded. That's like 24,000 man-hours a day."

They were supposed to wake him up in 2001.

Kendall now lived with a permanent cringe, expecting the heavy knock of the police at any minute.

The chimes sounded "Beauty's Only Skin Deep."

"What's wrong?" Ronnie said.

"Nothing," Kendall said, getting to his feet and walking through the house. He peered through the peep hole. It was Torrance carrying his laptop. Kendall let him in. His heavy metal neighbor looked grim.

"What's up, dog?" Kendall said.

"Is now a good time? I wanted to show you what I found about the stones."

"Sure. Want some coffee? You have dinner?"

"I'm good."

Torrance greeted Ronnie with a hug. They took their coffee into the studio and sat side by side on the sofa while Torrance set his laptop up on the coffee table.

"Where's the dog?" Torrance said.

Kendall took a deep breath. "He got hit by a car. Had him cremated"

Torrance looked stricken. "Mannn, I am so sorry! That sucks, man. I will pray with you if you like."

"What did you find?"

Torrance dialed up the photo he'd taken of one of the stones showing a female figure in the style of Egyptian hieroglyphs carrying a basket on her head from which jutted five or six rods. The stone was old and very worn, and the image was fuzzy.

"This stone was taken from the Temple of Enlil in the ancient Sumerian city of Kish. It depicts the female deity Nadras Bek, a nightmare figure who collected penises. That's what's in the basket."

Kendall's throat went dry. "How do you know this?"

"My friend is Professor of Ancient Civilizations at UCLA. He said the stone was probably taken from the British Museum and it's a felony to possess. Don't worry. I never mentioned your name."

"What about the others?"

"There are two others."

Torrance brought up a fresco in the manner of the Mayans. "This was probably taken from a Toltec temple in Belize."

The picture showed three women: an old woman on the left as indicated by her hair and posture, a mature upright woman in the middle, and a girl on the right.

"A Toltec deity. They call her Nowad RebI."

"I see three figures. Which one is Nowad Reb?"

"They all are."

"Did you come across someone named Nedrebo?"

Torrance looked at him. "No. But the names are similar. What's Nedrebo?"

"I don't know. You said there are three."

"Yeah," Torrance said stroking the keys. He took a sip of coffee while the image came up. It showed a woman wearing a turban riding a dragon-like creature with seven heads. "This is a Russian icon from the 7th century and was probably looted from a church. It's the Whore of Babylon."

A centipede ran down Kendall's spine. "What do you think it means?"

Torrance swallowed. "There's something in the house."

"What?"

"I don't know. I've been praying for you. I'm going to consult with Pastor John this weekend. He's a good guy. He might have some advice. You're welcome to come."

"He's going to tell me to sell the house," Kendall said with surprising bitterness.

"It may be that Smith had an ulterior motive. I don't claim to be an expert on the occult, but it seems to me Smith designed this place to incorporate powerful spiritual forces."

"Fuck!" Kendall said.

Torrance clapped Kendall on the shoulder. "Cheer up! Jesus loves you. We will figure it out. I got friends in the Latino community maybe could put us in touch with an exorcist."

"Yeah."

"Come on. Forget about it! What's new?"

"Hey, I'm going to San Diego. Ripon's got a booth, and they want me down there. It's this weekend. I'll be gone from Thursday until Monday. Could you keep an eye on the place? Pick up my mail and newspapers?"

"No prob."

Kendall reached in his pocket. "Here's the key to the front door."

Torrance took it. "Say, I wished you would have stuck around after the memorial. They had our songs on the jukebox!"

"I'd like to trade comics for your CDs."

"You bet," Torrance said standing.

Kendall rose with him. "How's the wife and kid?"

"Great, great. Tommy's prepping for the science fair. He'll be a freshman this year at UC Irvine. Gonna cost me an arm and a leg."

"Yeah. Let's get together when I get back and listen to some tunes."

Torrance held up his fist. "Right on."

Kendall bopped fists. "You've got my phone number."

Kendall let Torrance out, making certain the door was locked behind him.

Ronnie and Kendall went to bed. He couldn't get it up.

Ronnie put her arm around him. "Don't worry, baby. It happens to all men."

"Not to me."

"You want to tie me up?"

"No!"

"Why not? That was the hottest fuck you ever had."

The thought of fucking her bound made him hard.

"Never mind. Where were we?"

SIXTY-FOUR
NIGHT WITCH

WEDNESDAY MORNING

The Avalon started instantly. Kendall sat in the driver's seat with a stick up his ass. Since he'd bought it used at 40,000 miles, it had been stone reliable. The only glitch in its long and honorable career had occurred the previous morning. He knew there would be no more problems.

The Corvette had showed him what it wanted to show. The question remained what action he should take. Perhaps an anonymous tip. Best give the critters enough time to lay waste Shapiro's collarless body. All the shelter pups had chips implanted, but the LAPD had better things to do than check for chips in rotting animal carcasses. He'd do it when he returned from San Diego.

He drove to Pasadena in a fog but snapped into focus when he sat at his desk. *Off the Pig* was ahead of schedule and he had time to work up three Detonator scenarios. Russian gangsters, Islamic terrorists, right-wing nut jobs. He threw himself into the work so he wouldn't have to think about the swords over his head.

He quit at six and joined the queue on the 110. As he sat stuck in traffic, he looked around. At least half the drivers were on the phone. Well, why not? What else was there to do on the 110?

Obviously, the séance didn't work. He needed an exorcist. But where did you find someone who could exorcise a house? Torrance would bring in a *brujo* with a bone through his nose. Crazy thoughts flitted like purple ravens. Hire an arsonist. But that was a felony and would endanger the whole neighborhood. There had to be someone—some system—that could clear his house of whatever it was that lived there. He had no doubt that whatever was in the house opened the front door allowing Shapiro out. The house's power obviously extended to the Corvette.

It took him ninety minutes to traverse the fifteen miles between Ripon and the house. He microwaved a pizza, drank Odell's, watched *Rolling Thunder*, and went to bed. He slept poorly because of the beer and woke to the faint echo of a woman screaming.

Ripon had provided a limo for employees wanting to go to SDCC, but Kendall preferred to take his car. He packed a decent jacket and shirt for the industry parties, and whatever else he needed, including his laptop, sketchpad, and pencil case. He filled a fat water bottle, checked tire pressure, and turned the key.

Whine, whine, whine. Panic seized him. It grew out of the shadows at the end of the street and smacked into him. He sweated through his fresh clothes, heart hammering.

Dear God, what now? Why did it want him to take the Stingray? It was too late to grab the limo or make other arrangements. If he tried to deviate, he'd only make matters worse. With a lead ball in his stomach, he transferred his bags to the Stingray and headed south on the I-5 beneath an overcast sky. The car obeyed his commands.

At least from the I-5 he had occasional glimpses of the ocean. He would get out there one day soon with his Silver Surfer board. Maybe Tommy could teach him. WAVE played Laurie Biagini, The Bye Bye Blackbirds, and Lisa Mychols. He crept into San Diego around three thirty surrounded by tour buses and trucks. Ruben had somehow booked a suite of rooms at the

Grand Hyatt, a feat akin to a manned moon landing. The con was already in full swing as scores of policemen did their best to hold the human tide of freaks, geeks, nerds, monsters, and superheroes at bay. It was past four when Kendall finally pulled under the porte cochere and handed off the keys to a bug-eyed valet.

Kendall handed him a five-dollar bill. "That's my baby, understand?"

"Yes, sir!" the kid said, gently sliding into the leather seat.

Kendall entered the terrarium-like lobby and immediately spotted two comic book writers he knew drinking at a table. Kendall turned away and got small. He did not want to get dragged down in lobby discussions. The lobby was such a screaming zoo nobody noticed him.

"Oh, yes, Mr. Coffin! We have a reservation for you," said the young Indian in a brown suit behind the counter. He gave her his credit card for incidentals and rode up in the eerily silent elevator to the ninth floor. When he got in his room, his phone light was blinking. Message from Patty.

"We're all meeting in the lobby at seven for dinner. Let me know if you need anything."

He called her back and confirmed, then called Ronnie. Her phone went straight to message.

"Took me seven hours door to door, but I'm here. Love you, babe. Call me when you get a chance."

He showered, changed into khakis, light blue shirt, and sports jacket, and went to the lobby. He was early, so he sat at the bar and had a martini.

"Kendall!"

He turned. A slight middle-aged man with soulful eyes and a mustache. For an instant, he drew a blank then the name popped up.

"Bill!" They embraced.

Bill Reinhold had drawn the *Badger, Punisher, Batman,* and *Silver Surfer* among many other titles and had been a longtime

SDCC attendee. "Haven't seen you for ages. What are you up to?"

Kendall brought Bill up to speed.

"So sorry about Shirley," Bill said.

Kendall waved it off.

"You quit Wyrick?" Bill said in disbelief.

"I'm much happier designing games."

"I hear they're going to sneak a new *Star Wars* film this weekend."

Kendall saw Ruben across the room wearing a black suit over a white shirt with an open collar. Patty was with him in a sleek, shimmering blue cocktail dress, her honey-colored hair in a bob.

"There's my party, Bill. Talk to ya."

Patty had reserved a room at Sally's on the Water. Ruben, Patty, Wayne, Roger, Tonya, Ralph, and Kendall sat at a long table with a view of the bay, white yacht masts sticking up over the trees. Ruben made a speech praising God, Allah, and Crom.

He held up a handful of laminated passes on lanyards. "Here are your passes. We got them early because we ... got ... THE POWA!"

Patty led the enthusiastic applause. The table drank and waxed effusive. Kendall excused himself, went out on the patio warmed by an inland breeze, and phoned Ronnie. Again, he got her answering service, hung up without leaving a message.

At nine thirty he quit the party, buzzed from three martinis, and made his way through the lobby, which was even more crowded than when he'd checked in. He stuck to the walls wishing to avoid any contact and made it to the elevator in peace.

Got off on the eerily quiet ninth floor and walked to his room. As he was about to insert his key card, he heard a sound like a rumbling stomach and looked up. He froze, neck rigid, and backed away with a silent scream in his mouth.

An old woman with a dandelion head of white hair, her withered hand clasped around a stick, shuffled toward him in a shapeless burlap dress. She was the picture of Baba Yaga, a night witch from Lord of the Rings, a creature from the darkest recess of Kendall's imagination.

She extended a gnarled hand toward him. Kendall put a hand to his throat and gurgled.

She straightened up and grinned. "Hey! Relax! It's just cosplay."

Kendall forced a grin as he reinserted his key. "I knew that."

SIXTY-FIVE

THE PHONE RANG

Since the phone call, Portia barely ate or slept. She was at an age where she had few friends and no family. A ringing phone had been a happy sound, connecting her to the world. No longer. The spirit in the house had killed that for her.

Racked with indecision. Should she get rid of the phone altogether? It terrified her. She couldn't pass it now without cringing. Those old Princesses, there was no way to turn off the ringer. All she could do was unplug it. She had no other link to the outside world.

She'd had a computer, but when she went online an interstellar storm raged in her skull: a screaming cacophonous fit as of a million banshees, heavy metal bands, carnival barkers, jihadists, fundamentalist preachers, movie previews, scandals, and crimes against humanity. She sold it within a week.

The so-called smartphones were just a personal hell you carried in your purse.

She knew she had to tell Kendall about the call, but she was so terrified of the phone she wouldn't go near it. She knew that the instant she touched it, it would ring. She decided to walk down to the 7/11 and use the pay phone. The thing couldn't possibly track her there. She went to the big bowl in which she dropped business cards, carried it into the living room, sat on the sofa, and placed it in her lap. Ozzy jumped up and lay down in the bowl.

"No, my dear," Portia chided, lifting the cat up and setting it aside.

"Meooow," Ozzy protested.

Portia shook out a Camel and lit it with a Bic. She inhaled deeply and blew out a lustrous cloud of gray smoke. She went through the cards, wondering where she'd got them. Realtors, bankers, tattoo artists, tattoo removal, lawn services, catering. At last, she found Kendall's card; a tiny Doc Strange casting a spell in color with Kendall's signature, a stylized 'K' inside a tiny coffin, his email and phone.

She set the bowl on the table and pulled herself up with a grunt puffing smoke. Ozzy wound around her legs like Shriners on mini-bikes.

"What is it, Ozzums?" she coughed. "Are we humgrems?"

She went into the kitchen and opened a can of Friskies Beef Brisket, forked it out into Ozzy's bowl. "Fuckin' cat lives better than third world children," Portia growled.

She got her walking boots out of the closet, sat down in a wood chair to put them on, grabbed her purse, and left her house. It was nine o'clock Thursday evening. Overcast skies had brought the smog. Funny how pollution like oil in a lake or a layer of smog could produce such beautiful colors. The night glowed.

She walked west toward the gentrified recrudescence. There was a commercial block two blocks down with the convenience store. She was sure she'd seen a pay phone there. She passed a couple of boys with backward-turned ball caps lounging against a '99 Mustang with the trunk open blasting Kanye. Portia kept her eyes straight ahead and walked by them. They were in for a big surprise. This wasn't Compton. The cops would give you a ticket for creating a public nuisance.

The commercial block contained Cup o' Joe—filled with earnest young things staring into their laptops, tablets, and

Razrs—Cost Cutters, Fong's Laundry, The Miracle Lounge, and the 7/11 on the corner. Portia went into the 7/11. A young Pakistani man behind the counter smiled at her. She looked around.

"Where's the pay phone?" she said.

"We never have pay phone," the proprietor said.

Portia looked perplexed.

"Is it an emergency?"

Portia went over to the counter. "In a way. I'm Portia DeManning. I live down the block."

"Yes, I see you in here sometimes. You have the cat."

Portia smiled. "That's right. I need to make a phone call, and my phone isn't working."

The man reached into his pocket and proffered his phone. "Use mine."

"Thank you, Mr. ..."

"Eugene. You call me Eugene."

"And you call me Portia, Eugene."

Amicable relations established, Portia took the phone toward the rear where there was less noise. She opened it up, pulled out Kendall's card, and put her finger to the face.

The phone rang. She jumped. She took the phone back to Eugene and handed it to him.

Eugene put the phone to his head. "This is Eugene."

He listened quizzically for a minute then handed the phone back to Portia. "It's for you."

Dread stretched barracuda jaws as she took the phone. "Hello?" she croaked.

"Ladybird, ladybird fly away home, your house is on fire, and your children are gone. All except one and his name is Ozzy. Better get going, he ain't looking too rosy."

Portia gasped and coughed at the same time. She couldn't get a breath. Eugene looked alarmed, headed for the end of the counter but Portia was out of there, dropping his phone and running for the door.

She stumbled across the street heading east, barely noticing the blinking orange light. She was still in the street when the light changed. Loud honks. She stumbled on feeling a sharp ache in her side, past the strobing cop car, the cop writing the rap boys a ticket. A young woman out for a walk with her Sheltie stared at her in alarm as she pounded past. She was so exhausted by the time she reached her house she hung on the stair rail doubled over wheezing like a sucking drain.

A sudden tremor flashed from the base of her skull down her left arm. Her left leg wouldn't cooperate. She had to drag it up the steps holding onto the banister with both hands. Heaving and wheezing she unlocked the door and went inside. She was having a stroke. She had to call 911.

Where was Ozzy?

She went into the living room, turned on the light, and screamed.

Ozzy dangled from a thin rope attached to the overhead fan.

The phone rang.

SIXTY-SIX

THE WYRICK PANEL

K endall met Wayne and Mick for breakfast at Sally's off the lobby. Kendall had a throbbing headache from the night before and had slept poorly. He'd tried Ronnie again that morning and went straight to voice mail.

Wayne and Mick could barely suppress their excitement. This was Mick's first trip to the Comic Con.

"I hear Ryan Gosling's here!" Mick said.

"Fuck that noise!" Wayne said. "Zoe Saldana's here!"

They walked along the harbor to the convention center surrounded by thousands of fans, many of them outrageously accoutred as their favorite characters. Many others were their own creations. There was an unusually large percentage of the morbidly obese and people who had rendered themselves unemployable via facial tats and piercings.

Foot traffic was slow. People were everywhere.

"I've counted five Wolverines," Wayne said.

"I got six Wolverines and four Deadpools," Mick said.

"I'll raise you two Elektras and a Jessica Rabbit," Wayne said.

They joined the line marked VENDORS behind hundreds of others anxious for the doors to open at ten. The line shuffled forward. They picked up their program booklets and goody bags from the PRO table and entered the main hall, a vast room that could and did hold 125,000 people. Even at that hour of the morning, the floor was jammed. Within minutes it would become so packed it was virtually impossible to walk in any direction without waiting for someone to step aside.

Armed with a map they made their way slowly toward the Wayfarer booth. Lego had blocked off a huge area for an immense recreation of Middle Earth. Marvel's booth featured a larger-than-life sized animatronic Hulk and Spider-Man. DC's featured a life-sized recreation of the Bat Cave holding six different Batmobiles. A sign said George Clooney was set to sign on Saturday.

Fans and pros called out to Kendall on the way, exchanging greetings and cards. Everybody kept pushing forward. The PA system blasted incomprehensible gibberish with a Max Headroom voice. A nine-foot dire wraith staggered their way on hidden stilts. Kendall didn't see how he was able to keep his balance. Light and sound strobed and shrieked from every other booth.

It was no place for epileptics.

And here came a rotund hausfrau pushing a double-wide tram containing two adorable children dressed as Smurfs, running into shins, issuing serial apologies, always moving forward. "So sorry ... whoops ... very sorry ..."

A Harley Quinn eased her way through the crowd carrying a mallet the size of a bass drum. The Justice League of America trooped by. The Wayfarer booth jutted forth like the prow of a ship. In fact, it *was* the prow of a ship, like Orson Welles's pulpit in *Moby Dick*. The next Detonator film took place on a warship in the Persian Gulf. A ten-foot Ryan Gosling covered with camo looked determined. A tall epicene man in a dazzling sharkskin suit with a skinny tie and glasses stood behind the counter talking to Ruben. Kendall and the boys went behind the table.

"Ah," Ruben said. "Here they are. Boys, this is Matt Mason, head of Wayfarer. Matt, my head designer Kendall Coffin, Wayne Barkley, and Mick Runge."

They shook hands.

"We're having a panel Friday at five," Mason said. "I'd like you boys to be on it. It's in the program book. We're going to announce the Detonator video game and Kendall, later I'd like to pick your brain about a possible Detonator comic."

"You want us at the booth for any reason?" Kendall said.

"Feel free to use this as a base while roaming. A lot of your fans have been asking about you, Kendall. I told them you'd be here signing at some point."

"Any time," Kendall said.

Kendall, Wayne, and Mick pulled up folding chairs and sat behind the table which offered free Detonator and Ripon posters, a bowl of candy, and Detonator pens with the release date. A young man dressed as the Riddler swished up and down in front of their table swinging a cane and proclaiming as fruitily as possible, "When is a room not a room? When it's a mush room!"

"I'm gonna kill that guy," Wayne said.

"Hold on," Kendall said. "The crowd will sweep him away."

An instant later the Riddler was gone.

A steady string of comic fans sought Kendall's autograph and implored him to return to comics. Wayne and Mick wandered. They went out on the terrace for lunch around one. Wayne held up the con program.

"Dudes! There's a Wyrick Panel at two! They're gonna talk about the whole year's releases. Galaxy War, Ultra Pigeon, maybe a new line of comics!"

Kendall reached for the program. "Let me see that." Nate Polis was appearing on the panel.

At two Kendall, Wayne, and Mick were among the last admitted to the Wyrick Panel held in a room that could accommodate 400 people. They found three seats in the back row on the left. The room bristled with anticipation. Five people including Nate and Alice Sommers sat behind the table on which rested three mikes and two pitchers of ice water.

A mesomorph in a blue suit over a *Galaxy Wars* T-shirt and a bad combover sat in the middle. "Folks, I'm Wilson Milner, Vice

President in charge of film production at Wyrick Films. On my left are Paul Brenner and Tim Cahoon, who are producing the new *Galaxy Wars* movie. On my right are Nate Polis and Alice Sommers who are producing *Night Shifts*."

Nate described it as an erotic thriller. He and Alice offered a little boilerplate, ignoring a determined young woman in the first row in severe haircut and glasses who kept raising her hand. "We'll get to audience questions, shortly," Milner said.

Brenner and Cahoon showed stills from the new *Galaxy Wars* to much approval. Forty minutes in Milner said, "We now open the panel for questions."

The young woman sprang to her feet. "Mr. Polis, there are rumors that *Night Shifts* involves bestiality and sodomy. How does this fit into the Wyrick canon?"

"While it's true *Night Shifts* is an erotic thriller, we ask you to withhold judgment until you see the movie. As you know, context is everything."

"Is it true this will be the first Wyrick with an 'X' rating?"

"Are you a blogger?" Nate said.

"So what if I am?"

"Well, San Diego is for fans. This isn't a news conference …"

The young woman barked in disbelief. Milner grabbed the mike. "Do we have any *Galaxy Wars* questions?"

The young woman was shouted down.

Kendall didn't even notice the new *Galaxy Wars* material. He was sorry he'd come, but there was no way to get up and leave without drawing attention to himself.

He leaned forward and surveyed the crowd to his right. Every seat was taken. Across the center aisle against the wall, he spotted an older gentleman in a beret and sunglasses who looked familiar. It wasn't until the gentleman, perhaps feeling the weight of Kendall's gaze, turned and looked at him that Kendall realized who it was.

SIXTY-SEVEN
COFFEE WITH THE MAN

Kendall told Wayne and Mick to go on without him and waited in the hall as the room emptied for the next panel. Robocops and Rogues vogued up and down the broad corridor. There was no place in the city free of costumed super persons.

Wyrick was one of the last to emerge. Kendall fell into step beside him.

"Remember me, Mr. Wyrick?"

"Of course, young fellow. Really not surprised to see you here. What's your name?"

"Kendall Coffin. Want to get a cup of coffee?"

Wyrick put a hand on Kendall's arm. "I will, but understand I wish to remain incognito."

They left the convention center and walked up to Seaport Village where Kendall bought two coffees at a Starbucks. They sat at a wrought-iron table with an umbrella looking out to sea. An aircraft carrier anchored in the distance. White gulls swooped and dived screeching. The Village was busy but blessedly free of superheroes.

"Sir, how is it you're getting around so well? Didn't you suffer any after-effects from suspended animation?"

Wyrick smiled. "Let's just say I hold several patents which

are not generally known. I must say I'm grateful to you and the young lady, Kendall. If you hadn't come along, I doubt anyone would have revived me. I doubt it very much. The Wyrick I see today is not what I envisioned."

"How is it you haven't been missed?"

Wyrick exposed lupine teeth. "All that security and nobody knows nothin'. I want it this way. Once I reveal myself, all hell's gonna break loose."

"So you plan to reveal yourself?"

"At a time and place of my choosing. In the meantime, I would appreciate your discretion on this matter, and the young lady's."

"Of course. No one would believe us anyway. Sir, as I mentioned before, I'm living in the house built by Frank Wallanda."

"That son of a bitch ... excuse my French," Wyrick said through gritted teeth. "Surprised he didn't die of AIDS. Good filmmaker though."

"I think the place is haunted."

Wyrick leaned back and lowered his sunglasses. "Why?"

Kendall told him everything that happened since moving into the house.

"Sorry to hear about your wife and your dog."

"Not a problem."

"So what do you want from me?"

Kendall sighed. Darryl Wyrick was not an exorcist or ghost buster. "I don't know. I spoke to Bree briefly before she died, and she warned me against something called a nedrebo."

"I'm sorry I don't know what that is."

"Sir, did you know your granddaughter Lannie?"

"A delightful child. How is Lannie doing?"

Kendall stared at his plate.

"Tell me."

"The house came with a Corvette," Kendall began and then recounted the events involving his excursion in the park. When he was finished, Wyrick took off his sunglasses and looked out to sea. Wyrick was no fossil. He seemed sharp as a razor.

"You're telling me the car drove you to Lannie's grave."

"I have no other explanation."

"I see. Let me dig around and get back to you."

"You don't happen to have a cell phone, do you sir?"

Wyrick reached inside his jacket pocket and produced a Razr. "When I retired, these didn't exist. I wake up, and everything Dick Tracy predicted is true. A young lady showed me how to work this. I spent four hours in a Best Buy the other day learning how to navigate the internet. I don't have a computer yet, but I'm going to get one. We predicted something like this in *Velva Visits Venus*."

Kendall handed the magnate his card. "Sir, if you need anything please don't hesitate to ask."

"I appreciate that, young man. Let me give you my phone number."

Kendall entered it into his phone. No one had called. "Are you going back to the con?"

"No," Wyrick said. "I'll catch a taxi. I have a room at the Double Tree."

"You must have prepared well," Kendall said.

The old man smiled. "I was a Boy Scout. Their motto used to be 'Be prepared.' Now it's 'Celebrate diversity, fisting, and perversion, take it up the ass that's what we're urgin.' Excuse my French."

Kendall headed back to the con. By the time he returned he was due at the Ripon Panel. The room was nearly full when he arrived, with Ruben, Patty Hansen, and Wayne on the raised dais behind the table. Kendall joined them. Ruben introduced them and briefly described the games. No one objected to the premise behind *Off the Pig*. They cheered when Ruben announced the Detonator game. He opened it up for questions. A tall, thin buzz cut sleeved in blue tats which highlighted the whiteness of his skin stuck his hand up.

"This is for Kendall Coffin. Will you be returning to comics?"

"Sometime I'm sure."

Buzz Cut was waiting for him when he left the room, clutching a thick stack of *Doc Stranges* each in its own plastic bag with backer board. "Mr. Coffin, I hope you don't mind …"

"Not at all, but you're gonna have to filet them for me." They found a place on the wall and sunk down. The man began removing comics.

"Should I make this out to anyone?"

"Make it out to Lowell. Man, you drew the forbidden agonies of cham in that book. Aren't you worried that the church is going to come after you?"

Kendall looked quizzically at the man, but he appeared to be serious. Up closer, he was older than he first appeared, possibly in his forties but in excellent shape. He had a silver bolt through his nose.

"Not really," Kendall said signing as fast as he could.

"'Cause obviously you have the Gift, am I right? I mean, these comics, they're just a form of power you practice when you're not doing your real job."

"What's that?" Kendall said already bored.

"Fighting evil."

Kendall finished signing the books and handed them back. "Here you go, thanks for your support!"

Kendall headed toward the escalators as fast as he could, which wasn't fast.

"LIKE YOUR HOUSE, MAN!" Buzz Cut yelled after him.

Kendall swung around, but the man was gone.

SIXTY-EIGHT
BAD MANOR

The Wayfarer party took place at Trader Joe's downtown. The place was packed by the time Kendall arrived at eight. Ruben had been hobnobbing with gamers, movers, and shakers all day, inviting everybody. He stood by the bar, face flushed, shirt open, regaling a rapt audience with stories. As Kendall entered the room, a familiar voice called out, "Yo! The man!"

Kendall turned to find Nate, with one arm around a fresh young thing and the other clutching a cocktail, heading his way. Nate seemed genuinely glad to see him. There were no feuds in San Diego; at least not face to face.

Nate let go long enough to slap Kendall on the back. "How the hell are ya?"

"Great, Nate, great. Who's your friend?"

"This is Heather," Nate said.

She was a good-looking honey blond, all curves. "Hi!" she said. "Heather Collins."

Kendall put out his hand. "Kendall Coffin."

Heather's eyes went wide. "Are you the Kendall Coffin who drew Doc Strange?"

"Guilty."

"Oooh, I want to talk to you. Did you know they're making a movie starring Keanu Reeves?"

"I heard it was that Brit guy who played Sherlock."

Nate's head swiveled. "Hey, I gotta go talk to a guy, be right back."

Kendall and Heather were left alone in a corner. They sat next to each other on a love seat.

"I looooove your art," Heather said breathlessly, placing a hand on his arm. "I work for a small game designer called Human Head Studios. We're putting together a game I think might be right up your alley."

Kendall smiled. "That's great, but I'm working for Ripon now. That's why I'm here."

"Well, you can't be working all the time! We would pay you as a consultant. The reason I think you're the man for the job, the game is called *Bad Manor*, and it's about a haunted house. Like the houses you drew in Doc Strange! You did that one Victorian three-story for that story about the giant hand …"

"*House of Blood*. We did that through Marvel Max because it was adults only."

"I have them all. *Bad Manor's* this house in Louisiana that was designed by an insane architect …"

"What's his name?" Kendall said.

Heather stopped with lips parted. "Excuse me?"

"What's the architect's name in your game?"

"Gideon Geiser. Why?"

"Just wondering. Names are important."

"Aren't they! We would like you to design the house."

They exchanged cards, hers said, Heather Collins, VP Development, Human Head Studios, San Diego.

"Oh, you're from here."

"Yes, I have an apartment in La Jolla. In fact, I have all your comics there. Could I get you to sign them?"

"Of course."

"There you are," said a female voice. Kendall turned. Alice Sommers approached smiling. She looked like a Motown star.

Kendall rose to shake Alice's hand.

"I was so sorry to hear you left the project," she said. "You were doing a fantastic job."

"Thank you, Alice. Alice, Heather. Heather, Alice."

Heather waved with a forced smile.

"Well, I won't take too much of your time. Why did you quit?"

"To tell you the truth, Alice, the subject matter made me extremely uncomfortable."

A crease of concern formed between Alice's brown eyes. "Really? Are you a religious person?"

"Not extremely. I guess I'm just a prude."

Alice shook her head slowly. "I never would have thought that."

"Where's your partner?" Kendall said.

Alice looked surprised. "Who?"

"Desmond."

"Said he had too much work to do. Probably has a new girl-friend." She shook her head pityingly. "That boy can never get enough pussy."

Alice spotted someone important across the room and excused herself. Kendall sat down next to Heather who put her hand on his knee.

"How'd you like to come over to my place and sign my comics?"

Kendall grinned. "I'd love to, but I'm in a committed rela-tionship."

Heather went wide-eyed. "Really?"

"I know. Quaint, ain't it?"

"You must not be from around here," she said.

"Nope."

"Well now, I'm really attracted to you, but I respect you, too, so I guess I'll take my cute little butt somewhere else."

SIXTY-NINE
DEAD MAN'S CURVE

Kendall drank more than he ought, took a taxi back to the hotel and it still took a half hour. Hours after the convention center closed its doors the streets were awash with superheroes, villains, manga characters, and uniquely styled individuals. The hotel bar was chock-a-block including several industry colleagues. Kendall made himself small and skirted the lobby on his way to the elevators.

He got to his room without incident, peeled off his clothes down to his jockey shorts and went to bed, knowing the alcohol would prevent him from getting any rest. He fell into REM sleep, accepting the troubling dreams as the price of passage through the night.

He was at a party at his old house in Omaha. Ronnie was there, as were Torrance, Greg, and Heather. Shirley entered the room looking for him. In his dream, he felt deep disappointment and betrayal. She was supposed to be dead! It wasn't fair! Just when things were looking up. He had to get out of there.

He left the house, which was no longer in Omaha but now in Los Angeles, and looked for his car. There were cars parked up and down the street but none of them were his, and he had only the vaguest recollection where he'd left it. Fuck it. He'd hunt it down on foot. A police car cruised slowly by shining its spotlight on him. He put up his hands to shield the glare and waited for the inevitable, but the police car kept going.

His relief was short-lived. A new dark-green XKE followed the cop car, bass blaring Hard Core King. The driver abruptly shut off his system resulting in a vast withering silence. Kendall watched the taillights with dread as the XKE crept slowly up the street and turned the corner.

Kendall woke covered with sweat at one thirty, took a piss, and went back to "sleep." The dream picked up where it had left off. He was looking for his car, thought he spotted it on a side street but when he got there it was an empty parking spot. His Corvette cruised by with no one at the wheel. Kendall chased after it yelling, "Stop! Stop!" but the Vette was heedless and peeled out leaving two broad black strips on the street. A moment later, it passed him going the other way with a rotting corpse at the wheel.

Disgusted, he walked back to his house. The entry stairs seemed Mayan in length and grade. It took him forever to reach the gates and enter the foyer. He entered an empty house barely visible through a predawn half-light. Dust lay everywhere as in a freshly opened sarcophagus.

His phone rang. He reached his hand into his empty pocket.

Kendall woke up. His eyes went to the radio/clock. It was four in the morning, and the house phone blared loud enough to wake the dead. He fumbled for the receiver.

"Hello?" he said heart racing.

"Hellooo," said a seductive female voice.

"Ronnie?" he said, knowing as he said it that it wasn't her.

"Noooo, but I'm a big fan of your work."

"Heather!" he said, proud of his memory and feeling an absurd prick of guilt.

"Noooo …"

Kendall gripped the receiver white-knuckled. "Who is this?"

"Let's just say it's a house call."

"Who are you?"

"This is your house calling."

"Where's Ronnie?"

"She's here with me. And she's not alone."

Kendall held the receiver away from his head. The earpiece released an electronic crackle, and he slammed it down, got up, threw on his clothes, threw his belongings into his suitcase, went down to the front desk, and checked out. The sun rose as he hit the freeway heading north. At that hour, the traffic was relatively light, but as he approached Oceanside, he saw a long line of stalled traffic stretching north. Accident. Stuck in traffic, seething, he pulled out his phone to call Torrance.

The phone was inert, battery dead. Kendall rummaged around in the center console for his charger then realized he'd left it at the hotel, plugged into a socket in the bathroom. He was in a frenzy, electricity shooting out his fingers. He had to calm down before he did something stupid, like driving up the shoulder which would only garner a citation from the CHP if not worse.

The Stingray's license plates were from 1965. It was unregistered. Merkle had croaked in his house. Next day the dog dies. Cops didn't believe in coincidence. Where there's bass, there's drums.

He considered just talking to a cop, but what would he tell them? They had better things to do than listen to his nonsense. He inched along another forty-five minutes before exiting east on 78, which was crammed due to like-minded motorists fleeing gridlock.

"Please God," he said, "let her be okay."

In frustration, he stabbed the radio. "He rolled down the window of his shiny new Jag and challenged me then and there to a drag …"

The irony of the beach/car thing was not lost on Kendall. Here at the edge of manifest destiny, the land of surfing and cruising, the freeways resembled long narrow parking lots where drivers exchanged gunfire over perceived slights. He turned north on the 15 at Escondido, but this too was filled with traffic heading north. It was eight thirty Saturday morning, and the whole world seemed to be on the move. Tractor-trailers vied for space with enormous campers towing Jeeps with canoes on the roof. Low-riders hopped up and down in frustration. Crazed bikers split lanes.

Traffic lurched north like blood in a clogged artery. The intersections were weak points in the artery where the corpuscles went crazy driving on the shoulder, honking, flipping the bird trying to gain an advantage. Kendall cut west on 78 along with half the population all apparently intent on reaching Los Angeles. He crept along between twenty and thirty miles per hour resisting the urge to mash the accelerator and lay on the horn.

He pulled off at Oceanside and went into a Marie Callender's to relieve himself and phone Torrance. The restaurant was old enough to have pay phones in the back corridor leading to the rest rooms. Kendall ran his credit card through the slot and phoned Torrance. It rang four times and went to voice mail.

"Torrance, it's Kendall. My phone's dead I'm using a pay phone. Listen, do me a favor, willya? Go next door and see if everything's all right. Be careful. Maybe you shouldn't go alone. Take Tommy. I'll phone you as soon as I get a chance."

He bought a cruller and coffee to go, gassed up at a Quik Stop, and joined the thrombosis oozing north on the I-5. Traffic thinned north of Oceanside, and he got the Stingray up to seventy. A Porsche and a Ferrari passed him on the right doing at least a hundred. Two miles down the road they were pulled off on the shoulder surrounded by flashing light bars and armed cops.

Clouds grew out of the west covering the coast with a gray shroud. The radio said Angelenos should brace for possibly heavy rains that evening. He switched around AM until he found an all-news channel. Not a word about the bodies found in Griffith Park. A new day brought new bodies.

Although there was nothing of which Kendall could think connecting him to the body he'd dumped, he'd read enough true crime to know there were dogged detectives out there who simply never gave up. His imagination ran wild. Perhaps they would find his tire tracks and match it to his car. Perhaps there were hidden cameras in the park spying on people. They said that in every homicide the perp leaves some trace of himself at the scene. Kendall had killed no one, but still, that boy had died in his window well. What if there were something in the well: a button, a needle, some scrape of DNA?

The rains couldn't come soon enough.

It took him five hours to drive from Newport Beach to Long Beach. At one point, he got out of his stopped car, shinnied down the embankment, and pissed in the bushes. He was not alone. A tractor/trailer had overturned and burst into flames on the 605 effectively closing the highway. Kendall had no choice but to drive up the coast as clouds scudded in until the city was overcast, and the air smelled of rain. While inching along on the 405, he heard shots behind him and minutes later the wail of sirens.

He switched back to WAVE which played surf music as if the world were Beach Blanket Bingo. Keepin' that dream alive. They played Explorers Club's "One More Kiss" followed by Lauri Biagini's "Run to the Sun." The ocean was battleship gray with silvery highlights as the endless waves rolled in.

Endless Summer. Eternal youth. That inchoate longing that lies at the heart of all great pop.

The 710 and the 110 were even worse than the 405. Kendall was forced to drive all the way to Santa Monica by which time the rain began, gently at first, then with increasing frequency until it was a steady downpour. Nothing like the torrential rains of the Midwest, but to Angelenos unused to any but the most benign conditions, it was apocalyptic. The CHP could barely keep up with the fender-benders not to mention the road rage. Traffic shuttled Kendall along like a bull in a chute. Until, at last, he pulled off on Topanga Canyon Road which he planned to take north to the 101.

After the sclerosis of the highways Topanga Canyon was like one of those car commercials where you got in your Lexus or

Cadillac or Mercedes, and suddenly the highways were deserted. Kendall had plenty of experience driving in rain and snow and pushed the Stingray to 70 on open stretches. He glanced in his rearview. Headlights rapidly approached.

He came to a near stop where sand and gravel had washed across the road, and the car that had been following him pulled up on the right, half on the shoulder. It was a British Racing Green XKE. The windows were fogged. The Jag's driver's window opened revealing Desmond Krout wearing a hipster trilby, grinning at Kendall and waving.

"Want to drag?"

SEVENTY

HOUSE OF THE SETTING SUN

Desmond looked high on coke. "Fuck off!" Kendall said pulling ahead. The speed limit was 45, which he scrupulously obeyed. No sense losing it on a winding canyon road. He had gone perhaps a mile, leaving the producer behind a bend when the Jag surged up behind him and passed doing at least a hundred miles an hour.

You didn't need to be high or drunk to drive like an idiot. But it helped. The rain slackened to an intermittent drizzle, and Kendall opened his windows a crack. Seconds later, he heard a horrendous crash, the bone-bending screech of metal on metal. He slowed as he rounded the next curve dreading what he would find.

The Jag had exited the highway through a guard rail and ended up in the canyon. A plume of smoke rose from the twisted metal. Kendall pulled ahead onto the shoulder, got out, stepped carefully over the twisted guard rail, and began to inch down the steep wet incline sideways when the wreck burst into flames, the expanding ball of gas nearly pushing him back up the slope. He retreated, ran to his car, and grabbed his phone out of sheer habit.

Dead.

A Ford heading west pulled over on the opposite side as a handful of people emerged from the homes that dotted the canyon. The Ford's driver, a middle-aged woman, approached with her hand at her mouth.

"What happened?" she said.

"He drove off the road."

"Oh, how terrible."

"Do you have a phone? Dial 911!"

She took out her phone and dialed.

He got in his car and booked it, glad the accident was behind him. By now it was early evening, and the only light came from traffic and the odd house clinging to the canyon.

The final stretch on the 101 moved with agonizing slowness due to the rain and the sheer press of vehicles. At times like these Kendall's loathing for humanity peaked, and he wished them all to disappear. Who were all these people preventing him from reaching his destination?

It was eight thirty by the time he finally turned onto Franklin and drove the mile to his house. The street was completely parked up. Some jackass had parked his pickup right in front of Kendall's garage, and he was forced to park three blocks away and return in the rain. He jogged the whole way, passing Ronnie's car a block away. A lead ball rotated in his gut.

At the base of his steps, he looked up breathing heavily. Mist rose from the stucco walls, a faint yellow glow emanating from the hexagonal opening above the door. The entry alcove was as cold as a meat locker as he slipped his key into the door. He entered the house, struck by the eerie silence; the silence of a tomb. No click of clock, hum of refrigerator, or rush of air through the vents. Utter silence. He held his breath and listened, afraid to speak.

Plimsouls' "The Zero Hour" blasted from his pocket. His ringtone. How could that be? The phone was dead! Digging it out he looked at the screen: Ronnie.

"Ronnie!" he answered breathless.

"Hellooo, darling," said the female voice. "Welcome home."

"Who is this?" he hissed. "Where's Ronnie?"

"We're here. We're all here. We've been waiting for you."

The phone went dead. Rain drummed on the ceiling. Kendall removed his shoes, and stealth-walked into the den. He removed the Picasso from the wall exposing his safe, dialed it, opened it, and took out his father's .45. He cocked it beneath a throw blanket to stifle the sound.

There was something in the house. He felt it like a rock in his shoe. The walls radiated menace. It had always been there, but now it was bulked up on death. Death was everywhere. Kendall had gone west to forget the shadow of his late wife and fallen into a hecatomb.

JDuWayne Heller, Merkle, Crystal Feathers, and now Shapiro had died in the house or because of the house. The house was insatiable and had only been waiting for a donor. A single yellow lamp illuminated the hall. Kendall turned it off and crept slowly down the left corridor clutching the pistol before him in both hands. Rain drummed against the skylights and lightning flickered providing intermittent illumination. The lightning shown on Smith's angular furniture casting German expressionist shadows on the walls.

"IT'S THE LITTLE OLD LADY FROM PASADENA!" erupted from the den radio causing Kendall to jump. He raced back in and savagely yanked the cord from the wall. His heart was the loudest thing in the house. He four-cycled his breath until he brought his pulse under control and listened. The house ticked. The rain drummed. Thunder rolled. He went down the hall gripping the pistol with both hands. He edged through the living room as lightning splashed bizarre angles on the walls. He paused outside the bedroom, back to the wall.

He spun around into a shooter's stance and trained his gun on the bed. At first, he didn't see anything, but the lightning flashed, and he saw a white body tied spread-eagled to the bed, held in place by the eye bolts. It took a second to realize it was Ronnie. She lifted her head with pleading eyes trying to speak around the gag ball.

He stepped into the room, and something slammed into the back of his head like the earth rising, and everything went black.

SEVENTY-ONE
TRUNK MUSIC

I t was nine and raining by the time the meeting ended. The
three remaining members of Gearhead met at Reggie's place
in San Jacinto. Eddie and Reggie were both keen on the reunion
tour. Reggie needed money. Reggie had a huge child support
nut, and Eddie was just bored. The drummer wouldn't be a
problem. You couldn't swing a guitar on Sunset without hitting
five drummers and twenty-seven lead singers. They'd get some
hot young kid with tats and good hair to bring in the little girls.

Butch Vig had expressed interest in producing the new
album.

Eddie and Reggie groaned when Torrance ended the meeting
with a prayer.

Eddie was a little buzzed on reefer when he left Reggie's
house and headed south on the I-5, but he had years of stoned
driving experience. Torrance steered his Volvo station wagon
away from the house, Def Leppard on the sound system. Red
and blue strobes through the rainy windshield at the first inter-
section.

Having grown up in Michigan Torrance could only laugh. He
wasn't surprised that both accidents involved 4X4s. People
thought they could slip into four-wheel drive and put the pedal

to the metal. The computer would take care of everything. But it wasn't so easy! Four-wheel drive didn't guarantee traction.

Torrance ran through the new songs in his head. He had six, Eddie had four, and even Reggie had kicked in two. That was an album right there. They'd played their songs for each other on guitar and keyboards and made suggestions, just like the old days. Reggie and Torrance worked on two new songs together. *Melody Maker* had once compared Reggie and Torrance to Lennon and McCartney, which the boys found ironic as they were excellent judges of their own work and both knew deep in their hearts they couldn't hold a candle to the Beatles. Sure, they wrote some good songs. But to be compared to the Beatles you had to write hundreds of great songs.

Bronx Cheer was the title of the new album, and the cover art showed a top fuel dragster doing a spinout and belching flame in front of the Apollo on West 125th Street. Dean Raggits had built the Gearhead dragster in 1984 in Dearborn, and it had campaigned for several years through the Upper Midwest. Torrance already had the art.

He switched off the music and tuned into KNX 1070 for traffic news. There were fender-benders, slide-offs, and shootings throughout Los Angeles County. Business as usual: all fucked up. Emergency vehicles with lights flashing passed him as he passed downtown.

It was ten by the time Torrance finally pulled into his steep drive in Los Feliz. He pulled the car all the way in back to the garage and parked next to Tommy's Subaru in the three-car garage. He entered the house through the patio and yelled, "Marge!"

"In here!" she called from the den. Marge sat in front of the big flat screen watching *The Sing Off* and knitting a sweater that showed Big Foot trudging through snow-covered pines. Torrance bent down and kissed her.

"You're wet!" Marge said. "How'd it go?"

"Great! We're all on the same page. Hope they still feel that way when it's time to sign on the dotted line."

"I wanted to call you to ask you to pick up some eggs, but you left your phone on the dresser."

"Yeah, I figured that out a couple hours ago. Chalk it up to senility, my dear."

Torrance went to the bedroom, stripped off his clothes, and took a hot shower. He dressed in baggy jeans and an XXXL Buzzcocks T-shirt. He'd always been chunky, even as a youth and had left it to Reggie, Eddie, and Ziggy to carry the skinny-ass punk torch. Rock and rollers were not supposed to be fat, Leslie West excepted.

He knelt by the bed. "Thank you, Lord, for returning me safe. Amen."

Just as he reached for his cell phone it sounded his ring tone, Blue Oyster Cult's "Don't Fear the Reaper." He picked it up. It was Reggie.

"Hey man," Reggie said, "could you shoot me over that song?"

"What song?"

"The one about the Yeti."

"Yeah, okay."

Torrance slipped the phone into his pocket and went into his office which looked like a Guitar Center showcase. Torrance had more guitars than he could comfortably store, including a '59 Les Paul Gibson, a 1941 Martin, and a '67 Strat signed by Stevie Ray Vaughan. Torrance made his way around the amplifiers and electronic keyboards to his desk which looked like a dump truck had backed up and unloaded files, papers, and magazines. CDs peeked out from beneath stacks of paper, and as Torrance pulled out his chair, he started an avalanche which dumped several CDs and four inches of paper on the floor.

On the wall was a framed poster: "Beloved, do not take part in any of these components of Satan's Spiritual Structure. They are doorways to demonic possession." The list included yoga, astrology, Church of Satan, Ouija boards, rock and roll, and heavy metal.

He dialed up his Gateway PC. He got as far as the Blue

Screen of Death. The computer had been failing for months. Torrance had seen the handwriting on the wall but had procrastinated, and now here he was with a dead computer. Fortunately, he'd backed up all his files with barracuda.com so at least they were safe. He could always access them from Marge's or Tommy's computer.

Torrance got up and went into Marge's office where she sat before her monitor talking to friends on Facebook.

"Everything all right?" Marge said without looking up.

"Just ducky. My computer died."

"Torrie, you've known that for months. You may as well just bite the bullet and get a new one!"

"I know. I'll use Tommy's."

Torrance went to Tommy's room which had an Emperors of Wyoming poster taped to the door. Inside lay chaos. Tommy's bed was unmade, clothes and sporting equipment littered the floor. The walls were covered with posters: AC/DC, Maroon 5, Beyoncé, Pacific Rim, Akira. Torrance had to step carefully to avoid crushing the plastic CD cases littering the floor. He hated the plastic CD cases, but they were still better than downloads.

Torrance had grown up in an era when media meant something you could hold in your hands. Album covers used to be huge. He and his friends would pore over the apocrypha accompanying the Beatles's White Album or The Who's *Tommy* for hours. Now, what did you get? A download. Often not even an album, just a single song. Not that Gearhead didn't plan to take full advantage of the new media. They planned to hire a PR manager for the roll-out, one song at a time.

Torrance sat and booted up Tommy's Mac. A password prompt appeared on the screen. Torrance got up and went to Marge's office.

"What's Tommy's password?"

"How should I know?"

"When will you be off your computer?"

"Go away, little man!"

Sighing, Torrance returned to his son's bedroom and sat in

front of the enigmatic Mac. He typed in Tommy's name, birth-date, and the name of their late cocker spaniel. Nada. He typed in Tommy Lee. He typed in David Grohl. He typed in David Grohl with the number zero instead of an o. Bingo! He was in.

Torrance went online, retrieved the file from Barracuda, opened up his own email, and sent it to Eddie. He tried closing out the program but inadvertently opened his son's documents and files. Torrance gazed in affectionate awe at his brilliant son's handiwork: songs for Tommy's band, a paper he was writing on Elizabethan Theater. Bemused, aware that he was snooping, but it was all right because he was a responsible parent, Torrance opened up Tommy's picture file.

Tommy surfing. Tommy in *The Iceman Cometh*. Tommy with his buddies playing rock. Oddly enough there were no pictures of Tommy with girls. In a way, it was a relief. Torrance had had that talk with Tommy, the talk he never had with his own father, and if Tommy wanted to concentrate on other activities what parent wouldn't say no?

There were too many pictures to view. Torrance casually scrolled to the end. They were stored chronologically and brought up the last couple. At first, he wondered at what he was looking. There was nothing exceptional about them; a street scene with tourists. Then he noticed the girl in the background dressed as a magician in a black/blue suit with top hat.

The next picture was taken much closer and caught the girl in profile, her white-gloved hand extended, a dazzling white pigeon flapping to the delight of two little girls behind her. It was Kendall's girlfriend, Ronnie. It looked as if Ronnie was unaware of being photographed. Next was a telephoto pic of Ronnie in civvies entering a typical West Hollywood apartment building. Next was a photo of the rear of an old Ford Focus showing the license plate number.

Fear wormed its way into Torrance's head, of what he did not know. But there was something profoundly unsettling about the photos, about the idea of Tommy taking pictures of unaware women. Torrance quickly scrolled up and found a few more like them, featuring a different girl. One picture was obviously taken from inside Tommy's Subaru. It showed the dash cowl and the fuzzy dice hanging from his rearview mirror.

Torrance logged off and sat there. He heard a faint cackle from Marge's office as she talked with a friend. Torrance rose like a sleepwalker, went out through the back, and walked through the rain to the detached garage. He opened the door of Tommy's car noting that the light did not go on and popped the trunk.

He went back to the trunk and looked inside. There lay a massive dark blue nylon gym bag. It clanked when he lifted it. Torrance undid the zipper and spread its jaws. Duct tape, leather straps, handcuffs, and women's jewelry.

SEVENTY-TWO
MING THE MERCILESS

A blast of cold water jolted Kendall from blackness. Pain throbbed like a muscle in his skull which was full of black thoughts and jagged confusion. He tried to wipe his face and discovered his hands were tied to the foot posts of the bed with plastic harnesses. He sat on the floor at the foot of the bed staring up with his mouth open.

"I got tired of waiting for you to wake up," Tommy said wearing a flamboyant purple robe with an enormous standing gold collar, like something Ming the Merciless might wear. Beneath that he wore nothing but a shiny purple codpiece, his lithe young body rippling like Michelangelo's David.

Lightning strobed the room like a recalcitrant black and white projector.

"Where's Ronnie?" Kendall said, coughing.

"Right behind you, where she was when you came in. Of course, she can't talk right now. What do you think of this robe, dude? Found it in the basement. And this ain't all I found in your basement. I've been sneaking in here for about two years now. What happened to all the videos, dude? Don't tell me you destroyed them. That shit was worth a fortune!"

"What the fuck are you doin', man?"

Tommy shook Wallanda's Oscar in Kendall's face like a medicine man. "Don't you get it, dude? I'm the Kardashian Killer!"

Kendall stared in disbelief. "You?"

"Yeah, man. It doesn't matter because at the end of the day, guess who the Kardashian Killer really is? You!"

Kendall was thirsty, and his bladder was full. He hoped he wouldn't wet himself. "What are you talking about?"

"Oh yeah!" Tommy did a little shimmy around the room shaking the Oscar like Screamin' Jay Hawkins with his fetish pole. "I found those drawings you were doing for Wyrick. What do you think the news people will make of those when they find you hanging from a chandelier, having killed yourself in a fit of remorse? Duuuuuude! I had no idea you did such bodacious work! I might even save some for my private collection. You should see my collection. I really wish I could show it to you!"

Kendall shut up. He knew enough about psychopaths to understand he had no hope of changing Tommy's mind. He should have trusted his instincts! The kid seemed hinky from the git-go. Why hadn't Illeana cast off her bonds and slipped out of the house? What had happened to her magic?

There was no magic. There was just evil in the world. Kendall didn't blame the house, and he didn't blame Tommy's parents. Evil just was. You could give a kid every break in the world, and he could still turn out bad.

Tommy picked up the .45. "Or I could use this. Which do you prefer? Hanging or blowing your brains out?"

Kendall looked away.

"The house has a certain reputation to uphold, don't you think?"

Kendall wondered what would happen if Tommy got close enough for him to kick the kid in the knee. Tommy went into the bathroom and filled the glass with water. He came back and threw it in Kendall's face.

"I asked you a question."

"What's a nedrebo?" Kendall said.

Tommy looked at him quizzically. "Fuck if I know! Did you even watch those films?"

Kendall stared at a corner of the ceiling. Tommy delivered a kick to his thigh. "Come on, bitch! Talk to me! Don't act like you're holier than thou! I saw your art, dude. Remember?"

"Tommy, why would you throw your life away, raping and killing young women? Is it the sex?"

Tommy barked. "Dude, I've been sneaking into this house since I was twelve. Don't try to make me out to be some kind of pervert. I saw what the Great Wallanda did to women. Was he ever arrested? No. People loved the Great Wallanda! Having you buy the house is better than the lottery, you know why? 'Cause now I can hang it all on you and nobody will suspect a thing. You're the perfect patsy. Just more weirdness from the old Wallanda House."

"What about your folks?"

Tommy's face twisted into a grotesque mask as he kicked Kendall savagely with the point of his shoe, over and over on the same spot on the thigh. White hot pain strobed through Kendall's body as he writhed and twisted trying to get away.

"Fuck my folks! My old man and his constant Bible spouting, I don't buy that holier-than-thou shit! You know what? You know what I found out? My old man musta fucked a thousand women when he was on the road. How convenient for him to suddenly find God when he can't get it up anymore.

"You know what ahmina do now? Ahmina rape your girlfriend with Wallanda's fucking Oscar. Yeah, found that sucker in your bedroom. Then I'm either going to string you up, or you shoot yourself—undecided—and then ahmina set fire to this pile of weird and be home sleeping in my bed when the fire trucks come."

Tommy jammed the pistol into his leather belt. He held the Oscar in front of Kendall so he could read the inscription. "Whaddaya think? Vaseline or no Vaseline?"

Kendall pistoned his left leg, smacking his heel as hard as he could into Tommy's right knee. Tommy howled in pain, staggered back a step, and collapsed. He grabbed his knee and lay on his side groaning.

"You piece of shit motherfucker! Now it's gonna go hard."

"Ahhh, is poor widdle Tommy going to cry?" Kendall said.

With a snarl, Tommy lunged forward and cracked the golden statue across Kendall's forehead, stunning him. "Now you're gonna listen to your bitch wail!"

Grunting, he got to his feet and leaned on the bed post panting. "I've always wanted to fuck a Wyrick girl."

Torrance strode into the room like an avenging grizzly bear, seized his son by the neck, and hurled him to the floor. "I have born Satan's child," he said.

With a snarl Tommy rose, swinging the Oscar at his father's head. The massive Torrance effortlessly caught Tommy's wrist, ripped the statuette free, and swung it in an arc into Tommy's temple. Tommy dropped like laundry in a chute and lay inert, his father standing over him, fists clenched, snorting like a bull.

"What comes out of a person is what defiles them. For it is from within—out of a person's heart—that evil thoughts come: sexual immorality, theft, murder, adultery, greed, malice, deceit, lewdness, envy, slander, arrogance, and folly. All these evils come from inside and defile a person."

"Torrance," Kendall said.

Torrance looked at him, reached into his pocket, withdrew a pocketknife, which he clicked open, and sawed through the wrist restraints. Kendall got up rubbing his thigh and held his hand out for the knife. He flexed and went rigid, staring.

Ronnie was gone.

SEVENTY-THREE
SNIPE HUNT

Incredulous, Kendall turned to Torrance. "Where'd she go?"

Torrance looked around as if seeing the room for the first time. "I don't know. I heard what Tommy said ... Do you mean Ronnie?"

"He had her tied to the bed. Look!" The nylon ropes and the gag ball lay on the bed. Kendall picked up his pistol and jammed it in his belt.

"Is there someone else in here?" Torrance said softly.

"Ronnie!" Kendall said, startling them both. He looked into the bathroom. Nada. It made no sense. Where would she go?

Torrance stared at his dead son. His hands dropped. "God forgive me, what have I done?"

Kendall put his arms around the big man as best he could as Torrance broke into heavy sobs. It was like holding up a horse. Gradually the sobs subsided, and Torrance pushed himself away. "Brother Kendall, I don't know what to do."

Kendall steered the big man out of the bedroom into the living room and sat him down in one of the sofas. He went into the kitchen, poured water from the tap, and took the glass to Torrance. He went to the sideboard in the dining room and poured three fingers of Glenlivet in a tumbler and set it down on the coffee table.

Someone had to tell Marge. It wouldn't be right for her to learn it from the cops. Kendall watched his neighbor drain the water glass followed by the whiskey. Torrance was in shock.

So am I, Kendall thought. He had to call the cops this time, but first, he had to find Ronnie.

"Torrance." Nothing.

"Torrance."

Torrance looked up and grunted.

"I've got to find Ronnie. Will you be all right here? Do you want me to call anyone?" He almost said Marge.

Torrance set the glass down and stared at his hands with a stricken look. Kendall worried that he might do something stupid, but he had to find Ronnie.

"Stay here, okay?"

His neighbor gave no sign. Kendall returned to the bedroom, took his gun, grabbed a flashlight in the kitchen and ripped through the first floor in less than a minute. The door to the basement was open, and the lights were on. He descended watching his breath frost, wondering how it could be so cold. Music erupted from the theater, hit the wall hard and ricocheted. The power chords and then, "After six hours of school you've had enough of the day—you turn the radio on and turn it up all the way ..."

Applause, yelling, and laughter tumbled from the golden doors.

"DENNIS GET DOWN!"

An incoherent animal howl ripped upward like a buzz saw until it passed into a dentist drill. Kendall froze, afraid of what he'd find. Insane shadows gyrated on the wall opposite the theater, half jitterbug, half war dance. He took the gun out of his belt, stuck the flashlight in his pocket, and jacked one into the chamber.

It sounded like there was a fucking riot going on. He walked to the open doors and went inside.

Empty. A great silence echoed through the hall. His ears popped. Quickly Kendall ran up the steps to the projection booth, checked inside. He worked his way around the basement. Next was the furnace room beneath the foyer. Hushed voices flitted from the open door.

"Eye-talian black marble?" said a wise guy voice. "How much is that gonna cost me?"

"Relax," said a cultured older man with a hint of Welsh. "You can afford it. This is my masterpiece, Frank. This is one for the history books. A thousand years from now, the tour buses will bring the yokels to stare at this house from the street."

"You got fuckin' eye-talian black marble in the bathrooms, zebrawood cabinets, ironwood chairs …"

"I know, I know," said the older man. "But every dime is where you can see it."

"So Roark, maybe we could work out a little trade."

"What kind of trade?"

"Have you seen Miss Stephanie Squibb? Miss Cross Plains last year. She's a huge fan of your work."

"Oh?" said the older man.

"Indeed. You're coming to my party, aren't you?"

Kendall held his breath gripping the gun like a lifeline until he stepped slowly in front of the open door holding the gun before him. The room was silent and empty. Kendall shivered. It had to be close to freezing in the basement. He went to the wine cellar and opened the door, gun in hand.

Disaster.

Every bottle had been smashed on the concrete floor leaving a sticky black lake punctuated with shards of glass like icebergs in an Arctic sea. A subterranean rumble rose out of the earth. The floor danced, each glass shard the center of expanding rings, the glass itself getting up and dancing through the wine.

Earthquake. Kendall braced himself in the door frame and waited with his heart in his mouth. Was it the Big One? Would he emerge to find Los Angeles in flames and sirens wailing? The rumbling and vibration died away.

He moved on to the wardrobe room. Racks lay on their sides, clothes strewn about the room.

All that remained was the Toy Box. The door was shut, but light shone from beneath. Gun in his right hand, Kendall used his left to open the door. A wave of revulsion swept through him. The room smelled of sex, sweat, and pain. The gynecologist table waved its stirrups in the air like insect antennae beyond obscene.

A heavy thud rained down from above. Kendall slammed the door shut and sprinted for the stairs, taking them two at a time. He ran into the living room. Glasses lay on the hardwood floor their contents spilled. Torrance lay on his back, an expression of horror frozen in his staring eyes, ice pick buried to the handle in his chest. Kendall knelt next to his neighbor, felt for a pulse. The big man was dead. With a grunt of anger and frustration, Kendall set down the gun, yanked out the pick, and used his fists to pound on Torrance's chest. He straddled the big man using the heel of his palm to push down on the heart. One potato two potato.

"It's no use," said a sultry voice behind him. Kendall picked up the gun and swiveled.

Ronnie wore the white gloves, hot pants, black satin vest, and bustier of Velva Voom, along with Illeana's top hat. Kendall's heart jammed in his throat.

"Ronnie!" he exclaimed getting to his feet and rushing to embrace her. She felt limp and cool in his grip and laughed softly in a voice that wasn't Ronnie. He held her at arms' length and searched her face. She'd used highliner and mascara to grotesquely enlarge her eyes, lashes from a rainforest fern. Ronnie vogued into a provocative pose, one hand on her hip, butt and breasts thrust out, the other with a finger in her mouth.

"Who are you?"

"I'm the Nedrebo."

SEVENTY-FOUR

NEDREBO

S he is Isis's avenging spirit, Our Sister of the Lost Cause, the deity of desperate damsels, avenging goddess of the raped and murdered. She is the dark side of He who bestowed animal lust on men and made us defenseless. Modern man may mock us. Muslims, Mennonites, and morons may subjugate us, but sooner or later the veneer of civilization comes off, and I emerge. I am in the stones and the earth. This ground is soaked with my blood. This house was only waiting for my return."

Thunder rolled over the house obliterating sound.

The thing radiated raw hate, a thousand tiny teeth on Kendall's skin. He didn't know this creature. Lightning flashed. The nedrebo posed like a swastika. She approached Kendall as a series of stills separated by darkness, placed the flat of her hand against his chest, and shoved him effortlessly backward, sending him crashing into the big leather sofa which jerked back a half inch. Something poked Kendall in the butt. It was the bottle of merlot Torrance had brought over the night of the séance. Kendall closed his hand around the neck.

The nedrebo's voice fell to a hoarse whisper.

"Do you want to know what nedrebo means?" it hissed wide-eyed in his face. "A man fucks his daughter. She has a baby girl. The man fucks the baby girl. She has a baby girl. That child has powers. If the man lived long enough, he could fuck his great-great-granddaughter and produce a double nedrebo with even more powers. Alas, poor Popsie. He strangled himself trying to achieve an orgasm. The Great Wallanda!"

"Wallanda was your father?" Kendall croaked.

"My father, my grandfather, and my great-grandfather. Lannie was my mother. He killed her and farmed me out to the state. Frank impregnated Dorothy when she was fifteen. Frank claimed Lannie was Bree's daughter, but she was Dorothy's."

She opened her hand and held a saucer-sized, spiked tarantula cadaver. She tossed it to Kendall who batted it away and lurched back.

"Where's Ronnie?"

"Someone told Frank Crystal was seeing another man so they strapped her down to the table, took turns raping her, and good Dr. Manglebaum cut out her uterus, sawed her in half, and removed her pinky fingers so she would more closely resemble the object of their desire."

Kendall smashed the wine neck against the table. Wine and glass flew. Kendall stood and swung the bottle in a vertical arc soaking the nedrebo. Its eyes went wide. Its mouth formed a seductive 'O.'

Kendall raced to the sideboard, uncapped the vodka, and sloshed it over the floor, furniture, and drapery. He stooped next to the curtains and lit them with Portia's lighter. They caught with a dynamic whoosh and shot toward the ceiling. Blue flames marched across the floor.

The radio in the den went nova.

I'M PICKING UP GOOD VIBRATIONS—SHE'S GIVING ME EXCITATIONS

Kendall scooped the mesmerized nedrebo, threw her over his shoulder, and ran to the front door, surprised at how little she weighed.

A wall of flame gathered itself and pursued them like a tidal wave. As he entered the foyer, the nedrebo came alive, twisting, kicking, and scratching. She fell from his grasp and sprang at him with her fingernails. He caught her by the wrists and they struggled as flames lapped at the ceiling and heat pushed like a bulldozer.

"Ronnie!" he cried.

For an instant, he saw recognition in her green eyes and a look of desperate longing.

"I'm sorry," she said. "I'm sorry."

The last trace of Ronnie vanished, the magician's final trick. The nedrebo effortlessly shook off his grip and looked at him sideways, all trace of humanity gone. A black, pointed tongue flicked from its lascivious lips, and it sprang at him, shoving him against the front door hard. Kendall slid to the cool stone floor. The nedrebo stood over him tongue flicking, turned with an agonizing howl, and ran back into the raging inferno.

The smoke was so thick Kendall couldn't see as he reached up and opened the front door, dragging himself out on his belly, looking down at the street, seeing the flames reflected in automobile windows, seeing that same woman with the Chihuahua, that same expression of shock and disbelief. Heaving and choking, he staggered down the steps hanging on to the side rail with both hands.

A kid in a Lakers jersey and shorts who'd been shooting hoops in his driveway ran across the street and helped Kendall the last few feet.

"You all right man?" he yelled, the flames a dull roar. Kendall stood with his hands on his knees fighting for his breath.

He ran to warn his neighbors.

SEVENTY-FIVE

STOCKHOLDER'S MEETING

Despite rain, the fire burned so hot it was twenty-four hours before arson inspectors could enter the site. There was nothing left of the house. It might as well have been made of magnesium. Kendall hovered helplessly on the periphery enduring an unending series of questions. It didn't take long for police to realize it was the same address at which Stan Merkle died, and the owner's dog got run over.

News that Kendall's wife died of a drug and alcohol overdose only increased their scrutiny, but try as they might they found nothing remotely criminal in Kendall's past or behavior, and as the sky lightened to a dull gray he was free to go. He saw Marge standing on the sidewalk with her arms crossed, her face a mask, talking to a pair of detectives. He longed to comfort her, but she was surrounded by cops, friends, and neighbors, and he did not know how she would react.

Kendall spent the night at a Motel 6.

Forensic specialists found the remains of six bodies encased in cement off the "Toy Box."

Detectives found Tommy's collection in the Subaru's trunk. The freak show dominated the news cycle for a week and went national. Kendall didn't know what to do so he did what he always had, kept his head down and went to work.

A 4.2 earthquake centered in Reseda had struck the region.

The Big One waited.

The Ripon folks were supportive as hell, and there was a barely concealed undercurrent of glee at Kendall's notoriety. This could only help sales.

Kendall was at Ripon working late. It took his mind off his troubles. It was eight fifteen when his phone rang. The screen said "Darryl."

"Mr. Wyrick," Kendall answered.

"Mr. Coffin. I understand you've had a tough row to hoe these past few days. You have my deepest condolences, sir."

"Thank you, sir. How's it going?"

"Splendidly, young man. Splendidly. You know the annual stockholder's meeting is next week."

"No, I didn't."

"Are you a stockholder?"

"No, sir, I am not."

"Well, you are now. You should have got a FedEx package today. In any case, I'd be very pleased if you would attend that meeting. You might get a kick out of it."

ABOUT THE AUTHOR

Mike Baron is the creator of Nexus (with artist Steve Rude) and Badger, two of the longest lasting independent superhero comics. Nexus is about a cosmic avenger 500 years in the future; Badger, about a person with multiple personality disorder, one of whom is a costumed crime fighter. For  comics, Baron has written The Punisher, Flash, Deadman, Star Wars, and many other titles. He has won two Eisners and an Inkpot award.

Baron has published fifteen novels including *Banshees* (a Satanic rock band that returns from the dead), *Helmet Head* (Nazi biker zombies), *Whack Job* (spontaneous human combustion), *Skorpio* (a ghost who only appears under a blazing sun), his Biker series (a reformed biker hoodlum turned private investigator), and *Florida Man* (which is exactly what you think it is).

He lives in Colorado with his wife Ann and some dogs.

IF YOU LIKED ...

IF YOU LIKED *DOMAIN*, YOU MIGHT ALSO ENJOY:

Banshees
by Mike Baron

Rock Band Fights Evil Vol 1-3: Band on the Run
by DJ Butler

Rescue from Planet Pleasure
by Mario Acevedo

OTHER WORDFIRE PRESS TITLES BY MIKE BARON

A Brief History of Jazz Rock
Banshees
Helmet Head
Nexus: A Novel
Skorpio
Whack Job

Our list of other WordFire Press authors and titles is always growing. To find out more and shop our selection of titles, visit us at:
wordfirepress.com

www.ingramcontent.com/pod-product-compliance
Lightning Source LLC
Chambersburg PA
CBHW050515110726
47899CB00005B/1471